Praise for *A Song of Me and You* . . .

'Moving, uplifting, unforgettable. Mike always writes from the heart and creates stories we fall in love with'
Lisa Jewell

'Touching, funny, beautifully characterised and undeniably romantic, this may be the escapist page-turner of the summer'
Sunday Times

'I was swept away by Ben and Helen's story, equal parts relatable and fantastic but always, always pulling on my heart strings. Mike Gayle, then, now and forever one of the best'
Lindsey Kelk

'Public service announcement: Mike Gayle's latest is going to toy with your emotions, churn you up, and spit you out – but it's totally worth it . . . powerful storytelling and well-drawn characters'
Heat

'A wonderful story about the things that really matter in life – family, friendship and falling in love – and a poignant reminder to cherish them while we can. It's the perfect book to celebrate Mike's 25 years as an author!'
Ruth Hogan

'This second-chance romance comes from the sure hands of Mike Gayle, known for his ability to pluck the heartstrings'
Daily Mail

'Funny, real and unexpected, a story that will keep you hooked to the very last page'
Alexandra Potter

**Mike Gayle: emotions you'll never forget,
stories you'll want to share**

MIKE GAYLE

A Song of Me & You

HODDER &
STOUGHTON

First published in Great Britain in 2023 by Hodder & Stoughton Limited
An Hachette UK company

This paperback edition published in 2024

1

A CIP catalogue record for this title is available from the British Library

Paperback ISBN 978 1 529 34480 6
ebook ISBN 978 1 529 34484 4
Hardback ISBN 978 1 529 34481 3

Typeset in Plantin Light by Palimpsest Book Production Limited,
Falkirk, Stirlingshire

Printed and bound in Great Britain by Clays Ltd, Elcograf S.p.A.

Hodder & Stoughton policy is to use papers that are
natural, renewable and recyclable products and made from
wood grown in sustainable forests. The logging and manufacturing
processes are expected to conform to the environmental
regulations of the country of origin.

Hodder & Stoughton Limited
Carmelite House
50 Victoria Embankment
London EC4Y 0DZ

www.hodder.co.uk

To Monkey One and Monkey Two,
love you to the moon and back.
Consider this your shoutout!

Bluelight

Bluelight are a British **rock** band formed in London in 1996. They consist of vocalist, guitarist and pianist, **Ben Baptiste**, guitarist, **Andy Cartwright**, bassist and keyboard player, **Leona Ferreira**, and drummer **Jason 'Chip' Henderson**. They formed after meeting at London's **Glow-worm recording studio** in **Deptford**, first calling themselves Myriad, then Baptiste before settling on the name Bluelight.

After being spotted by the music manager **Rocco Roberts** playing at **King's Cross Water Rats**, Bluelight signed with **EchoPlus Recordings** a subsidiary of **Warner Brothers Music**, in one of the biggest ever deals for an unknown UK act. The band's first album, *Bluelight* (1997), debuted at number one in both the UK and US charts and included their number one debut single **"She Walks in the Stars."** The album received a **Brit Award for British Album of the Year**, a **Grammy Award for Best Alternative Music Album** and won that year's **Mercury Prize**. Their second album, *In The Red* (1999), won a Grammy and a Brit in the Album of the Year category and the singles **"Love Will See Us Through"** and **"Ground Down"** took both the top slots in *Rolling Stone*'s annual top 100 singles of the year poll. The band's third album *Speak* (2002) was the **best-selling album of the year** worldwide, an achievement later repeated by its successors, *Corsair* (2005) and *Makes Us Stronger* (2007).

Since then, Bluelight have diversified their sound with their subsequent releases *Small Hands Clapping* (2010), *Life Form* (2013), *Monocle* (2016), *Comet Dreamers* (2019) and *In Theory* (2021), each album exploring new themes and adding new musical styles to the band's original sound.

The band are well known for their "energetic" live performances, which *Pitchfork* described as "a semi-religious experience." In 2019 a documentary about the band's Monocle tour directed by the **Turner Prize**-winning artist **Christina Butcher** was premiered at selected cinemas around the world to widespread critical acclaim.

With 120 million albums sold worldwide, Bluelight are the **most successful band of the 21st century and one of the best-selling music acts of all time**. According to the UK music website *NME*, they are also the second-most-awarded group in history. Other notable achievements include the **highest-grossing tour of all time**, eight of the 50 highest-selling albums ever in the United States, and the most ever nominations and wins for a band in **Brit Awards** history. *The New York Times* described Bluelight as "Rock Icons," and *The LA Times* included both *Speak* and *Corsair* on their **"100 Albums to hear before you die"** list and the singles **"Home," "Lovesick"** and **"The Heart is a Warning,"** in their **"100 Greatest Songs"** list. Their music has been variously described by critics as "lifechanging, " "enthralling" and "passionate" and their frontman, Baptiste, as "captivating, " "magnetic" and "charismatic."

Part 1

1

Helen

As Helen stood at the front room window watching her husband's car pull up outside the house, she thought she might throw up. Then, once she was sure she wasn't going to be sick, her next instinct was to march upstairs to her son Frankie's room, grab his cricket bat from the side of the wardrobe where he kept it, and then use it to smash the living daylights out of Adam's Audi A3. It was, she thought, the very least he deserved, to witness his pride and joy being destroyed by the hand of the angry perimenopausal woman he had so cruelly abandoned. She resisted the temptation, however, as she was, for the children's sake, trying her best to be civil, and she was pretty sure that wrecking her estranged husband's car was about as uncivil as things got.

Stepping out into the hallway, Helen called up the stairs to the kids and told them to hurry up. After several moments, however, when they hadn't even acknowledged her summons let alone responded to it, she called out again.

'Frankie, Esme, your dad's here!'

Silence.

She tried again. 'Come on, kids, your dad's here! He's waiting.'

Yet more silence.

Finally, Helen screamed at the top of her voice, 'If you two aren't down here in the next five seconds I am going to lose it, do you hear me? Absolutely lose it!!!'

Helen hated yelling up the stairs to her children more than anything. It made her feel like she was a bad mother, something she'd felt day in day out to some degree ever since her daughter Esme was born eighteen years ago, a feeling that had only intensified on the arrival of her son Frankie four years later. What she hated most about yelling was that it was never her first chosen method of communication. Every single time she needed her children to do something she would start calmly by calling out a gentle request, which would, without fail, need to be repeated a second and a third time. Eventually, it would dawn on her that her children, her own flesh and blood, the two people she had brought into this world and who had caused untold damage to her body in the process, had heard her but for reasons best known to themselves had chosen to ignore her. That's when she'd become apoplectic with rage and start yelling. And it would be then, and only then, that her children would finally appear, faces aghast at their mother's meanness.

'Honestly, Mum,' said Esme, looking outraged as she came down the stairs trailed by her brother. 'Is there really any need to shout like that? You're not on a building site, you know!'

Helen didn't reply. She couldn't, not when these last few moments with her children would have to carry her through the next seven days without them. Drawing in a deep breath, she held it for the count of ten before letting it out slowly just like they did in yoga class. Finally, she forced a smile on to her face, kissed them both on the forehead and told them that she loved them.

'Right then,' she said, trying her best to sound cheery. 'Have you got everything? Phones, chargers, medication . . .' She paused, looked at Frankie and added, 'Clean underwear?'

Frankie scowled at her in outrage. 'Of course I've got clean underwear.'

'Enough for the whole week?' countered Helen.

Immediately Frankie looked slightly less sure of himself. 'Yeah.'

'How many pairs?' asked Helen, well aware that her son was bluffing.

Frankie snorted in disgust. 'I'm not going to count them in front of you.'

Helen wondered if perhaps as Frankie was the youngest she might be guilty of babying him. After all, he was fourteen now, more man than boy, and was probably more than capable of packing his own case, counting his own pants. Anyway, if it came to it, it wouldn't be her two days from now driving around the north Wales countryside trying to find a local shop that sold teenage boys' underwear. That would be Adam's problem.

'Fine,' she said resignedly. 'But just remember there's a limited number of times you can turn them inside out.'

For a moment Frankie continued to glower, his hands shoved deep in his pockets, but then suddenly he let out a pained groan of annoyance before dashing back up the stairs, undoubtedly to get more pants. Job done, Helen turned her attention to Esme and the rucksack and two suitcases she'd somehow managed to drag down from her room.

'Wow, Es, have you got Josh stashed away in one of those? You do know you're only going for a week.'

'There's nothing in any of these bags that I can do without,' Esme announced while simultaneously tapping out a message on her phone without even glancing at the screen. 'I know Dad said to pack light but I've been through everything three times and it's all essential.'

Even though Helen had her doubts about her daughter's under-standing of the concept of 'essentials' she decided not to labour the point. After all, Esme was eighteen now, had a boyfriend and would, all being well, be heading off to the University of Nottingham at the end of the summer to start a new stage of her life. There would be many moments in the future when Helen wouldn't be there to tell her daughter what she should and shouldn't do, and she had to trust that she'd figure it all out somehow. And well, if Adam had to crush his and his new girlfriend's bags by stuffing all of Esme's things into his car, that would only be a bonus.

'I'm sure it'll all be fine,' said Helen as Frankie came back down the stairs clutching several pairs of pants in each fist, which he shoved into his bag while refusing to meet his mother's gaze.

Helen stood for a moment staring at her two children, missing them already even though they hadn't yet gone. Unable to resist the urge, she pulled them fiercely to her chest and there they stood, in an awkward but nonetheless heartfelt group hug, until the doorbell rang. Letting go of each other, they looked towards the front door but no one moved. Then, drawing a deep breath, Helen summoned every last bit of courage she had, walked over to the door and opened it to reveal the figure of her husband, Adam.

In the immediate aftermath of his moving out Adam had at least had the grace to look reassuringly awful every time she'd seen him. His eyes were always red-rimmed, his hair lank, and after losing so much weight his frame was virtually skin and bones. In the past few weeks, however, it appeared that the guilt and shame that had led to this dishevelment must be on the wane because now, gallingly, her husband looked like a slimmer, more handsome version of the man she'd given the best years of her life to.

'Hey guys,' he said, shooting a grin at the kids over Helen's shoulder. 'Who's ready for some sea air?'

As Esme and Frankie put their trainers on and rustled about in the kitchen for last-minute snacks Helen and Adam stood, not talking, barely looking at one another, on the doorstep.

'Any idea what the forecast is for the week?' asked Helen when she could bear the awkwardness no more.

'A bit of everything,' replied Adam. 'Cloudy some days, rain others, and a bit of sun in between.'

'Well, I'm sure you'll have a nice time whatever the weather.' Helen hadn't meant it as anything other than a mild pleasantry but it somehow came out sounding bitter and resentful, and Adam immediately bristled.

'No one's stopping you from taking the kids on holiday,' he snapped in a low voice.

'Yes,' replied Helen, 'I suppose the world's my oyster now that I'm a single girl about town trying to make ends meet on a part-time teacher's salary.'

'Well, no one's stopping you from going full time, are they?' hissed Adam. 'It's not like the kids are small any more.'

Helen felt herself fill with rage. 'This is so typical of you, always rewriting history to cast yourself in a favourable light. If you remember, it was you who said I shouldn't go back full time because at least one of us needed to be around for the kids given that you were at work all the time . . . or at least that's where you told me you were.'

Adam shook his head in disgust. 'Here we go again . . . Saint Helen of Didsbury . . . always looking down on us mere—' He stopped, the animosity on his face replaced in a flash by a smile, and Helen turned to see the kids reappear in the hallway, laden down with what looked like the entire contents of the kitchen snack cupboard.

'It's a good job neither of you are car-sick any more,' said Helen, even though she wasn't entirely sure this was true of Frankie.

'Right, kids,' said Adam, 'give me your bags and I'll load up the car while you say goodbye to your mum.' As if repelled by an invisible forcefield, rather than coming into the house and grabbing the kids' cases Adam waited on the doorstep for them to bring them out to him, his eyes widening at the sight of how much luggage there was. Helen noted, however, that Adam made no comment. As the parent who had left, the one who had caused all the damage, he was clearly all too aware of his need to be Fun Dad, Cool Dad, Dad-that-doesn't-make-a-big-deal-out-of-things like Mum does.

As he struggled down the front path with the bags Helen took the opportunity to have one last hug with her children.

'Make sure you text to let me know you've arrived safely,' she said, squeezing them tightly, 'have a good time and if you need anything, absolutely anything at all, promise you'll call me, okay?'

It took everything Helen had to hold it together as she followed them down the front path to the car, a feat made all the more difficult when she caught sight of Adam's girlfriend, Holly, occupying the very seat where Helen herself had sat at the beginning of countless family holidays over the years, the very seat Helen herself would've been sitting in now had it not been for her weak-willed, cheating scumbag of a husband. Holly's long glossy chestnut hair was tumbling over her shoulders, eyes hidden behind expensive-looking designer sunglasses, and lips slick with sophisticated nude lip gloss. Helen wished more than anything that she too had had the foresight to wear sunglasses, because at least then she wouldn't have had to worry so much about the tears pricking at her eyes. Determined not to upset Esme and Frankie, Helen hung on for as long as she could, which turned out to be just long enough for Adam's car to reach the end of the road but nowhere near enough time for her to make it back inside the house. And so there, on the pavement, she crumpled like a cardboard box in the rain as the tears she'd been holding back all morning finally breached her defences.

Returning inside, Helen closed the front door and was immediately struck by how quiet the house was. It wasn't the same quiet as when the kids were at school or out with their friends, this was a different sort of quiet altogether; it was harsher, more menacing, the sort of quiet the makers of horror films use to scare audiences out of their wits. The silence was so unbearable that Helen doubted she'd be able to face an hour of it, let alone the seven days she would have to endure before the house was full of life and noise again. Still, she would have to learn to bear it at some point, and there really was no time like the present.

Spotting her phone on the hallway table, she picked it up and called her best friend.

'Hey Gabs,' she said, clutching the handset just a little too tightly as she tried her hardest not to cry. 'I'm really sorry, but I don't think I'm going to make it to yours this morning after all.'

'Oh mate,' said Gabby gently. 'Was it awful?'

Helen bit her lip and momentarily squeezed her eyes shut. 'It was worse than awful,' she said, forcing out the words. 'Much worse. But I don't want to get into that right now, all I want is to take a long, hot bath and go back to bed.'

'I get it,' said Gabby, 'I do, but are you sure you should be alone right now? Wouldn't you be better coming over to mine like we said? I've got all the food and prosecco you could want and I've even packed Rav and the kids off to the outlaws so we'll have the place to ourselves.'

'Sounds like bliss,' said Helen. 'But could we maybe do it another time? I'm not exactly the best company right now.'

'You don't need to be. I just want to help, that's all.'

'I know you do, and I love you for it but I think I'll just stay at home if that's okay. I'm sure I'll feel better soon but right now I feel like I've just been run over by a truck.'

Gabby fell silent, clearly wanting to do the right thing by her best friend but not being entirely certain what that might entail. 'Are you sure? I'm more than happy to come over to yours if that'll make a difference?'

'No, I'll be okay, but thanks. I think I just need some time to myself, some time to get my head around everything.'

'Understood,' said Gabby. 'But promise you'll call if you change your mind, or just want to talk. Day or night, I'm here for you, okay?'

'I will,' said Helen. 'I promise.'

'Good,' replied Gabby, and then she added firmly, 'And don't forget Lisa's birthday brunch tomorrow. I'm calling for you at eleven, and don't even think about bailing. I understand you need a bit of space but you also need your friends around you at a time like this, so I'm afraid tomorrow's non-negotiable.'

Helen knew better than to put up a fight and anyway, maybe Gabby had a point; after a day and a night alone, a boozy brunch with her friends might be just the tonic she'd need.

'Okay, I'll see you tomorrow at eleven . . . and thanks again, Gabs . . . for everything.'

Ending the call, Helen headed upstairs to run a bath but the kids had left the bathroom in such a state in their hurry to pack that she had no choice but to clean it from top to bottom. Then once that task was done, she caught sight of the overflowing laundry hamper in the hallway, and soon she was hanging out an earlier load of washing in the garden before refilling the machine and switching it on. While it wasn't what she'd planned, there was something soothing about the familiar monotony of everyday chores, and before she knew it she was upstairs working her way through the small mountain of ironing she'd been putting off all week.

A couple of hours later, as she stood marvelling at the empty ironing basket, Helen decided that now was the perfect time to finally reward herself with her bath. Running the water, she added a generous glug of the Jo Malone bath oil she normally reserved for special occasions, and was about to start getting undressed when the doorbell rang. Her gut instinct was to ignore it, after all it wasn't as if she was expecting anyone, but then she recalled something Esme had said over dinner the night before about a package from ASOS she was waiting for. The last time Helen hadn't answered the door to a courier her Amazon package had been left under the car and she'd accidentally run over it reversing off the drive. So she headed downstairs. Sighing heavily, she opened the door and immediately did a double-take. The face looking back at her didn't belong to a harried parcel courier, postman or even a double-glazing salesman. Instead, it belonged to someone she hadn't seen for a very long time, someone who, in what now felt very much like another universe, she had once loved more than life itself.

2

Helen

The last time Helen had been face to face with the person now standing on her doorstep was over twenty years ago. She had, however, seen him in the pages of *Hello* the previous summer when she'd been getting her hair done in Salon Solo on the high street. At the time her head had been covered in silver foils and she'd been enjoying a free cappuccino and an indulgent flick through a pile of celebrity magazines when she'd come across a spread entitled, 'Bluelight's Ben Baptiste enjoys secret getaway with new lover, Italian supermodel Cristina Taticchi.' The 'article' consisted of a series of 'intimate portraits' of the lead singer of the British rock band Bluelight accompanied by a stunningly beautiful long-legged creature with glossy raven hair and perfectly bronzed skin. There were shots of the happy couple sunbathing and diving off the deck of a luxury yacht into a turquoise sea, together with long-lens candid snaps of them applying sunscreen to each other's lithe bodies.

It had all looked very glamorous and unobtainable, the kind of thing that was nice to look at in order to divert oneself from the everydayness of life while having one's grey hairs covered over. But if Helen knew anything, it was that the sorts of people who graced the pages of *Hello* rarely appeared on the suburban south Manchester doorsteps of mere mortals. It just couldn't be real, could it?

'Ben?'

The tall, slim man flashed her a dazzling megawatt smile that made her feel quite lightheaded. She studied him again: his expensive-looking sunglasses in which she could see her own reflection, the short dreadlocks poking out from under his baseball cap, his slightly unruly beard, flecked with grey, his practically ageless dark brown skin. It certainly looked like Ben.

'I know it's a cunning disguise and everything, H, but come on . . .' Still smiling, he removed his sunglasses to reveal deep brown eyes with a sparkle she knew only all too well. Helen momentarily stopped breathing. It really was him.

'I . . . I . . . I don't understand,' she said, her head teeming with a million different thoughts and feelings all at once. 'What . . . what on earth are you doing here?'

'Now what sort of a greeting is that to offer an old mate? Especially one you haven't seen in so long?' He threw open his arms, wrapping Helen in them tightly, squeezing her to his chest and sending a slight shiver of something she couldn't quite define down her spine. His touch felt at once familiar and yet strange, instantly awakening long-forgotten memories that were hard to reconcile with the man before her.

'It's so good to see you,' he said as they parted. 'You look exactly the way I always remember you.'

'Well, now I know you're lying,' said Helen, blushing. 'I mean . . . for one thing there's a bit more of me now than there used to be. But anyway . . .' she added quickly, hoping to save herself from the embarrassment of having to listen to Ben scratching around for compliments, 'you still haven't answered my question. What on earth are you doing here? Are you playing a gig or something?'

'Nope, no gigs scheduled until the tour starts in October.'

'So, what then, are you doing some sort of promotional work?'

'Something like that,' he said. 'I'm only here in Manchester for a flying visit but when I found out I had a spare hour or two I thought, I know, I'll go and drop in on my old mate Helen Greene and see how she is.'

'How did you even know where I lived? The last address you would've had for me would've been in Leeds.'

Ben tapped the side of his nose in an annoyingly knowing fashion and gave her a wink. 'Let's just call it magic.'

Just then a car pulled up across the road and, seemingly automatically, Ben pulled his cap down and put his sunglasses back on. It was clearly the action of a man accustomed to hiding his identity and it dawned on Helen that perhaps he should be safely inside her house, not standing out on the street for all to see.

'Come on in,' she said, grabbing Ben by the arm and pulling him into the house. 'I'll get the kettle on and we can have a proper catch-up.'

As Helen ushered Ben along the hallway to the kitchen diner she shook her head in disbelief, still not able to accept that this was really happening. Her hugely famous ex-boyfriend, a man she hadn't seen in decades, a man whose life was the polar opposite of her own – full of glamour and excitement, private jets and celebrity friends – was actually in her house. It didn't make any sense, it didn't feel real. Was she having some sort of mental episode? Had the stress of the past few months finally caught up with her, causing her to see things that weren't really there? As they reached the kitchen it was all she could do to stop herself from putting a hand out to touch him, to make sure that he was made of flesh and blood just like her.

'This is so weird, Ben,' she said, coming to a halt by the kitchen island. 'I just can't believe you're really here. How long's it been?'

'Too long . . . far too long.' He grinned. 'But the important thing is I'm here now.'

'Indeed you are,' said Helen. She'd meant her comment innocently, but somehow to her ears it had come out sounding more than a little suggestive, a feeling not helped by her sudden awareness of his physicality. He was taller than she remembered, his shoulders so much broader, and, even though it was hard to tell, she sensed that under his jacket he was so much more muscular too.

Fearful that he possessed the ability to read minds, Helen quickly turned away, grabbed the kettle and began filling it. But then as she set it down and turned to grab a couple of mugs she suddenly noticed the state of the place. While her morning of housework had made upstairs look reasonably respectable, downstairs was a different story. The kitchen was a disaster zone. There were cereal bowls and crumb-laden plates strewn across the dining table, and dirty pots, pans, plates and dishes on the counter that she hadn't had the energy to deal with the night before.

'I'm so sorry about the mess,' she said, quickly opening the dishwasher and shoving a few random things inside. 'Kids, eh?'

Ben raised an eyebrow. 'Wow, you've got kids? Of course you do. It really has been a long time since we've seen each other, hasn't it?'

Helen inexplicably felt her cheeks flush scarlet. 'Two, a girl, Esme, and a boy, Frankie.'

'Oh, that's great. So, where are they both? Out causing trouble in town with their mates?'

Helen hesitated. Should she simply tell the truth, or would it be okay to tell a teeny bit of a lie in order to save herself the embarrassment of having to relate the whole sorry story of Adam's leaving?

'No, my husband's taken them camping in Wales for a week for a bit of a dad bonding trip before Esme goes to uni,' said Helen.

'And you didn't fancy it?'

Helen pulled a face. 'Camping isn't really my sort of thing. Anyway, we're all going for a proper family holiday together in August, so to be honest I'm glad of the time to myself. It's the only way I'll be able to get all the jobs that need doing done before we go away.'

Gesturing for Ben to sit down, Helen picked up a pile of post from the counter, pushed it into one of the dresser drawers near the dining table and then caught sight of her reflection in the mirror on the wall. She looked terrible. Absolutely monstrous. Her eyes were still puffy from her earlier tears, her make-up was a mess and, if that wasn't enough, the T-shirt she was wearing had some sort of stain on it just above her right breast.

'Listen,' she said, turning back to Ben and trying her best not to sound panicked, 'I've just remembered I've got to do something. Make yourself at home, and I'll be back in a little while.'

Exiting the room, Helen pulled the door to the kitchen shut behind her and then raced up the stairs to the bathroom. All too aware that time was not on her side, she opened the cabinet over the sink, removed her bottle of cleanser and frantically scrubbed away at the streaks of mascara and remnants of her foundation. Running the tap, she splashed her face with cold water, patting it dry with a clean towel before applying some of Esme's ultra-expensive moisturiser, then, scooping up her make-up bag from the floor by the sink, she hastily applied a layer of foundation. Grinning at herself crazily in the mirror to find the right spots, she added a bit of blusher before dusting her face lightly with translucent powder. A few sweeps of mascara and a slick of lip gloss later and she was done, with only her hair and clothes left to sort out.

Dashing to her bedroom, Helen flung open the wardrobe door and rifled through the contents looking for something nice but not too showy to wear. As she did so she couldn't help wondering about the lie she'd told Ben. Why hadn't she been truthful with him? Why hadn't she told him that Adam had left her and taken their kids away on holiday with his new girlfriend? If she was being honest she already knew the answer: she was ashamed. It was the reason it had taken her days to tell Gabby what had happened, why it was weeks before she'd told her own mum, and why, even though there had been plenty of opportunities before the end of the school year, no one at St Joseph's, the primary school she taught at, knew either. She hated lying, she really did, but she hated feeling like a failure even more.

The breakdown of her marriage was hard enough to admit to the ordinary people in her life but how could she not feel like an even bigger failure in the presence of someone like Ben? It would have been hard enough confessing the truth if he'd been just a regular ex-boyfriend who she hadn't seen in decades, but the fact he was the drop-dead-gorgeous lead singer of the band Bluelight, a global superstar, former husband of the Hollywood actress Allegra Kennedy and an eight-time Grammy Award winner somehow made it about a billion times harder.

She thought about him sitting downstairs in her kitchen. Even now it seemed surreal that he was here. Over the many years since they'd split up she'd seen him and his band go from strength to strength. In the beginning she'd read about him from time to time in the music press but then they'd hit the big time and were soon splashed across the front covers of every tabloid newspaper and magazine there was. She'd seen Ben being inter-viewed by Jools Holland at New Year, recordings of him playing live to a crowd of thousands of muddy people at Glastonbury, and even featured on a documentary about the best-selling bands of all time. He was success personified. He was living life as good as it gets and Helen . . . well, Helen felt like she was the polar opposite. A washed-up, middle-aged, part-time primary school teacher, with a broken marriage and her best years behind her.

Despite having seemingly made no effort at all with his appearance, Ben looked almost exactly as he had done in the pages of *Hello*. Okay, close up she had noticed a touch more grey in his stubble and in the hair around his temples, and there were laughter lines around his eyes too, but these only served to make him appear even more handsome than she remembered, not less. Not for the first time she cursed the fact that men and women aged so differently. Every day that passed it seemed that men of her generation got better looking without doing a single thing, while women her age had to spend a small fortune just to maintain what they already had.

Shedding her T-shirt and tracksuit bottoms on the floor, Helen hurriedly tried on several options before opting for jeans, a white shirt, and a hideously expensive necklace she'd ordered online in the middle of the night while she was still very much in the depths of her misery. Checking herself out in the full-length mirror on the wardrobe door, she was, if not exactly pleased with the results, then at least satisfied that she had done the best with the time that she had and what she had to work with. She looked, she thought, like a generic off-duty mum, smart enough but not exactly anything you'd look twice at.

Still, it would have to do for now. If she'd known he was coming she could've presented a better version of herself; as it was, she hadn't, so there was no choice but to get on with things. Shoving her feet into a pair of newish white trainers that Esme had encouraged her to buy last summer, she returned to the bathroom and with no little effort managed to tame her hair into something more respectable. Finally, she spritzed on some of the perfume Adam had bought her for Christmas, then taking a deep breath, she descended the stairs, her heart racing like a giddy teenager's.

3

Helen

'Oh, you've changed,' said Ben, sounding slightly perplexed, as Helen returned to the kitchen. 'Hope it wasn't on my account?'

Helen felt her face glow red underneath all her make-up. 'I was in the middle of doing the cleaning when you arrived,' she said quickly. 'Hence the scarecrow outfit I was wearing, which to be honest no one deserves to see.'

'Well,' said Ben, 'not that my opinion is worth much but you looked great then and you look great now too.'

'Thanks,' said Helen, and she busied herself by trying to make the kitchen look a bit tidier. 'Once again, I really am sorry about the state of the place. I've been trying to train the kids to clean up after themselves since they were tiny, and well . . . Esme's eighteen now so you can see how well that's gone.'

'Of course,' said Ben, 'you said your daughter's going off to uni, I don't know why it's taken until now to realise just how mad that is.'

'I know,' sighed Helen, who had been struck by this thought nearly every day since her daughter's birthday back in January. 'It doesn't feel like any time at all since we were that age ourselves, does it?'

'It's one of those things, about getting older,' said Ben. 'Time seems to both slow down and speed up.' He gestured to an old snap of Frankie stuck to the fridge.

'And is this your son?'

'Yeah, that's Frankie,' said Helen, smiling at the picture of her son aged ten dressed as *Where's Wally?* for World Book Day. 'Although he's fourteen now and wouldn't be seen dead dressing up for any kind of fun activity. In fact, he wouldn't be seen dead in anything unless it had a designer label and had been doused in half a can of Lynx Africa first.'

Ben laughed. 'He sounds like a typical teenage boy.'

'You can say that again. I went into his bedroom the other day to retrieve his dirty laundry and it was like going on an archaeological dig. Along with clothes I found plates, bowls, mugs, an actual frying pan and even my spare pair of hair straighteners.'

Ben smiled. 'Still, I bet you're missing him something rotten. How long did you say they are away camping for?'

'Just a week,' said Helen, and then she added quickly, 'And then, like I said there's still the family holiday to look forward to.'

'Where are you heading? Anywhere nice?'

'Portugal,' replied Helen, plucking a destination out of the air.

'Oh, I know Portugal really well,' said Ben, and Helen's heart sank. Why hadn't she chosen somewhere she at least vaguely knew something about? 'Whereabouts are you going? Lisbon or the coast, or a bit of both?'

'A bit of both,' said Helen quickly. 'I can't remember where exactly off the top of my head.'

'Well, if you get the chance you should definitely check out Madeirã and Alentejo. I spent some time in both a couple of years ago and I'd highly recommend them.'

'I'll certainly try,' said Helen, desperate to change the subject. Thankfully just then the kettle clicked off.

'I forgot to ask,' she said, opening a cupboard, 'are you still a tea drinker or is coffee more your thing now? Before you answer I should add that although we have a fancy coffee machine it's Adam's baby and I literally have no idea how it works.'

Ben smiled. 'Tea will be great thanks.'

'And that is the correct answer,' said Helen. 'Why don't you make yourself comfortable over there,' she pointed across the room to the sofa positioned opposite the French doors that led to the garden, 'and I'll bring your drink over.'

As Helen set about making the tea it occurred to her once again just how bonkers this whole situation was. More than anything she wanted to pick up the phone, call Gabby and tell her what was happening: that her ex-boyfriend and lead singer of Bluelight, Ben Baptiste, had come to see her, but it felt wrong somehow, like she would be cashing in on Ben's celebrity rather than just enjoying being with an old friend.

Drinks made, she rummaged in the top of one of the cupboards and took out a box of posh biscuits, which had, along with a forty-pound John Lewis voucher, been a gift from one of the mums at school at the end of term. As end-of-term teacher presents went, this had been far more generous than most, but then again, this mum's daughter had been a complete and utter nightmare all year, so to a large degree Helen felt like she had earned it.

'So,' she said, setting down Ben's tea in front of him along with a selection of the biscuits, 'tell me more about this thing you're in Manchester for.'

'It's nothing special,' he said, helping himself to a foil-covered biscuit. 'Just a TV thing at Media City over in Salford.'

'You mean like an interview?'

'Yeah, that sort of thing.'

'Ooh, exciting. Who's it with and when will it be going out?'

'To be honest I've no idea who the interviewer is,' he said, peeling the foil from the biscuit and dunking it into his tea. 'And I'm none the wiser about when it's going out either. Sometimes they film these things so far in advance that by the time they go out I can barely remember doing them.'

'Lifestyles of the rich and famous, eh!' said Helen, and then immediately hated herself for saying it.

'You wouldn't believe how tedious these things can be,' said Ben, thankfully ignoring her comment. He paused and took a bite of the biscuit. 'If I never had to talk about myself with a total stranger again, I think it would be too soon.'

'I've only ever been interviewed once,' said Helen. 'It was when one of the kids I used to teach raised a load of money for a children's hospital doing a sponsored walk. I was quoted in the *Evening News* as saying something boring like, "I always knew he'd do well, but he's surprised us all!" Talk about squandering your fifteen minutes of fame!' She laughed self-consciously and, desperate to stop gibbering, asked Ben another question.

'Do you ever get nervous doing interviews and stuff? I saw you on *Graham Norton* once, and you seemed completely at ease.'

'It's been a long time now so I'm used to it, I suppose. But occasionally I have a sort of out-of-body experience where I'm in the middle of an interview and I think to myself, "Where am I going with the answer to this question?"'

Helen laughed. 'That would be me all the time if I was in your shoes. How about going on stage? I mean what you do now is a world away from when we were kids and you were fourth on the bill at the Basement Club. Do you ever get stage fright playing in front of such huge audiences? I saw you at Glastonbury a couple of years ago, I can't believe you can do what you do in front of so many people and look so at ease.'

'You were at Glastonbury the year we headlined?' asked Ben. 'You should've said, I would've sorted out backstage passes.'

'Oh, I wasn't there in person,' admitted Helen, feeling distinctly uncool, 'I watched it on TV with the kids. I haven't been to a festival in years, not since my student days. They've never been Adam's cup of tea and so I suppose I just got out of the habit.'

'Do you remember that year we went to Reading?'

Helen smiled. 'How could I forget, three days and two nights of music, no sleep and mud.'

'And a tent missing half its tent poles! If it hadn't been for my guitar propping up the middle we'd have been homeless. Good times though, eh?'

'Some of the best,' said Helen wistfully. 'Although I'm not sure I could do it now at my age with all the standing up for hours on end, drinking and staying up late.'

'You're talking like you're past it,' said Ben, 'which as we're the same age would mean I am too.'

Helen laughed. She and Ben might have been the same age but they were nothing like each other, not any more. 'Time moves differently in the suburbs.'

'Rubbish,' said Ben. 'Age is just a state of mind.'

'Precisely,' said Helen, 'which probably explains why after a day at work I sometimes feel like I'm a hundred and three.'

'Are you still teaching?'

'For my sins,' said Helen, feeling even more boring than she already had been. 'I've been at the same school for the past twenty years.'

'Nothing wrong with a bit of stability,' said Ben. 'Nothing wrong with that at all.'

There was a brief lull in the conversation as they both sipped their drinks, and Helen wondered if she was boring him. While it was lovely, albeit surreal, to see him, she still couldn't help wondering why he'd chosen now to drop by after all these years. Bluelight had played in Manchester loads of times since they'd lost touch and he'd never got in contact then, so what made this time different? She was still puzzling over the answer to this question when Ben spoke.

'So, how's your mum, she okay?'

'Still the same: stubborn as ever,' said Helen. 'Refuses to see a doctor, thinks illness is just a matter of will power and won't let anyone do anything for her if she can help it.'

'That sounds just like Sue,' said Ben. 'Good to hear that some things don't change. And your sister?'

'Oh, Amanda, she's okay, I suppose,' continued Helen, 'still up herself as always. She's living down in Devon with some bloke she met – get this – on a bread-making course in Umbria. I couldn't tell you what she does for a living, to be honest I don't think she does anything at all. He's a bit older than her and made a stack of cash in the city in the Nineties and as far as I can tell from her Instagram, all she does is walk their three dogs on the beach and post memes about how grateful she is to the universe for her good fortune. Sometimes I want to write in her comments that I remember the days when she used to drink White Lightning in the park with her mates until she passed out, but then I worry she might get the universe to manifest some sort of spiritual voodoo nonsense, and I chicken out.' She smiled and took a sip of her tea. 'Do you ever hear from any of your family at all?'

Ben shook his head and Helen raised an eyebrow. 'What none of them?'

'No, and that's the way I like it. I haven't spoken to Dad since . . . well, since I left and after all that stuff with Nathan . . . well, how could I trust him again?'

'He's an idiot,' said Helen. 'That's for sure. I actually bumped into him in town must be about five or six years ago. To be honest he looked a bit of a state, but we started making small talk and of course we ended up talking about you. When I asked if you and he were in touch he just pulled a face like a slapped backside and there wasn't much more to say after that.'

'Sounds like my kid brother, all right,' said Ben. 'All I can do is apologise.'

'No need,' said Helen. 'All families are weird in their own special way.'

'Anyway,' said Ben, clearly keen to change the subject. 'This is a lovely home you've got here. Have you been here long?'

'About fifteen years now. We bought it as a bit of a wreck and did it up, back in the days when we both had energy for that sort of thing. It took us ages, cost a fortune, and there were points, particularly after Frankie was born and we had water coming through the bedroom ceiling, when I wondered what we'd taken on but thankfully we got through all that and I'm pleased with how it all turned out.'

'Well, you've done a great job. What made you pick Didsbury?'

Helen groaned inwardly and wondered how to make prosaic life choices sound more dynamic than they had been, but she came up short. 'It's going to sound boring but it was for the usual reasons,' she said, 'you know, school catchment areas and the like.'

'That sounds like a good enough reason to me. I mean, the last thing you'd want is for your kids to end up at somewhere like Cheadle Road, it's a wonder we survived.'

'Ah, Cheadle Road!' said Helen mock wistfully, of the primary school on the council estate that she and Ben had both attended. 'Never have quite so many supply teachers regretted their career choices so profoundly.'

'It really was little more than a holding pen,' said Ben. 'I think you did well to get your kids into a good school.'

'To be honest,' said Helen, 'it was all Adam's doing. He had a real bee in his bonnet about the kids going to the "right" primary school which fed into the "right" secondary school. It's all so strategic, the sharp-elbowed middle classes calculating every last move in order to get the best resources for our kids. The teenage socialist me would've accused me of being part of the problem, but the harried middle-aged mum of two me would probably just whack her over the head with her own copy of *Socialist Worker* and tell her to mind her own business.'

'Sometimes I miss the days when everything seemed simpler,' laughed Ben.

'Me too,' said Helen. 'But then you get older, life intervenes and you suddenly realise that things aren't always as black and white as you first thought.'

She paused, deliberating over whether she should have another biscuit, and in doing so recalled the lithe and slender body of the bikini-clad supermodel she had seen Ben with in the pages of *Hello*. Women like that didn't have first biscuits, let alone seconds. But she reasoned she wasn't one of those women and didn't particularly want to be either, and so she helped herself to another, telling herself that in doing so she was somehow striking a blow for feminism.

'Anyway,' she continued, 'it's really nice around here. Plus, the kids love it and their secondary school isn't that far away either.'

'And Adam, your husband, is he the guy you were going out with when we were last in touch?'

'Yes,' said Helen. 'That's the one.'

'How long have you been married?'

Helen swallowed hard and then took a sip of her tea. 'We've been together twenty-two years, and married almost twenty.'

Ben raised his mug in the air as if in toast. 'Congratulations! In this day and age that's no mean feat. What's the secret of your success?'

It crossed Helen's mind that this would've been a good point at which to correct her earlier lie and tell Ben the truth about her and Adam but then her phone rang. She picked it up from the coffee table in front of her, saw Esme's name on the screen and immediately felt a knot of worry tighten in her stomach. Esme almost never used her phone to speak on, so the fact that she was calling sent alarm bells ringing. It had to be trouble.

'Sorry,' she said, standing up, 'it's my daughter, probably just telling me she's forgotten something vital. I'll be back in a minute. Help yourself to another drink if you want one.'

Closing the door behind her, Helen went to the living room and then, taking a deep breath to compose herself, answered the call, hoping and praying that she didn't sound like a woman who had a megastar ex-boyfriend sitting in her kitchen.

4

Helen

'Hello, sweetie,' said Helen. 'Everything all right? You're not there already, are you?'

'We're at the services,' said Esme with a sigh. 'Frankie needed a wee after downing two bottles of Coke one after the other.'

Helen couldn't help but shake her head in despair. 'And apart from that is everything okay?'

There was a slight pause. 'I suppose.'

'You suppose? Why only suppose? What's wrong?'

'Come on, Mum, what do you think's wrong? It's her, isn't it? She's really doing my head in trying to be all pally like we're best mates or something.'

'Oh, I'm sorry, Es. I'm sure she's only trying to be friendly.'

'Oh, come on, Mum, stop being so reasonable and just hate her like I do! That bitch broke up our family, she doesn't deserve to be treated nicely!'

Helen closed her eyes and tried to calm herself down. She had been truly horrified when Adam had first floated the idea of taking the kids away with Holly. After all, it had only been a couple of months since he'd started having them over for the weekend and a week's holiday was a whole different beast altogether. In the end she'd agreed to it for precisely the same reason she'd given her blessing for weekend visits, because, no matter what had gone on, he was still their dad and she wanted them to have a relationship with him.

'Look, Essie,' said Helen. 'I know you didn't want to go and

I'm grateful that you're doing this for Frankie's sake, and I know it must be hard but just try to be positive. It'll all be over before you know it and you'll be back home in no time at all.'

'Sorry, Mum,' said Esme after a moment, 'I think I'm partly in such a bad mood because I just miss Josh so much. This is the longest we've ever been apart.'

Helen smiled at the thought that a week away from a boy Esme had only been seeing for three months could be so painful.

'Have you spoken to him yet?'

'We've been messaging but the signal got so bad that I had to give up until we got here.'

Sensing that any more talk of Josh might lead to tears, Helen decided to try to change the subject.

'And how's the traffic? Is there much on the road?'

'It's not bad, I suppose.'

'And is Frankie okay?'

'You can talk to him if you like, I'll pass you over.'

Helen listened to the sound of rustling and muffled voices and then finally Frankie came on the line.

'Hey Mum.'

'Hey Franks, are you having a good time?'

'It's okay, I suppose.'

'Have you seen the sea yet?'

'No, not yet, I think Dad said we might in a bit when we carry on.'

'Oh, that will be nice.'

Frankie said nothing.

'What's the weather like? Is it sunny?'

There was a long silence that Helen assumed was Frankie making some sort of meteorological assessment.

'It's a bit cloudy, and a bit windy too.'

'Well, hopefully it'll clear up later.'

Frankie again said nothing, and the next thing Helen knew Esme was back on the line.

'Hey Mum,' said Esme. 'I think we're getting back on the road now so we'll have to go.'

'Of course,' said Helen, trying to sound upbeat. 'Try to have a nice time, won't you, sweetie? Send me a text when you get there and remember how much I love you.'

'Sure, gotta go,' said Esme, and then the line went dead.

For a moment Helen stood with the phone pressed against her ear, swallowing down the ball of emotion stuck in her throat. She thought about last year's summer holiday, the cottage they'd rented in the Suffolk countryside. It had rained almost every day, and the kids had complained so much – about the weather, the wi-fi and the weird smell in the bathroom – that at one point she'd lost her temper and screamed that she was never taking them on holiday again. And yet now, when she looked back it wasn't so much those things that stood out but the small moments she remembered. The morning Esme and Frankie decided to make a surprise breakfast of American pancakes for them all. The afternoon the four of them sat playing board games and eating toasted tea cakes while outside it poured with rain. The evening they'd spent sitting in a companionable silence, the kids on their phones, Helen and Adam reading their books, all safe and secure together under the same roof.

At the time she hadn't known it was their last holiday as a family. At the time she'd thought they still had at least one more left before Esme went off to university. Had she known then what she knew now she would've mentally recorded every minute, every second of that final holiday. Had she known then what she knew now, she would have held them all a bit closer, treasured each moment just a little bit more.

Had it not been for Ben's presence in the house, Helen was almost certain she would've collapsed in tears for the second time that day but as it was, she told herself she'd have to hold it together for a while longer. Taking a deep breath, she fixed a smile to her face and returned to the kitchen. Placing her phone back on the coffee table, she took her seat next to Ben.

'Everything okay?'

'Yes, fine,' said Helen, brushing non-existent fluff from her lap. 'Although the weather's not up to much, apparently. Still, that's what you get for going on holiday in the UK. I bet LA is wall-to-wall sun all year round.'

'Pretty much,' said Ben. 'Although, I do miss the changing seasons you get here, even if a decent summer isn't always guaranteed.'

This time without any qualms, Helen helped herself to another biscuit. 'So, whereabouts in LA are you based? Still Bel Air?'

Ben shook his head. 'I've moved around quite a bit over the years but currently I've got a place in Malibu.'

'Sounds lovely, is it close to the beach?'

'Not far,' he replied, sounding just a touch embarrassed.

Once again an image of the leggy Italian supermodel from *Hello* popped into Helen's mind. Not having kept up to date with her celebrity gossip, she had no idea if Ben was still dating her or had moved on to pastures new, but she found she couldn't resist trying to dig for a little more information.

'And do you live there alone?'

Ben smiled wryly, clearly aware of Helen's clumsy attempt to ask about his love life. 'At the moment,' he replied. 'You know I was married, don't you?'

Helen nodded, wondering how much she should admit to knowing. After all, both his wedding to the actress Allegra Kennedy ten years ago and their subsequent divorce six years later had been all over the news.

'I think I heard something about it,' she replied. 'I was sorry to hear that it didn't work out. It's always horrible when relationships end.'

Again, Helen felt guilty for not being honest with Ben about Adam's leaving, but once more decided against it. She hadn't seen Ben in so long and who knew when or if she'd see him again, so was there really any point in souring a nice visit for no reason?

'We both just wanted different things, I suppose,' continued Ben. 'But we're still good friends. In fact, I spent last Christmas with her and her new husband at their ranch in Connecticut.'

It crossed Helen's mind that if Gabby had been here right now her eyes would be popping out of her head. Ben's ex-wife was married to none other than Christopher Jordan, star of that impenetrable series of superhero films Frankie and his friends were so obsessed with. It seemed utterly bizarre that she was now, thanks to Ben, party to the sort of insider celebrity gossip that magazines like *Hello*, and for that matter her friend Gabby, existed for.

'Well,' she said, trying her best to sound casual, 'that all sounds very grown up and civilised.'

Ben laughed. 'Believe me, it took us quite a while to get to this point, but I think it helped that when we drilled down to it, in the end we both realised that some things just weren't meant to be.'

'And you didn't have kids?'

The question had seemed innocent enough when it had crossed her mind, but now it had left her lips she felt awful. There could have been a million reasons why Ben and Allegra hadn't started a family, and not a single one of them was her business. She chided herself for not being more sensitive.

'I'm sorry,' she said. 'That was rude. Just ignore me.'

Although Ben offered her a forgiving smile there was a hint of sadness in his eyes when he spoke. 'You're not being rude. It's a natural enough question. It's just a long story, probably one for when we've got a bit more time.'

He stood up, as if to bring that topic of conversation to a close. 'I don't suppose there's any chance I could use your bathroom, is there?'

'Of course,' said Helen, and she had just opened her mouth to direct him to the downstairs loo when she suddenly remembered that Frankie had managed to block it that morning with one of his increasingly substantial bowel movements. 'Upstairs, second door on the left, you can't miss it.'

Helen refilled the kettle to make them both a fresh cup of tea and while it boiled had another go at making the kitchen look half decent. As she loaded the dishwasher, wiped down the surfaces and emptied the overflowing bin she wondered what Ben must think of her. With her strange behaviour, intrusive questions and boring suburban existence, was he regretting coming to see her? She couldn't help but think so. Even she was bored by the sound of her own voice. Most likely he was thinking he'd had a lucky escape when they'd split up all those years ago, because if they hadn't perhaps this might have been the life he'd have ended up with. She made up her mind that she wasn't going to talk about herself any more, she was just going to ask him question after question about himself until he left, to avoid boring him any further.

Crossing the room, she picked up her phone, opened up her music app and put on a playlist that Esme had made for her consisting of songs from Helen's youth. The moment she heard the opening bars to Jeff Buckley's 'Mojo Pin' playing over the speaker she immediately felt several degrees more relaxed. It made her remember her old self, her young self, the person she used to be who didn't agonise over every little thing she said.

With her phone still in her hand, she checked her emails and when she saw there was nothing particularly exciting there she opened Instagram. Helen, who had the sum total of three followers, had initially only joined to look at her friends' photos and nice pictures of food, but over time she had become so sucked in that now her feed consisted of everything from cute puppies to heart-warming stories of enormous basketball players helping tiny old ladies across the road with their shopping. She looked up Esme's profile but had already seen the most recent pictures there. It crossed her mind to search Ben's name to see if he had a profile, but this felt so stalkerish that in the end she closed the app altogether. She was about to put her phone down when it occurred to her that she could quickly catch up on the news, and then instead of just wittering on about her own tedious existence she might be able to drop a few things into her conversation with Ben that might make her sound a little more intelligent and informed.

Opening the BBC News app, Helen was met by a photo of Ben looking back at her. Her first thought was that she was having a senior moment and had inadvertently opened Instagram again, but then a closer look revealed that she hadn't made a mistake at all, Ben really was the lead story on the news. She read the headline, then read it again, then finally the article that went with it, and was utterly perplexed, so much so that the next thing she did was cross the room and turn on the TV. There too, on *Sky News*, Ben's face loomed large and the scrolling caption underneath echoed that of the BBC news article: '. . . fears grow for troubled Grammy Award-winning Bluelight singer now missing for over seventy-two hours.'

The picture of Ben was then replaced by footage of a large bald man dressed in a Hawaiian shirt, apparently giving some sort of press conference. Helen turned up the volume. 'We just want Ben to know,' the man was saying, 'that we all love him and care for him and want him home safe and sound.'

It made no sense, why were they saying Ben was 'troubled' when he looked absolutely fine to her? Why were they saying he was missing when he was here in Manchester for publicity? It had to be some sort of mistake.

Just then Ben himself returned from the loo, and she turned to look at him just as he caught sight of the screen. His previously calm features twisted into a look of horror and in that instant Helen knew that she hadn't been the only one keeping secrets.

5

Ben

Ben exhaled deeply but didn't meet Helen's gaze. He hadn't expected things to catch up with him quite so quickly. He'd been totally sure that he'd have more time.

'I know what you're going to say but I promise it's nothing to worry about.'

Helen raised an eyebrow. 'Nothing to worry about? Ben, you're all over the news. What's going on?'

'It's a long story . . . and a complicated one too and given my age it's also more than a bit embarrassing . . . but essentially . . . well . . . I suppose . . . what it boils down to is that . . . I've run away.'

He felt a mixture of relief and discomfort. While it was good to have finally confessed the truth to someone, at the same time he didn't even know how to begin to explain what had led him to this point.

'Run away?' said Helen, a look of confusion on her face. 'From what, from who?'

Ben swallowed hard. 'From the band . . . my manager . . . my life, well from everything really.'

Crossing the room, he sat down on the sofa as Helen switched off the TV before sitting down next to him. He felt the weight of the past few sleepless nights suddenly descend on him, obliterating every last bit of the energy he'd managed to summon for his visit with Helen. He owed her an explanation before he left, that much was certain. He couldn't just turn and go without at least trying to throw some light on the events that had brought him to this moment, but at the same time he couldn't just tell her the unvarnished truth either; even after all these years her respect still meant something to him.

'It's hard to know when things started to go wrong,' he found himself saying. 'For instance, I could go all the way back to when I was a kid and talk about losing my mum or, as you know better than most, my crappy relationship with my dad. I could even talk about the pressures of making it big so young, and all the ways that screwed me up too, and all the crazy things I did to try and even things out. I could talk about the exhaustion of relentless touring and the strain of being in the public eye. Or about the trail of broken relationships I left in my wake, up to and including my failed marriage. To be honest, there wasn't just one thing that made me want to run away, just lots of things building up over a very long time. But I suppose if I had to pick one key event that tipped the balance, it was the release of the new album back in April.'

'What? Wasn't it received well?' asked Helen.

'The critics loved it,' said Ben, 'and so did the fans. It wasn't the music that was the problem, it was everything else: the band, the promotion, all the big plans for the tour. It all got a bit too much, and well . . . I ended up in a mess and for the past three months I've been in . . . not rehab exactly . . . but you get the idea.'

It wasn't the full story, not by any means, but it was all he could manage at the moment. He briefly lifted his gaze from the floor to see Helen looking back at him, her eyes full of pity. She reached out and put a hand on his arm. 'Oh, Ben, I'm so sorry, I had no idea you've been struggling.'

'No one did,' he replied. 'That's how good my manager, Rocco, the guy in the loud shirt that was just on the news, is at controlling media narratives.' He stopped and smiled. 'He actually leaked a story that I've been out in the Brazilian rainforests with Ridley Scott preparing to make my film debut as a cover for me being in rehab, can you believe that? And what's more, people actually bought it! Me, who didn't even get a speaking part in the school nativity, in a Ridley Scott film!'

'So, after your stint in rehab or whatever . . . are you okay now?'

Ben took a breath and then another, hoping that each might fortify him. How exactly to answer this question? While he wasn't in the dark place he had once been, this latest turn of events was certainly taking its toll. 'Yeah, I'm getting there. I mean, I have good days and bad like everybody else, but for the most part, I'm fine. The place I was staying, the Compono, it's easily one of the best facilities in the world. And my time there really helped me get a bit of perspective. It really helped me get my head straight, helped me understand that I wasn't happy any more, and probably hadn't been for a very long time.' He looked briefly at Helen again, before returning his gaze to the floor. 'It's really difficult to talk about, and is probably just going to sound really spoiled, but I reached a point where everything just felt so meaningless, it was all just more of the same. It's hard to explain but . . . I don't know . . . it felt like an endless round of more money, more parties, more girlfriends but none of it meaning anything, none of it having any substance . . . and life just felt pretty . . . I don't know . . . empty.' He half smiled, embarrassed. 'First world problems, eh?'

'Not at all,' replied Helen. 'I'm so sorry you felt so low.'

Ben shrugged and smiled, keen to change the direction of the conversation. 'If I hadn't been I wouldn't have ended up at the Compono, and if I hadn't gone there I wouldn't have visited the library.'

Helen looked puzzled. 'The library?'

'Residents at the Compono aren't allowed phones, the Internet or TV, so the library is where it's at when it comes to entertainment,' Ben explained. 'Anyway, one day I was in there just browsing the shelves – I'd just read *The Power of Now* – and I was looking for something a bit less . . . I don't know . . . "woo woo" when at random I picked a book up off the shelf. It turned out to be about the most remote places on earth. I started reading, thinking it might help pass the time, but then in a few hours I'd finished it and I was completely blown away. I just fell in love with the idea of getting away from it all, of taking myself off the map, and that same night I made up my mind that when I got out of the Compono I wasn't just going to take a break, I was going to quit the band for good and move to one of the places I'd read about. It took a second read to narrow down my destination to two: either Barrow Island in Alaska or Ittoqqortoormiit in Greenland. In the end Greenland won because . . .' he paused and smiled, 'I don't know . . . I liked the idea of living in a place that half the world wouldn't be able to pronounce, let alone get to. The moment I made the decision it was like the rest suddenly fell into place. I'd turn my back on everything, sling a few clothes in a bag, along with an eight-track and my acoustic, and live a simpler life away from all the madness.'

'So, what happened?' asked Helen.

'Rocco is what happened,' said Ben, his stomach tightening at the thought of the man. 'Last week, a few days before I was due to leave the Compono, a new guy arrived, a film producer who I vaguely knew. Anyway, we got talking and to my surprise he congratulated me on the tour selling out. I told him that he must have made a mistake because Rocco had told me he'd cancelled it and that it was all taken care of. But then later, this guy took me to one side, produced a phone he'd managed to sneak in and showed me a *Rolling Stone* article confirming what he'd told me.'

'Your manager lied to you?'

Ben nodded and ran a hand across his beard thoughtfully. 'Rocco is such a very convincing liar and can make anyone believe anything. He'll tell you whatever it is he thinks you want to hear and then when you confront him with his lies he'll deny them so vehemently you convince yourself that you must have made a mistake. I've seen him do it to countless people over the years but usually for the benefit of the band. But seeing that article, I knew he'd been lying to me, telling me the tour had been cancelled, to shut me up and keep me sweet. I should've known better than to believe him, but there it was in black and white: we'd sold out fifty dates, across twenty-six countries, netting over $500 million worth of ticket sales and *Rolling Stone* were calling us the biggest band in the world. Of course, there was no way he was going to let all that go just because I'd had a bit of a "meltdown". This was his moment, his way of proving to the world that he was the best in the business.'

'Couldn't you have put your foot down?' asked Helen. 'Told this Rocco guy you'd had enough, that you weren't doing the tour, that you wanted out of the band? Surely he works for you and not the other way around.'

Ben sighed. 'You mean, like the three times I'd tried before?' He shook his head sadly. 'Telling Rocco anything he doesn't want to hear is pointless, all he does is talk and talk until somehow you end up agreeing with him. All he does is tell you, "I hear you, mate, really I do, and I promise you there's definitely an end point to all this but now is not the right time." And of course, there never is a right time. And there and then, standing in this guy's room looking at his contraband phone, I realised the right time was never going to come unless I made it happen.'

A look of outrage flashed across Helen's face. 'Your manager sounds like a complete and utter snake.'

'He is,' said Ben. 'But that's part of the reason he's so good at what he does. He's ruthless, you wouldn't trust him as far as you could throw him – and believe me he's a big man – but he's also the deal maker to end all deal makers. Bluelight wouldn't be the band it is without him.'

'I'm sure that's not true,' protested Helen. 'You're the band you are because you're amazingly talented.'

Ben shook his head. 'There are lots of amazingly talented people in the world. I meet them all the time driving Ubers, tending bars and waitressing in restaurants, all waiting for their big break. Talent is good, but it only gets you so far. The things that push you over the top, the things that make the difference are power and connections, and Rocco has both in spades.'

'But once you'd found out he'd lied to you about the tour couldn't you confront him?'

'There wouldn't be any point,' said Ben. 'Rocco isn't in it for the money, he already has more cars and houses than he knows what to do with. He's in it because he loves power, and being the manager of Bluelight gives him that. He's never going to let that go without a fight. If I'd told him my plans to quit the band he'd have had me wrapped up in the mother of all legal battles before I'd even finished talking, and to be honest I just don't think I'd have the strength for it. I knew it would just be easier if I disappeared. So, I put the plan I'd come up with at the Compono into action. I bribed a porter to get me my phone, then that night let myself out of a back window and escaped.'

'I can't believe it,' said Helen. 'It sounds like something out of a film.'

'That's what it felt like,' said Ben. 'Like it was all happening to someone else.'

He told her about getting a cab to his house in Malibu and his frantic dash around his home gathering together everything he might need: clothes, cash, bank cards, passport and a notepad in which he scribbled down some phone numbers and email addresses before switching off his phone and hiding it under a pile of T-shirts in his walk-in wardrobe. Then how, under the cover of darkness, he made his way to LA-X and got a flight to London.

Helen looked at him confused. 'Why London if you were going to Greenland?'

Ben sighed. 'I know this is going to sound weird . . . especially as we haven't seen each other in years . . . but I got the flight to London because I wanted to say goodbye to you.'

'To me?' Helen was completely taken aback. 'Why would you want to say goodbye to me of all people?'

He wanted to tell her about the time his therapist at the Compono had asked when he'd last felt happy, how the answer that had immediately sprung to mind had been the twenty months he and Helen had been together. He wanted to tell her how much he missed spending time with someone who'd known him before he was famous, when he was just plain old Ben, not the lead singer of Bluelight. He wanted to tell her how grateful he was to have had her in his life, and how much he regretted not making more of an effort to maintain their friendship. He wanted to tell her all this and more but he didn't quite know how.

'Because . . . I suppose . . . because we used to be so close . . . and I don't know . . . I've always regretted that we lost touch. It was my fault I'm sure, never prioritising what was really important. I mean over the years I've thought about you a lot . . . wondering where you were and what you were up to . . . but I just never got round to making the call. But I knew if I was planning on disappearing for good, then this might well be my last chance to see you. So, I decided I'd make a quick detour, see you for a few hours and then carry on to Greenland afterwards.'

'Wow,' said Helen. 'I don't really know what to say except . . . well . . . I'm glad that you came. I've always regretted that we didn't stay in touch too. But life's been so busy and other stuff always got in the way somehow.' She smiled awkwardly as though embarrassed and then immediately changed the subject. 'So, how was getting from London to Manchester?'

'Surprisingly fine,' said Ben. 'Or at least I thought so at the time. I got the train to Paddington, a Tube to Euston and then finally the train to Manchester, and as far as I'm aware no one recognised me.' He paused and glanced in the direction of the TV. 'Until a few moments ago, I thought . . . I don't know . . . that I'd got away with it, that after seeing you it would be goodbye England and hello Greenland, but now thanks to Rocco that's not going to happen. The press conference, all that stuff on the news and I guess by now all over the Internet, about me being "mentally fragile", it's all designed to smoke me out from wherever I'm hiding, to make it impossible for me to disappear. This is Rocco sending a message that he's not going to rest until I'm back in LA, back on tour, back writing songs and back making money for him. This is his way of making sure I never ever get to step off this stupid merry-go-round.'

This last sentence tumbled out and he could see that Helen was confused and maybe a little frightened. He stood up, face grim. 'I'm going to have to go. The last thing I want is to drag you into all this.' And then without another word he bent down, kissed Helen gently on the cheek and headed to the hallway, frantically trying to work out what to do next. He'd barely reached the front door when Helen slipped round him, blocking his exit.

'Ben, stop,' she said firmly. 'Just take a minute to think about what you're doing. You're all over the news, which means the minute you open this door there's a good chance someone somewhere will spot you and tip off the press.'

He shrugged. 'It's a risk I'll have to take.'

'Not if you stay here, it isn't,' said Helen.

'I can't stay here. It just isn't an option.'

'So, what's your big plan then?'

'To take my chances, make my way to the airport, fly to Reykjavik and get my connection to Ittoqqortoormiit.'

'That's your big plan?' said Helen, sounding oddly assertive. 'To go to an airport full of people on the same day you've been headline news and do what . . . cross your fingers and hope that no one notices you because you're wearing a hat and sunglasses?'

Ben smiled. Helen was right. It really wasn't much of a plan. 'Okay, so maybe I'll book myself into a hotel somewhere and wait until things quieten down.'

'And how's that any better? There'll still be people around to recognise you, and even worse you'll be a sitting duck if they contact the press. No, you'll have to stay here with me.'

'But what about your family?'

'What about them? They're in Wales for the week, by which time hopefully this will have all blown over.'

'But what if it doesn't? I'm sorry but I can't risk dragging you all into this.'

He reached past her to open the door but Helen pushed his hand away. 'I'm not joking, Ben, you're staying here, and I'm not going to take no for an answer!'

He couldn't help but smile. The Helen before him, so assured, so confident, reminded him so much of the Helen he used to know. 'I want to say yes, Helen, really I do, but I just can't do this to you. I know you had a taste of what it's like to be in the middle of a media storm when the band first took off but believe me if word gets out that I'm here it'll be much, much worse. There'll be newspapers camping on your doorstep, journalists turning over every inch of your life, and well . . . I wouldn't wish that on my worst enemy let alone one of my oldest friends. I'm sorry, but I can't risk them blowing your life apart. I just can't.'

Helen shook her head, determined. 'You can, and you will. And anyway, good luck to anyone trying to blow my life up any more than it has been already.'

Puzzled, Ben looked at Helen. 'What do you mean?'

She sighed. 'I feel really stupid saying this to you now, when I should've been honest with you from the start but . . .' she said, her voice breaking with emotion. 'I've been lying to you, Ben. My kids aren't really on a dad bonding trip . . . the truth is . . . the truth is we've split up and he's taken them away on holiday with his new twenty-five-year-old girlfriend.'

6

Ben

A pensive Ben was sitting opposite Helen and they were both cradling fresh mugs of tea that he suspected neither of them actually wanted. Helen's news had really taken him by surprise. All these years he'd always pictured her living pretty much the perfect life: a loving family, a comfortable home, a life filled with substance and meaning. The very life he'd always thought she deserved, the kind of life, if he was being honest, he would've liked to have had himself. So, to learn that this wasn't the case, that her life wasn't as flawless as he'd assumed, had stopped him in his tracks. Seeing her like this, so hurt, so lost, he knew he couldn't just walk away and leave her, he had to do something, even if that was merely to listen if she wanted to tell him her story. Suddenly his own problems receded into the background, and all he cared about was making sure that Helen, this woman who long ago, in what felt like a different life, he'd loved more than his very soul, was okay.

'You don't have to talk about it if you don't want to,' said Ben after a while. 'But if you do, I'm happy to listen.'

'I'm almost embarrassed to talk about it,' she began. 'Honestly, Ben, he made me feel like such a fool.' She sighed and stared bleakly into her mug of tea. 'I only found out by chance. I was checking the pockets of one of his suits one morning before taking it to the dry-cleaners when I came across a receipt for an upmarket restaurant in Manchester. It was on a night when he'd told me he was going to the pub for a work colleague's birthday. It was such a cliché, but I suppose clichés are clichés for a reason. My guess is he'd been careful for so long and hadn't been caught out that he'd simply become lazy. The receipt got me thinking. Things had been off between us somehow since the previous summer, small arguments over nothing, being short-tempered with each other, that sort of thing. He'd also been working a lot. Even though we'd always tried hard to keep the holidays free for spending time with the kids from the moment school broke up, aside from the one week we were away, he always seemed to have some work emergency or other that needed to be dealt with: exam board appeals, staffing issues for the new term and problems with the new sports block that was being built. At the time I'd tried to be supportive because I knew he was gunning for promotion, but I think even back then, deep down I knew there was more to it. Anyway, after finding the receipt I couldn't stop thinking about it and so the first opportunity I found I checked his phone. While I didn't find any incriminating texts or emails, his banking app told a different story. A story of bills, for hotel rooms, expensive dinners and numerous presents, and not a penny of it had been for my benefit.'

Ben found it hard not to get angry. If anyone deserved better than to be treated like that, it was Helen. 'So, what did he say when you confronted him?'

'He denied it of course, but I still had his phone in my hand at the time and I told him I was going to ring every number in his contacts until I found her.' She laughed bitterly. 'You should've seen his face, he went so pale I thought he was going to pass out and then finally he admitted it.'

'And who is she? Someone from work?'

'It's always someone from work, isn't it?' Helen paused and absently fiddled with her necklace. 'Her name's Holly, she's a not-that-long-qualified teacher at his school and he admitted it had been going on for a while but wouldn't confirm or deny any dates, not that it mattered. Anyway, long story short, he moved out the next day to stay with his parents, saying that he needed space to think things through, while I, naïve fool that I was, booked us in for counselling with Relate. We managed the sum total of one solitary session before he confessed that there was no point in carrying on because he'd already moved in with her.'

Ben shook his head. What was it about men that made them such idiots? 'Classy.'

'Exactly,' replied Helen. 'That's my husband for you.'

'And how have the kids taken it?'

Helen bit her lip. 'I think that's the worst of it. Esme was livid when she found out and didn't talk to Adam for a whole month after it all happened, and Frankie, well he might be fourteen, but he's still a little boy really. Although it's impossible to get him to talk about it I can't help feeling like this whole situation has just wrecked him. He adores his dad, absolutely worships him, so he must be devastated.'

'And the holiday?' asked Ben. 'Is this your ex's attempt to get the kids used to his new set-up?'

Helen rolled her eyes. 'Who knows? Believe it or not it was supposed to be our family holiday. Adam always does the booking, he likes doing all the research and bagging the deals, and it's one less thing for me to do so I've always let him get on with it. After he left, of course, the holiday was the furthest thing from my mind. Then bold as you like, after he's had the kids stay with him a couple of times, he announces casually that he's taking them on our family holiday with his new woman.'

'I bet you had something to say about that!'

'To be honest, I didn't feel like I had much of a choice. I could've kicked up a fuss, I could've threatened to get nasty with divorce lawyers and the like, but at the end of the day, it's all about making sure the kids are all right, isn't it? I might want to wring his neck but the bottom line is he's their dad, and I want them to be able to have a relationship with him. Anyway, he's not all evil. He's agreed I can have the house, so at least the kids won't have to move.'

'How very generous of him after blowing up your life like that.'

'To be fair it's the only upside in what has been from start to finish an absolute and total nightmare. Still, if it's true that "what doesn't kill you makes you stronger", this time next year I'll be Wonder Woman.' She smiled sadly and looked at Ben. 'So, you see, as I said earlier, my life's already a mess. And while I'm sure you'll be safe here, while I'm sure the media won't track you down to the house of a boring middle-aged woman in south Manchester, even if they do find you, there's not much more damage they can do to my life that hasn't already been done by my husband. So, what do you say? Will you stay?'

Ben considered the question. There were a million and one good reasons to say no and yet he heard himself saying the opposite.

'Good,' said Helen brightly as she got to her feet. 'Then grab your bag, and I'll show sir to his suite.'

Marvelling at the strange twists and turns life can take, Ben did as he was instructed, and Helen led him upstairs and along the hallway to a door that opened into a small room with white walls and a dark brown laminated floor. There was a wardrobe against one wall, with a bed next to it, and two desks, one positioned under the window and another against the adjacent wall.

'This is our guest bedroom-cum-study-cum-ironing-room-cum-place where we stick all the stuff we don't know what to do with,' said Helen, hefting a huge pile of folders off the bed and on to one of the desks. 'I'm afraid the kids' rooms are a total pit at the moment so it's the best I've got to offer you.'

'No need to apologise,' said Ben, 'you're doing me a massive favour and anyway, it looks great to me.'

'Are you sure?' she asked, picking up a washing basket from the floor and shoving it into the hallway. 'I'm guessing it's a bit of a comedown compared to the kinds of luxury hotels you're used to.'

'Take it from me,' said Ben, 'that kind of thing can get very old very quickly. This is perfect, thank you.'

'Well, in that case, I'll leave you to get settled in,' said Helen. 'I'll put some clean towels out in the bathroom, so help yourself to a shower or even a soak in the tub if you like. Take as long as you need and I'll see you downstairs whenever you're ready.'

The moment Helen closed the door behind her Ben flopped down on the bed exhausted. His every muscle hurt, his head felt so foggy he could hardly think straight and he was clenching his jaw so tightly that the whole of his face ached. How could he have been so naïve? How had he not seen this coming? He should've known that Rocco was never going to just sit by and let him walk away. He should have known he was always going to do everything in his power to make sure that Ben knew who was in charge.

Back in the Eighties, Rocco Roberts had been a market trader in London's East End before going on to become a doorman at a whole host of West End nightclubs. That would've probably been the sum total of his career had it not been for an early-Nineties dance music act scoring a number of underground hits. In desperate need of management but wary of going with someone they didn't know, the act had asked Rocco, a former school friend, to help out, and overnight Rocco Promotions and Band Management Services was born.

In the years that followed Rocco made a small fortune managing three more dance acts, two boy bands, and a brace of singer-songwriters before accidentally coming across Bluelight playing third on the bill at King's Cross Water Rats. While Rocco happily admitted he was indifferent to Bluelight's music, he always said that the moment he saw Ben on stage he knew he was watching a star in the making. As soon as Bluelight finished their set, forgetting all about the singer-songwriter he'd actually come to see, Rocco went backstage and invited the band to join him for dinner at the Groucho Club.

That night, somewhere between the first bottle of Champagne and the fifth, Rocco persuaded Bluelight to sign him as their manager and six months, two producers and a change of drummer later, he landed them a four-album deal with EMI so huge that, without releasing a single record, Bluelight ended up gracing the covers of every significant music magazine in the UK and America. That's how good Rocco already was at his job.

It occurred to Ben that the fact Rocco had turned to the press in order to smoke him out was a good indicator that, for the moment at least, his manager had no idea where in the world he was. How long this would remain the case, however, he didn't know but guessed it wouldn't be long. He was only too aware of the resources Rocco had at his disposal and this, combined with all the media attention, the Twitter hashtag #findbluelightben and the fact that, thanks to Rocco, international authorities now believed him to be in a vulnerable mental state, meant that effectively there were eyes everywhere.

Feeling suddenly sick, Ben leaned across the bed to his bags, rooted through them and plucked out some fresh clothes and underwear. Making his way to the bathroom, he closed the door behind him and turned on the shower. As the room filled with steam he shed his clothes on the floor and then stepped into the stream of just-below-scalding hot water.

Closing his eyes, he felt his skin grow accustomed to the water's sting and churned over his thoughts about the day. Was it only this morning he'd landed at Heathrow? He'd assumed his visit to see Helen would be little more than a pit stop, an opportunity to catch up with an old friend followed by a night in an anonymous hotel before getting his flight to Reykjavik in the morning. Now here he was, his face all over the news, hiding from the world at the home of a woman he hadn't spoken to in decades, a woman he'd dated for less than two years before they'd split up at the tender age of eighteen. The whole situation seemed like madness and yet at the same time he couldn't help feeling that something about it felt right too. Because Helen wasn't just anybody; there had been a time when he had loved her more than life itself. She was one of the few people who had believed in him before he became Ben from Bluelight. She was one of the few people in the world who'd known him before fame and fortune got their hooks into him. Though he hadn't planned it he knew that if he had to wait out this storm anywhere, then here with Helen was just about the best place he could think of.

After his shower Ben dressed before heading back to his room and could easily have crawled under the covers and fallen asleep. But after years of touring he'd learned the hard way that getting on to local time as quickly as possible was the best cure for jet lag and so, fighting the urge to give in to his fatigue, he picked up his bag, rifled through it and pulled out the brand-new phone he'd bought for cash on his way to Euston. Removing it from its box, he inserted a new SIM card, switched it on and then took out the notebook in which he'd frantically scribbled down all the numbers and email addresses he'd thought he might need before he left.

Turning the book's pages, Ben found the code for accessing his old number's voicemail messages. It felt strange dialling his own number, and for a moment he imagined himself answering it, like some sort of *Twilight Zone* episode where the old Ben was carrying on with his life as usual, blissfully unaware that his other self was halfway around the world. When the call went to voicemail he tapped in the PIN number and was horrified when the electronic voice coolly informed him that he had forty messages waiting for him.

Steeling himself, he listened to the first message, which was innocuous enough, just his bandmate Leona checking in with him: 'Hey Ben, Rocco's saying you've gone missing from some rehab place. I didn't even know you were in rehab. Some friend I am. Anyway, if you can, please call me back when you get this and let me know everything's okay, will you?'

The next few were pretty much in the same vein, the other band members all wondering where he was, although with each message their tone became increasingly anxious. Then came a call from Rocco. 'Ben,' he said, and Ben felt an involuntary chill run down his spine, 'it's midday and you're nowhere to be seen. Either you call me in the next fifteen minutes or I'm going to come looking for you.'

From anyone else those might have been interpreted as words of concern but knowing Rocco as he did, Ben knew they were a threat. He skipped through a few more messages, which were mostly of Rocco calling him every name under the sun, but then about twenty messages in he heard a much gentler voice, one he was glad to hear.

'Hey Ben, it's me. It's all over the news about you going missing. I'm really worried about you, so please, if you do hear this just get in touch and let me know you're safe, okay? I don't need to know where you are, I don't need to know why you've gone, I just need to know you're safe.'

Allegra.

Ben felt awful. In all his calculations around his escape he hadn't factored in the worry he might be causing the people he cared about. Not that there were many, but Allegra was one of them. His instinct was to call and reassure her everything was okay, but that would only make her a target for his manager. Allegra would've been one of the first people Rocco would've called looking for Ben, and with his ability to smell a lie from a thousand paces he was glad that she had nothing to hide. He'd have to think of a way round this, there was no way he was going back to LA, back to the life he'd been living before he'd arrived at the Compono. No way at all. But as for a solution, he was too tired to come up with one now and so, throwing the phone down on the bed, he stood up, left the room and headed back downstairs to rejoin Helen.

7

Helen

When Helen awoke after a somewhat fitful night the first thing she did was check her phone to see what time it was. To her surprise she discovered that somehow she had overslept and it was 10.05 a.m. Helen couldn't remember the last time she'd slept this late and could only think that on some level her unconscious mind, knowing that the kids were away, had given her a special dispensation. Yawning, she stretched her arms above her head and, somewhat wrongfooted by the fact that she was still in bed this late in the day, she was reaching out an arm to pull back the covers when suddenly her stomach lurched as the memory of the previous day's events came flooding back to her. With sudden clarity she recalled the fact that she had a fugitive rock star ex-boyfriend sleeping in her spare room and the entire world was looking for him.

Once she'd calmed down Helen found herself smiling, not just because of the strange turn her normally predictable life had taken, but also at the memory of the lovely afternoon and evening she and Ben had spent together. Following a very unglamorous and hastily thrown-together late lunch of tuna pasta they had chatted all afternoon, reminiscing about the old days. And later, after a dinner of frozen pizza and oven chips, they had chatted more about the same, which had led to Helen retrieving an old box of photos from the loft. Over a bottle of wine they had rummaged through the box, each picking out their favourite of all the photos. Helen's had been a black-and-white shot of an eighteen-year-old

Ben singing on stage at the Barrel Organ with his very first band, Only Creatures. He'd been so skinny back then and all sharp cheekbones, tight jeans and youthful optimism. Ben's favourite, meanwhile, was a polaroid of Helen wearing a vintage tea dress and bright red baseball boots at the sixth-form Christmas party. She was seventeen in the photo, and so full of the arrogance of youth that she had stared defiantly straight into the camera lens as if daring it to capture her image.

'Look at us though,' Helen had said as she and Ben stared at both the photos side by side. 'We were such babies back then, thinking we knew it all.'

'But we hadn't got a clue, had we?' Ben had replied. 'Not a single clue.'

Reaching across to the bedside table, Helen picked up the polaroid of herself, which she'd brought up to bed with her at the end of the night. She could see elements of Esme in her features, and even some of Frankie too, but it was the parts that were just her that she marvelled at most, that awe-inspiring confidence, that self-assured look in her eyes. Where was that young woman now? Helen wondered. Had she disappeared completely or was there still some small trace of her left?

Returning the picture to her bedside table, Helen picked up her phone again, took a deep breath and then unlocked it, hoping beyond hope that some other big news story might have broken overnight to knock Ben out of the spotlight. But it hadn't. Instead, the papers were full of Ben, and more Ben. One tabloid had led with a story about a psychic who claimed that Ben had been kidnapped, and another had quoted 'anonymous sources' claiming that following an unspecified incident Ben was undergoing extensive plastic surgery in South America. Meanwhile on Twitter the hashtag #findbluelightben was trending high as was #lightacandleforben and #bluelightfansforben. In addition, there were numerous reports about a group of Internet sleuths working around the clock to track Ben down who were now speculating there was a good chance he was in the UK, most likely London or Manchester.

Helen swallowed hard; the net really was closing in, and she got out of bed, walked over to the bedroom window and very gently pulled the curtains aside a fraction, her breath bated. Thankfully, there were no hordes of journalists and photographers standing on her drive, in fact the street was empty apart from an elderly man walking a tiny Jack Russell, but even so she felt unnerved. She wondered briefly if it had been the right thing to do to ask Ben to stay. After all, she didn't really know anything about the strange world he inhabited, and for all her bravado the day before she couldn't help wondering what her reaction might be if the press started rummaging through her life. What if they found out about Adam? What if all their dirty laundry was set out for complete strangers to ogle at? Helen shuddered at the thought. But then taking a deep breath, she reminded herself that although they hadn't seen each other in years, Ben wasn't just anybody, he was her first true love, one of her oldest friends, a friend in need of help.

When he'd revealed that he'd been in rehab Helen hadn't known what to think. Everything she knew about that kind of world – which admittedly wasn't very much at all – was from media stories of celebrity breakdowns over the years. Actors, singers and models taking time out in places that to Helen's eyes looked a lot like posh hotels to recover from drug and alcohol abuse. But from the way Ben had talked about his time at the Compono, Helen sensed that it hadn't been an addiction that had taken him there. It seemed like there was more to the story but she hadn't wanted to press him. Ben would tell her when he was good and ready. At the rate things were going it looked to be a question of *when* they would track him down, not *if*, so she wanted to do all she could to be a friend he could rely on.

Closing the browser on her phone, Helen texted the kids good morning then slipped on her dressing gown and, wary of Ben seeing what she liked to call her 'morning face', she gently opened her bedroom door, ears straining for any sign that he was awake. Once she was sure the coast was clear she dashed across the hallway to the bathroom, showered in record time and was back in her bedroom in under five minutes.

Half an hour later, having dressed and done her hair and make-up, Helen went downstairs and turned off the alarm before heading to the kitchen to make a start on breakfast. She opened the fridge, but there was barely anything inside, as knowing that the kids would be away she hadn't felt like doing a food shop. Opening the freezer, she searched for inspiration and was rewarded, after excavating through the permafrost at the back of the bottom drawer, by the discovery of a pack of M&S croissants and half a pack of IKEA cinnamon buns.

Warming up the oven, she decanted both packets on to two baking trays and was just wondering if she should make the effort to nip out to the shop at the end of the road to grab some fresh orange juice when the kitchen door opened and in came Ben.

'Morning,' he said blearily. 'That was the best sleep I've had in ages. I could easily have stayed in that bed all day.'

'I'm glad you got some rest,' said Helen brightly. 'I've just put some bits in the oven for breakfast. Are you hungry?'

'Ravenous,' said Ben. 'But listen, I hate that I'm putting you out like this. Please, don't go to any trouble for my benefit. Why don't you let me pay for breakfast to be ordered in? It's the least I could do after you've put me up like this.'

'Really, it's no trouble,' said Helen, 'it's not like I've been up for hours making stuff from scratch. And anyway, compared with two constantly hungry, impossible-to-please teenagers I'm normally making breakfast for, you're a dream—'

The front doorbell rang, making Helen jump. She looked at Ben and he looked at her and their gaze asked only one question.

'Probably just the postman,' said Helen breezily, 'but to be on the safe side keep out of sight and I'll deal with it.'

Wiping her hands on a tea towel, Helen left the kitchen and as she made her way to the front door a strange feeling came over her as if she had forgotten something. She wondered if it was something to do with the kids, or perhaps something she needed to do with the car? Or perhaps it was a bill that needed paying. Whatever it was, she couldn't get a hold of it, until, that is, she opened the door and saw a smartly dressed Gabby looking back at her.

'Lisa's birthday brunch!' exclaimed Helen. 'You said you'd call by on the way, didn't you?'

'You hadn't forgotten, had you?' asked Gabby. 'I suppose you've had a lot on your mind. Anyway, just grab what you need and we'll get going.' Her friend then stepped into the hallway, just as she had done countless times before, sending Helen into an immediate panic.

'Where are you going?' said Helen as Gabby started walking towards the kitchen.

'I was just going to get myself a quick glass of water while I wait for you to get ready,' replied her friend, giving Helen a strange look. 'I was late leaving and I dashed over here so quickly that I'm parched. It's okay that I get myself a drink, isn't it?'

'Of course,' said Helen quickly. 'It's just that the kitchen's a tip. Let me get it for you.'

Helen dashed into the kitchen but to her surprise Ben was nowhere to be seen, which was just as well because instead of staying put, Gabby had followed her.

'Are you baking?' she asked, eyebrows raised as she sniffed the air and then spotted the empty croissant packet on the counter. 'Far be it from me to look down on anyone who likes to indulge in a little pre-breakfast breakfast, but you know as well as I do that they always serve too much food at those brunches. I'm just worried you'll burst!'

'You were right, I had forgotten about this morning,' said Helen, wondering where on earth Ben had got to. She switched off the oven and then hesitated. If Gabby saw the amount of food she'd cooked it might give the game away. Instead, she grabbed a glass, filled it from the tap and handed it to her friend.

'Thanks,' she replied, and then taking a sip she gave Helen a funny look. 'Aren't you going to take those croissants out? They'll burn otherwise.'

Helen laughed nervously. 'Of course, I don't know where my head's at this morning.' She opened the oven and removed both trays and her friend's quizzical expression was impossible to avoid.

'Wow,' said Gabby, 'far be it from me to food shame you, but that's a lot of pastries.'

'Honestly,' said Helen, 'what was I thinking? I must have been on autopilot thinking I was doing breakfast for the kids.'

Setting down her glass on the kitchen counter, Gabby gave Helen a hug. 'You must be really missing them. How are they getting on, have they called yet?'

'I spoke to them just after they arrived yesterday,' said Helen. 'They seem to be trying to make the best of a bad situation.'

Gabby's lip curled in disgust. 'I could really thump that husband of yours.'

'Join the queue,' said Helen.

'Anyway,' said Gabby, 'let's get going. The sooner we leave, the sooner we'll be face down in our bottomless brunches!'

Helen wasn't sure what to do, leave Ben alone in the house or tell Gabby she wasn't coming and run the risk of raising her suspicions even more than they already were.

'Okay,' she said, her voice raised slightly in the hope that it might reach Ben wherever he was hiding, 'Lisa's birthday brunch here I come! Just wait here and I'll get my shoes and coat.'

A puzzled Gabby gave Helen a strange look. 'Why are you shouting like I'm a ninety-year-old with an ear trumpet?'

'Sorry,' said Helen, 'I'm so used to yelling at the kids that I forget normal human beings don't need to be shouted at.' She grabbed her trainers and denim jacket from the hallway, slipped them on, and then the two of them made their way outside.

Helen waited until they were halfway up the road before she suddenly exclaimed that she had left her phone back at the house even though it was actually in her jacket pocket.

'Won't be a minute,' she said, and without waiting for Gabby's response she quickly turned, ran back to the house and, once she was inside with the front door closed, she called out: 'Ben! Where are you?'

'I'm in here,' came a voice from the direction of the living room, and as Helen entered Ben emerged from his hiding place behind the sofa.

'All clear?' he asked.

'Not quite. I'm so sorry but I've got to go to a friend's birthday brunch. If I don't go they'll get suspicious, and for now at least we need things to look as normal as possible.'

Mike Gayle

'Don't worry, you go, I'll be fine.'

'Are you sure?'

'Absolutely,' said Ben, and then he grinned and added, 'and anyway, that just means a bigger breakfast for me.'

By the time Helen and Gabby made it to Milk and Honey, the rest of their friends were already seated at the rear of the restaurant looking out on to the garden. While Helen had been in contact with all her friends individually at various points across the past two months, this was the first time she had seen everyone together since Adam left. And while she was sure that things would be fine, she couldn't help but feel a moment of trepidation wondering how they would be with her. She didn't want their pity, and neither did she want their outrage on her behalf. All she wanted, all she needed was for things to be normal, like they used to be before her life got turned upside down.

'Sorry we're late,' said Helen after they had all exchanged greetings, 'it was my fault, I forgot my phone and had to go back.'

'No worries,' said Lisa, 'I'm just glad you came. It feels like ages since we've all been out together. Now, let's pour you a mimosa, order some food and then crack on with the present opening!'

Pleased to have the attention taken away from her, Helen took a sip of her drink and allowed herself to enjoy this moment with her old friends. They'd all met when their kids started preschool fifteen years earlier, when they were new mums. Despite the years that had passed and the additional children that had come along, they had remained solid friends, seeing each other through the loss of parents, two cancer scares and, in the case of Lisa herself, the breakdown of her first marriage. For all their jokey banter and playful insults, they had always been there for each other and Helen was incredibly grateful to have this group of women in her life.

64

After they ordered food, a delighted Lisa opened her presents and then as usual they set about putting the world to rights. They covered everything from a rise in local car thefts through to nervousness about their children's upcoming A-level results, but then the food arrived, momentarily disrupting the flow of conversation.

As the waiters left, Helen was about to ask whether anyone else was thinking about getting a dog to fill the void left by children heading off to university, when from the other side of the table Sura broached a new topic for discussion.

'So, what do you guys think about that singer who's gone missing?' she said, balancing a mouthful of eggs Benedict on her fork. 'It's strange, isn't it? No one knowing where he is?'

Helen felt sick, as though it was completely obvious just from looking at her that she was complicit in the story that had captured everyone's attention.

'I bet he's just off on some desert island with some young starlet,' said Yas with a derisive snort. 'Didn't he used to go out with that red-headed singer from that band all the kids are mad about?'

'Yeah, he did,' said Lisa. 'And I think before that he was with Allegra Kennedy.'

'And their marriage only lasted ten minutes, didn't it?' said Sura. 'I'm sure I read that somewhere.'

'Yeah, you're right,' said Yas. 'I remember it was all over the—' She stopped mid-sentence and looked at Helen. 'Are you okay? You look a bit pale.'

Before Helen could reply, Gabby nudged her with her elbow. 'Go on, Helen, tell them.'

'Tell us what?' said a wide-eyed Lisa, as the table's attention turned to Helen.

Helen gripped the sides of her chair and her mouth went

suddenly dry. Had Gabby seen something back at the house after all and for some reason left it until now to make her big reveal?

'Tell them what?' Helen said, barely able to squeeze out the words.

'You know,' said Gabby, raising a prompting eyebrow. 'About you and . . . you know who.'

'I have no idea what you're on about,' bluffed Helen, even as a memory of a long-ago conversation began to come into focus. She tried to change the subject. 'Anyway, I don't know about you guys but my scrambled eggs are—'

'Helen used to go out with him!' blurted out Gabby. 'That guy Ben, the singer from Bluelight, the one who's gone missing! Helen used to be his girlfriend!'

8

Helen

There was a moment of stunned silence that seemed to go on forever, and then finally the table exploded in a cacophony of shock and surprise so loud that everyone else in the café turned to look at them. Helen was mortified. Not just because Ben was hiding in her home, not fifteen minutes' walk away, but also because over the course of the past twenty-five years she had learned to hate being asked about Ben. The conversation always went the same way. People would be surprised, almost insultingly so, that someone like Ben, with his good looks, talent, fame and fortune, could ever have dated someone as 'ordinary' as Helen. Then they'd become insatiably curious, practically begging her for salacious details about their relationship, which she would never give. Once it was clear that she wasn't about to reveal anything interesting they would then always ask for details about the split, which again Helen would refuse to discuss. Then, disappointed at the lack of gossip, they would inevitably ask their final and most humiliating question: how does it feel knowing you've missed out on being the wife of one of the world's sexiest, richest and most talented men?

The only reason Gabby knew about Ben was because Helen had made the mistake of getting horribly drunk on margaritas during a girls' trip to London five years earlier. The occasion had been Yas's fortieth and after a day spent shopping, they had gone for a posh meal after which they'd ended up at a nightclub with a two-for-the-price-of-one cocktail deal. Around midnight, and very much the worse for wear, they had hit the dancefloor just as the DJ started to play one of Bluelight's early hits, 'Holding On To You'. Momentarily forgetting herself, Helen had stupidly yelled to Gabby that, 'This song is about me!' Even though Helen had immediately tried to take it back, Gabby had been like a dog with a bone for the rest of the night until finally, swearing her friend to secrecy, Helen had relented in the ladies' toilets.

'Nooooooo!' screamed Sura at the top of her voice as everyone fired questions at Helen. 'Is it true? Did you really go out with Ben from Bluelight?'

Helen glared at Gabby but there was no way of avoiding it now.

'Yes,' she admitted, 'I did used to go out with Ben from Bluelight or just plain old Ben Baptiste as I knew him back when I was seventeen.'

The whole table erupted once again in a paroxysm of screams.

'I can't believe I'm hearing this!' said Lisa, scandalised. 'He's absolutely gorgeous!'

'Did you see him in that music video,' asked Yas, 'you know, the one where he's wearing that really tight T-shirt in the rain?'

'Did I ever!' said Lisa reflectively. 'Much to the embarrassment of my kids it was my screensaver for a while. Helen, how are we only finding out about this now?'

'Because I knew you'd all make a big deal out of it,' she replied, trying her best to dismiss the image Yas had conjured up of a muscular Ben in a tight-fitting wet T-shirt. 'It was years ago, we were both at sixth form, we split up when I went to uni, end of story.'

'End of story?' said Lisa incredulously. 'I don't think so, we're going to need details . . . about everything! And before you think about refusing, remember it is my birthday.'

'Nice try, Lise,' said Helen, 'but there's nothing to tell. It was a teenage romance that fizzled out, that's all.'

'Only he went on to become a world-famous rock star,' joked Lisa.

'That's right,' said Helen, 'and I went on to become an excellent primary teacher and mum of two.'

'Yeah, yeah, yeah,' said Sura naughtily. 'We're all very proud of your achievements, but let's get back to what we all really want to know. First things first, how did you guys meet?'

'I've already told you, at sixth form. We went to the same primary school, but different secondaries, then we got talking on the bus one day and realised we were both at the same sixth-form college and that was that.'

'And how long were you together?' asked Sura.

'Two years,' said Helen.

'And was he your first *proper* boyfriend?' asked Lisa, placing unneeded emphasis on the word 'proper' so that everyone burst out laughing.

Helen took a fortifying swig of her cocktail and sighed. 'All you need to know is that it was a very sweet and very ordinary teenage romance that ran its course.'

Lisa laughed. 'So, is that your way of saying that you broke his heart by copping off with someone else at the school disco?'

'No, it is not,' replied Helen firmly, 'it's my way of saying that we were very young and both wanted different things and that's all there is to know.'

'And did you keep in touch?' asked Sura.

Helen sighed again. 'How many of you are still in contact with boys you went out with nearly thirty years ago?'

Sura laughed. 'Good point.'

'That said,' chipped in Lisa, 'if the ex-boyfriend in question was a super-hot rock star rather than Billy McSpotty Face, I think I'd have probably made the effort.'

'Wow,' said Yas dreamily, 'just think how different your life could've been if you hadn't split up. You'd be Mrs Ben Baptiste, living in some swanky mansion in the Californian hills . . .'

'. . . holidaying every summer with George and Amal,' added Lisa.

'. . . or even Harry and Meghan,' said Sura. 'Just imagine that, bezzie mates with Harry and Meghan.'

'. . . and don't forget Oprah,' said Yas, 'all the major celebs are mates with her and Stedman too.'

'Thanks, everyone,' said Helen. 'It's always great to be reminded of how fabulous my life could've been.'

'You know we're only teasing,' said Lisa. 'We're just jealous, that's all. It's not every day you get to have brunch with the ex-girlfriend of one of the world's biggest rock stars.'

'And now he's missing,' said Sura. 'Do you have any idea where he might be?'

Helen took another sip of her drink and her voice was incredulous when she spoke: 'Why on earth would I know where he is?'

'Well, on the news,' said Sura, 'they said something about him being "troubled", whatever that means. I really do hope he's okay.'

'Of course he is,' declared Lisa. 'I think "troubled" is just media shorthand for "got a bit of a coke problem". He'll be fine, I'm sure. He's gorgeous, successful and has more money than he knows what to do with. Who wouldn't be all right with all that?'

Thankfully just then their waiter arrived with a fresh pitcher of mimosas and began topping up glasses, thereby allowing Helen to stop biting her tongue. In a matter of moments Ben was no longer the primary topic of conversation. Instead, Lisa was telling Yas about the posh minibreak she and her husband had booked for the following weekend, while Gabby was quizzing Sura about whether she'd recommend her plumber to fix their leaking shower.

Never before had Helen been quite so grateful for the mercurial nature of female conversation.

Two hours later, having put the world and everything in it to rights, the brunch was over and everyone was preparing to leave.

'I can't tell you how good it's been to see you all,' said Lisa, slipping on her jacket. 'I know we say this every time but we really should do this more often.'

'Especially if we're going to get quality gossip of the "I used to date a celebrity" kind,' said Yas, picking up her bag from the table. 'I still can't quite believe it. Helen, you really are a dark horse.'

'Isn't she just?' said Sura, adding some coins to the tip on the table. 'If that was my gossip, I'd be shouting it from the rooftops.'

'Me too,' said Lisa. 'I'd have cards printed and would just hand them out to strangers at random. "Yes, I may look like a regular boring mum of three, but let me tell you, I've had it away with Ben from Bluelight".'

'You lot really are awful,' said Helen, smiling in spite of herself as they all began making their way outside. 'And if you think I'm going to tell you all about me and my time with Keanu, you're going to have a very long wait on your hands.'

As the group said their goodbyes outside the café Lisa came over to Helen. 'Thanks so much for coming today,' she said, 'and for being such a good sport about Ben. But that was quite some news. I know we tease, but we really do love you, you know.'

'I know,' said Helen. 'And when I get the chance, believe me I'll be teasing you right back!'

'I'll look forward to it,' said Lisa and then, lowering her voice, she added, 'Having been there myself, I know the last thing you want is to talk about Adam in front of everyone but if you need anything . . . even just to let off some steam, I'm here for you.

Let me know when you're free and we can grab a coffee and have a proper talk. I can give you the name of my divorce lawyer for starters. She was worth her weight in gold.'

As the rest of the girls went their separate ways Gabby linked arms with Helen and they began walking in the direction of home.

'I'm so sorry for not keeping my mouth shut,' said Gabby. 'You're never going to confide anything in me ever again, are you?'

'To be honest I'd forgotten that I'd told you,' said Helen. 'And the girls weren't too bad so consider yourself forgiven.'

'I'll tell you what,' said Gabby, 'next time we're all together you can reveal one of my secrets. Anything you like . . . even that story about Ravi and me and that time on holiday in Marrakech!'

Helen winced, recalling the details of Gabby's story. 'I'm not sure I wanted to hear that story myself in the first place, let alone inflict it on anyone else.'

'It is weird though,' mused Gabby as they paused at the edge of the road to let a stream of traffic pass by. 'You know . . . that Ben . . . your ex has gone missing. I mean why would he just vanish like that?'

'I don't know,' said Helen, feeling slightly guilty for lying to her best friend. 'Maybe it's like Lisa said, and he's just sunning himself somewhere with some young actress or other.'

'But what if he isn't?' said Gabby as they crossed the road. 'What if it's something more serious?'

'Then I'm sure the police or whoever will track him down.'

'I'm sure you're right,' said Gabby, sounding reassured, 'I mean, he's one of the most famous men on the planet. Where exactly could he go where he's not going to be recognised?'

Just then Gabby's mobile dinged from inside her bag. She fished it out, checked the screen and groaned.

'Everything okay?' asked Helen.

'Just Rav reminding me to pick up his dry-cleaning and of course I've completely forgotten. I'll have to head back to the high street. You can come with me if you like, if you've got nothing else planned.'

Gabby obviously thought she was being nice, saving Helen from going home to an empty house, but as it was Helen already felt awful for leaving Ben alone this long.

'Actually,' she said, 'I've got a bit of a headache, probably one too many mimosas. I think I'll just head home if that's okay.'

As Helen continued on her way alone, she let out a huge sigh of relief. These past few hours had been a nightmare. First Gabby going into the kitchen while Ben was in the house, then having to leave Ben alone all this time, and then to top it all Gabby revealing to everyone that she and Ben used to date! It had taken all the strength she had not to leap to Ben's defence when her friends were all speculating about his life, especially Lisa's comment about Ben having a drug problem and questioning his right to be unhappy just because from the outside he appeared to have it all.

Still, Helen thought, as she turned the corner into her road, her friends' comments weren't anything she hadn't said herself about other celebrities, ones she didn't know, ones with whom she didn't have a personal connection. It was all too easy, she thought, to believe that the lives of the rich and famous weren't plagued by the same problems we all suffer from. It was all too easy to think that money and fame were the answer to everything. No one ever considered that perhaps these things brought problems of their own.

As one of her neighbours drove past and waved Helen wondered how Ben had filled his time alone. Had he gone back to bed to catch up on his sleep, turned on the TV and lost himself in mindless Saturday-afternoon telly, or had he spent all that time on his phone scrolling through everything the Internet had to say about him? All of the crackpot theories, wild speculation and, most damaging, the endless uninformed vitriolic comments about entitled celebrities and their rarefied existences. Was it any wonder people in the public eye struggled so much when all around them were so intent on stripping their humanity from them? On the spot she decided she would never read another celebrity magazine again. The whole celebrity gossip industry from top to bottom was trash.

Feeling better about herself, Helen decided that with what was left of the day she would try to lift Ben's spirits. She would make him lunch, and then if the sun was still out maybe they could sit outside, so long as they sat close enough to the house that the neighbours couldn't see them. Just as she was calculating how much food she had in the house and whether she would need to go shopping Helen looked up to see a car pulling across her drive. Her first thought was that perhaps it was another parcel delivery for Esme but, as she looked at the make and model of the car, a jolt of panic went right through her. This wasn't just any car, it was one she knew well, and one she hadn't been expecting to see until the end of the week.

9

Helen

'Adam! What's wrong? What's happened? What are you doing here?' called Helen frantically, as she looked from Esme to Frankie, satisfying herself that there were no visible injuries to either of them.

'I think you'd best ask the kids that question,' he replied, slamming the car door shut, his face grim as Helen noted for the first time the absence of Holly.

'Go on, then,' continued Adam, leaning against the car, with his arms tightly folded. 'Tell your mum why I've brought you both back early.'

Helen looked at her children standing sulkily on the pavement, their gaze, fixed firmly to the ground.

'Do I have to repeat myself?' snapped Adam, no longer, it seemed, inclined to be 'Cool Dad'.

'I called Holly . . . I called Holly . . . a stupid bitch,' mumbled Esme.

'You called her what?' asked Helen, outraged.

'She kept telling me what to do when she's got no right,' snapped Esme, with a petulant raise of the chin that reminded Helen of countless stand-offs when her daughter was a toddler.

'All she did was ask you not to have your phone glued to your eyes over breakfast,' snapped Adam. 'She asked you several times politely, only to have you ignore her, and then the one time she asks a bit more firmly you have the audacity to speak to her like that.'

'I'm eighteen, Dad, I'm an adult and I'm going away to university in September! She was talking to me like I'm a kid!'

'You were behaving like a spoiled brat and so she treated you like one!' replied Adam. 'And then of course Frankie joined in.' He glared at his son. 'Go on, tell your mother what you said to Holly.'

Frankie, who had so far remained silent, looked mortified.

'I'm waiting, Frankie,' prompted Adam, sounding very much like the assistant head teacher he was.

Sighing, Frankie mumbled something under his breath that Helen, even after all her years of teaching small children, hadn't a hope of deciphering.

'Clearly!' demanded Adam.

Ashamed, Frankie looked to his mum, eyes pleading for leniency, but Helen offered none.

'I called her a skanky whore,' said Frankie, 'and told her to shut her stupid face.'

Helen was rendered speechless. While she was aware that her son was no angel, and knew from overheard fragments of conversation while he played video games online with his friends that his language could be reasonably fruity, for him to have said something like that to another adult in front of his dad was unheard of.

'I can't believe you two,' said Helen, 'I don't care if you think you were in the right, your dad and I brought you up better than that.'

Esme exploded. 'You're unreal, Mum! Taking his side after everything he's done? Stop being such a doormat!'

Esme's words stung Helen like a slap and her daughter looked horrified that she'd said them and immediately burst into tears, throwing her arms around her mother.

This is a total nightmare, thought Helen. A complete and utter nightmare. But then as a furious Adam unloaded the kids' bags from the boot and began carrying them towards the front door of the house, she realised that the nightmare was actually only just beginning.

'Just leave those by the door thanks, Adam,' said Helen quickly, as she peeled a still tearful Esme's arms from around her neck, wondering what on earth she was going to do about Ben.

'It's no problem,' said Adam, a touch calmer than he had been, grateful, she suspected, that she had been on his side.

'I know,' said Helen calmly. 'But just leave them for now thanks. I'll get the kids to take them in but right now . . .' She turned and looked at Esme and Frankie, 'I want them to call Holly and apologise.'

Esme gasped in outrage. 'There's no way I'm apologising to that—' She managed to stop herself mid-sentence, catching sight of the warning look on Helen's face.

'Not only will you apologise to her,' said Helen, 'but you're also going to apologise to your dad. I'm not kidding either. You will both apologise.'

There was a brief stand-off but then, sighing, Esme said, 'Fine,' and then held out her hand for Adam's phone, which he handed to her.

'Hello, Holly, it's Esme here, I'm sorry for the things I said to you this morning,' she paused and looked at Helen sheepishly, 'it was rude and I shouldn't have done it.' Esme then went quiet, presumably listening to Holly's response, then finally she handed the phone to Frankie, who mumbled a word-for-word rendition of his sister's *mea culpa* before handing the phone back to his dad.

'Right, well, thank you,' said Adam to Helen, seemingly wrong-footed by her support. 'I suppose I'll be getting off then.'

Adam got into the car and started the engine and the three of them stood and watched as he drove away. Finally, Helen turned to face her children.

'I'm really disappointed in you both,' she said. 'I know this whole situation must be incredibly difficult for you, and I know

77

that neither of you asked for things to be this way, but we just can't have things like that going on. Your dad's made his choice, and while we might not like it we've got to respect it. He loves you both with his whole heart, and we've just got to hold on to that while we get used to this new way of being.'

To their credit, both Esme and Frankie looked suitably chastised and so Helen pulled them both in for a hug, and there they stood for several moments, oblivious to the cars and people passing by on the street, until eventually Frankie broke the spell.

'Mum,' he said, so earnestly that for a moment Helen thought he might be about to spontaneously tell her how much he loved her, 'can we go inside now? I really need a poo.'

'Aww, rank,' said Esme, as Helen tried to conceal her amusement. 'No wonder the car stank so much on the way home.'

'Shut your face,' said Frankie. 'As if you never stink the place out. Next time Josh is over I'm going to drag him into the loo after you've been just so he can smell for himself how dead your guts are.'

Ordinarily, Helen would've intervened to stop this bickering but as it was she had other things on her mind. For a moment she considered making up some excuse to take the kids to her mum's so that Ben could lie low for a few days more but before she could think of one, Frankie, who almost never remembered to take his keys with him, suddenly sprinted round her, produced a set from his pocket and let himself into the house.

The fact that Frankie didn't immediately let out a yelp of surprise was a good indicator that Ben had at the very least heard the commotion going on outside the house and had taken the opportunity to squirrel himself away out of sight. Quite where was another question. Frankie raced first to the downstairs loo, only to be confronted by the blockage he himself had created the day before, forcing him to head up to the family bathroom.

Esme, meanwhile, dropped her luggage in the middle of the hallway and then, texting one-handed, made her way into the kitchen, where for reasons known only to herself she proceeded to assemble the equipment and ingredients required to make a smoothie.

Trying her best to look casual, Helen did a sweep first of the kitchen, before moving to the living room. When she had satisfied herself that he wasn't downstairs, she made her way discreetly up the stairs to the spare room, entertaining the possibility that he was so tired he had slept through the entire drama. Not only was he not in the room, however, but his bags and clothes had vanished too. Frantic, Helen checked the kids' bedrooms and her own, but there was no sign of him and a horrible image filled her thoughts of Ben dashing through the suburban gardens of south Manchester, desperately trying to find somewhere to hide.

Returning downstairs, Helen was about to explore the garden to see if Ben had taken up residence in the shed when out of the corner of her eye she noticed that one of her old coats, one she only ever wore for gardening, was on the floor. As she picked it up and hung it back on the peg attached to the door to the cellar an idea struck her. She opened the cellar door, switched on the light and descended the cobwebby stairs to the basement and, sure enough, there crouched between an old chest of drawers and a huge pile of decorating equipment was Ben.

'What's going on?' he whispered. 'I heard some noise outside, looked out the window and saw people on the drive and so I grabbed my things and came down here.'

'Sorry,' whispered Helen, 'you'll never believe it but Adam's brought the kids home early and right now they're upstairs.'

'And do they know I'm here?'

Helen shook her head. 'My plan is to make up some excuse and take them to my mum's, then I'll come back here and we'll figure out what to do next.'

Grinning, Ben shook his head. 'This is like some sort of French farce, first I'm hiding from your best mate, next I'm hiding from your ex and your kids. I really am sorry, Helen, I told you I should never have stayed.'

'Well for starters,' said Helen, 'Adam's gone so it's just the kids. And as for you staying here, I've told you, I'm not going to let you go out there alone. We'll work all this out, I promise, just give me a while to get the kids sorted.'

Tiptoeing back upstairs, Helen opened the door at the top of the stairs just as Frankie was walking past to the kitchen.

'What were you doing down there?' he asked. 'You never go down there. You always send me, you always say it's too full of spiders.'

'Well,' said Helen, closing the door firmly behind her and making her way to the kitchen. 'I thought I'd give the kitchen a bit of a facelift so I was just checking to see how we're fixed for rollers and stuff.'

Shrugging, Frankie made his way to the fridge, took out a carton of orange juice, gave it a quick shake and then lifted it to his lips and started drinking.

'Oh, Frankie, get a glass!' exclaimed Helen. 'What have I told you about drinking from the carton?'

'There's barely anything in it,' said Frankie defensively. 'I checked first.'

'He's just being a pig, as usual,' said Esme, who had herself turned the kitchen counter into a bombsite of banana peels, frozen-fruit packets and splats of yoghurt. 'You might as well give up now, Mum, he's never going to be a civilised human being.'

Helen scooped up some of the empty packets around the blender and put them in the bin. 'I was just telling your brother that I'm going to be decorating in here over the next few days so I'm thinking it might be for the best if you both go and stay at your gran's.'

'Do we have to?' groaned Frankie. 'I like Gran and everything but we're not kids any more. All my stuff's here, plus, Gran's got no wi-fi.'

'Well, I'm certainly not going,' said Esme flatly. 'Josh is coming over tonight and I'm making him dinner . . . which reminds me, have we got water chestnuts, bamboo shoots, frozen prawns and . . . angel-hair noodles?' She paused, looked at the screen of her phone. 'Oh, and black bean sauce, but not the cheap stuff, you know the one I mean, the organic one from Waitrose.'

Helen almost wanted to laugh; her daughter's inability to understand how the real world worked never ceased to amaze her. How that child was going to last a single day at university she could only wonder.

'I don't care what either of you say,' said Helen. 'Given your recent performance you really don't have any say in the—'

'Mum,' said Esme thoughtfully as she pointed across the room. 'Whose is the jacket on the back of that chair?'

Helen felt the colour drain from her face as she saw Ben's jacket draped across the back of one of the dining chairs. How on earth had she missed that during her sweep of the kitchen?

'It's mine,' she said. 'I bought it while you were away.'

Esme frowned, walked over to the jacket and slipped it on. It drowned her and clearly was far too big for Helen too.

'Mum,' said Esme, 'this is a limited-edition Belstaff jacket that probably cost more than you earn in a month. This is not your jacket. So, whose is it?' Before Helen could reply Esme's eyes widened and her hand shot to her mouth as she gasped in shock. 'You've got a boyfriend, haven't you?'

'Don't be daft,' said Helen, just a little too quickly. 'Of course I haven't.'

'Yes, you have,' said Esme. 'It all makes sense now, you were weird about Dad bringing our stuff into the house, and when I came into the kitchen there was a half-drunk mug of black coffee on the side still warm, and you never drink black coffee. Then there's you suddenly wanting to get rid of us to Gran's. Just admit it, Mum, you've got a new boyfriend, and he's still—'

Esme's face froze, and she stopped mid-sentence, looking at something over her mother's shoulder. Helen turned to see what her daughter was looking at and to her shock Ben was standing framed by the kitchen doorway.

'Hi, guys,' he said, 'I'm Ben.'

10

Ben

Helen's children were both staring open-mouthed at Ben. It was a look he had seen countless times before in the years since he had become famous. It was a look people gave whenever they saw him grabbing a bite to eat from his favourite food truck, going for a Sunday morning hike along Corral Canyon or pulling up next to them at traffic lights. It was a look of utter disbelief, and confusion. One that said, 'Woah, you look like that guy . . . that guy from that band.' One that said, 'I want to say you're Ben from Bluelight . . . but how can that even be?' It was one that said, 'I must be dreaming, this can't be real.'

It was Esme who spoke first, or at least tried to. 'You're not . . . you can't be . . . but I mean you really look like . . . but you're in our kitchen so . . . but . . . I don't know . . . you really look like Ben Baptiste from Bluelight.'

Ben grinned. 'You've got it in one. I am indeed Ben Baptiste from Bluelight. But you can just call me Ben, it saves a lot of time that way.'

Frankie frowned and shook his head. 'You're not Ben from Bluelight,' he said dismissively. 'What would he be doing in our kitchen?'

'Yeah,' chimed in Esme forcefully. 'What *would* he be doing in our kitchen?'

'I dropped in to see your mum,' said Ben. 'She and I go way back.'

There was a long silence as Esme and Frankie looked at each other, then at their mother and then back at Ben. Finally, Esme shook her head as if trying to rearrange her thoughts into something that made sense and turned back to her mother.

'Mum, come on, stop messing about, who is this really?'

'He's just told you, Essie.'

Laughing, Esme began frantically looking around the kitchen. 'I can't believe it!' she exclaimed. 'Frankie, we're on one of those TV wind-up shows! We must be. See if you can work out where the hidden cameras are.'

'You're not on a TV wind-up show,' she said patiently. 'He really is Ben Baptiste. Ben and I are old friends.'

'Like I'm really going to buy that,' said Esme sarcastically. 'No offence, Mum, but there's no way on earth you are old friends with Ben from Bluelight.'

'Why, because I'm not cool?'

'Well . . .' began Esme, 'no offence, Mum, but you're not, are you?'

'Thanks very much,' said Helen. 'I'll have you know that back in the day I was very cool indeed and I had very cool friends like Ben.'

'If that's the case how come we're only hearing this now?' said Esme, flashing the equivalent of a mic-drop grin at Frankie. 'Nice try, Mum, but we're not buying it.'

'Actually,' said Helen, 'there are lots of things you don't know about me, and Ben's just one of them.'

Esme frowned, uncertain. 'Like what?'

'Like the fact that, I don't know . . . I once broke my arm—'

Esme interrupted, '—playing netball when you got tackled by a huge girl who went on to represent England in the discus in the 1996 Olympics. Yeah, I know that story, Mum.'

'Okay,' said Helen, slightly flustered, 'well, you don't know that when I was eighteen I got a hundred pounds and a job offer—'

'—from the local building society when you were economics student of the year,' said Frankie. 'Mum, you've told us that story a million times.'

'Fine,' said Helen, exasperated, 'okay, so I might have bored you to death with most of my anecdotes but Ben . . . I suppose he was a story I just hadn't got around to telling you about.'

Esme nodded sarcastically. 'So, you're telling me that when we all watched Glastonbury on the telly when Bluelight were head-lining, it never even crossed your mind to bring up the fact that you knew the lead singer?'

'It did actually,' said Helen, 'but I don't know . . . it had been so long . . . plus your dad was there and I don't know . . . it would've been weird I suppose.'

'Yeah right,' said Esme. 'I rest my case, this is a wind-up. Come on, Mum, who is this bloke? A rent-by-the-hour look-a-like?'

'Of course he isn't,' said Helen. 'He really is who I've said he is.'

Esme remained unconvinced and for a moment no one spoke but then Frankie, wearing a thoughtful look, said: 'Actually, Es, what you said doesn't make any sense.'

'It does,' snapped Esme. 'Of course it does.'

'No, it doesn't,' continued Frankie. 'Think about it: why would Mum have organised a look-a-like to wind us up today when she didn't even know we were coming back?'

Ben couldn't help but smile as he watched Esme trying to wrestle with her brother's logic. 'But that would mean . . .'

'That it could actually be him,' said Frankie, who, Ben noticed, had now got his phone in his hand. 'Look,' he said, turning the screen to his sister, 'this guy looks exactly like him.'

Esme looked from the phone to Ben and back, then let out part of a high-pitched squeal before clamping a hand over her mouth and taking several steps backwards.

'Mum, Ben Baptiste from Bluelight is in our kitchen!' she said, in an almost tearful voice. 'He's in our kitchen!'

'I know,' said Helen, 'it's weird, isn't it?'

'But what's he doing here?' said Esme. 'I don't understand. Didn't I read somewhere that he'd gone missing or something?'

'All will be revealed,' said Helen, 'but first I'm going to need you to promise to keep what I'm about to say to yourself. I mean it, no one can know. Not your mates, not Josh, not even Dad can know what we're about to tell you.'

Staring wide-eyed at their mother, Esme and Frankie nodded meekly and then Helen told them to go and wait in the living room while she made them all some drinks.

'Who knew having a rock star staying with you could be so fraught with difficulty?' she said as they closed the door behind them. I feel like I've aged a decade since this morning when Gabby turned up.'

'Well, I did try to warn you,' said Ben. 'Do you think they'll be okay?'

Helen smiled. 'They'll be fine.' She flicked the kettle on and took out three mugs from the cupboard and a glass for Frankie. 'What made you come up from the cellar?'

'I was listening at the top of the stairs when they were accusing you of having a boyfriend over,' confessed Ben, passing a hand through his hair. 'I thought maybe it would be easier for you if I just came clean.'

'Thanks,' said Helen, removing a carton of orange juice from a cupboard behind Ben, 'it was getting a bit hairy there.'

She made the drinks and then Ben helped carry them through to the living room. The moment he opened the door, Esme and Frankie, who had clearly been deep in conversation about him, suddenly stopped talking, sat up straight and stared wordlessly.

'Right,' said Ben, after Helen had handed out the drinks, 'I'm guessing you're both wondering why I'm here.'

The two nodded but said nothing.

'Well, the thing is,' said Ben, 'your mum and I really are old friends, in fact back in the day, we actually used to go out together.'

At this revelation Esme's jaw literally dropped open and Frankie, who had been mid-sip, actually spat out some of his orange juice.

'You . . . you . . . went out with Mum?' said Esme incredulously as Helen passed Frankie a box of tissues to dry himself off. 'You mean that woman sitting next to you?'

'Come on, Es,' said Helen, 'it's not that unbelievable! I used to be really quite hot when I was seventeen.'

Frankie pulled a face of such revulsion that Ben almost laughed. 'Euuurrrgghhh, Mum, just stop it, will you?'

'Your mum's right,' said Ben. 'She was absolutely gorgeous when she was seventeen . . .' He grinned and then quickly added, 'And obviously she still is now.'

'Thanks,' said Helen. 'But there'll be no convincing these two that I had a whole other life before them. They think I came into being the moment I became their mum.'

'Well,' said Ben, 'I can certainly vouch for her having a life before you guys. And yes, we really did date. But that's not why I'm here. I'm here because I flew into London yesterday and I had some spare time and I thought, as I hadn't seen your mum in years, that I would drop by and say hello and that was going to be that. But the thing is something's happened, something that means there's a strong chance I'm going to have to lie low and stay here with you guys for a couple of days.'

'What?' asked Esme.

'It's complicated,' said Helen, jumping in, 'but put simply Ben was trying to take some time off and get away from it all but his manager is spreading rumours that Ben has gone missing. Now pretty much the entire world's media is looking for him.'

'I don't get it,' said Frankie. 'Why is your manager spreading rumours just because you want to go on holiday?'

Ben and Helen exchanged a meaningful look, both trying to gauge how much to share.

'Okay,' said Ben after a moment, 'the truth is I want to quit Bluelight and my manager doesn't want me to.'

'Hang on,' said Esme. 'I thought famous people could do whatever they wanted?'

Ben smiled sadly. This is what people always thought and what he himself had thought when he'd dreamed of making it big. Sadly, however, the reality was very different.

'Well,' he replied, 'while in theory my manager works for me and it should just be a case of me telling him what I want and him doing it, the fact is it's not as easy as that. Which is why I didn't tell anyone where I was going and why he's using the press to track me down.'

'That's awful,' said Esme, sounding outraged. 'Isn't there anyone you can tell, anyone that could help you?'

'At the minute,' said Ben, 'I'm afraid the only people I can really trust are in this room.'

Esme was so shocked by this that she covered her mouth while Frankie, after a moment's thought, said, 'So, what, you're like, going to stay in our house with us?'

'That's the plan,' said Ben. 'At least if that's okay with you guys.'

'I can't believe it,' said Esme. 'Ben from Bluelight is staying at our house!! My mates are going to go insane when I tell them.'

Helen shook her head. 'Have you been listening to a word we've been saying, Es? You can't tell anyone about Ben being here. Not a soul.'

'But I can tell Josh, can't I?'

'No, you can't.'

'But why not? We tell each other everything.'

'Because it's got to be a secret,' said Helen firmly. 'Because the more people that know, the more chance there is of someone telling someone else and before you know it, everyone knows.'

'But he wouldn't say a word, I swear.'

Helen shook her head again. 'I know it's a lot to ask, sweetie, but the only way this is going to work is if we all keep this to ourselves. And if you can't promise that then, well . . . Ben will have to look for somewhere else to stay.'

'What about Dad?' asked Frankie. 'We can tell him, can't we?'

'No,' said Helen. 'No one outside of this room can know anything about Ben. I mean it, no one at all.'

Esme and Frankie exchanged a wordless look and then turned back to face Helen.

'Okay,' said Esme.

'Okay,' said Frankie.

'Thank you,' said Ben. 'I owe you guys, big time.'

Just then Helen's phone rang. 'It's my mum,' she said, turning to Ben. 'I'd better take it or she'll be coming round to check on me. I shouldn't be too long. Will you be okay?'

'Of course,' said Ben. 'It'll give me and the kids chance to get to know each other a bit better.'

As Helen left the room a silence immediately descended. Ben picked up his mug and took a sip and could feel the kids watching his every move. Desperate to break the tension, he opened his mouth ready to engage them in some mild chitchat about school, exams and university but before he could say a word, Esme shifted in her seat and, turning to look at him, said, 'You didn't really go out with Mum, did you? You were just mates, weren't you?'

'No,' said Ben, 'we really did go out together. We were proper boyfriend and girlfriend for almost two years.'

'Two years!' exclaimed Esme. 'But that's like a serious relationship.'

Ben tried his best not to smile. 'I suppose . . . it was . . . yeah.'

'This is so weird,' said Esme, 'my mum . . . my actual mum, dated an actual celebrity.'

'Well,' said Ben, 'for a start I wasn't a "celebrity" as you put it, back then. I was just plain old me, and for another thing as I said before, your mum was a total fox and utterly cool with it.'

Esme looked unconvinced. 'Are you sure you're talking about my mum? The same woman who wouldn't let me get my ears pierced until last year, the same woman who buys her trainers from Sainsbury's, and who regularly falls asleep on the sofa by nine thirty?'

Again, Ben tried not to laugh. 'Yes, that woman. And I'll tell you what as well, I was lucky she even gave me a second glance. Let alone agreed to go out with me. Your mum was amazing.'

Esme laughed. 'This makes no sense at all. It's like totally blowing my mind. My actual mum going out with Ben from Bluelight . . . it's crazy. I mean where did you two even meet?'

'It's kind of a long story,' said Ben. 'But here goes . . .'

11

Ben

'My earliest memory of seeing your mum was on my first day at Cheadle Road primary,' said Ben. How long had it been since he'd thought about that time? How long since he'd allowed himself to revisit the past in such detail? 'I was having a proper meltdown because I didn't want to go and my mum was on the verge of taking me back home when the teacher took me by the hand and said, "I know someone who'll look after you." The next thing I knew she was introducing me to this little girl called Helen, who very kindly showed me where to hang my coat.'

Frankie laughed. 'That sounds like Mum, I bet she was a right teacher's pet.'

'It's mad that I can even remember this after all these years,' continued Ben, 'but I'm pretty sure we spent the morning painting. I think I did a picture of a dinosaur and your mum did one of her mum and gran, and afterwards we had lunch together. When my mum came to collect me at the end of the day she was shocked at how happy I was and after that, whenever she told the story of my first day at school she always joked that it was my new girlfriend, Helen, who had saved the day.'

'Wow,' said Esme, 'how cute, you and Mum had a thing even back then.'

Ben pulled a face. 'I'm afraid my infatuation only lasted a day or two tops, because I soon ended up making friends with some boys and that was that really, I was off with them.'

'Typical boy!' sniffed Esme. 'Dumping your girlfriend to play football with your mates. I bet she was heartbroken.'

'Hardly,' said Ben, 'we were four! But even back then your mum was one of the popular girls everyone wanted to be around and she wasn't short of admirers. Anyway, I don't remember saying another word to your mum for years after that, even though we lived on the same estate.'

'So, how did you two get together then?' asked Esme, while Frankie sat next to her trying and failing not to look interested.

'We'd gone to different secondary schools but ended up at the same sixth-form college. Anyway, it was my first week there, when I was on my way home and I left my guitar on the bus.'

'Your guitar?' asked Frankie.

'Yup, my acoustic guitar,' said Ben, 'although technically it wasn't mine, it was on loan from college. I was doing A-level music and although I had my old one at home, the one from school was about a million times better and was really swanky and expensive. I'd only just been given it, but because I had loads of other things with me as well – rucksack, sports kit, art folder and the like – I didn't realise I didn't have it with me until it was too late and I'd left it on the back seat. Of course, I ran up the road shouting like an idiot for the driver to stop but it was no use, it was gone.'

'That happened to a friend of mine with her laptop,' said Esme. 'By the time she'd called her mum and they'd called the bus company it was gone.'

'Well, that's exactly what I assumed would happen to it,' said Ben. 'And it was all the worse because in order to get it from the college my dad was supposed to have signed a permission slip agreeing to pay for any damage or loss while I had it. Well, he was broke and even if he hadn't been he'd never have signed it in a million years, so I did something I shouldn't have – I forged his signature.'

Esme looked gleefully scandalised. 'You didn't?'

'I'm afraid I did,' said Ben. 'Not that I'm condoning that sort of behaviour, obviously. Anyway, there I am, freaking out because I'm about to get into a whole world of trouble when out of nowhere your mum appears. Of course, I remembered her straight away from primary school but it really wasn't the moment for a reunion. She could see how stressed out I was and asked me what was wrong and so I told her the problem. Cool as you like she held out her arm and flagged down the next bus that came along but the funny thing was all she did was talk to the driver and then jump back off.'

'What did she say to him?' asked Frankie, his curiosity overcoming his shyness.

'She wouldn't tell me at first,' said Ben. 'She just started crossing the road towards the bus stop on the other side and told me to follow her. I didn't know what else to do and so I just trailed after her. Anyway, a little while later a bus turned up, your mum got on and the driver handed her my guitar.'

Esme was rapt. 'How did she manage that?'

'That's exactly what I wanted to know,' said Ben, 'and do you know what she said?'

Esme and Frankie both shook their heads.

'Magic,' he said with a grin, 'and I was so in awe of her that I think I almost believed her at the time. It was only later that I found out that her uncle drove the number 35 and so she knew a load of the drivers and they'd radioed around to get the guitar back.'

'Oh yeah,' said Esme, laughing. 'Mum's Uncle Terry used to drive on the buses, didn't he? So, was that your big meet cute then?'

'I suppose,' said Ben. 'I've never thought about it that way.'

'So, when did you and Mum get together, as in "get together"?' asked Esme as Frankie blushed scarlet and looked at his feet.

'Well, after the guitar incident,' continued Ben, 'it felt like overnight your mum was everywhere I went: on the bus, around college and even the estate too. Perhaps she'd always been there and I just hadn't noticed her, but it was as if I couldn't stop seeing her. And gradually, I suppose, I realised I really liked her and eventually I plucked up the courage to ask her out on a date.'

Frankie looked puzzled. '*You* were scared to ask *Mum* out?'

'Terrified,' said Ben. 'Like I said, your mum was really cool.'

'This is madness,' said Esme to her brother. 'Ben from Bluelight was afraid to ask our mum out!' She shook her head in despair. 'It's absolute torture not being able to tell Josh and my mates about this!'

Ben smiled. 'Maybe you can when this has all blown over . . .'

'Do you think?'

Ben shrugged. 'Maybe.'

'But for now,' warned Frankie, 'you've got to keep your big gob shut.'

'Shut up, loser,' said Esme. 'At least I've got mates to tell.'

'I've got mates,' said Frankie.

'I mean real ones,' said Esme. 'Not creepy weirdos you meet online playing *Call of Duty*.'

'*Anyway*,' said Ben, keen to defuse the tension building between the siblings, 'I was playing guitar in a band at the time—'

'It wasn't Bluelight, was it?' interjected Esme.

'No,' said Ben, 'it was just me and some mates from school.' He shook his head in embarrassment at the memory. 'We were called Only Creatures, after a quote from Albert Camus, which I know is pretty pretentious. And to make matters worse we were awful too. We mostly played covers, with a couple of songs that I wrote myself thrown in for good measure. Anyway, terrible though we were, someone's brother got us on the bill at the Scott Arms on a Saturday night and so when I bumped into your mum at college a few days later, thinking I was all fancy I asked her if she wanted to come along and see us play.'

'And what did she say?' asked Esme.

'To my surprise she said yes, and then asked if she could bring a friend along too.' He paused and sipped his tea. 'So, when Saturday rolled around I was really excited. I thought, This is it. She's going to see me on stage, think I'm really cool, and just like that we'll be together.'

'Only it didn't go like that,' said Esme, jumping ahead. 'What happened, didn't she turn up?'

'Oh, she turned up,' said Ben, 'but we'll get to that in a moment. For now, picture the scene: a seventeen-year-old me turns up at the gig, completely excited about seeing your mum, when he finds the rest of the band were in total panic mode. It turned out that Olly our lead singer had been caught smoking something he shouldn't have been in his bedroom by his parents and they'd grounded him, meaning that we were now a band without a singer.'

Esme interrupted. 'So, you mean you weren't the singer?'

Ben shook his head. 'Back then I was just a guitarist and did occasional backing vocals and I was way too self-conscious to even think about putting myself in the spotlight like that.'

'So, what happened?' asked Frankie. 'Did you call off the gig?'

'Well, that's what I wanted to do,' said Ben, 'but everyone else wanted to carry on with me on lead vocals. I told them no of course but they kept on at me until finally I gave in.'

'How did it go?' asked Esme, cringing in anticipation.

'Awful,' replied Ben. 'Absolutely awful. For starters we were fourth on the bill so there was barely anyone there when we came on stage, then mid-set my mind went blank and I forgot the lyrics to the song I was singing and then worst of all, your mum arrived . . . with a boy from the year above and he had his arm draped around her.'

. 'Plot twist!' screamed a genuinely shocked Esme. 'My mum, the heartbreaker! I didn't see that coming at all.'

'Neither did I,' continued Ben. 'I was so devastated that I cut the set short and rushed off stage, wanting to get out of there as quickly as possible. And I almost made it too, but then just as I was heading out of the pub, I heard someone call my name and I turned round to see your mum standing there.'

'Did she have this boyfriend all along and hadn't told you?' asked Esme eagerly. 'She did, didn't she? So, what did she say?'

'Actually, she didn't say anything at first,' said Ben, 'because I didn't give her the chance. Before she could open her mouth I garbled something about how awful we were and apologised for dragging her down there and wasting her time. And then I told her she should go back to her boyfriend and try and make the most of what was left of the night.'

Esme looked at Ben completely rapt. 'So, what did she do then?'

Ben shook his head. 'She just laughed and said, "That's not my boyfriend, that's just my mate Dan. Why on earth would I bring a boyfriend with me when I'm only here because of you?"'

'Wow,' said Esme. 'Mum really was cool. And so, what happened then?'

Ben grinned. 'Well . . . I suppose . . . we kissed.'

At this Esme and Frankie gasped in unison, but before they could ask any more questions Helen returned to the room. For a moment there was total silence as they all stared at Helen and then, as if unable to hold in the tension any longer, they all burst out laughing.

'Well, I see you guys are hitting it off,' said Helen, puzzled. 'What's so funny?'

'Nothing,' said Esme, still smirking. She grabbed her brother by the arm and, steering him out of the room, she called back over her shoulder at Ben, '. . . to be continued!'

'They've gone upstairs to talk about me, haven't they?' asked Ben as the door swung shut.

'I'd bet my life savings on it,' said Helen. 'After all, it's not every day that you get to sit down and have a chat with a world-famous rock star.'

'I think they're actually over me being famous,' said Ben. 'I think they're more wowed by hearing about you when you were young.'

Helen winced. 'What exactly did you tell them?'

'Nothing bad,' said Ben. They were asking about how we met, that's why they were giggling so much. I'd just told them how you turned up to see me play with some kid draped all over you.'

Helen laughed. 'Dan Woolley! Now, there's a blast from the past. I think he's living in Australia now and works in IT.' She laughed. 'You could put a gun to my head and I literally wouldn't be able to tell you why I thought it might be a good idea to drag a boy I didn't even fancy to a gig where the boy I actually had the hots for was playing. Honestly, teenagers are so clueless some-times.'

Ben shrugged. 'That's the vagaries of youth for you.' He laughed and added, 'That would make a pretty good name for a band, though, wouldn't it?' He adopted an over-the-top transatlantic drawl and said, 'Ladies and gentlemen, put your hands together for The Vagaries of Youth!' He chuckled and took a sip of his tea. 'How was your mum by the way?'

'She's fine,' said Helen, 'she and her mates—' The doorbell

rang, cutting Helen off, and was quickly followed by the sound of footsteps coming down the stairs and Esme calling out, 'I'll get it, I think it's my ASOS parcel!'

Ben was about to ask Helen to carry on with her story when her expression changed and she held up her hand to quiet him as she listened carefully at the door. Ben listened too; he could hear that it was a woman's voice but couldn't quite make out what she was saying and, judging by the confused look on Helen's face, neither could she. Helen reached to open the living room door just as it swung open to reveal a panicked Esme.

'What's wrong?' asked Helen. 'Who was it?'

'It wasn't my parcel,' said Esme, her voice shaky, 'it's a woman, she says she's a journalist, and she's asking for you, Mum. She wants to talk to you about Ben.'

12

Helen

When Helen looked at Ben there was sheer panic in his eyes.

'It's all over,' he said, voice heavy with resignation. 'They've found me.'

'Maybe not,' said Helen. 'Maybe they're just sniffing round on the off chance I know something. Listen, don't worry. I'll get rid of her. Just stay here and don't come out no matter what, okay? I've got this.'

Wishing she felt as confident as she sounded, Helen took a deep breath to compose herself, then stepped into the hallway, closing the living room door firmly behind her. As she made her way towards the door she immediately recalled all of the numerous encounters she'd had with journalists over the years since Bluelight became a global phenomenon.

It had started around the time their debut album reached number one on both sides of the Atlantic. Helen had been at university in Leeds when they had tracked her down to her dingy student terrace in Woodhouse, desperate to interview her. Now that the whole world was obsessed with Bluelight and Ben in particular the media were desperate for stories about them, and what better story was there than the girl who let the most desired man in the world slip between her fingers. Helen had told the journalist who had tracked her down, in no uncertain terms, exactly what they could do with the five grand they were offering her for an exclusive interview. She wasn't for sale, and that was never going to change. Despite this, for several weeks she could barely leave the house or answer the phone without being bombarded with questions from journalists.

When one particular tabloid offered her double the money of the first for an interview and personal photos of her together with Ben, Helen's housemates thought she was crazy. How could she even think about turning down that kind of money, they reasoned, when she was so broke that her bank had taken her credit cards from her? And what did it matter if she spoke to the press when she wasn't even going out with him? In return Helen told them Ben was her friend, and even though they weren't a couple she wasn't, and would never be, the sort of person who would even dream of selling out her friends.

Even after that initial frenzy, from time to time whenever Ben was in the news some journalist somewhere would dig up her name and come looking for quotes. Like when he started dating a beautiful Australian pop singer ten years his senior, or the time he was spotted holding hands at a festival with a real-life princess from a European royal family. And when the news broke of his engagement to Hollywood star Allegra Kennedy, so many journalists had called her home and mobile asking for her reaction that in the end she'd changed both numbers. So, when it came to dealing with the press Helen was no novice, and she was quietly confident that she would be able to send this woman, whoever she was, packing just like she had all the rest.

'Hi there, are you by any chance Helen Morley, formerly Helen Greene?' asked a dark-haired smartly dressed young woman in a black trouser suit, when Helen finally opened the front door.

'I might be,' said Helen, her tone clipped. 'Who's asking?'

The woman smiled, clearly trying to get Helen on side, but it didn't reach her eyes. 'My name's Chelsea Maher, I'm a reporter for the North News Agency based here in Manchester and I was just wondering if I might be able to ask you a few questions. I don't know whether you're aware but your former boyfriend, Ben Baptiste of the band Bluelight, has gone missing.'

Helen thought about feigning total ignorance but at the last moment decided against it, reasoning that it might arouse suspicion.

'Firstly,' said Helen, 'Ben and I dated as teenagers over a quarter of a century ago, love, so to call him a former boyfriend is stretching things a bit. Secondly, I've not seen or heard from him in years. And thirdly, and finally, yes, of course I've heard he's gone missing because I don't live under a rock.'

Clearly thrown by Helen's demeanour, the woman blinked several times before recovering herself and trying a different tack.

'I'm sorry,' she said, 'I know this is a massive pain but this is a huge news story right now and my bosses are putting pressure on me to dig up something, anything, we can use to put a fresh angle on things. And while I appreciate you must value your privacy, I'm sure you must want Ben to be found as much as we do, and I really do think your input would help.'

This woman was good, thought Helen. And had it not been for the fact that the man she was looking for was just a few feet away in her living room she might well have succumbed.

'I'm sorry,' said Helen, 'I don't talk to the press. In fact, you'll know from your research that I never have.'

'Indeed, I do,' said the journalist, 'and I really admire your integrity. But this is different, I'm not here for salacious details about you or your time with Ben, I just really want to help find him. All the reports are saying he's in a really vulnerable state, so obviously the sooner he can get the care and support he needs the better.'

Helen was about to issue another firm but polite refusal when it occurred to her that perhaps talking to the journalist this one time wouldn't be such a bad thing after all. In fact, if she kept her cool and was careful, she might not only be able to stop other journalists from coming to the house but also throw the media off the scent entirely.

'Fine,' she said, 'come in, I'll give you five minutes maximum and then I just want to be left alone, not just by you, but all your lot.'

All too aware that the journalist would leap on any detail whatsoever of Ben's presence, Helen carefully guided her through the hallway, to the kitchen diner and the sofa overlooking the garden.

'It's such a lovely home you've got here,' said the journalist, sitting down while Helen sat in the chair opposite, 'have you been here long?'

'Clock's ticking,' said Helen, trying her best to be firm and businesslike even though she not only wanted to take the compliment but also offer the woman a cup of tea.

'Yes, of course,' said the journalist, taking a notepad and pen out of her bag. 'So, first question, and I know it's an obvious one: given that we now know that Ben flew into Heathrow, do you have any idea where he might be?'

'Is that definite?' asked Helen. 'The last thing I read they thought he might be in New York.'

'There are, of course, all sorts of rumours floating about,' said the journalist. 'But we know for a fact that he flew into London, and to the best of our knowledge he hasn't left the country yet. So, what we need to know is where in the country he might be.'

'How would I know?' said Helen. 'London's a big place.'

'He lived there for a couple of years, didn't he?'

'Yes, back in the mid-Nineties, but I couldn't tell you where.'

The woman consulted her notebook. 'Camberwell, Camden and Belsize Park, apparently. Can you think of anywhere in those locations Ben might have sought refuge, maybe somewhere he thought of as special during your time together?'

Helen tried her best to look like she was considering the question. 'Nothing immediately springs to mind.'

'And how about outside of London?'

She again pretended to think. 'Well . . . we did once enjoy a lovely couple of days at a campsite in Wales if that's any use.'

The journalist's eyes lit up and she immediately sat forward in her seat. 'Whereabouts in Wales, do you remember?'

'It was a long time ago,' said Helen, frantically trying to recall the details of the holiday that Adam had taken the kids on. 'It was on the coast I think, not far from Conwy Castle.'

The woman took out her phone, tapped the screen several times and then turned it round, revealing a map of north Wales. 'Can you see it anywhere here?'

Helen studied the map for a moment, and then shook her head. 'I'm sorry,' she said, handing the phone back, 'as I said it was a long time ago.'

'That's okay,' she replied, 'by the looks of it there are quite a few campsites in the area you mentioned. Obviously given his considerable wealth it's unlikely he'll be living under canvas, but who knows? He might have gone to ground in the area because it held happy memories for him.'

'It's possible I suppose,' said Helen.

The woman scribbled something down on her notepad before looking back at her. 'Is there anywhere else you can think of, perhaps even somewhere here in Manchester?'

'You think he's in Manchester?' asked Helen, trying her best to sound surprised.

'Well, this is where he's from, isn't it?' replied the journalist. 'That's part of the reason the nationals got in touch with the agency I work for, that, and the fact that being on the ground here we could make contact with his family and friends.'

'And what have they said?' asked Helen. 'His family and friends. Do they have any idea where he might be?'

'I reached out to Ben's brother, Nathan, yesterday,' said the woman. 'He declined to speak to me, but to be honest from what I gather he hasn't heard from him in years – I understand there's some sort of bad blood between them. And I've spoken to a few old school mates and old neighbours from the estate he grew up on, but I've drawn a blank there too.'

'Well,' said Helen, 'as you said, Ben's a pretty wealthy man now, so even if he had stopped off in Manchester my guess is he could be absolutely anywhere by now.'

'You're not wrong there,' said the journalist, 'it's like trying to find the proverbial needle in a haystack.'

Helen stood up, signalling that the five minutes were up. 'Well, I'm sorry I couldn't be of any more help, but like I said I haven't seen or heard from Ben in years.'

The other woman looked as though she was about to try her hand asking another question but then, presumably thinking better of it, she shoved her notepad and pen in her bag and stood up too.

'Thanks so much for your time, Mrs Morley,' said the journalist, 'I really do appreciate it.'

'My pleasure,' said Helen, walking the woman to the hallway.

At the front door the journalist reached into her bag and handed Helen a business card. 'In case anything occurs to you later,' she said. 'Day or night, don't hesitate to call.'

Sliding the card into her pocket, Helen, whose heart was thumping so loudly she was sure it was audible, gave a curt nod but said nothing.

'Once again,' said the journalist, 'thanks for your time,' and for a moment Helen allowed herself to feel relieved that the encounter was over, but then halfway down the drive the woman turned back.

'Just one last thing,' she said, 'and I know I should've asked this earlier but I wonder if you might have a message for Ben?'

'A message? What do you mean?'

'A message, you know, in case he reads the article and needs encouragement to come back home?'

'Oh, I see,' said Helen, feeling like she might just spontaneously throw up at any moment. 'I suppose I'd say, "Ben, we all love you and want the best for you, please get in touch and let us know you're safe." How's that?'

'Perfect,' said the journalist, taking out her pad and pen again, and jotting down Helen's words before looking back at her, a questioning expression on her face. 'Mrs Morley, for the record can I just double-check how old you are?'

'No, you can't,' snapped Helen. She slammed the door shut, then turned and leaned against it feeling completely and utterly drained.

Dismissing the praises of Ben and the kids on how she'd dealt with the situation, Helen barely slept that night for worrying that she'd somehow inadvertently let something slip that would ultimately give the game away. The following morning, the first thing she did was reach for her phone and scan every single news site for mention of herself. Finally, she found it, a tabloid piece with the headline, 'Missing Star's Ex Claims Singer Ben in Wales'. A frantic Helen then went on to read a completely distorted account of her encounter with the journalist, in which she was variously described as 'mum of two', 'pretty part-time teacher', and 'an attractive forty-something'. Throughout the article she was also said to be looking 'drawn', 'tearful' and 'anguished' at the 'unknown fate' of her 'former lover'. As much as it made her roll her eyes at the ingrained misogyny of the British media, Helen was relieved not to have given away any clues to Ben's whereabouts. She was satisfied that for now at least he was safe. The question that remained, however, was – safe for how long?

Part 2

13

Ben

It was morning and Ben was sitting opposite Helen at the kitchen table. They had both just finished eating breakfast and were silently scrolling through the news on their phones. He'd been lying low at Helen's for a week now, in theory more than enough time for interest in his story to have petered out. Yet whether it was due to the summer and there being a dearth of other news stories to fill the void, the fact his disappearance had given a much-needed boost to dwindling newspaper sales, or indeed Rocco working his dark arts behind the scenes, the story stubbornly refused to die.

In fact, rather than waning, appetite for stories around his disappearance, no matter how trivial, seemed to be growing. Newspapers were scraping the barrel running interviews with former school friends and even an old teacher or two. One article he read claimed that a number of bands, inspired by Ben's disappearance, were in early talks to release a recording of the Beatles' 'With a Little Help from My Friends' in aid of mental health charities. Strangest of all was an interview with a so-called psychic claiming to have seen in her dreams that Ben was hiding out in the jungle in Borneo. Sighing, he put down his phone just as Helen, who had been gazing at hers, let out a gasp.

'What's up?'

'They know you're in Manchester. Or at the very least that a week ago you were at Piccadilly station.' She handed her phone to him and sure enough, under the headline 'Breaking News' was a blurry photo of Ben at Manchester Piccadilly followed by a few sentences quoting officials confirming that they still believed he was in the country.

He passed the phone back to Helen, his heart feeling like it had turned to lead. Maybe he should just hand himself in and go back to LA. It would be the end of him of course, but at least this madness would stop and Helen and her family could get their lives back. He looked at Helen ready to voice his thoughts but she was already looking at him, her face stern.

'Don't even think about saying you'll go back,' she said. 'We've already been over this and like I said, we just need to stick with the plan, sit tight and this will all blow over, I promise.'

Over the past few days Ben and Helen had discussed the situation many times. They had talked about the pros and cons of hiring a private plane to make his escape, investigated the viability of getting hold of a fake passport on the dark web, and even considered the possibility of Helen driving him to France via the Channel Tunnel with him in the boot of the car, but they always came to the same conclusion: the best thing they could do was wait it out.

While Helen seemed fine with this, Ben hated putting her in such an awkward position. This was her life he was occupying, her summer holiday he was eating into, not to mention the risk she was putting herself and her family at in helping him. When this was all over, he told himself, he would find a way to thank her for everything she was doing. This wasn't just helping a friend in need, for some reason she was willing to go above and beyond.

Just then Helen's phone buzzed, and she checked the screen then let out a heartfelt groan.

'What's up? More bad news?'

'Yeah, but thankfully it's nothing to do with you this time. Adam's back from Wales and he wants us to meet up and talk.'

'Talk?' said Ben. 'About what?'

'I have no idea,' she said wearily. 'But it can't be good. Normally if he's got something to say he does it by text or email.'

'So, what do you think asking for a face-to-face means?'

Helen shrugged. 'It's too early for it to be about divorce proceedings but I suppose . . . no . . .' She shook her head and grimaced as though a particularly painful thought had just occurred to her. 'If he's got that stupid Barbie he calls a girlfriend pregnant, I swear I'll kill him with my bare hands.'

'It might not be anything like that,' said Ben, trying to be the voice of reason. 'I mean, he's just had a week away with her, and you know what they say about holidays being make or break . . . maybe he's having second thoughts.'

Helen shook her head. 'Believe me, he isn't.'

'How can you be so sure?' he asked, wondering if Helen would take her husband back if he asked her to. 'I've known plenty of men my age who have done the mid-life crisis thing only to wake up one morning and realise what it is they've thrown away.'

Helen looked unconvinced. 'Like I said, I doubt it. Still, the only way to be sure is to go and meet him I suppose.' She tapped out a quick reply to Adam on her phone. 'Will you be all right here on your own for a bit? I'm sure the kids will be up and about later but you don't need to mind them, they'll do their own thing.'

'Of course, don't worry about me. I'll be fine.'

Insisting that Helen should go and get ready, Ben cleared up the kitchen and then carried on doom scrolling until half an hour later she left to meet Adam. Flicking on the kettle, he wondered how much more of this enforced captivity he could stand. He couldn't remember the last time he had spent this much time indoors. He was desperate to go out, take a walk somewhere that wasn't in the house or in Helen's overlooked garden, and for a moment he wondered if it really would be so bad if he went outside for just a few minutes.

The kitchen door opened, bringing his train of thought to a stop, and Esme strode in wearing a grey hoodie and navy-blue tracksuit bottoms.

'Morning,' she said brightly as she made her way over to the cereal cupboard. 'Where's Mum?'

'She's gone out to meet your dad, I think.'

Esme frowned, then took the milk from the fridge and set it down on the kitchen island. 'That doesn't sound good. Did she say what it was about?'

'I think they're just talking,' said Ben.

'They don't just talk,' said Esme matter-of-factly as she poured muesli into a bowl, fishing out a few of the raisins as she did so and putting them straight into her mouth. 'Not any more. Normally they just text or email, so if they're meeting up face to face it must be something big.' She groaned. 'What if Dad's got Holly pregnant? It happened to a mate of mine at college. Her dad left her mum for some woman at work and then a few months later he announced that she was with child! Honestly it was so grim. My mate nearly died of embarrassment!'

'I'm sure there's nothing to worry about,' said Ben, keeping the fact that Helen had jumped to the same conclusion to himself. 'Chances are he probably just wants to check in with her.'

'Hmm,' said Esme sceptically, 'we'll see.'

She sat down, poured milk on her cereal and, as she started tucking in, Ben couldn't help but marvel at how at ease she was in his company. After less than a week of knowing him she had gone from constantly asking questions ('Do you know Drake?', 'Is Taylor Swift really as nice as she seems?', 'Do you know who Billie Eilish is dating since she split up with her ex?') to being able to chat comfortably to him about all the dramas going on with her friends.

'Do you remember me telling you about my friend Ellie?' said Esme, with her gaze fixed to her phone lying flat on the table next to her bowl.

'I think so,' said Ben. 'Isn't she the one who dyed her hair purple and her parents went mad?'

'That's the one,' said Esme. 'Well, it looks like she's having second thoughts about going to uni in Aberystwyth. It's the only offer she got and she went there to visit last week with her boyfriend because she hadn't even seen the place yet and the first thing she said to me is, "I hate it! It's the anti-Manchester." I told her she should take a year out and reapply next year but I know she won't because her dad has said if she does that then she'll have to get a job, and I'm not being funny but Ellie is like seriously the laziest bitch I know.'

Even though he knew he probably shouldn't, Ben chuckled. 'And how about you? How are you feeling about going to uni?'

'To be honest how I feel changes every day. Of course, I'm looking forward to it – it will be a relief to get out of this madhouse and live my life – but I don't know, I'll miss Mum, and though it pains me to say it . . . probably Frankie too. How did you find going to uni?'

'I didn't,' said Ben, and for a moment he thought about that particular road not taken. What would graduate Ben have been like? Would he still be a musician or something else? 'I had a big bust-up with my dad just before I was supposed to sit my A-levels and so I packed my bags and moved to London.'

'Wow,' said Esme. 'I didn't know that. So, is that why . . .?'

'Me and your mum split up?'

She nodded.

'Yeah.' Ben fiddled with his phone for a moment, remembering that time, and all the pain and confusion that went with it. 'I wanted her to go with me, and of course she wanted to do her exams and go to uni, so that was that really.'

Esme stared at Ben in shock. 'So, you mean, if you hadn't fallen out with your dad, you and Mum might still be together?'

'I don't know,' said Ben, feeling suddenly awkward, trying to pretend that he'd never once entertained the idea. 'I suppose it's possible.'

'That's insane,' said Esme. 'I could've been Ben from Bluelight's daughter, and I would've had lovely light brown skin that could take the sun instead of being as pale as milk and having to wear factor fifty all year round.'

Ben laughed. 'But you wouldn't have been you. You'd have been someone else.'

'Someone much cooler and much richer,' said Esme longingly. She finished her cereal and then, lifting the bowl to her mouth, drank the last of the milk. Wiping her lips with the back of her hand, she fixed Ben with a questioning stare. 'So, what was moving to London like?'

'Difficult,' said Ben, 'really difficult. I missed your mum, I missed my brother, and to top it all what little money I had didn't go very far. In the end I moved into a squat in Camberwell, then worked in a bar to make ends meet while playing in a few different bands. After a while I managed to wangle a job as tea boy at a recording studio in Camden and it was through people I met there that I ended up forming Bluelight.'

'Talk about living the dream,' said Esme wistfully.

'You wouldn't say that if you'd seen the toilet in the squat,' said Ben. 'I promise you it was about as far from "the dream" as it gets.'

'But you made it,' said Esme, refusing to be put off. 'You believed in yourself and you made it happen and that's all that matters.'

Before Ben could correct her, tell her about all the rejections and the setbacks, the false starts and mistakes along the way, her phone dinged several times in succession. Leaving her empty bowl on the counter and with her eyes fixed to the screen, she typed furiously with one hand, and said, 'Got to go, friend drama!' and with that she promptly left the room.

Aware that he ought to feel slighted but unable to resist being charmed by her insouciant manner, Ben picked up Esme's bowl and loaded it into the dishwasher just as Frankie, all legs and elbows, bumbled into the kitchen.

'Hi,' said Frankie. 'Where's Mum?'

'She's just had to pop out,' said Ben, unsure if Frankie was old enough or indeed would want to know about the potential trouble brewing between his mum and dad. 'She shouldn't be too long. I was about to have a cup of tea, do you want one?'

'No thanks,' said Frankie, 'I'll just have some cereal and take it up to my room.'

'There's no need on my account, I was thinking about taking my tea back up to bed anyway.' Unlike his sister, Frankie hadn't said very much to Ben, at least not when there wasn't someone else around. Ben hated the idea that his presence might be making the poor kid feel uncomfortable in his own home and he thought the very least he could do was try to bond a bit with him. 'Actually,' he began, 'I don't suppose you'd fancy a quick game of *FIFA*, would you?'

Frankie's face was a picture of disbelief. 'You play *FIFA*?'

'I'm in a band,' said Ben, 'what do you think we do all day when we're on the road, read books?'

Grinning, Frankie helped himself to cereal then directed Ben to the living room, where he set up the game. For the first few minutes Ben played deliberately badly in the hope of bolstering Frankie's confidence around him but it soon became clear that the kid was a lot better at *FIFA* than Ben, and in no time at all he was 3-1 down.

'For someone who says they play a lot,' said Frankie, as his striker scored another goal, 'you're not very good, are you?'

'I was going easy on you,' chided Ben. 'Give me a bit longer to warm up and I'll really show you.'

Frankie won the first game 6-1, a second 6-2, and a third 5-1. And it took a fourth game before Ben manged to hold him to a draw. In the middle of a fifth game, just as Ben took the lead for the first time, out of nowhere Frankie said: 'So, are you and my mum going to . . . get together or whatever?'

Taken aback, Ben looked across at Frankie, whose eyes were firmly fixed to the screen. 'No,' he said. 'Your mum and I are just friends. What made you ask that?'

Frankie shrugged and tapped the controller, making one of his players jump for a header.

'I'm only here because of the press,' continued Ben, as one of Frankie's defenders tackled his striker. 'Me and your mum are just mates. I promise there's nothing more to it than that.'

He looked over at Frankie again, hoping for a response, but there was none, he just carried on playing and even managed to score another goal. But then, with two minutes and twenty-eight seconds of the game left, he said, 'I dunno . . . I really miss my dad sometimes.'

Ben thought about saying something, anything in the hope of making Frankie feel better, but then he recalled the awkwardness of youth, and how difficult, nigh on impossible it was to communicate your feelings to anyone at that age, let alone someone you had only known for a week. This moment didn't need a big speech, or even words of encouragement, it just needed Ben to listen and Frankie to know that he had been heard. So, Ben, who in this moment felt that he identified more with this fourteen-year-old boy than he did with anyone else on the planet, said nothing. Instead, he looked down briefly at his controller and tried his best to score another goal.

They played for another half an hour, after which Frankie announced that he was going to have a shower. A few moments later Ben heard a squabble break out upstairs as Esme accused her brother of using the last of her expensive shampoo.

'I only used a little bit of it yesterday because there was nothing else,' Frankie protested. 'How was I supposed to know it cost a fortune? It smelled just like the ordinary stuff to me!'

'I'm surprised you can smell anything over your own stench,' snapped Esme. 'Touch my stuff again and you'll be sorry!'

As one door slam was quickly followed by another, Ben couldn't help but smile as he recalled spats like this between him and his brother when they were kids. It was all part of the cut and thrust of having a sibling, they could annoy you like no one else on earth and yet at the same time stand shoulder to shoulder with you when you most needed it, or at least that's how it should be.

Picking up his phone, he began looking at the latest round of stories about his disappearance. On one news site there was an article about other celebrities who had gone missing over the years. On another there was a think piece about the pressures of stardom written by a former boyband member, and even the *Telegraph* had run an in-depth profile on Rocco, of all people. As Ben considered reading it, a thought in part inspired by Frankie and Esme struck him: why, in the countless articles he'd read over the past week, hadn't there been a single interview or even a brief quote from his brother, Nathan? It made no sense, especially given his past behaviour. He hadn't heard from Nathan in years, he didn't even know if he was still in the country let alone Manchester. A dark thought occurred to him: what if something had happened to him? What if his brother had passed away and Ben hadn't even known?

Desperate to put his mind at rest, Ben put his brother's name into a search engine and scrolled through the results. And there, sandwiched between a listing for a financial advisor and a LinkedIn entry for a logistics manager, was a link on Check-a-Trade, for a Manchester-based window fitter. Ben clicked through and found the company's website. Sure enough, alongside one of the client testimonials was the grinning face of his brother. Overcome with relief and without pausing to talk himself out of it, Ben punched the mobile number on the site into his phone, and sent the following text: 'Hey bro, it's me'.

14

Helen

'You got my text that I was running late, didn't you?' said Adam as he stood at the table where Helen had been nursing a long-since-cooled coffee for the past half hour.

'Yes, I did,' said Helen tersely, only just resisting the temptation to add, '. . . about ten minutes after I'd already bought a drink and sat down.'

'Yeah,' said Adam, somewhat smugly, 'the thing is living in town now, I'm always forgetting just how long it takes to walk places. Anyway, let me grab a drink and I'll be right with you.' He glanced at Helen's untouched filter coffee. 'Can I get you anything?'

'No,' said Helen, not wanting to feel beholden to him for anything. 'You sort yourself out.' She bit her lip fighting the urge to add, 'Like you always do.'

'Are you sure?' he asked. 'Can't I even tempt you with a slice of cake? They do a killer red velvet in here.'

Helen eyed Adam suspiciously. Was he trying to be nice in order to butter her up for some reason yet to be revealed, or was he simply trying to fatten her up in order to make Holly look even thinner by comparison? Quite frankly, knowing him as well as she did, either option was plausible.

'I'm fine thanks. But feel free to get one for yourself.'

As Adam joined the queue at the counter, Helen used her time alone to think about Ben and the seven days they'd spent living under the same roof. Technically speaking, it should've been a nightmare: an unexpected guest dropping round for a quick visit and ending up having to stay for an indefinite period of time. Add to the mix the fact that the guest in question was not only an ex-boyfriend but also a world-famous rock star being hounded by the media, and it would be the perfect recipe for a nervous breakdown. Yet here she was in exactly this position, and she was more stressed by this meeting with Adam than she was by any of the other strange events in her life. Spending time with Ben had been an unexpected delight, making her feel alive in a way that she hadn't done in years, reminding her of the person she used to be. Ben didn't talk over her, dismiss her opinions, or make her feel worthless as Adam often had. He really listened when she spoke, and actively sought out her counsel as though he valued her point of view. And whereas, to all intents and purposes, her husband had run away from her like he was fleeing a burning building, Ben had run towards her, as if she was his safe harbour, his refuge from the world. And while she had no idea how long this situation could carry on for, she found, much to her surprise, that she was in no hurry for it to end.

Having placed his order, Adam returned to the table and sat down in the chair opposite Helen. 'So, how have you been?'

'Fine,' said Helen, wishing he would simply get to the point of their meeting. 'You?'

'I'm good,' he said, and he slipped off his jacket, which, Helen noted, was a new one, and hung it on the back of his chair. 'That week away was just what I needed after the madness of the last term.'

'I'm sure it was,' said Helen dryly.

Although Adam gave her a withering look to let her know that her sarcasm had been noted, he said nothing, which set Helen on edge even more than she already was. He wanted to deliver some bad news, she could feel it in her bones; the question was, how bad would it be, and when exactly would he pluck up the courage to deliver it?

A young, pretty barista with a nose ring and an angular haircut arrived at the table. 'Tall, Half-Caff, Soy Latte at 120 Degrees?' she said brightly.

'That's me,' said Adam as she set down the drink in front of him and disappeared back behind the counter.

'Since when?' asked Helen, nodding towards Adam's drink. 'You always used to say if we were meant to have milk from soy beans they'd have teats.'

'People can change,' he said nonchalantly.

'Yeah,' said Helen. 'Can't they just?'

Again, Adam, who had never needed much in the way of provocation to defend himself, failed to take the bait. Instead, he opened a pack of brown sugar, poured it into his drink and gave it a stir, then sat for a moment or two, looking anywhere but at Helen. Finally, as if something had just occurred to him, he leaned forward, and briefly held her gaze. 'So, I take it you've heard about your old boyfriend going missing?'

Helen nodded, and wondered for a moment if this was why he had dragged her here.

'It's all over the news, Adam, of course I have.'

'It's a strange one, isn't it?' he continued, again refusing to react to Helen's tone. 'What's your take on it? Where do you think he is?'

Part of Helen wanted to say, 'Well, I imagine right about now, he's reading the weekend papers in the house you used to live in and hopefully helping himself to an espresso from that pretentious coffee machine of yours,' just to see her husband's smug face crumple.

Despite the fact that Ben and Helen had been split up for at least three and a half years by the time she and Adam got together,

Adam had always had a bit of a thing about Ben. She'd first told Adam about her and Ben during a late-night conversation about exes, when they'd been together just over a month. Adam had brought the conversation up, she'd guessed, in order to humble-brag to her about his series of quite mad but stunningly beautiful exes. And everything had been fine until he'd asked her to share about her past in a similar fashion.

'Well,' she'd said, knowing full well that what she was about to tell him would blow all of his exes out of the water, 'you know that band Bluelight?'

'You mean the one with that really cool black guy as the lead singer?' Helen nodded. 'What about them?'

'Well, the . . . as you put it, "really cool black guy" is my ex-boyfriend.'

Initially Adam had assumed that Helen was joking, but then she'd shown him a photo of her and Ben kissing at a New Year's Eve party when they were eighteen. This along with a cutting from an old copy of *Melody Maker* that suggested that Helen was the inspiration for Bluelight's hit, 'Not Over You', and the framed disc under her bed Ben had sent her when his band's debut album went platinum had gone a long way to convince Adam that she wasn't just pulling his leg.

After that, Adam became touchy whenever the subject of Helen's famous boyfriend came up. It was part of the reason she'd never told the kids about Ben until now; she'd always been worried about stirring up old jealousies. But, in the light of everything Adam had put her through over the past few months the tempta-tion to reveal just how much she knew about Ben was strong. Very strong. But even so, she couldn't.

'I don't have a take on Ben's disappearance,' said Helen firmly. 'As you well know I haven't seen him in years.'

'True,' said Adam. 'Chances are he's off somewhere tropical with one of those starlets he's always being photographed with. He's quite the player these days, isn't he?'

The subtext of Adam's statement was of course that, while Ben might once have thought Helen worthy of his affections, that was clearly no longer the case, as she wasn't twenty-five or a model or a singer. And while Helen didn't doubt for a moment that there might be an element of truth in this, she saw no need to give her husband the pleasure of formally acknowledging it.

'Like I said,' she replied. 'I wouldn't know. Now, if you don't mind, let's just cut the chat and get to the point: what is it that's so important you needed to talk to me face to face?'

'Oh right,' said Adam, feigning offence, 'so it's like that, is it?'

'It was the minute you took up with that skank behind my back,' snapped Helen, her voice raised. 'So, come on then, let's have it. Have you knocked her up? Have you caught some STD from her which I now need to be tested for? Come on, Adam, whatever it is just be a man for once and spit it out.'

'Fine,' said Adam, his face now a cold mask of fury, 'you want me to just spit it out, well here it is: I want my half of the house.'

This was even worse than the thought Holly might be pregnant. She'd been nothing but disappointed in Adam ever since his affair came to light, but just when she'd thought he'd reached rock bottom he'd shown her that he had a whole other level of depths to plumb. Realising that an angry Adam was less likely to back down than a calm one, Helen fought hard to conceal her own rage.

'But Adam . . . you promised . . . you gave me your word . . . you said when you left that I could have the house.'

Adam at least had the grace to look shame-faced and when he

spoke his tone was a little more remorseful. 'You're right, I did. And I really meant it at the time . . . but . . . the thing is . . .'

'The thing is what?' prompted Helen.

Adam exhaled heavily. 'The thing is I don't want to have to start over from nothing. I shouldn't have to. We both paid into the house so . . . I think it's only fair that I take my share.'

'Fair?' Helen's voice was raised again, this time loud enough for people at neighbouring tables to turn and stare. 'How's going back on your word fair? How's forcing the kids out of the only home they've ever known fair?' Another wave of nausea washed over her. The kids, their poor kids.

'They won't be forced out of anything,' Adam sniffed indignantly. 'They'll have two homes instead of one.'

Helen had to laugh. 'Two homes? Do you seriously think I have any chance of getting anything decent on half our equity and a part-time teacher's salary? You haven't thought it through, have you? You haven't thought it through at all.' She looked him straight in the eye. 'I get it that you don't love me any more, I get it that you've got someone new, but Adam, seriously, this is wrong and you know it . . . I'm begging you, don't do this, please, don't do this.'

For a moment he looked so contrite that Helen thought she might have managed to talk him around, but then he cast his gaze down to his coffee cup and without looking at her said, 'I'm sorry, but my mind's made up. You need to either find a way to buy me out or we put the house on the market.'

For a split second Helen felt nothing, not hate or despair, not worry or anguish. But then, as if a switch had flipped in her head, all the anger, all the hurt she had been holding back since the day she found out about his affair boiled over. Standing up so quickly that her chair toppled over, crashing to the floor, Helen grabbed her cold, untouched, overpriced coffee and flung it into Adam's face. Then, as her husband sat blinking in outrage, she turned on her heel and stormed out of the café.

Pulling up outside the house a short while later, Helen sat for a moment trying to compose herself before facing the kids. She couldn't tell them about their dad's cruel change of heart, not yet, not until she'd had the time to think her way around the situation, not until she'd had time to figure out how to make this whole thing go away.

Taking a deep breath, she got out of the car just as the front door opened to reveal Esme.

'Hey Mum,' she said. 'How did it go with Dad?'

'He just wanted to talk through some financial things, that's all, nothing to worry about.' Helen took a breath and smiled. 'You off to Josh's?'

'We're meeting in town, then I'm going back to his for a while because obviously I can't bring him here as we're . . .' she added a knowing tone to her voice, '*in the middle of decorating and the house is a tip.*'

Helen smiled. Josh was certainly going to be surprised when he next came over and discovered that the house looked just as it had always done. Still, that was a problem for another time.

'It won't be forever,' she said, 'I promise you'll be able to have Josh over to hang out soon. Where's Frankie?'

'He was playing *FIFA* with Ben a little while ago but I think he might be in his room now.'

'Okay,' said Helen, and she wrapped her arms around her daughter just a little too tightly for a little too long.

'I love you too, Mum,' said Esme, wriggling out of Helen's grip, 'but you do know I've got a few more weeks before I head off to uni. No need to squeeze the life out of me yet.'

'Sorry, love,' said Helen. 'Can't help myself sometimes. Have a good time, and give my love to Josh, won't you?'

Letting herself into the house, Helen kicked off her trainers just as Ben came bounding down the stairs with his phone in his hand. He looked happy, as if he had something to tell her, but then his expression changed as he reached the bottom step and they came face to face.

'Are you okay?'

Helen forced a smile. 'Yeah, I'm fine. Just a little tired, that's all. You look like you've had some good news. What is it?'

Ben shoved his phone into his back pocket. 'It's nothing that can't wait.' He looked at Helen, his face full of concern. 'Something's happened with Adam, hasn't it?'

Avoiding his gaze, she walked into the kitchen. As she began filling the kettle for a cup of tea she heard Ben come in behind her and close the door.

'Helen, I can see something's wrong. You can talk to me, you know.' He reached over and put a comforting hand on her shoulder and with that, all her resolve crumbled and she burst into tears.

'Hey, it's okay,' he said, pulling her into his arms. 'Whatever it is, we can talk about it.'

'It was awful, Ben,' said Helen through her tears. 'Really awful.'

'Why? What happened?'

Helen bit her lip. Much as she wanted to confide in Ben what had happened, to vent her rage and fury to this man she knew would be on her side, she stopped herself. She knew that his immediate response would be to leap into action and offer her the money to buy Adam out. He'd always been generous, even when neither of them had very much, and when Bluelight had become successful he'd remained the same even though they were no longer a couple. He'd offered to bail her out of messes several times when she was a student but his offers of help were never made in a showy manner, the boy done good wanting to flash his cash. Rather they were born out of a genuine desire to help a friend in need, and nothing more. But she'd turned him down every time. She'd been Ben's friend for the person he was, not for what he could give her, and all these years later she felt just the same. She didn't want him to feel like she was asking him to fix things, for him to feel like she was just one more person in the long queue of people who wanted something from him. Right now, standing in his arms, she'd got all she needed.

'I'm fine,' she said, holding him a little tighter. 'I don't want to talk about it, but I promise I'm fine.'

15

Ben

The following morning Ben was in the kitchen putting the finishing touches to a tray laden with toast, boiled eggs and a cafetiere of coffee when Helen came into the room.

'You're awake,' he said, 'I was just about to bring this up to you.'

'Wow, thanks, that's really sweet.' She stopped suddenly and looked at him, eyes wide. 'What have you done to your beautiful hair? And your beard too!'

Ben rubbed a hand over his freshly shorn head. 'Don't worry, it'll grow back with time. I just needed to make myself look as different as possible because . . . well, because I need to go out today.'

He hadn't wanted to ambush her with news like this but since her tears in the kitchen after her meeting with Adam yesterday she just hadn't seemed herself. He'd tried to get her to talk about it but she'd refused, insisting she was okay. With no choice but to accept her decision, Ben had thought it best to keep his news about contacting Nathan to himself, not wanting to give her anything else to worry about.

'Out?' said Helen. 'You can't possibly do that. Why on earth do you need to go out?'

Ben exhaled heavily, only too aware of how reckless he was going to sound. 'I've . . . I've . . . well . . . I've sort of arranged to see Nathan.'

'You've been in touch with your brother?'

He nodded. 'Yesterday. I found him online, we exchanged a couple of messages and arranged to meet today.'

Helen looked horrified. 'He could be selling you out to the tabloids as we speak. Or worse still, your manager.'

Ben had to acknowledge that Helen had a point, it was a possibility. But even so. it was a risk worth taking. Being around Helen and the kids had reminded him of the importance of family, of the value of that sort of connection, and, while at the time he had been sure cutting Nathan out of his life had been the right thing to do, it had not been without consequences. He missed his brother, missed being around someone he could share memories of his mum with, that sense of belonging and comfort that comes from a common history. He wanted to believe that Nathan might have changed, that he could be trusted. 'I know he's not exactly been the best brother in the world,' he told Helen, 'but he's the only one I've got, and all the family I have left . . . well, at least the only one I can bring myself to care about. I need to see him, Helen, I just do.'

He saw in her eyes that she was trying to understand his reasoning. 'I get it, really, I do,' she said, 'but this is a massive risk you're taking, a really huge risk, one I'm not willing to let you take alone. I don't know what you had planned but I'm happy to drive you wherever you need to go and if it doesn't feel right, or if I think there's anything dodgy going on then we're out of there, okay?'

For a moment Ben studied Helen, taken as he was by her desire to protect him. He wanted to do the same for her, and wished desperately that she would open up to him and tell him what it was that Adam had done. He'd wondered if perhaps her guess had been right after all, that her husband had got this new woman pregnant. Or maybe it was some issue to do with custody, possibly about Frankie's living arrangements. It had crossed his mind that Adam might even have told Helen he wanted to come home, and that her tears were an indicator of her mixed-up feelings about having him back. Whatever it was she was wrestling with, he wanted nothing more than to help her, to sort it out and bring her peace. She was a wonderful person and deserved to be happy, but for the time being all he could do was wait, and hope that she would open up to him soon.

At Helen's suggestion Ben put on some of Adam's decorating overalls and an old fishing hat Esme had found in a bag of things destined for the charity shop. While Ben had certainly looked odd in this get-up, what he definitely didn't look like was the lead singer of a world-famous rock group and so, after waiting for Helen to start up the car, he quickly dashed outside and straight into the passenger seat. And as they headed to Heaton Park as arranged, Ben's thoughts turned to his brother and the moment he'd found out that Nathan had betrayed him.

It had been Rocco who had first alerted Ben to the fact that someone close to him was leaking information to the press about his forthcoming wedding to Allegra. 'We've got a rat,' Rocco had said, showing him the front page of a UK tabloid featuring a paparazzi shot of Ben with his fiancée headlined, 'Bluelight Ben's wedding woes'. The article had detailed an argument between Ben and Allegra about how their wedding plans were spinning out of control. Only a handful of people had known about it, and Rocco had no doubt at all where the leak was coming from. 'My money's on that no-mark brother of yours,' he'd said. 'I told you from the start you should cut him loose, but you wouldn't have it. Well, now he definitely has to go.'

At Rocco's instigation a sting operation was set up: Ben was to leak fake wedding details to his brother and then wait to see if they made it into the news. It took less than twenty-four hours for the information Ben had fed Nathan to appear in the tabloids, leaving Ben no choice but to cut all ties with his brother. Nathan, in turn, had reacted exactly as Rocco had predicted, bringing his treachery out from the shadows in the form of a double-page tabloid spread entitled 'Bluelight Ben's Secret Heartache'. The story not only included a slew of private family photos, but in addition Nathan had laid bare the story of the loss of their mum to cancer when Ben was just twelve. And, as an added bonus, the following day Nathan had shared with the same paper the story of Ben's subsequent estrangement from their father too. It had been a mean-spirited, heartless thing to do, the kind of thing from which there should have been no coming back. But Ben was nothing if not hopeful.

As they pulled into the car park Ben immediately spotted Nathan sitting at the wheel of a rusting Ford Transit with a cigarette in his hand.

'Are you absolutely sure about this?' said Helen, scanning the surrounding cars for signs of trouble.

'Yeah,' said Ben. 'Or at least I think I am.'

Getting out of the car, Ben made his way over to the van, opened the passenger door and slid into the seat next to his brother.

'The wanderer returns,' said Nathan. 'How goes it, bro?'

Ben tried his best not to choke on the cigarette smoke. 'Not so bad. You?'

'You know me,' said Nathan. 'I always land on my feet.'

There was a long pause, and the thought reluctantly crossed Ben's mind that Nathan could easily be recording their conversation.

'You want to check and see if I'm wearing a wire?' said Nathan as if reading his thoughts.

'You're not, are you?' asked Ben.

'Of course I'm not,' said Nathan, 'but I suppose I deserved that.' He fumbled in his pocket, reached for his phone and handed it to Ben. 'If I was going to be recording anything it would be on this.'

Ben shrugged. 'You could have a second phone stashed somewhere on you.'

Nathan wound down his window and stubbed his cigarette against the side of the van before flicking it away. 'Search me then, search the whole van if you like, I've got nothing to hide.'

Ben held his brother's gaze. 'I wouldn't be here if I thought you had. The papers have been in touch I take it.'

Nathan nodded. 'I didn't say a word to them, even though one offered me three grand for an exclusive.' He shook his head partly in dismay, partly in disgust. 'You have any idea how long it would take me to make that kind of money? I couldn't believe it when I heard myself turning it down. But it was the right thing to do, I'm not that man any more.'

Ben thought for moment; his brother sounded sincere and he so wanted to believe him. He sighed heavily. 'You'd better not make me regret this.'

'I won't,' said Nathan.

'Fine,' said Ben. 'In that case let's take a walk.'

Nathan gave Ben a funny look. 'Haven't you got to stay out of sight?' He glanced at Ben's clothes. 'Isn't that what this whole get-up is about?'

'Yeah,' said Ben. 'But come on, who's really going to look twice at a painter and decorator taking a walk with a window fitter?'

The day was fairly mild, so much so that Nathan was only wearing a T-shirt, but Ben, accustomed as he was to the Malibu sunshine, was glad that he at least had the protection of the overalls. They walked in silence, passing the occasional dog walker or jogger, Ben always taking care to angle his face away whenever anyone approached. Finally, they came to a path that, after passing through a line of trees, eventually ended at a small pond known to locals as the Secret Lake.

'I have to say I was surprised when you got in touch,' said Nathan as they sat down on a bench overlooking the water. 'When I read about everything going on in the papers I just thought it must be some sort of publicity stunt your manager had come up with. Then when they started going on about . . . you know . . . you being in rehab or whatever . . . I don't know . . . I started to worry.' Nathan reached into his front pocket, pulled out a pack of cigarettes and offered one to his brother.

'I don't smoke,' said Ben.

'Fair play,' said Nathan. 'I should probably give them up myself.' Sighing heavily, he lit his cigarette, then took a deep drag on it, sending a large plume of smoke into the air.

'So, are you going to tell me how all this started?' continued Nathan.

'We can do all of that another time,' said Ben, feeling fatigued at the thought of telling this story again. 'I think the more important thing to talk about is why you did it. Why you sold me out. I trusted you, Nath, everyone around me told me not to but I trusted you because you're my brother. So why do it? It can't have been the money because I was giving you more than enough, and would've given more if you needed it. So why?'

Nathan glowered into the middle distance for a while and then in a calm voice he said, 'Because I thought you owed me.'

'Owed you? For what?'

'For walking away all those years ago and leaving me with Dad!'

Ben was speechless. All this time, all these years, it had never once crossed his mind that Nathan had felt abandoned.

'You sold me out because I left home?'

'You make it sound like we had a normal home with a normal dad,' replied Nathan, 'but you know as well as me that it was nothing like that. Dad was a drunk, Ben, you left your sixteen-year-old brother in the care of a drunk and you didn't look back once.'

'Of course I did! I called, didn't I? I called as much as I could. And as soon as I started making money, didn't I tell you to come down to London and live with me?'

'And you think that changes the fact that you left?' said Nathan. 'Is that what you really think?'

Ben couldn't think of a reply, at least not one that seemed adequate.

'Your leaving meant that I couldn't,' continued Nathan. 'Someone had to stay and look after him, didn't they? And it couldn't be you, of course, could it, because you had all these big plans, these big dreams. What about me? What about my life, my big plans, my big dreams? Or did you assume just because you were the golden child that I didn't have any?'

'You could've left too, no one was stopping you,' said Ben, even though in his heart of hearts he already knew what Nathan would say.

Nathan sniffed. 'And leave him to drink himself to death? I couldn't have that on my conscience even if you could.'

'So, you sold me out for what . . . spite?'

Nathan laughed bitterly. 'Yes spite . . . if that's how you want to put it! You wouldn't have had the career you've got if it wasn't for me. I know you, Ben Baptiste, you're like me even if you don't want to admit it. If I'd done what you did, if I'd walked out first, you'd never have left, because there would be no one to pick up the pieces. So yes, I sold you out, and while I am sorry it hurt you I can't lie, for as long as it was going on it felt good to be the one with a bit of power for a change, the one calling the shots, to have people listening to me.'

Ben didn't know what to think, or what to say. Finally, he heard himself asking a question he had vowed to himself that he would never ask.

'So how is Dad? Is he still . . .?'

'Alive?' Nathan snorted. 'Yeah, just about.'

'And is he still at the old place?'

Nathan shook his head. 'Not for a while now.'

'Oh,' said Ben surprised. 'Where is he?'

'In a care home in Stockport,' said Nathan. 'He had a stroke a year ago and he's pretty much been there ever since.'

16

Helen

Helen had just pressed send on a text asking Gabby if she was free for a chat later in the day when, out of the corner of her eye, she noticed Ben and Nathan returning to the car park. Both their faces were equally impassive, making it impossible to guess how their meeting had gone. Had they been women, Helen thought, it would've been completely obvious, and not for the first time she wondered at the mysterious nature of male relationships, and men's ability to conceal their emotions.

'How did it go?' she asked as soon as Ben got back in the car.

'Okay,' he replied, as Nathan's van drove away. 'Although I did discover that my brother has held a grudge against me for the past twenty-seven years. Oh . . . and he told me that my dad's had a stroke and has been in a care home for the past year.'

Helen listened as he told her everything Nathan had said and when he finished she reached out and put a hand on his shoulder. 'Oh, Ben. That's an awful lot to process. How do you feel?'

'To be honest,' he began, 'I don't really know. I wasn't expecting Nathan and me to have some sort of tearful family reunion but pretty much everything he said was news to me. I don't know, maybe he's got a point. Maybe I wouldn't have left if it had meant abandoning Dad to his fate, maybe I did just assume he would pick up the pieces, or at the very least would be the one to have to make the decision to leave Dad on his own.' Pausing, he took his hat off, tossed it on the dashboard and ran a hand across his scalp that was now damp with sweat. 'As for my dad, I'm even more confused. Nathan's asked if I want to go and visit him, and I don't know what to do. When I left all that time ago, I swore I was done with him . . . but now he's an old man in a care home and . . . I don't know . . . maybe it's time I forgave him . . . maybe it's time I tried to move on from the past.'

'Maybe,' said Helen. 'But you can only do what you think is right.'

'The thing is,' said Ben, 'I have no idea what that is.' He looked over at her. 'And are you all right now? I've been worried about you.'

He was talking about the day before, when she'd sobbed in his arms after her meeting with Adam. 'I'm okay now,' she said. 'I've just got to work a few things out, that's all.'

'Anything I can help with?'

'No,' said Helen firmly. 'But thanks.'

She glanced in her rear-view mirror and noticed that the car park had started to fill up now the early cloud had blown away and the day was looking brighter. 'We should probably go,' she said, starting the engine, 'the last thing you need right now is to be spotted by a passer-by on top of everything else.'

When they reached home, Helen waited until the coast was clear before ushering Ben inside the house. He looked utterly exhausted, as if everything was suddenly catching up with him, and she told him he should take it easy for the rest of the day.

'I think you're right,' said Ben. 'I'm absolutely shattered. I think I might go and get my head down for a bit if that's okay?'

Helen smiled. 'Ben, you don't need to ask my permission! Of course, do whatever you want. I might pop out in a bit, and the kids are out so you'll have the place to yourself. I'll text them to be extra quiet when they get back in case you're sleeping.'

As Ben headed upstairs, Helen's phone buzzed. She checked

the screen and saw a message from Gabby. 'A catch-up would be lovely,' it read. 'Why don't you come round to mine around two?'

'So, what's going on?' asked Gabby, pouring tea into vintage china cups as they sat at her kitchen table. 'I could tell something was up just from the tone of your text. Is it Adam? What's he done now?'

'He wants me to buy him out,' said Helen.

Gabby froze, teapot in mid-air. 'He what?'

'I know,' said Helen, comforted by the outrage on her friend's face. 'I feel like it's just come out of nowhere.'

'But didn't he say you could keep the house, that he didn't want any part of it?'

Helen nodded. 'Clearly that was just the guilt talking. Now his remorse has all but dried up he wants what's his.'

'What an absolute git,' said Gabby as she poured milk into both cups and handed one to Helen. 'And I'm guessing you can't afford to buy him out?'

'Not in a million years.'

Gabby shook her head in disgust, picked up a knife and cut into a freshly baked Victoria sponge with a little more gusto than was necessary, before placing a slice on each of two waiting plates. 'Honestly, just when you think he can't sink any lower . . . how Rav can still bear to be friends with him is beyond me.'

'So Rav doesn't know anything about this?' Helen knew she shouldn't ask, the last thing she wanted to do was cause trouble between Gabby and Rav, but she couldn't help herself.

'If he did and he'd told me, you'd be the first to know, trust me. I can't believe Adam's putting you in this position. What will you do?'

'I've no idea,' said Helen. 'I've barely been able to sleep for worrying about it. Obviously, I can call the head and see if there's a full-time post going at school but to be honest, if there was it'll probably have gone by now. I also thought about asking the bank to extend the mortgage, but even if I miraculously managed to wangle a full-time job for September I doubt they'd say yes without at least six months' worth of payslips.' Helen sighed heavily, fearing she might cry. 'I think my only serious option is going to be to sell, and get something smaller in a cheaper area.'

Clearly outraged, Gabby was about to reply when Helen noticed her friend's expression change. 'Well . . .'

'Well, what?' said Helen. 'You've had an idea, haven't you? Tell me.'

'I have,' said Gabby, 'but . . . I don't know, it's a bit . . . how can I put it? Radical.'

'Go on. I'm liking the sound of "radical".'

'Well, I was thinking . . . maybe you could try appealing to Holly.'

This hadn't been at all what Helen had been expecting her friend to say. 'What, you mean talk to her?'

'Well, it doesn't have to be face to face or anything, it could be a letter or an email, even a text.'

'Saying what exactly?'

'I don't know,' said Gabby. 'Maybe try appealing to her woman to woman, you know, play the sisterhood card. Chances are Adam didn't even tell her he'd promised you could keep the house in the first place, maybe she'd be just as outraged as we are if she knew the truth. Maybe she'd be able to talk him round.'

'I don't know,' said Helen. 'Even the idea of sending her a text makes my skin crawl.'

'But think about it,' said Gabby, 'all she knows about you is what Adam's told her. Maybe if you explained the situation from your point of view, you know, how he's going back on a promise he made, how you'll have to sell the only home the kids have ever known, I don't know . . . maybe it'll give her pause . . . maybe she won't see you as whatever kind of crazy bunny boiler or cold, unloving ice queen Adam's undoubtedly made you out to be . . . and maybe instead, she'll see you for you, a woman trying her best to keep it all together.'

Helen spent the next two days going over her conversation with Gabby and agonising about what to do. She thought about calling Lisa, and getting the number of the divorce lawyer she'd told her about, but then she saw a thread on Mumsnet about the exorbitant fees these people charge and she thought better of it. She texted Adam to see if he'd agree to another meeting but his response was a flat-out no. She even considered calling his parents to see if they'd be willing to try to talk some sense into him, but then she remembered that they were away for three weeks on a cruise around the Mediterranean. All out of ideas, she reconsidered Gabby's suggestion. As she didn't have Holly's email or phone number, contacting her that way wasn't an option. She tried to compose a letter but she couldn't get the tone right. And anyway, even if she did finish it and find the courage to post it, what if Adam recognised her handwriting and intercepted it? In the end she decided there was only one way forward, which explains how she found herself lingering on the Wednesday evening across the road from Yoga Spirit, an upmarket city-centre yoga studio whose entrance was sandwiched between a co-operative office working space and a vegan patisserie.

As the doors to the studio opened, a flurry of people emerged, some men, but mostly women, all under thirty, and all disgustingly healthy-looking. It suddenly occurred to Helen that she hadn't really thought any of this through properly. What would Holly think if Helen approached her? She'd be terrified. And what would

Helen even say? 'Hi there, you stole my husband from me, can we chat?' Helen shuddered at the thought and almost turned around and headed back home. But then she pictured the kids' faces as she told them they were going to lose their home, and she knew she had to follow through. There was simply too much at stake not to.

Scanning the faces of the people who had just exited the building, Helen spotted Holly, a rolled-up yoga mat tucked under her arm, her hair piled up in a loose knot. She was dressed in an all-black ensemble consisting of leggings and a tight sleeveless top and was laughing and chatting with a small group of people next to her. Before she could change her mind Helen quickly crossed the road.

'Excuse me.' There was no mistaking the look of recognition and alarm on Holly's face when Helen stood next to her.

'Helen,' she said, 'what are you—' She took several steps away from her friends, enough to be out of earshot but clearly close enough to call for help if needed. In a lowered voice she continued, 'Have you followed me here?'

'No,' said Helen, 'I saw on one of your Instagram posts that you were a regular here and then I read a comment you'd written on the yoga studio's Facebook page about you being at the seven o'clock class and so here I am.'

'Wow,' Holly replied, her expression growing more alarmed. 'That doesn't sound at all stalker-y. What do you want?'

'Just five minutes of your time,' said Helen, 'and then I promise I'll leave you alone.'

Holly eyed her suspiciously. 'I don't think so.'

'Please,' said Helen, hating herself for sounding so pathetic, 'after everything that's gone on lately I don't think five minutes is too much to ask, is it?'

At Holly's suggestion they went into the vegan patisserie, where she ordered an oat milk cappuccino and Helen, a chai tea. Though the café was fairly empty Helen couldn't help but notice that Holly chose a table near the counter, in full view of the bored young man with numerous piercings standing at the till.

While Helen didn't want to make small talk, she was aware at the same time that Holly was going to need warming up if she was going to agree to help her out.

'I've never been here before,' she asked. 'Have you?'

'I've been a few times.' Holly's tone was clipped and guarded. She clearly wanted nothing more than for Helen to get to her point.

'So, are you a vegan?'

'Yes.'

'How long for?'

'Eight years.' She really was giving Helen nothing to work with. Once again Helen noted the fear in the other woman's eyes. Did she really think Helen would physically attack her? What had Adam said about her?

'Listen,' began Helen, 'I promise you I'm not here to cause any trouble, so really there's no need to look so worried. All I want to do is talk.'

'Okay.' Holly's voice was still wary. 'Talk away, I'm listening.'

Helen wasn't quite ready to get to her point. Some more small talk was needed to establish some sort of rapport. 'Where's Adam, back at the flat?'

'No, I think he's gone for a drink with Rav.'

Helen couldn't help herself. 'Are you sure about that? I mean I'm guessing at least half the times he told me he was with Rav he was seeing you.'

'So, that's what this is about?' Holly picked up her yoga mat from the seat next to her and stood up. 'No thanks.'

Helen cursed herself for giving in to temptation. 'Holly, wait, don't go. I'm sorry. Please just sit and hear me out.'

Holly stood looking at her for a moment and then sighed and sat back down. 'Fine, but just get to the point please. We're never going to be friends so let's just cut the small talk.'

'Okay,' said Helen, and then their order arrived, so she had no choice but to wait until the barista had resumed his position behind the counter. There was a moment of awkwardness as they both stared at their drinks and then finally Helen took a deep breath and looked at Holly. With her perfect skin and deep brown eyes, she really was quite beautiful. Helen couldn't imagine what Holly must make of her. She'd thought long and hard about what to wear for tonight before opting for a denim jacket and the navy-blue jumpsuit Esme had persuaded her she looked cool in. But now in the face of Holly's youth and natural beauty she felt about as glamorous as an overflowing bin bag.

'The reason I want to speak to you is because I need a favour.'

Holly's curiosity was clearly piqued. 'A favour? What kind?'

Helen cleared her throat and summoned every last ounce of strength she had. 'I don't know if you're aware but when Adam left he promised that the children and I could have the house. He promised he wouldn't try and take any money from it and to cut a long story short, a few days ago he went back on that promise, and I'm hoping, well begging really, that you might have a word with him and try and talk him round. It's my home, Holly, it's the kids' home too, the only one they've really known. It would break my heart to have to tell them they've got to move.'

Holly took a sip of her drink, then sat back in her seat and regarded Helen carefully. 'Adam warned me you might try something like this but I didn't believe him. He told me all about the so-called "promise" but he also told me how the only reason you were able to afford your house in the first place was because of the money he inherited from his grandfather. So, really he isn't asking for anything that isn't rightfully his.'

Helen felt her anger begin to simmer. 'So, you knew about this?'

'Of course, Adam tells me everything.'

'Funny, I believed that once too.'

Holly stood up again. 'I think we're done here, don't you?'

'Yes,' said Helen, 'I think we probably are but before you go, do you mind if I say one last thing?'

Holly sighed but didn't move.

'It's just a warning really,' Helen began. 'A warning that you won't always be young, a warning that one day, years from now you could find yourself in my position. And when that happens, when you're the one whose life is falling apart, just make sure you remember this moment, and what a complete and utter bitch you've been. You and Adam deserve each other, you really do, and if I never lay eyes on either of you ever again it'll be too soon.'

17

Ben

It was clear to Ben from the force with which Helen slammed the front door on her return that something was wrong. She'd told him she was going to check out a yoga class in town, but if it had been peace and tranquillity she was after it appeared she had come away without it.

'You okay?' he asked as he followed her into the kitchen and watched as she threw her bag and keys on to the counter, her eyes blazing with fury.

'No, I'm about as far from being okay as is possible right now!'

Ben closed the kitchen door behind him. While Esme had gone out, Frankie was in his room playing video games and though he had his headphones on, there was still a chance he might overhear.

'What's happened?'

'I'm fine, really.'

'You don't look fine. Is it something to do with Adam? Has he been in touch again?'

'I told you I'm fine. Can you just leave me alone please!'

Ben was surprised by how hurt Helen's words made him feel. She was clearly going through something but he just couldn't understand why she was refusing to open up to him given how close they'd become.

'Oh, okay, sorry,' he said, but as he turned to leave Helen apologised.

'I'm so sorry, Ben, I shouldn't be taking this out on you. It's completely unfair.'

'I get it. I don't want to get in the middle of your business but . . . I don't know . . . you've helped me so much I just want to be a good friend to you too.'

'And you are being, I promise.' She sat down at the kitchen island, and Ben sat down beside her desperately trying to read her expression.

'Whatever it is, you can tell me.' He reached across and took her hand in his. 'It can be as much or as little as you want, I just want to help.'

'You're right,' she said, 'it is to do with Adam. Remember I told you that, when he left, he promised I could have the house?' Ben nodded. 'Well, it turns out that promise was about as sincere as his wedding vows.'

'He wants half the house?'

Helen nodded. 'That's what our meeting was about the other day. I'm guessing he thought he'd try and soften the blow by offering me coffee and a slice of cake.'

'So where were you tonight? I'm guessing not yoga.'

Helen laughed bitterly. 'It wasn't a complete lie, I was sort of at yoga, but mostly I was making a fool of myself. I did a spot of online stalking, worked out where and when Adam's girlfriend went to yoga and decided to try and reason with her woman to woman. Crazy right? I don't know . . . I suppose I hoped I could make her see my point of view and persuade her to talk some sense into Adam.'

Ben squeezed Helen's hand. 'And I take it she wasn't very receptive?'

Helen shook her head. 'She basically told me where to go.' She started to cry. 'Oh, Ben, what am I going to tell the kids? I only work part time, and even if I went full time tomorrow there's no way on earth I could afford to buy Adam out. How do I tell them that on top of everything they've already been through they've now got to lose their home too?'

'You don't.' Ben got up and put an arm around Helen's shoulder. 'If there's one thing I've got more than enough of, it's money. I can call my lawyer in LA right now and have the money with you to buy Adam out by the morning. You don't have to worry.'

Helen bit her lip and gave Ben's hand a squeeze. 'That's such a kind offer but I can't take your money, Ben.'

'Yes, you can, believe me. This industry's taken a lot from me but in material terms it's given me a lot too, more than I could hope to spend in a lifetime. It's obscene really, and you'd be doing me a favour taking some of it off my hands.'

Helen stood up, tore off a piece of kitchen roll from the holder and dried her eyes. 'It's a lovely thing to offer, really it is, but part of the reason I haven't told you about this before now is because I knew you'd try and do something like this. Remember when I was a student and you offered to buy the house me and my mates were living in because the landlord was being a nightmare? Or the time you tried to get me a car when I got into teacher training college? I didn't want you to bail me out then, and I don't now.'

'But why, when it's such an easy thing for me to do? I literally wouldn't even notice the money had gone.'

'Because it would change things between us,' said Helen. 'And you can say it wouldn't all you like, but I know it would. I'm your friend, Ben, not because you're famous, rich or good-looking, I'm your friend because you're you, all the rest is just window dressing.'

Ben gave her a wry smile. 'You think I'm good-looking?'

Grinning, she playfully punched him on the arm. 'That's the one thing you've taken from everything I've just said?'

'Of course not,' said Ben. 'I want to help you, Helen. You've got a problem, I've got the means to make that problem go away, where's the harm?'

Helen rested her head against his chest for a moment before looking up at him. 'Because money changes things. You know that, it changes the way you see people and it changes the way people see you. I like the way I see you, Ben, I don't want it to change.'

In the wake of the band's early success Helen, unlike many people he could think of, had been funny about taking gifts from him. In his mind he'd simply been sharing his good fortune but he couldn't help thinking that Helen needed to prove it was him she cared about, not what he could give her.

'I get it,' he said reluctantly. 'I don't like it, but I get it even though I wish I didn't. But just so you know, the offer's there if you change your mind, no strings, nothing changing, just one friend helping out another.'

Burying her face in his chest, Helen hugged him with all her might, and they stood in silence, holding each other in the fading light of the day. After a while she looked up at him. 'Anyway, how are you? Have you decided about going with Nathan to see your dad? It's tomorrow, isn't it?'

'I still don't know what to do. I just keep going round in circles.'

'Do you want my advice?' He nodded. 'I think you should go. What your dad did was terrible, there's no two ways about it. But I think you've got to try to forgive him, if not for his sake, then for your own. I know when you dropped in to see me you didn't intend to stay more than a few hours, let alone over a week, but now you're stuck here you might as well use your time well. With everything you've told me, with everything you've been through I can't help thinking that deep down the stuff with your dad is part of it somehow. It seems to me like you've been carrying this round with you for a very long time . . . and now you've got the chance, maybe it's time you saw him and tried to start letting some of it go.'

Her words really made Ben think. All this time, all these years, he'd blamed his lack of happiness on the rigours of touring, the constraints of being a celebrity and the existential questions thrown up by having a fortune so vast that nothing was beyond his reach. But Helen had made him consider the possibility that perhaps the cause of his problems lay deeper and that, if he truly wanted to find peace, maybe he didn't need to run away to an island in the middle of nowhere to get it. It had felt good getting back in touch with Nathan and starting to rebuild what they'd had. So maybe the next step towards the healing he needed was to be found in trying to forgive his father.

The following morning at just after eleven the doorbell rang. Three short bursts, followed by two long ones just as Ben had agreed with Nathan.

'That'll be your brother,' said Helen, as they stood in the kitchen. She leaned forward and gave him a hug. 'I really do hope it goes well today, and please don't worry about anything here, just concentrate on everything you've got going on.'

Ben hesitated; it seemed like madness that he was leaving her worrying about her future when he could so easily solve the problem, and he opened his mouth to repeat his offer of help but before he could say a word Helen, as if reading his mind, shook her head. 'Don't worry about me,' she said again, 'I'll get this sorted. For now, just concentrate on doing what you need to get done.'

'Like the new look,' greeted Nathan, looking his brother up and down, 'much better than the painter-and-decorator outfit you had on last time.'

Grinning, Ben adjusted the waistband of the shapeless grey marl hoodie and matching jogging bottoms Helen had picked up from a supermarket especially for the occasion. The outfit, together with the sunglasses and baseball cap he was wearing, was to be his disguise for the day and the ensemble looked so unlike anything he would normally wear that with the hood up and his sunglasses on, he barely recognised himself and hoped no one else would either.

'If anyone asks,' said Ben, climbing into the passenger side of his brother's van, 'I'm your cousin, Alvin, visiting from Antigua.'

'Nice to meet you, Alvin,' said Nathan, amused. 'Buckle up, and we'll get you to the family reunion.'

As Nathan pulled off the drive and headed towards Stockport, for once Ben was grateful for the silence afforded by his brother's taciturn nature, and as Radio 5 Live played in the background he allowed his thoughts to once more drift to the past, specifically to the immediate aftermath of him and Nathan losing their mum.

Clifford Henry Baptiste hadn't always been a drunk. In fact, Ben wasn't sure when his father had first started drinking. Had it been when his mother had first been taken to hospital? Or later, when it was clear there was nothing the medical profession could do to save her? Whenever it was, by the time their mother passed away, both Ben and Nathan had been well aware that their father was no longer the man he used be.

The two brothers had no choice but to adapt to this new way of life, and quickly became accustomed to caring for and clearing up after their father. As the eldest, Ben took the lead, cooking every meal, making sure that Nathan made it to school every day, and everything else in between. It wasn't the easiest of childhoods, but with the help of various family friends and neighbours they made it through, all the time hoping that one day things might change, that one day Clifford might stop drinking. It didn't happen of course; no matter who tried to intervene, their dad simply couldn't or wouldn't change. Eventually he lost his job and had it not been for his GP signing him off as medically unfit for work, enabling him to claim incapacity benefits, there was every chance they would've lost their council flat too.

The one thing that had kept Ben going through those hard times, the one thing that had given him hope had been music. Ben's mum had always loved music, and the sound of the pop and soul records of the time had been a constant soundtrack to his early childhood. For the last birthday she would celebrate with Ben, his mother had given him a second-hand acoustic guitar, even though he hadn't professed a desire for one. 'I think you've got a lot of talent in you, Ben,' she'd said at the time, 'and maybe this could be a way for you to show it.'

Not long after, Ben had borrowed a book from the library and tried to teach himself a few chords, but his interest had quickly waned, and the guitar had sat gathering dust in the corner of the bedroom he and Nathan shared. But after losing his mother he'd picked it up again, and this time had stuck with it. In no time at all he'd graduated from the basics and was soon playing along to songs that he loved, everything from Aretha Franklin through to Led Zeppelin. When he played guitar, all his troubles faded away, all the grief for his mum, all the anger he felt towards his dad, and it felt like nothing else in the world existed but him and the sound he was trying to create.

As his love of music had continued to grow, Ben's thoughts had turned to his future, looking for a way to continue to pursue his passion, and he'd been thrilled to be offered a place on a music production course at Sheffield. This would be it, his way of doing what he loved all day long, and the perfect location, given the city's musical pedigree – ABC, Heaven 17, The Human League – to get another band off the ground. The realisation, however, that he would soon be leaving home had prompted him to think about Nathan, and how life might be for his brother without him around to stand in for his dad. More than ever, Ben needed their father to get his act together and stop drinking. One day, to this end, armed with a bunch of leaflets he'd picked up from the library, he had confronted his dad and begged him to get help. An almighty row had ensued, worse than ever before, and consumed by anger and bitterness his dad had begun wrecking the place. 'Don't you dare tell me what to do!' he had yelled, toppling over a cabinet full of his mother's prized china. 'You go to your university and don't come back! Me and your brother will manage fine without you!'

If the damage Clifford had caused had been limited to the living room, Ben might have found a way to forgive him. But when, having left the flat to escape his father's anger, he'd returned to find the guitar his mother had bought for him smashed to pieces in the hallway, he flew into a rage. Though he hadn't played it in a long while, spending most of his time on his electric guitar, as the last gift his mother had given to him it meant the world to him, and now it was broken beyond repair much like his relationship with his father. He'd packed his things, withdrawn his meagre savings from a part-time job glass-collecting at a nightclub in town, and told Nathan he was leaving.

'Come with me,' he'd said, but Nathan had refused.

'If we both go, you know he'll just drink and drink until he's dead.'

'I know,' Ben had replied. 'But I just can't stay.'

Just thinking about this moment was enough to bring a lump to his throat and it took all the strength he had not to reach out and touch his brother's arm. Instead, he swallowed down all the emotions he was feeling and, staring out of the window, continued replaying the memory of what happened on that day all those years ago.

After a tearful goodbye with Nathan a distraught Ben had made his way over to Helen's. It was his hope that she might agree to go with him, that this might be the ultimate turning point in their relationship, their first step towards spending the rest of their lives together. But even though he'd told her about the argument and begged her to join him, she had refused.

'Ben, this is madness,' she'd replied. 'We can't leave, we're only weeks away from sitting our A-levels. You're angry, that's all. Just stay at mine for a few days and you'll see things differently.'

Ben hadn't wanted to see things differently, he'd finally done the one thing he'd been wanting to do for a long time and the last thing he wanted was to be talked out of it.

'I have to go,' he'd told her and, although he cringed with guilt at the memory, he recalled adding, 'I need to go and if you really love me, you'll come too.'

It had been the worst kind of emotional blackmail, and Helen had immediately seen it for what it was. 'And if you love me as much as you say you do,' she'd replied, 'you wouldn't be forcing me to make a choice like this.'

He'd known she was right. Helen had worked hard to make sure she got the grades she needed to go to university. This was her ticket off the estate, her shot at making a better life for herself, and it was unfair of him to ask her to throw it away.

'You're right,' he'd said, 'I'm sorry. You should definitely stay.'

'But what about you, about us?' she'd asked, her eyes already brimming with tears.

He hadn't replied, he couldn't. Instead, he'd grabbed his bags and left without once looking back, for fear the sight of her might change his mind.

Across the weeks and months that followed, as Ben slowly built a life of sorts for himself in London, that image of Helen looking so lost and broken never left him, nor did his fury at his father. It fuelled every song he wrote, every chorus he created, and drove him to make the most of every opportunity that came his way. When he formed the band that would become Bluelight it was because of that day. When they performed the songs he wrote back then, he always sang them with all the passion, anger and tenderness he would've done had he been able to sing them to Helen or his father at the time. That night when Rocco stumbled across Bluelight in a dingy bar in King's Cross, the first words he'd said to Ben backstage were, 'That was absolutely stunning, son, absolutely stunning! You've got more passion and heart than any artist I've even seen.' Taking in the large, balding man wearing a loud Hawaiian shirt, Ben had wiped the beads of sweat from his brow and, meeting the man's penetrating gaze, he had replied, somewhat wryly, 'Thanks, mate, I owe it all to my father.'

18

Helen

'Okay, Pat,' said Helen, attempting to sound brighter than she felt as she tried to bring the conversation to a close, 'thanks so much for getting back to me, and please don't worry, really, I'm sure something will turn up. You have a great rest of your holiday and I'll talk to you soon.'

Helen ended the call and slumped back in the chair defeated. Although she knew it was a long shot she'd messaged her head teacher the night before, asking if there was any chance of making her position at St Joseph's full time. A worried Pat had called not long after Ben had left to find out what had prompted the question, leaving Helen no choice but to let the whole sorry tale come tumbling out. Having been through something similar herself a few years back, Pat was only too sympathetic to Helen's plight and, while there currently was no way to give Helen more hours, her boss had promised to make it her mission to find some way to help her out.

'Have we got any more orange juice?' asked Frankie, wandering into the kitchen. Momentarily startled, Helen sat up, quickly dabbed her eyes and then took several deep breaths to make sure her voice was steady. 'I didn't even know we'd run out,' she said, standing up. 'What have I told you about letting me know when we're running low on something? I'm not a mind reader, Franks, and I'm not a magician either!'

'I didn't say you were,' he snapped. 'I was just asking if we had any more.'

'Well, we haven't,' said Helen. 'So, you'll have to do without

I'm afraid unless you want to get out of your pyjamas and go out and get some. I mean it is practically midday after all.'

Shrugging, Frankie opened the fridge. 'I suppose I'll have this then,' he said, taking out a two-litre bottle of milk.

'Fine by me,' said Helen, knowing her son only too well, 'but I'm telling you now, if you drink straight from that bottle I will not be held responsible for my actions! Get yourself a glass and pour the milk into it like a normal human being.'

As Frankie left the room, glass of milk in hand, Helen's phone rang. She turned to pick it up from the coffee table, half hoping it was Pat calling her back with some good news, but to her dismay she saw that it was Adam. She could think of only one reason he might be calling: Holly must have told him about their meeting outside the yoga studio last night.

'What the hell were you thinking?'

Tempted though she was to bite back at him, Helen decided to meet his fury with calm. 'And good morning to you too, Adam. What can I do for you?'

'Well, for starters you can stop being such a spiteful bitch! What were you thinking waylaying poor Holly like that?'

'I didn't *waylay* anyone thank you very much. All I did was merely take an opportunity to have an adult conversation with someone who I hoped might be able to talk some sense into you.'

'Well, your little plan didn't work, did it? And now Holly knows first-hand what kind of a bitter, mean-spirited woman you are.'

'Indeed she does,' said Helen. 'Now is that you done yelling or is there more?'

'Yes, there's more: for starters I need to know what you've decided about the house. Are you going to buy me out?'

'Adam, you know everything about me there is to know, including how much there is in my bank account. You know full well I can't buy you out, so you can dispense with this pantomime. If you want your half of the money out of the house then there's no choice but to sell.'

Adam didn't even pause for thought. 'Well, that's fine by me.'

'Well, that's useful to know,' said Helen. 'I just hope when you tell the kids you'll sound a little less triumphant.'

The silence at the other end of the line was deafening. Finally, he recovered himself enough to speak.

'You want *me* to tell them?'

'Well, it's not me who's gone back on my word, is it? When you left you told me and the kids that we wouldn't have to move, that I could have the house. Now you've changed your mind you need to tell them.'

'You're being unfair,' said Adam. 'We're separated. This is just the next logical step.'

'Well, good luck explaining that to the kids when you see them on Saturday. You are still seeing them, aren't you? Or have you gone back on that promise too?'

'Of course I haven't,' he snapped. 'But you can't expect me to ruin my day with them by making me tell them about the house.'

'Oh, but it's okay for me to have my day ruined? No, Adam, this is all on you. If you want your money out of this house so desperately, you'll have to tell them yourself.'

Once the call was over Helen decided to bite the bullet and contact an estate agent to come and value the property. While she had a good idea what the house was worth, if her financial calculations were going to make any sense at all she needed them to be as accurate as possible. Much to her relief, they agreed to send someone round on Saturday morning at a time she was sure the kids would be at Adam's and she was assured the valuation would take no longer than half an hour. Ending the call, Helen rubbed her throbbing temples, and tried to quell the feeling of nausea that threatened to overwhelm her. She almost succeeded but then suddenly realised that she had just invited a complete stranger to wander around the house when she was currently harbouring the most famous missing person in the world.

At that very moment, to Helen's surprise the kitchen door opened and Ben himself walked in. She hadn't expected him back so soon but she could tell by the look on his face that things hadn't gone well.

'I couldn't do it,' he said, refusing to meet her gaze. 'I couldn't even bring myself to go in the building.'

'Oh, Ben, I'm sorry,' said Helen, and taking him by the hand she led him to the sofa and they both sat in silence looking out on to the garden. Helen felt awful. She'd encouraged Ben to see his father, thinking it might help, but now things seemed worse than ever. She wished more than anything that she could take his pain away, that she could somehow make everything all right.

'Are you okay?' she asked after a while. 'I feel like I pushed you into doing something you weren't ready for.'

'You were only trying to help,' said Ben. 'And to be honest, all the way there I really thought I could go through with it but I just couldn't. The thought of being in the same building was unbearable, let alone the same room.'

More than anything Helen wanted to comfort Ben, to put her arms around him and hold him tight, but she could see that he was trying to contain everything he was feeling. And so instead she took his hand in hers.

'It'll be all right,' she said. 'I don't know how, but it will.'

When Saturday came around Adam picked up Esme and Frankie as arranged, leaving Helen free to make a start getting the house ready for the arrival of the estate agent. With Ben's help she blitzed the kitchen before attacking the kids' bedrooms, tidying away what could be tidied, and bin-bagging everything else, loading it out of sight into the back of the car to deal with later.

She was just giving the downstairs a final tidy with Ben's assistance when a brisk knock at the door made them both jump. 'Damn,' she said, looking at her watch, 'he's ten minutes early. I'm so sorry about this but I think it's time for you to make your escape.'

Unlocking the back door, Helen watched as Ben made his way down to the shed as they'd planned, and waited until he was safely out of sight before running back to the hallway. She opened the door to reveal a young man, dressed in a slim-fitting grey suit and a loud red tie. He was carrying a briefcase in his left hand and an SLR camera on a strap was slung over one shoulder. He beamed at her as if they were long lost friends.

'Miss Morley! I thought I recognised the name! Do you remember me?'

Helen's heart sank. This kind of thing seemed to happen to her all the time these days, former pupils of St Joseph's who she'd taught when they were little kids of ten and eleven, now young men and women, out in the world with actual grown-up jobs, and sometimes even kids of their own. It made her feel old and decrepit, only too aware of the relentless march of time.

'It's Henry, isn't it? Don't tell me . . . Henry . . . Abimbola?'

The young man's face lit up. 'Wow, Miss, that's impressive! I can't believe you remembered my name after all these years, St Joseph's feels like a lifetime ago.'

'I'm sure it does,' said Helen. 'I take it you work for Holden Estates?'

'Three years now, started off at Dixon's, then moved to Purple

Bricks before coming to Holden's as a senior sales negotiator. You've definitely made the right choice, we're easily the best on the high street.'

She managed to keep her reason for moving as vague as possible, 'It just feels like the right time to move on,' and showed him around the house, allowing him to take all the photos he needed, answering all the house-related questions that he fired at her. Thankfully, despite taking pictures of the garden, he didn't insist on inspecting the shed where a Grammy Award-winning rock star was hiding amongst rusting bikes and assorted patio furniture.

'Well, miss,' said Henry as they stood at the door a short while later, 'thank you so much for showing me your beautiful home. I really can see it selling in no time at all, no problem. I'll email you the contracts and in the meantime, if you need anything or have any questions just give me a call, my number's on the card I gave you.'

Helen watched as her former pupil climbed into a white Mini Cooper plastered in the Holden Estates logo, then, waving him off, she closed the door, and walked down the garden to liberate Ben.

'How was it?' he asked, dusting himself off as he emerged from the cobweb-strewn shed.

'Okay,' said Helen, and then, unable to hold in the emotion she'd been feeling any longer, she began sobbing like her heart was breaking, and couldn't stop no matter how hard she tried.

It was a little after eight when Helen heard keys in the door signalling the return of Frankie and Esme. All afternoon she'd been checking her phone for calls or messages from her kids reacting to Adam's news about the house being sold but none came. Reasoning that perhaps Adam, coward that he was, had left it until the very last minute to break the news, as Ben went upstairs to give them all some space she steeled herself to cope with their upset. But to her surprise and confusion, as they tumbled through the door, both Esme and Frankie were all smiles.

'How was your day?' she asked casually, noting the multiple shopping bags they were both clutching.

'Wicked,' beamed Frankie. 'Dad bought those new trainers I wanted. What do you think?'

Helen looked down at Frankie's feet to see them encased in footwear that looked like some sort of ridiculous miniature space-ships.

'They're lovely, darling.' She looked at Esme who, judging from the carrier bags, seemed to have brought half of Primark home with her. 'And what have you got there?'

'Three jackets, five shirts, four pairs of trousers, two pairs of really cute shorts, and at least ten T-shirts, half of which I think I'll probably take back,' Esme replied. 'Dad gave me two hundred quid so I went a bit wild. I can't wait to wear it all out.'

Helen's heart sank. Neither of these kids looked like they had just heard the news that their home was going to be sold. Adam clearly hadn't told them.

'So, you've . . . had a good day?' she asked tentatively, determined to be doubly sure before she ripped Adam apart.

'The best,' said Frankie. 'We had lunch at that new burger place in town, I had the waffle burger. You should've seen it, Mum, it was huge, almost as big as my head.'

'And their spicy fries are to die for,' Esme chipped in. 'Frankie and Dad couldn't handle it but I know you'd love them.'

'I bet I would,' said Helen, trying her best to stay calm. 'I tell you what, why don't you go up and show Ben your new gear? I'm sure he'd love to see it.'

As they both raced up the stairs Helen took her phone out of her back pocket and called Adam. On her first try, it went to voicemail, as it did the half-dozen times she tried over the course of the next five minutes. Spotting Frankie's phone on the hallway table, Helen picked it up, punched in his code, went into the kitchen, and tried Adam again. This time round he picked up straight away.

'Frankie, mate, still loving those new kicks?'

'It's not Frankie, it's me!' hissed Helen and even from the end of the line she imagined she could hear Adam's blood freezing in his veins.

'Helen . . .?'

'Yes . . . Helen! What are you playing at, Adam? How could you not have told them?'

He was silent for a moment. 'I tried . . . I really did . . . but I don't know . . . I just couldn't.'

'You just couldn't? You just couldn't? Where was that sort of resolve when you were sneaking around behind my back? Just couldn't! Don't give me that! You could have, but you just didn't want to, because as always you want me to do your dirty work! Well, I'm not doing it any more, Adam, I'm not going to be the bad guy when you're the villain here. You're the one who had an affair, you're the one who chose to leave, and you're the one who's making me sell this house so that you can buy yourself a cosy love nest with—'

Hearing a noise behind her, she turned around to see Frankie standing in the open doorway, his face so pale with shock that there was no need to ask how much he had heard. Whether she liked it or not, she had done Adam's dirty work for him after all.

19

Helen

Helen was dreading the thought of the day ahead. As she lay under the covers she replayed the terrible scenes from the night before, as she had done over and over since it all happened, since Frankie had overheard her yelling at Adam over the phone.

'It's all your fault!' a distraught Frankie had yelled at her as she'd tried to comfort him. 'It's all your fault! And now because of you we're going to have to move!'

At the noise of the commotion Esme had appeared in the kitchen, closely followed by Ben. 'What's going on, Mum? Why's Frankie losing it?'

Helen had been so upset she'd been barely able to get the words out. 'Because . . . because . . . Frankie overheard me talking with your dad.'

'About what?'

'About selling the house!' spat Frankie.

Esme looked confused. 'You're not selling the house, are you?'

Helen's heart ached. 'I'm afraid so, Dad was supposed to tell you himself today but he didn't and I was talking to him about it on the phone when Frankie overheard.'

'He came down to get his phone,' explained Esme, 'he wanted to show Ben pictures of the burger he'd eaten.'

A tearful Frankie pushed Helen's arm away from his shoulder. 'And she had my phone and was shouting at Dad on it! She was saying we have to sell the house, Es. She was saying we have to move. Everything's going to change again and it's all her fault!'

Esme had turned to her mother, her pale green eyes full of accusation. 'Mum, why do we need to sell the house?'

'I'm afraid I've got no choice,' said Helen. 'Dad wants to buy a place of his own with Holly and to do that he needs the money he's got tied up here.'

'But that can't be right,' said Esme. 'Dad's got loads of money, look at all the stuff he bought us today.'

'I know,' said Helen, 'but he hasn't got enough to buy a house, not without selling this place.' She'd put an arm around Esme. 'I'm so sorry, darling, if it was up to me none of this would be happening.'

'But it is,' snapped Frankie. 'And you have to stop it, Mum, I don't want to move.'

'Me either. Isn't there something you can do?' said Esme plaintively. 'Some way around this? Can't you get another job?'

Helen bit her lip. 'I'm trying, sweetie, really I'm trying, but even if I got a full-time job tomorrow, that still wouldn't be enough for me to afford to keep this place on.'

That's when Esme had looked at Ben, her eyes pleading. 'Can't you do something? You're rich, you're famous, you've got money. Mum's helped you out, can't you help her?'

'Esme!' reprimanded Helen, springing to Ben's defence. 'That's enough of that! And I mean it!'

'But why not?' retorted her daughter defiantly. 'If he gave you the money to give to Dad that would solve everything.'

'I said that's enough,' snapped Helen. 'Not another word! You want to blame me for this, go ahead! You want to blame your father, then be my guest! But I'm telling you now, Ben's not the villain here, and this isn't his problem to solve!'

With that Esme, glaring daggers at her mum, had grabbed Frankie's hand and stormed out of the room. And since then, despite several attempts to offer an olive branch, neither Esme nor Frankie had said a word to her. And while she hoped today would be different, she had her doubts.

Forcing herself out of bed, Helen got dressed and went down to the kitchen and started frying some bacon, hoping that the prospect of a nice breakfast might lure the children out of their rooms. Sure enough, no sooner had she got the grill on than a scowling Frankie sloped into the kitchen.

'Oh, hi, love,' she said. 'I'm cooking some bacon, do you fancy some?'

Frankie said nothing. Instead he grabbed himself a bowl from the cupboard, filled it to the brim with cereal, poured on some milk and then, without acknowledging her, left the room. Worrying that her offering of bacon wasn't anywhere near as tempting as she'd hoped, Helen made Esme's favourite: scrambled eggs with smashed avocado on toast. As she headed upstairs with it she met her daughter coming the other way.

'Oh, hello, sweetie, I was just bringing this up to you. It's your favourite.'

'I'm not hungry,' scowled Esme.

'You must be. You haven't eaten since last night.'

'I told you I'm not.'

Helen decided to let it go. 'Okay, well, how about a drink? I bought some fresh orange juice yesterday, or if you don't fancy that how about a cup of tea?'

When Esme spoke her lips barely moved. 'I'm fine.'

All Helen wanted to do was wrap her darling baby in a hug, but she resisted the temptation for fear of making the situation even worse.

'Come on, Es, give me a break. Look, I get it, you're upset but—'

Esme cut her off. 'I'm not going to uni.' She spat the words at her mother with such vehemence it was as if she wanted to make sure they could never be taken back.

Helen looked at Esme in confusion. She didn't quite know what to say other than to echo her daughter's words with an added edge of total disbelief. 'You're not going to uni?'

'No,' said Esme firmly, 'and just so you know, when you're looking for a new house don't bother getting a bedroom for me. I won't need one. Me and Josh are moving to London and getting a place together.'

Helen was momentarily speechless. This was all Adam's fault, every last bit of it, yet another aftershock of his affair. 'Look, Es, I don't think you know what you're saying. Why don't we just have a cup of tea and see if we can't talk this thing through?'

'There's nothing to talk about, Mum, I've made up my mind. Josh and I are doing this and there's nothing you can do to stop me.'

Tempted though she was to say that there were indeed plenty of things she could do, up to and including locking her daughter in her room for the foreseeable future, for the sake of peace Helen decided against it. 'Come on, Es, please, let's talk.' She reached out to take Esme's hand. 'We can work this out, I promise you.'

'I'm not going to let you talk me out of this,' said Esme, snatching her hand out of her mother's reach. She then turned and stormed back up the stairs to her room, slamming the door behind her.

Helen thought briefly about going after her but knew that doing so would only inflame the situation. Esme needed to cool off and so did Helen, and so instead she sat down on the stairs, head in hands, trying her best not to cry. This was such a mess. Her daughter was going to ruin her life, throw away everything she'd worked so hard to achieve, squander all the wonderful opportunities that lay in front of her and all because of Adam. Sometimes she really wanted nothing more than to wring her husband's neck, to enact all the violent scenarios she'd fantasised about in her darkest moments, to make him hurt as much as she had since finding out about his affair. She'd never do this of course. Helen couldn't even bring herself to squash a spider, even the big ones with hairy legs, preferring instead to abandon a room for a while, in the hope that the creature might move on of its own accord. But the pain Adam was causing them all was intolerable, and sometimes she couldn't help wishing she was the sort of person who could take pleasure in revenge.

Returning to the kitchen, Helen scraped Esme's breakfast into the bin and leaned against the sink, trying to think what else she could do. Just then, the kitchen door opened and Helen's heart leaped, hoping it was one of the kids come to make peace, but instead it was Ben.

'Things still no better?' he asked, reading her face.

Helen shook her head and, spying her keys on the kitchen counter, she said, 'I feel like my head's going to explode. I need to get out of here. Do you fancy coming for a drive?'

Helen didn't say very much as they headed in the direction of the M60 and neither did Ben. Instead, as if lost in their own thoughts, they listened to the radio in silence, save for the occasional comment about the traffic. After a short while on the motorway, however, Ben spoke up as Helen turned on her indicator to join a slip road.

'Are we going where I think we're going?' he said gleefully, as a sign for Ashton-under-Lyne loomed into view.

Helen nodded. 'Hartshead Pike. I thought it might be fun. I haven't been here in years. Not since the kids were little.'

'Well, I haven't been since we last came with your mate . . . who was it again? . . . Amara . . . when she passed her driving test.'

'Practically thirty years ago now,' said Helen. 'You're about due another visit then, wouldn't you say?'

Back when they were all young and broke Hartshead Pike was the sort of place Helen and her friends would go to hang out if one of them had access to a car for a reasonable amount of time. Just half an hour from Manchester, it felt like you were in the middle of the countryside, and after a short uphill walk you were rewarded with the Gothic grandeur of the Grade II listed Hartshead Tower and stunning views of the surrounding area. On a clear day you could see as far as Cheshire and even Snowdonia.

The last time Helen had been there with Ben, it had been a warm spring day, the kind that feels like a foretaste of summer, full of possibilities and hope. Just one month later he would argue with his dad, and not long after that they would split up. So, it was strange to be back here with him after all these years, particularly when the place had changed so little, making it easier for all the memories to come flooding back.

'It hasn't changed a bit,' declared Ben as they reached the tower, its entrance covered by a graffiti-strewn reinforced metal door and windows that had been long since sealed up.

'Do you remember the stories we used to tell each other about some mad woman being bricked up inside there?'

Helen smiled. 'The Mad Woman of Hartshead, we used to wind ourselves up into a frenzy talking about her, especially if we came up here at night. I wonder if kids still scare themselves with that story?' They walked around the building before finally looking out towards Manchester, just able to make out the city through a bank of low cloud.

'Looks like we're out of luck with the views today,' said Helen, sitting down on the ledge surrounding the tower. 'Still, I'm glad we came. I think I was seconds from exploding when you arrived.'

'The kids still not talking to you?' asked Ben.

'Worse,' replied Helen. 'Esme's got it into her head that instead of going to uni she's going to shack up with Josh and move down to London.'

Ben groaned and, when Helen turned to look at him, he seemed embarrassed and awkward. 'What's wrong?'

'Nothing,' said Ben. 'It's just that I think that . . . well . . . that might have been my fault. When I first arrived, Esme was asking about my career and how I started off and everything, and of course I told her all about moving to London. I'm sorry, Helen, I just thought she was interested, I never imagined she'd take it as careers advice.'

Helen shook her head. 'You might have made it sound glamorous but believe me this is all my doing, or Adam's to be precise. She's doing this because she feels messed about, because Adam's making me sell the house. I suppose she feels like all the security of home has gone so she might as well make her own somewhere else with Josh.'

'But you're not going to let them go, are you?'

Helen sighed. 'Not while there's breath in my body! I'll have to have words with Josh's parents and of course Adam too, but I doubt it'll happen. Right now, it's just teenagers being . . .' Her voice trailed off and she bit her lip in an effort to stop herself from crying, a task made all the more difficult when Ben put an arm around her. 'What am I going to do, Ben? My family's falling apart in front of my eyes and I feel like there's nothing I can do to stop it.'

He leaned forward. 'Well, for starters you could let me give you—'

'Ben,' said Helen firmly, 'it's a really kind offer but like I said, I don't want your money.'

'Then what do you want?'

Helen smiled. It was a good question. 'Honestly? Right now, I feel like the thing I want most is to get away from it all.'

'Okay,' said Ben. 'Then let's do that. I've got a friend with a place down in Cornwall and they're always saying I can use it whenever I want. It's really tucked away, it's got loads of rooms and even has its own private beach. What if I gave them a ring and we all went down there for a few days? We could drive down – me, you, the kids, we could even let your mum in on me being here and bring her along too, if she's up for it. Come on, what do you say? If you won't let me help you with the house, at least let me give you a break from it all. I think it would do you the world of good.'

Helen rested her hand on his. 'It's so sweet of you, Ben, really it is, but I can't. There's so much to sort out with the house, with the kids, with my job, I couldn't afford to take the time out.'

'But that's exactly the reason you should,' countered Ben. 'You're going to burn yourself out if you're not careful. You're already running on fumes as it is.'

'I'll be fine,' said Helen, 'you know me, tough as old boots. I'll survive.'

Helen's phone rang and she checked the screen and saw her husband's name. There was only one reason he'd be calling her: Esme must have told him about her decision.

'I'd better take this,' she said, getting to her feet and, walking a little distance to give her privacy, she answered the call.

'What's all this about Esme not going to university?' Adam's voice was cold and direct.

'You know as much as I do,' she replied. 'Frankie overheard me talking to you last night about selling the house, and now all hell has broken loose.'

'Frankie overheard you? How could you have been so careless?'

Helen could barely believe the audacity of the man. 'Careless? Me? You're the one who left the family home! You're the one who's forcing me to sell the house! You're the one who's such an utter coward that you were begging me to tell the kids that you'd gone back on your promise! This is all on you, Adam! You alone!'

'And of course, now's the time to be apportioning blame when we've got a full-blown crisis on our hands! You've got to talk her round, Helen, you've got to fix this, you can't let her throw her life away!'

Helen felt herself flush with fury. Once again, her husband was trying to abdicate all parental responsibility, refusing to step up and be their children's father. 'Why's it always my job to clear up the mess you've created? Why am I the one having to pick up all the pieces of the things you've broken? Well, I've had enough, Adam, I'm not doing this any more. I'm not your skivvy!' Ending the call, she thrust the phone into her pocket and marched back to Ben.

'This holiday you were just talking about, is the offer still there?'

'Of course,' said Ben, standing up. 'Just say the word and I'll make the arrangements. Have you changed your mind then?'

'Yes,' said Helen. 'In a big way. I think you're right, I think a holiday is just what we all need.'

20

Ben

As the imposing black metal security gates at the entrance to the Sea House slid back to reveal not only a long, winding tree-lined drive but also a bank of security cameras pointing in every direction, everyone in the car, with the exception of Ben, let out a huge gasp.

'My goodness!' exclaimed Helen's mum, Sue, who was sitting in the back with Esme and Frankie. 'This place is like Fort Knox! Who did you say it belongs to again?'

'Nice try, Sue,' said Ben jovially, as Helen drove slowly through the entrance and continued along the drive. 'But you know I've already told you I can't tell you. All I can say is that it belongs to a good mate of mine.'

Sue laughed. 'By any chance is your "good mate" a famous singer like you, who likes outrageous outfits, big glasses and Watford Football Club?'

Ben couldn't help but smile. 'My lips are sealed.'

'I reckon it's Ed Sheeran's,' said Esme, unable to hide the excitement in her voice. 'He'd definitely have a holiday home like this.'

'We should check all the plugholes for ginger hair,' joked Frankie. 'If we find any it's definitely him.' At this, the kids and Helen's mum collapsed in a fit of giggles.

They rounded a bend and a breathtakingly beautiful modern-looking architect-designed house loomed into view. It was made up of a series of geometric shapes all piled artfully on top of each other – an elegantly proportioned rectangle here, the gentle sweep of an ellipse there, each form punctuated with huge floor-to-ceiling windows. It was at once imposing and inviting and reminded Ben a little of his home in Malibu.

'Well,' said Helen, as her mum, Esme and Frankie fell into an awed silence, 'whoever it belongs to it's very kind of them to let us stay, so let's stop speculating about who it is, because it's rude, and no snooping because that's rude too.' She paused and looked in the rear-view mirror. 'And I'm including you in all that, Mum! I know what you're like.'

Ben was glad Helen had agreed to accept his offer of taking her and her family on holiday. It felt like the very least he could do for her after everything she had done for him. He'd made the call to his friend out in LA the moment Helen had changed her mind and, while they had been surprised to hear from Ben given all that had been in the news, thankfully they hadn't asked any questions about what was going on. Instead, without any fuss they had told Ben they were glad he was safe, and told him to enjoy his stay at the Cornwall holiday home.

Armed with this news, Ben had given Helen the green light to tell the kids. Esme's first response had been to ask if Josh could come along too, to which Helen had replied that not only couldn't he come, but she couldn't even tell Josh where she was going. For a moment Ben had thought that Esme might not join them, but the lure of staying in a celebrity's house must have proved too great because after pausing for thought, she'd agreed to come and abide by Helen's rules.

Frankie, meanwhile, perhaps bored of spending all day on his PlayStation, had agreed to come to Cornwall with the minimum of fuss, and so next Helen had called her mum. Swearing her to secrecy, Helen had confessed all about Ben before extending his invitation to join them on the trip. 'I always did like that boy,' she'd said, 'and he's much better than what you actually ended up with! Of course I'll come.'

Then finally, early that morning, they'd all loaded their things into Helen's car and, after picking up her mum, had begun the long drive down to Cornwall. And though Ben had been worried that the whole of the six-hour trip might be undertaken either in frosty silence or peppered with barbed remarks, he'd been pleased to discover that as the journey progressed Frankie and Esme unofficially declared a truce of sorts. By Stoke-on-Trent Frankie appeared to have forgotten that he was angry at his mother, and by Birmingham Esme was even joking with Helen about the ancient swimming costume Sue had brought with her. Their problems were still there of course, but for now, at least, it felt like they might be able to take a break from them.

Opening up the huge cantilevered door, there was a flurry of activity as Esme and Frankie raced around the ground floor yelling back reports about everything they discovered. 'Someone's filled the fridge with food and Champagne!' called Esme. 'And there's a room with a massive screen and a popcorn machine and proper cinema seats and everything down here!' cried Frankie from somewhere down the hallway. Even Sue got in on the act, exclaiming excitedly, 'Ohh! The toilet seats are heated!' as she emerged from one of the two downstairs bathrooms.

'It is pretty amazing,' said Ben, grateful for the opportunity to see such luxury through the eyes of people who really appreciated it.

'Amazing?' said Helen, running a hand across the smooth pale grey marble island in the kitchen. 'This place is stunning.' She walked over to him and threw her arms around him, squeezing him tightly. 'Oh, Ben, how can we ever thank you for arranging all this?'

'No need,' said Ben, thrilled to see her looking so happy. 'Believe me, the pleasure is all mine.'

As everyone gathered back together Ben suggested they should all head upstairs. 'I think your mum should have the master suite,' he said to an excited Esme and Frankie. 'But there are five others to pick from, all en suite, and all with great views so you won't be missing out on anything.'

'Are you sure about that?' said Helen as her children raced up the stairs, followed at a more sedate pace by Sue. 'Why don't you have it? I don't need a fancy room.'

'Nobody needs a fancy room,' said Ben, 'but it's nice to have one every now and again, and I think you need a bit of spoiling far more than me.' Leading her upstairs, he took her all the way down a bright sunlit corridor before opening a door at the end to reveal an enormous bedroom with floor-to-ceiling windows looking out across the sea.

'Oh, Ben,' said Helen. 'This is amazing, I feel like I'm dreaming.'

'And this is just the bedroom,' said Ben, and, walking down a passage that ran the length of the room, he showed her the bathroom, a small gym and a sauna, before finally opening a set of large glass doors to reveal a private balcony with its own jacuzzi too.

'I'll see you in a week,' said Helen, taking in the views from the balcony. 'You're going to have to drag me out of here kicking and screaming.'

'Take as long as you need,' said Ben, preparing to leave. 'But maybe not a whole week. See you downstairs when you're ready, and perhaps we'll all go and check out the beach.'

After dropping his bags into one of the remaining empty bedrooms, Ben headed down to the kitchen and set about making a picnic lunch for them to take to the beach. He started looking through the fridge and cupboards and began filling two cool bags with things he thought people might like. As he put in a bottle of Coke for Frankie and a fruit smoothie for Esme, he thought how back in LA this sort of thing was normally done by his house-keeper, and yet here he was enjoying the opportunity to take care of a family, even if it wasn't his own. He realised that there was pleasure to be had in such a simple task, a certain contentment in considering and trying to meet each person's needs, a feeling he'd grown unaccustomed to since his divorce. He'd missed looking after someone other than himself, and he was glad of the oppor-tunity to do so now.

By the time he'd finished packing the picnic bags, everyone had come back downstairs, having changed out of their travelling clothes ready for the beach.

'Right then,' said Ben, handing one of the bags to Frankie and a collection of rugs and picnic blankets to Esme, 'let's go and see the sea.'

Together they walked away from the house through perfectly manicured gardens down a series of steps that led to a stunning sheltered cove. The sand beneath their feet was soft and white, the sea a gleaming azure blue, and the heat from the afternoon sun high above them was thankfully tempered by a gentle breeze coming in off the water.

'This is mad,' said Frankie, 'we've got the whole beach to ourselves. When we went to Wales with Dad, the sun came out and the beach was packed!'

'It's nice,' said Ben, not wanting Frankie to feel as if he was trying to outdo his dad. 'But on the downside, you'd never get a Mr Whippy van down those steps in a million years, would you?'

'Race you to the sea!' yelled Esme, hurling the beach towels at her brother before running in the direction of the water.

'That's not fair,' protested Frankie, dropping the cool bag on the sand and chasing after his sister. 'You wait until I catch up with you! I'm going to soak you!'

While Ben spread out the blankets and strategically positioned parasols in the sand, Helen settled her mum down on a lounger, before sorting through the food, ready for them to eat. Then a short while later Frankie and Esme returned from the water, wet and breathless, wrapping themselves in beach towels, before they all tucked into what was widely proclaimed by all to be little short of a feast.

'I could easily get used to this sort of life,' declared Frankie, brandishing a chicken drumstick like he was Henry VIII.

'Me too,' said Esme, saluting her brother with a glass of chilled Moët. 'It's proper killing me that I can't put any of this online, moments like this are made for Instagram!'

Sue plucked another succulent strawberry out of the bowl next to her. 'I must admit, Sir Elton, if indeed that is who this place belongs to, certainly knows how to pick a good spot! My tan's topping up very nicely indeed!'

'It is totally beautiful,' said Helen. 'I feel quite spoiled.' She turned and looked at Ben. 'Fancy a stroll?'

'Definitely,' said Ben. 'I could do with walking off some of that lunch otherwise I'll be fast asleep like a cat in the sun in no time.'

Helen turned to her mum. 'You'll be all right with the kids for a bit, won't you?'

'Of course,' said Sue, closing her eyes and lying back on the sun lounger. 'I'll get them peeling grapes and feeding them to me.'

Side by side, Ben and Helen made their way down to the water's edge, then slipped off their shoes before stepping into the surf. Once again Ben found himself thinking about his home in Malibu, and the early morning run he used to take along the beach. Though the water was far cooler here, the sense of calm he felt being so near to it felt the same.

'It's so peaceful here,' said Helen, as if reading his thoughts, as they walked along the shoreline. 'The real world feels like it's a million miles away. You were so right, I did need a holiday. Sometimes you convince yourself that the only option is just to carry on, put your head down and get on with it, when really, all you really need is to step off the merry-go-round and allow yourself to get things in perspective.'

Ben smiled. 'You could almost be talking about me, how I used to feel on the constant cycle of writing, recording, touring and promo.'

'And how are you feeling about it all now? Do you miss it?'

He thought for a moment; he was aware that Helen had been avoiding this subject, not wanting to push him to open up, but he found himself wanting to talk.

'It's hard to say,' he began, 'I mean it's pretty much all I've known for over twenty years, so how do I tell if I'm actually missing it, or just the routine that went along with it? When I was deep in that cycle, I didn't have to think, I didn't have to worry, I didn't have time because my every waking moment was scheduled, and . . . I have to say . . . there's a certain comfort in that.'

'I know it's not exactly the same,' said Helen, 'but I think I've felt similar. Sometimes between work, the kids and running a house, it feels like there's so much to do that you don't have time to ponder all the big questions of life: am I fulfilled, is this why I'm here on earth, is this what I really want? You haven't got the head space for any of that because . . . well . . . you're too busy living life, aren't you?'

'Exactly,' said Ben. 'But here's the thing: all that busyness, all that craziness, it doesn't take those questions away, it just hides them, covers them over, pushes them into the shadows and there they lurk, ready to take you by surprise when you least expect it.'

Reaching a line of rocks, they followed them round until they came across another set of steps that took them back up to the top of the cliff, opening out on to a wildflower meadow overlooking the sea.

'This place just keeps on giving,' said Helen, looping an arm through Ben's as they stood looking out across the water, watching tiny fishing boats bobbing along in the distance.

'I know,' he replied, 'just when you think you've seen everything, it surprises you.'

He turned to look at Helen and found that she was already looking at him. There was something different about her expression, about her whole demeanour, and for a moment he wondered if she might be about to ask him a question. But she didn't speak. Instead, she slowly tilted her head towards his, and as if drawn by an invisible force he leaned down towards her and they remained, for what to Ben felt like an eternity, then finally their lips touched, and gently, very gently, they kissed.

21

Helen

It was early evening and Helen and her mum were busy at the kitchen island preparing side dishes for dinner. Pausing as she shredded a white cabbage for the coleslaw she was making, Helen glanced through the open doors leading out to the terrace. On one side, Ben was manning the enormous professional-looking barbecue, ably assisted by Frankie, and on the other Esme lounged on a deckchair enjoying the dying embers of the sun as she chatted animatedly on her phone with, she presumed, Josh. Moments like this, she thought, were what all the best holidays were made of, everyone together and content, away from all the stresses and strains of everyday life.

'Nice to see everyone happy, isn't it?'

Brought out of her reverie, Helen turned to see her mum looking back at her.

'Sorry?'

Sue nodded towards the terrace. 'I was saying it's nice to see everyone happy.'

Helen smiled. 'Yes, it is, isn't it?'

'And it's all thanks to your old boyfriend! I certainly didn't see that coming.'

Helen felt herself bristle. 'See what coming?'

'You and Ben getting back together after all these years.'

Helen sighed. 'I've already told you there's nothing going on. Me and Ben are just friends and that's all, okay?'

Helen's mum raised a sceptical eyebrow. 'No need to jump down my throat, I believe you.'

Suddenly Helen didn't feel like a middle-aged mother of two, but a sulky teenager resistant to the idea of being interrogated about her love life. 'Yeah, it certainly sounds like it.'

'Well, you can hardly blame me, can you? Just think about it, he travels halfway around the world to see you only to end up staying at your house, and now he's whisked you away to Elton John's seaside palace, it couldn't be more romantic!'

Helen laughed. 'Because nothing spells romance quite like hiding from the world's media and taking your sulky teenage kids and your interfering old mother on holiday with you.'

Sue pointed the paring knife in her hand at her daughter. 'Oi, you, less of the old, thank you very much! I'll have you know I still get the odd wolf whistle when I walk past a building site!'

Helen grimaced; sometimes her mum really was too much. 'That's far more information than I need to know.'

'I'm still a sexual being, you know,' replied Sue, to Helen's intense discomfort. 'And so are you, by the way. Just because Adam's off sowing his wild oats doesn't mean you can't. You must be blind if you can't see how much Ben still fancies you.'

Helen blushed scarlet and was about to protest when, thankfully, Frankie came into the kitchen carrying a tray of barbecued chicken.

'Ben says these need to be kept warm in the oven.'

'Thanks, sweetheart,' said Sue, taking them from him. 'I'll sort them out.'

As Sue searched the drawers for kitchen foil Helen, prompted by her mum's observation, found herself thinking for the millionth time about her clifftop kiss with Ben. How had it happened? She hadn't had any designs on kissing him when she'd suggested going for a walk. All she'd wanted to do was thank him for giving her and the kids the opportunity to get away, something they would never have been able to afford to do on their own. But then it had been such a lovely warm day, and the sound of the waves lapping at their feet as they'd walked down to the water's edge had been so relaxing, and then there was that spectacular view of the horizon from the clifftop, which had made her feel so calm, so at peace that she'd allowed herself to get carried away by the moment.

After the kiss, they hadn't spoken. Instead they'd stood, holding each other as they gazed out to sea, each lost in their own thoughts. Wrapped in Ben's arms, Helen felt like she was eighteen again, like all the cares and worries of the past year belonged to someone else. It was the nearest thing she'd experienced to time travel, feeling like her youth, her vitality, her zest for life had been restored and with it her feelings for Ben. Had she ever stopped loving him, or had she simply locked all that away deep within herself all those years ago? Had this kiss been inevitable from the moment he'd knocked on her door, only she'd been too blind to see it until now? Whatever the answers to these questions, the one thing Helen knew for sure was that she hadn't wanted the moment to end. But then her phone had buzzed with a text, and if the sound hadn't been enough to break the spell between them then the sight of a message from Adam had certainly done the job.

Being away, she'd left all responsibility for dealing with requests to view the house with him, and the message was one informing her that he had just done the first viewing himself. Tucking the phone away, Helen had tried not to let the idea of strangers roaming around her home get to her, but even so it was with a heavy heart that she'd walked back to the others with Ben. Wonderful as this place was, as this moment with Ben had been, Adam's text had brought her crashing back down to reality. She wasn't an eighteen-year-old girl but a forty-five-year-old recently separated mother of two, in the process of having her life dismantled. And Ben wasn't the boy of her youth but rather a middle-aged man wrestling with a whole lot of problems of his own. The kiss then had been a mistake, a lovely one, but a mistake nonetheless. She would have to face facts, do the responsible thing and make it clear that it wouldn't be happening again.

It didn't take long for the rest of the food to be ready, and in no time at all there was a veritable banquet spread out across the table on the terrace. Though, like everyone else, Helen piled her plate high, in the end all she could manage was a few forkfuls of salad and a tiny bite of a burger, because of the knot of anxiety growing in her stomach. She needed to talk to Ben, to clear the air with him, to make sure that things were okay between them, that the kiss wasn't going to ruin everything. But this would be virtually impossible surrounded as she was by her family, and so she had no choice but to sit tight and wait for an opportunity to present itself.

Sometime later, once all the eating was over and the kitchen tidied, Frankie began lobbying to watch a film in the cinema room. He managed to get Esme and his grandma on board, but when it came to Ben he was unsuccessful.

'You go for it, mate,' said Ben. 'But I think I'm going to give it a miss tonight, if that's okay? It's such a beautiful evening, I thought I might stay out here and have a beer on the terrace.'

Frankie extended the same invitation to Helen, which she too declined. 'After all that driving I'm completely shattered,' she said. 'You carry on with Gran and Es, and I'll keep Ben company for a bit.'

'Suit yourself,' said Frankie. 'It's your loss. I tried out the sound system when we got back from the beach and it's off the hook! It was so loud my ears are still ringing!'

Helen winced; Frankie's frequent delight at the prospect of

damaging his hearing never ceased to amaze her. He wore it like a badge of honour. 'Well, not too loud please, if only for Gran's sake.'

'Don't mind me,' said Sue. 'My hearing aid goes up to eleven!'

As Frankie herded his grandmother and sister inside, Helen grabbed two beers from the ice bucket, opened both and handed one to Ben. 'Fancy a quick stroll around the gardens? They're so beautiful, aren't they?'

'Sounds perfect,' said Ben. 'Lead the way.'

They walked through the landscaped gardens past bougainvillea in bloom, honeysuckle and jasmine filling the air with their heady scent and palm trees rustling gently in the evening breeze. Finally, they reached a decked terrace overlooking the cliff edge and, stepping on to it, they made their way right up to the glass balustrade. Though the sun had long since set, the moon was bright, and sounds of the waves crashing on the rocks beneath once again made the scene dangerously romantic.

Helen kept her gaze fixed towards the horizon. 'We need to talk, don't we?'

'Not necessarily,' said Ben. 'We could always try not talking and see how that goes.'

Helen smiled sadly. He had a point. As uncomfortable as not talking about the matter in hand was, actually having to converse about it felt even more awkward. 'About . . . well . . . about earlier . . . I'm sorry . . . I shouldn't have let that happen.'

'Didn't you want it to?'

'That's not the issue. I don't want to muddy the waters between us.'

'What's so bad about Muddy Waters? "Mannish Boy", "Hoochie Coochie Man" and "Rollin' Stone" are all amazing tracks.' Ben pulled a face and groaned. 'I don't even have kids and yet here I am making "dad" jokes like a professional.' He took a sip of his beer. 'So, you think it was a mistake?'

Helen considered 'it' for a moment, the tantalising kiss that had almost made her go weak at the knees. Perhaps 'mistake' was the wrong word but the right one seemed to elude her. 'I just think that, for lots of different reasons, it shouldn't happen again.'

Ben was silent for a moment, avoiding her gaze at all costs, then finally he looked up and gave a barely perceptible nod. 'Understood.' His tone was casual, but perhaps a bit too much, as if he was overcompensating. Helen wanted to put her arms around him, to reassure him that if things were different, she would want nothing more than to kiss him again and again, but she knew to do so would undermine her decision to nip this thing in the bud.

Tipping his head back, Ben chugged down the remaining contents of his bottle. 'It's getting a bit cold. I think I'm going to head back to the house. Are you coming?'

Helen shook her head. He didn't really want her company now. All he wanted was to get as far away from her as possible, and who could blame him? 'I think I'll stay out here a bit longer.' She automatically went to put her arms around him to give him a hug but stopped herself at the last moment. 'Good night,' she said, a little awkwardly. 'Sleep well.'

When she finally made her way back to the house there was no sign of Ben in the kitchen. She assumed he must have gone to his room for an early night and so, poking her head around the door to the cinema room, she wished her mum and the kids a good night before heading upstairs herself.

As she entered her room, she was once again struck by its glamour. The floor-to-ceiling windows perfectly framed the moonlit gardens and the sea beyond, and she couldn't help but feel a little sad that she had no one to share the view with. She felt the same about the rest of the room, from the enormous Emperor-sized bed to the futuristic-style log burner in the lounge area with two plush expensive-looking armchairs positioned either side. Suddenly, she felt lonely, lonelier than she had in a long time, and, walking over to the table where she'd left her phone charging, she picked it up, got into bed and called Gabby.

'Helen, everything okay?' Her friend's voice was full of concern.

'Everything's fine. Sorry to call so late, I just needed to talk. Are you on your own?'

'No, I'm just watching telly with Rav, though he's been asleep for the past half hour. Why, what's up?'

'I need you to go somewhere you won't be overheard.'

Helen listened to the sound of rustling down the line and then finally Gabby said, 'I'm in the kitchen with the door closed, what's going on?'

Helen paused, weighing up the risk of what she was about to do. It could all go wrong, horribly wrong, but there was also a chance that it might make no difference at all. She decided to take the chance. 'Before I tell you what I'm about to tell you, I need you to promise that you'll keep it to yourself. And I don't mean like, keep it to yourself but it's okay to tell Rav, I mean you can't tell another living soul what I'm about to say.'

'Okay.' Gabby sounded unsettled. 'You're not about to tell me you've throttled Adam, are you? I can't even dig a hole big enough to put a rose bush in the garden so you're out of luck if you're looking for help getting rid of a body.'

Helen laughed. 'No, Adam's safe . . . for now at least. The thing is . . . you know how I told you I didn't have any idea where my

ex, you know Ben from Bluelight might be? Well . . . the truth is
. . . I lied. He's been living with me and the kids.'

There was a long silence, which Helen took to be the sound of
her words sinking in. Finally, her bewildered friend spoke: 'Are you
being serious? Are you telling me, the whole time the papers have
been hunting for the lead singer of one of the world's most famous
bands he's actually been hiding in your house in south Didsbury?'

'In my spare room,' Helen explained. 'Remember that day when
you called for me before we went to Lisa's brunch thing? Well,
Ben was in the living room the whole time.'

'No way!' exclaimed Gabby. 'I knew something was wrong, you
were being so weird that day but I just put it down to everything
else going on in your life. I can't believe it! My best mate harbouring
a world-famous rock star on the run, no wonder you need to talk!'

'Actually, that's not the reason I'm calling.' Helen took a deep
breath. 'The thing is, you know how I told you I managed to snag
a last-minute cheap break? Well . . . me, Mum and the kids are
actually away with Ben staying at his mate's swanky beachfront
holiday home in Cornwall.'

'Wow!' said Gabby. 'Whose holiday home is it? Is it Elton John's?
I bet it is.'

'That's beside the point,' said Helen. 'The point isn't where we
are so much as the fact that this afternoon . . . well . . . I kissed
him.'

The whole story came pouring out of Helen, right up to and
including her telling Ben the kiss had been a mistake.

'You did what?' Gabby's voice was only a couple of notches
down from a shriek. 'I think you must have lost your mind! That
man is gorgeous! And he's talented and loaded too! Why on earth
would you think it was a mistake?'

'Because I'm forty-five years old, Gabby!' exclaimed Helen. 'I can't go around kissing rock stars like some love-struck teenager! I've got responsibilities, I've got kids . . . think about it . . . I've technically still got a husband! And besides all that, every single one of Ben's exes is about twenty years younger than me, and is either a supermodel or world-famous actress! So, why's he slumming it with me?'

'Excuse me!' interjected Gabby. 'That's my best mate you're talking about there and I'll have you know that, rock star or not, that man would be lucky to be with someone as beautiful, funny and smart as you, so we'll stop with the "I'm an old bag" routine, okay? You're not, you're a total fox.'

'Thanks, Gabs, but you're not exactly impartial, are you? I think what I'm trying to say is that our worlds are just too different. And this, what happened today, is just some version of a holiday romance. He doesn't really want me, Gabs, it's just the situation: he's vulnerable, I'm vulnerable and the last thing I want to do is jeopardise what we've got just because I've let myself get swept up in the moment.'

'But have you though?' said Gabby thoughtfully. 'Could it be that what you've missed with all your overthinking is the one thing that's completely obvious? Ben isn't just some random guy, he was your first love. So, this thing between you and him isn't like starting over again . . . it's more like picking up from where you left off.'

22

Ben

There were black spots dancing in front of Ben's eyes and an unsettling whistling noise in his ears as he lay panting on the floor next to the treadmill. Still, he'd enjoyed every moment of his 5k run; the burning in his lungs and the pain in his legs at the pace he'd been going had proved to be the perfect distraction from the thoughts of Helen that had kept him awake all night.

Much as their kiss had taken Ben by surprise, it wasn't as though he hadn't thought about kissing her before that moment. He'd thought about it a great deal but had always managed to stop himself out of a desire not to make her life any more complicated than it was already. After all, she had an estranged husband, two kids who were struggling to come to terms with the end of their parents' relationship and a runaway rock star sleeping in her spare room. The last thing she needed was a romantic entanglement, especially with someone who came with as much baggage as him. So, he'd resisted, he'd held back, avoiding intimate situations and generally keeping himself in check. But then yesterday, standing on that clifftop, summoning all of his strength to fight the urge to kiss her, she had kissed him instead. That kiss had been every-thing he'd hoped it would be and so much more. It had been intoxicating, passionate and all-consuming, and because of their shared history it had been tender, comforting and familiar too, and felt a lot like coming home.

He hadn't wanted to ruin the moment by dissecting it and, judging by the silence they'd shared as they'd returned to the house, nor had Helen. But then last night, when they were alone again, she'd told him the kiss had been a mistake. Even without her saying a word, he could imagine the multitude of reasons she might have used to justify reaching such a conclusion. But while he could understand her reasoning, that didn't make her declaration any less painful. So, he'd retreated to his room like a lovesick teenager who'd been given the 'let's be friends' talk. Following a sleepless night he'd gone down to the gym in the basement at a little after five, in the hopes of stopping himself from going over and over the situation in his mind.

Picking himself up off the floor, Ben towelled himself down and headed back upstairs to grab a drink from the kitchen but was surprised to find that Helen's mum was there, making herself a cup of tea.

'Morning, love, you all right? You look like you've just run a marathon.'

'Morning, Sue.' He opened the fridge and took out a bottle of water. 'I was up early so I thought I'd try out the gym.'

'Rather you than me.' Sue flicked the kettle on again. 'Why don't you sit down and rest yourself? I'll make you a brew.'

As he sat watching her bustle about the kitchen Ben thought about all the time he'd spent at Sue's flat back when he and Helen were together. Helen's mum had always made him feel welcome, thinking nothing of regularly setting an extra place for him at the dinner table. He'd sometimes even pop round and chat to her when Helen wasn't there, never feeling the awkwardness he'd felt around other girlfriends' parents before or since. With her unfussy attitude to life she reminded him a lot of his own mum, and he'd always found her presence comforting.

'It really is so lovely of you to have laid on this place for us, Ben,' she said, setting down a mug of tea in front of him. 'A little break was exactly what Helen needed. I can't tell you how worried I've been about her over these last few months.'

'Believe me,' said Ben, 'the pleasure's all mine. She really has gone out of her way to look after me. This is the very least I could do.'

Sue took a sip of her tea. 'So, what do you think you'll do once things die down? Go back to America?'

Ben shook his head. Just the thought of going back to LA was enough to send a chill down his spine. 'I'm not sure how much Helen has told you, but the only reason this is all happening is because I wanted to leave that world behind. I was actually planning to head to Greenland.'

Sue laughed. 'And do what? Build igloos?'

'Get away from it all, I suppose,' said Ben. 'I was going to try to live a different life, one with a bit more substance, a bit more meaning.'

'And you need to go to Greenland to do that? Couldn't you do the same back in Manchester?'

Ben took a sip of his tea, wishing he had her straightforward view of the world. 'It's a nice idea but it wouldn't work. I need to get away, Sue, properly away. This business, the music business, it was killing me slowly from the inside out. I just need to get away from it all.'

Reaching across the counter, Sue placed a hand on his. 'Sounds like you were having a really tough time of it. Maybe getting out of America was the right thing to do. But this Greenland idea of yours doesn't make any sense to me. Surely, the last thing you need is to be in the middle of nowhere. Surely what you need right now is friends like Helen looking after you and fighting your corner.'

Ben sensed that there was perhaps more to Sue's words than

she was letting on. Had Helen talked to her? Had she told her about the kiss? 'Maybe you're right,' said Ben, 'but I think she's got enough on her plate with everything else that's going on in her life right now without me adding to it.'

'All the more reason you should stay,' said Sue firmly. 'She's looking out for you, and I know you're looking out for her, sounds like the perfect arrangement to me.'

Ben looked over his mug of tea at Sue. 'You're not trying to play matchmaker here are you, Sue?'

She grinned mischievously. 'I mean, you're single, she's single, and we already know that you're good together because you were a great couple even when you were kids! Would it really be so bad if I was?'

Before Ben could reply, suddenly the shrill shriek of an alarm going off filled the air. Panicked, Ben and Sue exchanged worried looks while they tried to identify the source, but then he remembered what he'd been told about the house's control room and all the security equipment in there. Sure enough, as he entered the room, a panel next to the door was flashing a warning message indicating that there was a problem at the front gate.

'What is it? What's happening?' Ben turned around to see Helen standing in the doorway.

'I think someone's trying to get in,' said Ben, turning to the bank of monitors on the wall and scanning the screens.

'Do you think it's burglars? Shall I call the police?' Helen's voice was panicked.

Ben shook his head as he spotted the explanation for the alarms going off on one of the screens. 'Not unless you want them to arrest your own daughter,' he said, pointing to a monitor displaying an image of a fraught-looking Esme frantically tapping the security panel at the main entrance.

'What on earth is she doing?' said Helen, leaning over Ben's shoulder to get a better look.

'I think this might explain things.' Ben pointed to another monitor where a hooded figure could be seen standing on the other side of the gate talking to Esme.

Helen sighed heavily. 'I bet you any money that's Josh and that my clueless daughter accidentally set the alarm off trying to sneak him in.'

'I can explain!' said a tearful Esme as her furious mum left Ben's side and strode towards her.

'What do you think you're playing at?' Helen demanded as Ben reset the keycode and opened the gate to reveal a terrified teenage boy looking back at him. Seeing Ben's face, the boy momentarily stopped looking scared just long enough to look confused.

'You're . . . you're . . . Ben Baptiste from Bluelight!' he said, pointing. He turned to look at Esme. 'What's the singer from Bluelight doing here?'

'It's a long story,' said Ben. 'How about you come in and after we've worked out what to do with you I might tell you.'

As they headed back to the house a mortified Esme tried to explain exactly what had happened. 'We were just missing each other so much,' she began, 'and he kept asking me where I was and I knew I couldn't tell him, but then he wouldn't stop asking and so I did tell him and then the next thing was I get a call from him saying he was at the front gate.'

As he recalled just how intense love could be at that age Ben couldn't help but feel sorry for the young man. 'So, let me get this right, you got the train here from Manchester?'

Josh shook his head. 'I couldn't afford the train so I got the coach to Plymouth instead because I thought it would be near, but then it turned out that it wasn't quite as close as I thought. I didn't have any money left so I thought I'd go back home, only I then found out that there wasn't another coach to Manchester until the morning so I slept at the station. But then when I woke up, a nice lady, I think she was a cleaner, got talking to me and I told her where I was trying to get to and she very kindly gave me the money for a bus ticket here.'

'Sleeping at a coach station!' exclaimed Helen. 'Have you any idea how reckless you've been? Anything could've happened to you. Do your parents even know where you are?'

'Not exactly,' said Josh. 'They think I've gone to a music festival with my mates.'

Sensing Helen's blood pressure rising, Ben decided to step in. 'Well, that was bang out of order, wasn't it?' The young man nodded. 'You'll have to call them straight away.'

'And say what?' interjected Helen. 'That he's sneaked off to Cornwall to stay at Elton John's holiday home with Esme and the missing rock star that's in all the papers?'

Josh gasped. 'This is Elton John's holiday home?'

'We don't know for sure,' said Helen. 'Ben won't say. But that's hardly the point, is it? The point is you shouldn't have come.'

'Well, he's here now,' said Esme. 'Can't he just stay? He won't say a word about Ben, will you, Josh?'

'No,' said Josh, and looked at Ben wide-eyed. 'Not a word, I promise.'

Ben looked at Helen to see that she was trying to weigh up this impossible situation. He took her aside, out of earshot of the rest of the group. 'It's totally your call,' he said. 'But for what it's worth I'm happy for him to stay.'

Everyone turned and looked at Helen anxiously. 'Well,' she said eventually, 'I suppose there is a room going spare he could use.'

She turned and looked at Ben. 'But what about you? Are you sure? What if he lets it slip to his parents or his mates that you're here? It feels like the circle of people who know where you are is getting so huge that it's only going to be a matter of time before word gets out.'

Ben looked over at Josh. 'You can keep a secret, can't you, mate?'

'Yes, absolutely. I promise I won't say anything to anyone.'

'See,' said Ben, looking at Helen, 'I think we can take a chance on him.'

Helen shook her head and sighed. 'This is absolute madness. But if you're okay with it, then I suppose I am. Plus he's more likely to keep his mouth shut if we let him stay than if we send him home.' She turned back to Josh and Esme. 'Fine, he can stay, on the condition that he sleeps in the spare room, and doesn't mention a word of this to anyone. I mean it, Es, not a word.'

Esme's face flushed with relief. 'He'll be fine in the spare room and I promise, he won't say anything about Ben or this place.' She ran over and hugged her mum tightly. 'Thank you so much for being cool about this, I'll never forget it.'

With the situation seemingly resolved for the moment, they all headed back to the house and started making breakfast, which thanks to the warmth of the morning they were able to eat out on the terrace. Then later, after they'd cleared up Esme, Frankie and Sue took Josh off for a guided tour of the house and grounds, leaving Ben and Helen alone for the first time since their awkward conversation about the kiss the night before.

'Well, that was certainly an unexpected start to the day,' said Ben, desperate for things between them to get back to normal. 'Still, it was quite sweet in its own way.'

'The impetuousness of young love,' said Helen, and she came

and stood next to him. 'Do you remember when you had to go away for a week on a field trip for geography A-level? I missed you so much I genuinely thought I might die.'

'And how about when you had that residential French course in Lyon? I think if I'd had just a quarter of Josh's daring back then I'd have followed you there.'

A wistful smile played on Helen's lips. 'Instead, you wrote letters to me every day. I think I've still got them somewhere.'

'You kept them?'

Helen smiled, embarrassed. 'Shouldn't I have?'

Ben grinned. 'Over the years and all the countless moves I've made I've managed to lose records from my collection, photographs and even my birth certificate, and yet somehow I've always managed to hold on to your letters, every last single one of them.'

Helen shifted even closer to Ben, so much so that he could see his own reflection in her eyes. 'I'm sorry about yesterday,' she said, holding his gaze.

'Don't be,' said Ben. 'There's no need to apologise.'

'But I think there is,' said Helen. 'Kissing you wasn't a mistake, the only mistake was me getting caught up in my own head.' She looked up and then very gently pressed her lips against his, then finally she took him by the hand and led him upstairs to her room.

Part 3

23

Helen

As Helen lay in Ben's arms her phone vibrated from somewhere on the floor next to the bed. Snaking down an arm, she scrabbled around frantically amongst the heap of discarded clothes until finally she located it in the back pocket of her jeans.

'Hi, Mum,' said Helen, trying her best to sound normal. 'Where are you, still giving Josh the grand tour?'

'No,' said Sue, 'we're all done with that, we're about to head down to the beach and just wondered if you and Ben were going to join us. There's no sign of Ben anywhere and I did try your door but it was locked.'

'Ah, yes,' said Helen thinking quickly. 'Well, since you were giving a tour, the last thing I wanted was for Josh to be mentally scarred accidentally seeing me in my pants, so I locked it. You carry on down to the beach and I'll see if I can track Ben down and hopefully see you down there in a bit.'

Ending the call, she flopped back on the pillows and let out a sigh. 'Did you hear Mum knocking on the door?'

Ben shook his head. 'To be fair my mind was elsewhere.' He leaned over and kissed Helen's shoulder. 'I take it they're looking for us?'

Helen nodded. 'Do you think Mum suspects? My door's locked, you've disappeared, it wouldn't exactly take a genius to put two and two together.'

'Equally, there could be a perfectly logical explanation just like the one you've offered. So, my guess is, she doesn't suspect a thing.'

Helen rolled on to her side, resting her head in the crook of Ben's arm, and flashed a filthy grin. 'I can't believe we just did that! And before nine o'clock in the morning too!'

Ben laughed. 'For future reference what sort of time would be acceptable?'

Helen playfully slapped him on the chest. 'You know what I mean . . . I'm a middle-aged mum of two, I don't do things like this.'

Ben raised an eyebrow knowingly. 'You might want to rethink that statement, unless of course you're an imposter and the real Helen is stuffed in a cupboard somewhere. This *is* you, Helen, and it actually turns out that you *do* do things like this; being "middle-aged" or indeed a "mum" doesn't mean you stop being a real person.'

Helen thought for a moment. Perhaps over the years she had buried her own wants and desires behind these labels. 'The thing is when you've got a busy family life, a husband, two kids, a demanding job and a house to run, it's really easy to forget the person you used to be, the person you probably still are in many ways. I can't remember the last time I just thought about myself and what I wanted . . . well, apart from just now of course.'

Ben tenderly kissed the top of Helen's head. 'I get it, it's so easy to lose yourself in a role, even when it's one you've chosen. I think that was my problem with the band, I got so used to being Ben from Bluelight that I didn't really know who I was outside of that. But the more I stuck to that role, the more unhappy I became.'

'Is that how you ended up at that rehab place you were at?' The question had left her lips before she'd had chance to think it through. She'd wanted to ask it ever since she'd learned about his troubles, but had sensed from the vague way in which he spoke about that time that he hadn't been ready to go into details. 'I'm sorry,' she added quickly. 'You don't have to answer that.'

'I want to,' said Ben. 'I need to.' He took a deep breath and exhaled. 'The truth is I tried to kill myself.'

Helen gasped, she couldn't help herself; it wasn't at all what she'd been expecting him to say. 'Oh, Ben, I'm so sorry.'

'It's fine,' he said. 'I'm not in that place any more. Thankfully my time in the Compono helped sort me out.'

'I don't understand,' said Helen. 'How did things get so bad?'

Ben exhaled heavily. 'Long story short, I think after my divorce I just lost it for a while. I started doing everything to excess – drink, drugs, women – thinking that was the answer to all my problems even though I knew from the early days of the band that it wasn't. After that, I convinced myself that happiness lay in making Bluelight the biggest band in the world, which is why I made sure that we recorded and toured constantly, and always had a new project on the go. For a while it seemed to work, my life was so busy that I didn't have time to give thought to the question of whether or not I was happy.'

'So, what happened?'

'The wheels came off,' said Ben flatly. 'What I didn't know then but what I know now is that I'd been depressed for years. The band's success, all the accolades we garnered, all it did was mask the problem not solve it. Anyway, to celebrate the release of the new album there was supposed to be a party at the rooftop bar of a hotel on Sunset, and I was in a hotel room getting ready for it when it hit me: I hated my life. Everything about it was facile, empty and worthless. In that moment I felt lower than I ever had before and I thought that's it: this is where it ends. I downed a bottle of vodka, took enough prescription painkillers to knock out an elephant and that was the last thing I remember. The next thing I knew, I was waking up in hospital, feeling like I'd gone ten rounds with Mike Tyson, with Rocco by my side.'

'So, someone found you in time?'

Ben nodded, and in that moment he looked so lost, so sad. 'I don't know who, it could've been my PA, it could've been Rocco himself but either way, whoever it was saved me.'

Helen couldn't believe that Ben had come so close to death. The very thought terrified her and she took his hand in her own, squeezing it tightly.

'I don't know how long I was in hospital for,' said Ben. 'A few days, maybe a week and then I'm guessing Rocco must have seen how much of a mess I was in because he got me discharged to the Compono.' He shook his head and laughed mirthlessly. 'A rock star takes a near-fatal overdose, gets taken to an emergency ward and then to a place like the Compono and not a word gets into the press about it. Think about it, all the hotel staff that must have known, the EMTs, the doctors and the hospital workers, and not a single one says a word about it.'

'Are you saying Rocco managed to keep all of those people quiet?'

Ben nodded. 'I don't know how he did it, but he did. But that's Rocco for you, he always gets what he wants.'

'And you, when do you get what you want?' Helen looked up at him and wrapped him in her arms. 'I hate that you've had to go through all of this. I hate that you felt so lost that you thought the only way to stop your pain was to end your life. I wish I'd been there to help you, I wish I'd been there to see you through that nightmare.'

'You're here now,' said Ben. 'And that's all that matters.' He pressed his lips against hers. The kiss was long and slow, and for a moment everything that wasn't Ben seemed to fade away. Finally, they parted and, holding her gaze, Ben said, 'I think we'd better make ourselves decent and then find the others before they come looking for us.'

A short while later, having showered and dressed, Helen went downstairs to find Ben waiting for her in the kitchen. During their short time apart she'd worried that perhaps the connection they'd established might have broken, so she couldn't help but smile as Ben's face lit up at the sight of her. He wrapped her in his arms, and as he kissed her the thought crossed her mind: The connection isn't broken. What we shared meant as much to him as it did to me.

Across the days that followed, they stole moments alone together whenever they could, taking it in turns to sneak into each other's rooms late at night when they were certain everyone was sleeping, always making sure to be back in their own rooms by morning. Helen felt a lightness that she hadn't felt in a long time and would often catch herself smiling for no reason. She was convinced the joy she felt being with Ben was clear for all to see, but thankfully, if it was, no one remarked upon it.

During this time, although she and Ben talked almost constantly about everything from music to politics and back again, the one subject they didn't discuss was their future together. When everything was so mired in complexity, when there wasn't a single easy solution to any of their problems, there seemed little point in spoiling the time they had by trying to figure it all out. Instead, they enjoyed being together, content to take each day as it came. Occasionally, however, while lying in Ben's arms in the depths of the night, Helen's mind would flash forward to the end of the holiday, wondering what exactly life would look like once they left this place, this idyll, their haven. She felt like every bad thing was waiting for them on the other side, the sale of the house, her return to full-time work, and the question marks around Esme's future. Meanwhile Ben had unfinished business with his father, his decision about his next move, and the unsettling fact that the world's media was still hunting for him. Still, as dawn broke, as the darkness receded so too would her fears. In the daylight it was so much easier to believe that everything would be all right in the end.

On the last full day before leaving, everyone went down to the beach for the afternoon. Ben started off a game of football with the boys, leaving the girls to read on sun loungers in the shade. Sue managed all of ten minutes before she was gently snoring, and shortly afterwards Esme set down the book she was reading, adjusted her sunglasses and turned to look at her mother.

'I don't think me and Josh are going to move down to London after all,' she said in a matter-of-fact fashion as if the turmoil of the past week hadn't happened.

'Oh,' said Helen, trying to resist the urge to cheer, 'how come?'

'Well, for starters Josh's parents threw a triple fit when he told them, and they threatened to stop paying for his phone, and everything, so he sort of backed down. But I'd already been thinking myself that it probably wasn't a great idea really. I mean, it's not like I can't move to London after I graduate, is it?'

Hearing her own words of advice repeated back to her, Helen allowed herself the luxury of a small smile. 'That's a good point, it's not like London is going anywhere.'

'Plus, I don't want to be too far away from you and Frankie with the house move and everything. Nottingham isn't too far, and Frankie can come and stay with me if you need a break from him sometimes.'

For a moment Helen felt like she might cry. Her little girl really was growing up. 'Thanks, Es, that really means a lot.'

'It's going to be tough though with me being in Nottingham and Josh being so far away in Exeter, I'm worried that we won't be able to make the long-distance thing work. I'm already imagining all the girls who'll be chasing after him in halls.'

'And what about all the boys who'll be chasing after you at Nottingham?'

Esme laughed. 'True, but that doesn't make it any easier. If we split up, I don't think I'd be able to handle it.'

'You would,' replied Helen. 'It would be tough but so are you.'

'You were my age when you and Ben split up, weren't you? How did you cope?'

Helen cast her mind back to that time, recalling all of the tearful phone calls and the heartfelt letters that had followed. 'It wasn't easy, but I got through it, and it made me a stronger person.'

'And did you ever regret it?'

'Breaking up with Ben?' Esme nodded. 'Regret's a funny notion. I mean no matter how hard some things are it's hard to regret going through them when ultimately they lead to such wonderful things.'

Esme laughed. 'Mum, I get it, you love me and Frankie, yeah, yeah, yeah, but I'm not talking about that. I'm talking about whether or not you regret breaking up with someone you cared about, and still care about nearly thirty years later.'

Helen flinched. Had Esme guessed about her and Ben? She decided to bluff it out. 'Ben's a good friend, and I'm glad we've been able to help him out.'

Esme lowered her sunglasses and directed a hard stare at Helen. '"Good friend", come on, Mum! Frankie might not see it but I'm not blind . . . and neither for that matter is Gran. In fact, only this morning we were saying how nice it is to see you happy again. Since we got here you've been like a different person. I keep seeing you laughing and joking and I've found myself thinking, Who is this woman and what has she done with my mum?' Esme laughed. 'Seriously though, I'm happy for you, Mum, really I am.'

Before Helen could reply, her phone vibrated on the lounger

next to her. It wasn't a number she recognised and she considered ignoring it until she recalled her head teacher's promise to pass on her details to anyone who might have a full-time position for her.

'Hello, am I speaking to Helen Morley?' The female caller's voice sounded vaguely familiar but Helen couldn't quite place it.

'Yes,' she said. 'Who's this?'

'We've spoken before, my name's Chelsea Maher. I'm a reporter for the North News Agency.' Helen felt her stomach flip; it was the journalist who had come to her house in search of quotes about Ben. What did she want now?

'Oh yes,' said Helen, 'I remember you, but I don't remember giving you my phone number.'

'Oh, don't you?' said the woman, vaguely. 'Perhaps you forgot.'

'I didn't forget anything,' said Helen. 'How did you get my number?'

'Right now, Mrs Morley, that's the least of your problems . . . I know you've been hiding Ben Baptiste, and I know that right now you're on holiday in Cornwall with him. And, if you don't want tomorrow's headline to be "Missing Rock Star Found in Love Nest with Married Mum of Two", I suggest you come down to the front gate and let me in so we can talk.'

24

Ben

Taking a seat opposite Ben and Helen at the table on the terrace, Chelsea Maher looked back at the house admiringly. 'Wow, this really is some place, isn't it?'

'Yes, it is.' Ben's heart was pounding and his tone was thick with barely concealed anger. 'But you're not here to do an "at home" piece. Why don't you just get to the point: what is it that you want?'

She smiled disdainfully, clearly aware that at this moment she held all the cards. 'I was just trying to be polite, but if you want me to be direct I can do that too. I want everything, Mr Baptiste, absolutely everything. I want a detailed account of your every moment since you left your home in Malibu twenty days ago. I want where you went, how you felt, and why you went missing in the first place. I want photos too, of you, this place; and for a little colour for the piece, any texts or messages you've sent that could be relevant. And finally,' she added with something of a flourish, 'I want an exclusive. No talking to any other news outlets or agencies, no talking to anyone about this but me.' She paused and looked at Ben. 'That, in a nutshell, is what I want.'

Across his twenty years in the business Ben had encountered plenty of loathsome tabloid hacks, people who were prepared to lie, cheat and steal, if it meant getting a good story. He'd had journalists paying off doctors' receptionists in order to gain access to his medical records, bribing security staff so that they could view his schedules, and even blackmailing a well-thought-of assistant into handing over copies of his personal emails. But as much as he despised each and every one of those scumbags for what they had done to him and his employees, he felt a special kind of hatred for the woman sitting opposite: the woman who had brought to such an abrupt and brutal end a week that had been one of the happiest of his life.

'And if I don't?' Ben gritted his teeth and stared hard at her. 'What happens then?'

Chelsea flashed a vulpine grin in Helen's direction. 'Do I really need to spell it out? Come on, Ben, you've been in the business long enough to know the drill. You know what I'll do. I'll drag your girlfriend's name through the mud and by the time I'm finished, there won't be a single detail of your private life, Helen – or indeed, that of your family – that your friends, neighbours and work colleagues won't be able to read about over their morning latte.' She reached into her bag on the table, removed a notepad, flicked it open and glanced down at it. 'For starters there's your husband's affair with a woman young enough to be his daughter, I think I could easily get a front-page splash with that. Then there's the public confrontation between you and your husband where you threw a drink in his face – granted not quite as juicy as the other story, but our female readers will love it nonetheless. And that's all before I get started on the remarkably clear images I've lifted off your daughter's Instagram of, how shall I put it, a considerable number of messy nights out. There's always an appetite for scantily clad young women falling out of nightclubs the worse for wear, and I think young Esme's connection to Ben will certainly add an extra—'

Filled with rage, Ben stood up so suddenly that the chair he'd been sitting on fell backwards, clattering to the floor with such force that Chelsea visibly flinched. Leaning across the table, his face twisted in anger, he jabbed a finger in the woman's direction. 'I swear to you, if I see even a single picture of Esme in your paper I will make it my life's mission to destroy you! I don't care how much money it costs, or how long it takes, I will make you regret it!'

Helen stood up, and rubbed a hand across Ben's shoulders. 'Don't let her rile you, Ben, she's not worth it.'

'You should listen to your girlfriend, Ben.' Chelsea's voice, though firm, belied a trace of apprehension, as if she wasn't fully convinced that she had the situation under control any more. 'You know I don't want to run nasty pieces about civilians, I don't want to run nasty pieces at all. I just want you to tell me your story in your words. Surely your fans who have been so worried about you over the past few weeks deserve that, at least?'

Scared of what he might do or say, Ben looked away. This was so much worse than he'd been dreading. It was one thing to do this to him, but the thought that Helen and her family might be dragged into the midst of a media feeding frenzy was too much to bear. There was no choice. He'd have to give her what she wanted.

He drew a deep breath and returned his gaze to Chelsea. 'I'll need some time to think it over.'

There was just a trace of a smile of victory on the journalist's face when she spoke. 'I'll give you half an hour. After that I'll have no choice but to go with what I've got.'

Grabbing Helen's hand, Ben marched inside the house and immediately pressed the button that slid the huge glass doors looking out on to the terrace back into place until they shut with a gentle thud.

'Oh, Ben,' said Helen, wrapping him in her arms. 'That awful woman! Are you okay?'

Ben looked down at her, unable to believe that just a few short hours ago they'd been lying blissfully content in each other's arms. 'I'm fine, really, I am, it's you and the kids I'm worried about. I can't believe the depths these people will sink to. It's like they haven't got a soul, like they're not even human.'

'But how on earth did she even find us? We've all been so careful.'

Ben shrugged. 'These sorts of people always find a way. It's second nature to them. But right now, we've got bigger things to worry about. I don't think I've got any choice. I'm going to have to do the interview.'

Helen's face was full of anguish. 'Ben, you can't, it's too dangerous. She'll dig into the reason you left, which means she'll force you into talking about the night of your launch.'

Ben's response was immediate. 'I'd sooner that than have her drag you and the kids into all this. I couldn't bear it.'

'Isn't there anything we can do legally? She's blackmailing you into doing something that you don't want to do, that's got to be against the law surely?'

'The legal route takes time and that's something we haven't got.' He stopped, turned towards the terrace and saw Chelsea on her phone, and once more he was filled with disgust. 'Look at her, she's probably talking to her editors right now, trying to work out how much room to dedicate to the story for tomorrow's papers. What I wouldn't give to be able to wipe that smug look off her—' Ben stopped in his tracks as a thought occurred to him. It was a thought that instinctively he recoiled from and yet he couldn't think of an alternative.

'What is it? What's wrong.'

'I've got an idea and I don't think you're going to like it but I've got no choice . . . I'm going to call Rocco.'

Horrified at the thought, Helen shook her head. 'You can't do that, Ben. He's the reason this is all happening in the first place. He told the world you'd gone missing when he knew it wasn't true. Why on earth would you call him?'

'Because he's the only person I know with the kind of power needed to make this go away.'

'But why would he even consider doing that? All he wants is for you to go back, to carry on doing what you're doing.'

'He'll want to negotiate, of course,' said Ben. 'That's just the way he is, but I'm sure I can talk him around. Explain how much I don't want to go back, maybe even remind him of how much money he's made from me and the band and use that as leverage to get this all to go away.'

'But what if you going back to LA is what he wants in return?'

Ben pushed this thought away. He wasn't going back to LA. Not now. Not ever. 'Then I'll have to think of something else. But I've got to try at least.' He glanced over his shoulder to look at Chelsea, who in response waved and tapped her watch as if to indicate that time was running out.

'Keep an eye on her,' said Ben, 'while I go and make the call.'

Heading upstairs, Ben searched around in his room for his phone before finally realising that he must have left it in Helen's room the night before. Sure enough, he found it on the floor next to the bed where it must have fallen out of his jeans. As he punched in Rocco's number, he tried to remain calm even though his every nerve felt shredded. What if Rocco wouldn't help him? What if he was so angry with Ben that he'd leave him to face the press alone?

'Who is this and how did you get my number?' Rocco's voice alone was enough to make Ben's stomach lurch.

He took a deep breath. 'It's me.' He felt as if he could almost hear the cogs whirring in Rocco's brain as he wrestled with the question of why Ben might be calling.

'You're in trouble, aren't you?' he said. 'And you need me to fix it.'

'A journalist from one of the tabs has tracked me down to Cornwall,' said Ben. 'She's using the threat of publishing stories about people I care for to bag herself an exclusive with me.'

Rocco snorted. 'And you want me to make it disappear? After the way you've treated me? Running off like that, making me look a fool . . . why should I even bother?'

'Look,' said Ben, 'I'm sorry for the way things happened, I'm sorry for running out on you like I did, but what choice did you give me? You lied about cancelling the tour. You knew what I was going through and yet you lied to my face, and told me it was all sorted. Doing a runner was the only way I was ever going to get away from you.'

'You would've been fine for the tour,' Rocco responded. 'I would've made sure of that. I always look out for you, you know that.'

'Then help me now,' said Ben. 'I'll sign over all my rights to the last album. It'll be yours to do whatever you want with, just help me out this one last time.'

Rocco laughed. 'You think I need your money? I got more than I know what to do with, son, you know that.'

'Then just tell me what it'll take.'

'I made you what you are,' snarled Rocco. 'Without me you'd just be some washed-up has-been chasing after your youth and knocking out music on the Internet that no one gives a crap about. It was me who plucked you and the rest of the band out of obscurity, and it was me who made history turning four nobodies into the biggest band in the world. And do you know what? I'm rather proud of that fact. So, when it comes to calling quits on Bluelight, I'm telling you now, that's going to be my decision not yours. I'll get rid of your tabloid toerag, no problem. But in return I want you back in LA, I want you back in the band, and I want the tour to go ahead just as we all planned.'

Ben felt sick. This was exactly what he'd been dreading. He couldn't go back to LA, he couldn't go back to that life. Going back to LA would take him away from Helen, away from the happiness he'd found and towards what? An existence he'd hated so much that he'd almost ended his own life. He had to try to find a way to change Rocco's mind.

'Okay, so you don't want the album rights, but how about I record a solo album for you? Completely new material, that way there's no complication with the rest of the band, and anything it makes is yours.'

Rocco sniffed. 'Not interested.'

'Fine, I'll sign over the rights to everything, all of Bluelight's back catalogue, it'll be yours to control.'

'Tempting,' said Rocco. 'I could certainly spin a few deals off the back of that, but still no. I've told you what I want, and I'm not going to settle for anything less. So, the ball's in your court. What's it going to be?'

Though he knew it was futile, Ben made a last-ditch appeal to Rocco's better nature, if indeed he had one. 'Come on, Rocco, you know how miserable I've been these past few years, you know how bad things got. For the first time in forever I'm happy, I feel like I'm actually looking forward to the future, don't make me give all that up. I'm begging you, just let me be.'

There was a short pause that Ben understood to be Rocco losing what little patience he had. He'd never been one to tolerate extended negotiations, you either agreed to his terms or he walked away, and this was no different. 'I've said what I've said, Ben, and I'll say no more beyond this: you've seen what the press can do to people, they chew them up and they spit them out, and they're never the same again. Never. They'll trawl through every little detail, they'll leave no stone unturned, they'll dig up every single piece of dirt they can find and if they can't find any, they'll make something up. If you really love this woman – and I'm guessing this is all about you falling for some woman or other – then you won't even think about putting her through all that. But like I say, the choice is yours.'

25

Helen

Helen checked her watch. The deadline Chelsea had given Ben was fast approaching and there was still no sign of him. What if he hadn't been able to get hold of his manager? What if he had but Rocco was refusing to help? The idea of both those scenarios made Helen's insides twist.

By this time tomorrow her private life, and that of her family, could be emblazoned across the front pages of a tabloid. She wasn't so much worried for herself, or even Adam, but for Esme and Frankie. Although Ben had warned her about the possibility of this happening when she'd first asked him to stay, it was unbearable to think how it might impact them, especially if Chelsea followed through with her threat to publish photographs of her daughter. Esme wasn't perfect, Helen knew that. And she knew better than to look through her other Instagram account, the one she thought Helen didn't know about. She had warned Esme countless times about the dangers of putting her life on the Internet but her advice always landed on deaf ears. Whatever these pictures were, she was sure they were harmless enough, but these sorts of things were always about context, and in the wrong hands she couldn't help but imagine how they might be misconstrued and the damage they might do to Esme in the future.

Checking her watch once again, Helen made up her mind to approach Chelsea herself. Perhaps she could make her see sense, or at least appeal to her humanity. She moved to open the doors to the terrace but stopped when she heard footsteps coming down the stairs behind her.

Rather than wearing a look of relief his expression was grim, and she could only conclude that his call with Rocco hadn't gone to plan.

'Ben,' she said, taking him by the hand. 'Did you get through to him? What did he say?'

Ben didn't reply. Instead, shrugging off her hand, he stormed over to the doors to the terrace, stabbed his finger at the button to open them and slipped through them the moment there was a gap big enough.

'You're cutting it fine, aren't you?' said Chelsea as Ben marched over to her. 'I take it you've made a decision.'

Ben leaned into Chelsea so that he was barely an inch away from her face, and there was a cold, hard edge to his voice when he spoke. 'I want you out of here. Now.'

Unsettled, Chelsea took a step backwards but then, after a beat, regained her composure. 'I think you're forgetting who's got the upper hand here,' she spat, and then looked pointedly at Helen. 'With a single call, I could destroy your girlfriend's life, and I'll do it. Just see if I—'

Just then Chelsea's phone rang, and she snatched it up from the table never once taking her eyes off Ben. Helen couldn't hear what was being said, but whatever it was clearly came as a shock to the journalist as all colour suddenly drained from the woman's face. The call was brief, a minute at most, and Chelsea didn't get to say a single word during it, not even, it seemed, goodbye.

With the call over she stood for a moment glaring at Ben in the most vile way, and then finally, grabbing her bag, she threw her phone inside and strode angrily in the direction of the main gate.

Without a word Ben returned inside, and Helen followed, watching as he pressed a button on the security panel by the main door to open the front gate. Together they watched the monitor in silence as Chelsea left the property and the gates slid shut behind her.

Helen turned to Ben, trying to read his face. Surely this was a moment for celebration but he looked defeated, almost broken.

'What just happened?'

He took a moment to reply. 'It's all sorted. There won't be anything in the papers about you or any of your family.'

A chill of apprehension ran down Helen's spine. 'Oh, Ben, you didn't agree to the interview, did you?' He shook his head. 'Then what?'

'I offered Rocco everything I had to bargain with, but there was only one thing he wanted, and to make this all go away, I had no choice but to give it to him.'

Helen felt herself reel. 'You've agreed to go back to LA?'

Ben nodded. 'It was the only way. I couldn't stand by and watch them tear into your family, I just couldn't. And I knew I couldn't give the interview without effectively granting them full access to every inch of my private life. Giving in to Rocco's terms seemed like the least-worst option.'

Helen was overcome with an immediate feeling of dread. 'But being in the band was killing you. You can't go back.'

Ben put his arms around Helen and held her close. 'I'll be fine. I've got through it before, I can do it again.'

'But what if you don't? What if it's all too much? What if you get so low again that you make yourself ill, or worse, end up harming yourself? Surely there's another way?'

Ben exhaled heavily, and afterwards seemed more beaten down than ever. 'There isn't another way, believe me, if there was I'd have taken it.' He looked into her eyes and held her gaze. 'This is just the way it's got to be.'

For a moment, Helen said nothing. Instead, she wrapped her arms around Ben tightly, as if by doing so she was keeping all the shattered pieces of him from falling apart. All she wanted at this moment was to make things right for him, to do something, anything that would magically solve all his problems. He was such a wonderful man, so kind, so generous and caring. He didn't deserve the hand he'd been dealt, he didn't deserve to be treated like some sort of indentured servant. For a moment, she felt so angry, so full of rage at the injustice of it all that she wanted to scream. Then a thought crossed her mind that the only reason they were in this situation was because someone, somewhere had betrayed them. In that instant, Helen silently vowed that she would find the culprit and when she did, she would make them pay.

Just then, Ben's phone vibrated in his hand. He took a step back from her and glanced at the screen. 'It's Rocco. He said he'd call back to talk details. I'd better take it.'

For a moment, Helen considered snatching the phone from Ben's hand and screaming at Ben's manager to leave him alone. While it might make her feel better in the short term, she knew it wouldn't really change a thing. Ben would still have to go. Instead, throwing her arms around his neck, she kissed him fiercely, passionately, before heading upstairs to confront the traitor.

Flinging open the door to her mum's room, where she'd told everyone to wait while she and Ben dealt with the journalist, Helen was met by a collection of questioning faces.

Sue got to her feet and rushed to Helen's side, closely followed by Esme and Frankie. 'What's happening, love? Did you manage to get rid of that woman? Where's Ben?'

Helen was determined not to cry. 'He's downstairs on the phone arranging his return to LA.'

'But why? I don't understand. What's happened?'

'Ben had to make a deal, it was the only way to get the journalist off all of our backs. He's got to go back to LA, back to the band.'

'But doesn't he hate it?' asked Esme. 'Isn't that why he ran away?'

Helen nodded. 'Yes, he loathes it. He doesn't want to go, but he has no choice because someone tipped off the press. The journalist, she knew everything, about where Ben had been, and where to find us.' Turning away from her family, Helen marched across the room to Josh, who was standing next to the window. 'How could you do it, Josh, after Ben made you so welcome?'

The young man looked horrified at the accusation, his eyes widening in surprise. 'I didn't do anything, Mrs Morley, I swear on my life! I haven't said a word to anyone.'

Esme pushed her way in between the two of them, glaring at her mother. 'What are you talking about, Mum? Josh really likes Ben, he wouldn't do this.'

'Then tell me exactly how she knew he was here?'

Esme shrugged. 'I don't know, do I? Maybe it was Ben's brother. Ben told me he's sold stories about him in the past.'

Helen's response was immediate. 'Ben didn't tell Nathan we were coming to Cornwall, so I know it's not him. So, it has to be Josh.'

'It wasn't me, Mrs Morley, you've got to believe me.' He reached into the back pocket of his shorts, removed his phone and handed it to Helen. 'Check it if you like, I haven't said anything to anyone about being here. I like Ben, I think he's amazing, why would I grass him up?'

'I don't know, money, fifteen minutes of fame.' Helen held the phone up to Josh's face and it unlocked, and without any qualms she began looking through his messages. Even after a thorough search she found nothing and, although he could have easily deleted anything incriminating, as she returned his phone to him she couldn't help but feel that he was probably innocent.

She apologised, but her mind was already racing ahead to the next suspect. And so it was with a heavy heart that she reached for her phone and dialled Gabby's number.

'Hey you.' Gabby's voice sounded normal, chirpy even. 'How's things with your hunky superstar? Has anything . . . progressed yet?'

Determined to get this over with, Helen jumped straight to the point. 'Please tell me you haven't told anyone about Ben.'

'Of course I haven't. You told me not to.'

Helen wanted to breathe a sigh of relief but Gabby wasn't out of the woods quite yet. 'And you absolutely swear on our friendship that you've kept it completely to yourself?'

'Of course,' said Gabby. 'Helen, I don't understand. Tell me, what's this all about?'

'We've had a journalist here in Cornwall,' she replied. 'It wasn't just a wild stab in the dark; they knew Ben was here, which could only mean that someone had told them.'

'Well, it wasn't me.' Gabby's voice suddenly sounded less certain. 'Unless . . .'

Helen closed her eyes. 'You told Rav, didn't you?'

'I didn't mean to, it just sort of came out. But I know Rav, and you know him too, he wouldn't dream of telling the papers. Not in a million years. This just doesn't sound like him.'

A thought gradually occurred to Helen. 'No . . . but I know exactly who it does sound like.' Assuring a tearful Gabby that she forgave her even though she wasn't quite sure that was true, Helen ended the call and made another. This time to Adam. It had to be him, didn't it? Helen was sure. It just made sense. Gabby had told Rav, Rav had told Adam, and then her jealous, mean-spirited and needlessly cruel husband, determined to make sure she should never be happy, had called the press.

'You just couldn't stand to see me happy, could you?' she said the moment he picked up. 'You just couldn't stand the thought of me being with someone else.'

'What . . . what are you on about?' Adam sounded bewildered, or like at least that's what he wanted Helen to believe.

'You know what you've done. How could you, Adam? They threatened me, they threatened Esme . . . they even talked about throwing you under the bus too. And all for what?'

'Have you been drinking? I have no idea what you're talking about. Who's threatening Esme?'

'The papers,' snapped Helen, 'we had a tabloid journalist here saying that if Ben didn't give them an interview they would drag us all through the mud instead.'

'Ben? Ben who? And what interview?'

'You always hated Ben, you hated the fact that I'd been involved with someone so successful before I met you, I can't believe your ego felt so threatened that you'd do something like this.'

Adam fell silent, and his intonation changed as if he was only just joining up the dots.

'Are you talking about your ex, the one that's missing?'

'Don't play the innocent, Adam,' said Helen. 'I know it was you. I've just got off the phone with Gabby, so I know Rav told you about me and Ben.'

There was another brief pause before Adam responded. 'You mean to tell me that you and your old boyfriend are back together?' His voice was incredulous now. 'That makes no sense . . . I mean for starters he's gone missing, hasn't he?'

'Stop making out like you don't know! I'm not an idiot. Gabby told Rav about me being in Cornwall with Ben, and he told you, and you're so bitter and twisted at the thought that I might actually be happy that you leaked it to the press.'

There was another pause, this time longer, and this time when he spoke he was angry. 'Are you seriously telling me you've taken my kids on holiday with that loser from Bluelight?'

Helen's resolve began to falter. Even though Adam had proved himself to be something of an accomplished liar in the past, she knew from experience that once found out he very quickly caved. None of this felt right. Could it be that she'd got it wrong? Was it possible that he was innocent after all?

'You're really telling me you had nothing to do with this?'

'I have no idea what "this" is, but I'm not liking the sound of it. Give me the address where you are, I'm coming to pick up the kids.'

Helen let the phone fall from her grasp and it clattered to the floor. She turned to face the others, feeling like she was unable to be certain of anything any more.

'Your dad says it wasn't him, and I just don't know whether to believe him.'

Helen's mum came and put an arm around her. 'It's okay, sweetheart. Really it is. So, you didn't find out who it was, but does it really matter?'

'Matter?' Helen flared with indignation. 'Of course it matters, Mum. For a brief second back there I was happy, really happy, and now because someone I trusted has betrayed me, that happiness has been ripped from me.' She started to cry. 'It's just so unfair, why aren't I allowed to be happy . . . why is it always my life that's falling apart?'

As her mum comforted her Helen heard someone else in the room let out a strangled sob. She looked up to see Frankie's face contorted in anguish, and, even though her own pain was so overwhelming, her instinct to protect Frankie was greater and she rushed to comfort him. 'I'm so sorry, Frankie, I shouldn't have got so upset in front of you, I'll be all right don't you worry.' At this, Frankie sobbed even harder, clutching his mother as if he was scared that he might drown. Then finally through the tears and distress Helen heard him say something she'd never imagined in a million lifetimes that he might say.

'I'm so sorry, Mum . . . I'm so, so, sorry . . . but it was me.'

26

Ben

It was after midnight when Helen pulled the car on to the drive, having dropped off her mum and Josh along the way. As she switched off the engine Ben looked up at the house and was struck by how much had changed since they'd left this place less than a week ago. Sometimes he felt like his life was on fast-forward, a series of blurry frames whizzing past, meaning it was almost impossible to make out the details.

Getting out of the car, Ben, no longer quite as afraid of being spotted as he once had been, but still cautious nonetheless, helped unload the boot and take the bags into the house. There was none of the excited chat and laughter that had seen them load the car for the holiday; now, everyone worked in silence to get the job done, locked away in their own thoughts as they had been since they'd left Cornwall seven hours earlier.

With the task complete the kids disappeared to their rooms without saying a word, leaving Ben and Helen alone in the kitchen.

Ben reached for the kettle. 'Do you want a drink?'

'I'd love one, but something stronger than tea I think.' She grabbed a bottle of red from the rack on the wall along with two wine glasses, while Ben opened a drawer, removed a corkscrew and followed her to the sofa. Sitting down, he opened the bottle as Helen reached down the side of the sofa as if searching for something. Eventually she produced a blue carrier bag, from which she removed a pack of cigarettes and a lighter. She lit one, then offered the pack to Ben, but he declined. 'You're right, I probably shouldn't either,' she said, standing up to open the French doors before returning to her seat. 'I only bought them in the wake of Adam leaving; until then I hadn't had a cigarette since I was a student.' She paused, took a long drag and exhaled. 'It's funny how in times of stress you go back to old habits.'

Ben poured the wine and handed a glass to Helen. 'I hope that's not how you see me.'

'Never.' She set her glass down on the table, stubbed out her cigarette on a saucer she'd brought along as a makeshift ashtray, and then, leaning her head on his shoulder, curled her arm through his. 'I don't know what I'd do without you, Ben . . . what I'm going to do . . . why couldn't things have been different? We've only just found each other again. It just feels so unfair . . . like life is always conspiring against us . . . like something somewhere is trying to keep us apart.'

Ben pressed his lips against her forehead, then, closing his eyes, rested his head against hers. The memory of the scene that had greeted him when he'd gone in search of Helen after his call with Rocco was still fresh in his mind. A distraught Frankie sobbing on the bed comforted by Helen, while Sue, Esme and Josh all looked on in concern. He'd had no idea what had happened, and his first thought was that perhaps despite his manager's intervention a story about them had been published online, maybe something hurtful about Esme, or her mum. Nothing had prepared him for the news that Helen broke to him: that Frankie had been the source of the leak.

'He didn't mean for things to turn out the way they have,' she'd explained. 'I don't think he had any idea about the consequences. He said he heard Mum and Esme talking about me and you being together and was scared that meant his dad and I would never have any chance of making a go of things. So, he looked up Chelsea

Maher online, found her on Twitter, set up a fake profile and messaged her that you were here, and well . . . you know the rest.'

At first Ben didn't know what to think. While he'd guessed that someone somewhere had leaked the information, Frankie would have been the last person he'd have suspected. He thought they'd been getting on well, especially during their time in Cornwall, but then he recalled the conversation he'd had with Frankie the first time they'd played *FIFA*. How he'd confessed just how much he missed his dad, and Ben had assured him that there was nothing going on between him and Helen. Viewed in that light, Ben was as much the betrayer as the betrayed.

'None of this is your fault,' he'd assured Frankie. 'I'd told you there was nothing between your mum and me, and though when I said it it was true I should've told you when things changed. This is all my fault, Frankie, not yours, you were just trying to keep your family together, and no one, least of all me, can blame you for that.'

Walking over to Frankie, Ben had held out his hand. 'Let's put this behind us, mate.' Frankie had stared at his outstretched hand for a moment, then with eyes full of pain had looked up, before flinging his arms around him. As Ben held him tightly, he was joined in the embrace by Helen, then Esme, and finally Sue. And there they'd stood, as one united around Frankie, until finally his tears had subsided.

A little later as Ben had packed in his room, Helen came to find him.

'Thank you for being so kind to Frankie, I think he thought you'd never speak to him again.'

'It's okay,' Ben said. 'He didn't mean any harm, not really, he just misses his dad, that's all.'

'But look at the chaos he's caused . . .'

'It was always going to happen one way or another,' Ben replied. 'That's the thing about secrets, they rarely remain buried forever.'

Taking his hand in hers, she'd asked him how long they had before he had to leave for LA, and this was the point at which Ben had broken the news that he was booked on a flight the day after tomorrow.

'That soon? Can't he give you any longer than that?'

Ben shook his head. 'Technically, all this time I've been away we should have been rehearsing,' he explained, gently brushing a tear from Helen's face. 'If the tour is going to go ahead then I have to leave.'

They hadn't spoken about what might happen next. It was as if they both knew it was a conversation too fraught with difficulty to undertake so soon after the turmoil of the afternoon. Ben couldn't bear the thought of leaving but, no matter how hard he tried, couldn't see a way to make staying work. His presence had already exposed Helen and her family to the threat of media intrusion and the misery that would follow, and he couldn't stand the thought of it getting any worse for the sake of his own happiness. So there was nothing for it. Though it broke his heart they would have to part, him returning to a world he hated, to a life he loathed.

That night back in Manchester, Ben and Helen stayed up until the early hours, saying very little but content to be in each other's arms, before finally, sometime around two, they went to bed, Helen insisting that he should stay in her room. 'I don't want to waste a single second of the time we have left,' she whispered as she led him into the bedroom. 'I want to make the most of every last moment.'

When Ben awoke the next morning, in that brief gap between sleep and being fully awake he imagined he was back in Cornwall, lying next to Helen. But then as he scanned the room he realised his mistake. He was back in Manchester, and this was it, his last day with her, his love, his final few hours of happiness. He reached across the bed hoping to feel the warmth of her body but instead found nothing but empty space. Throwing on some clothes, he made his way downstairs to find Helen chatting to Frankie and Esme as she buttered a slice of toast.

'Oh, you're up. I was just about to bring you breakfast.' Helen walked over to Ben and kissed him. To his surprise he felt himself blush. It felt strange that their relationship was, to the family at least, now out in the open.

'Did you sleep well?'

Ben looked at Esme, confused by the cheery tone in her voice.

'Hey Ben,' said Frankie before he could reply. 'Fancy a game of *FIFA* after breakfast?'

Ben looked at Helen's two children, trying to work out what was going on. Only a few hours ago they'd seemed so down they'd been unable to say a word, and now here they were acting like teenagers in a cereal commercial. Something wasn't right. Finally, it dawned on him: Helen must have told them how soon he had to leave, and this was them putting their sadness aside to give him a good send-off. Even though he didn't feel much like being happy, for the two of them and for Helen, he would make an effort to pretend that his heart wasn't breaking.

'Yes, I slept well,' he said to Esme and then, turning to Frankie, added, 'and yes to *FIFA*, but it might not be straight after breakfast because I have to go out.'

Helen looked at him surprised. 'Out? Where to?'

'To see my dad,' said Ben. 'I think it's about time I tried to make peace with him. I need to do it now, who knows if I'll get another chance.'

Later, as he and Nathan made their way over to Stockport, Ben took the opportunity to bring his brother up to speed with everything that had happened in Cornwall. Nathan listened in shocked silence before finally turning to him, eyes wide and a wry grin on his face. 'Well, bro, next time anyone asks me if I wish I could swap places with you, I'll definitely know what to say. Just hearing about all that is enough to make me feel like throwing up.'

Ben sighed. 'Thanks, Nath. That's just what I need to hear right now.'

Nathan gave Ben a playful nudge with his elbow. 'You know me, I'm only kidding. It's just that it's a lot, isn't it? And that's even before you've decided about what's happening with you and Helen.' He glanced quickly at Ben before returning his gaze to the road ahead. 'I am right about that, you haven't decided, have you?'

'We haven't talked about it yet. We haven't really had the chance. Everything happened so fast.'

'But you like her, don't you? I mean proper like, not just a fling?'

Ben grinned at the thought of Helen, and didn't even know where to begin to describe how she made him feel.

'She's amazing,' he said, only too aware of his failure to convey the strength of his feeling.

'Then figure out a way to make it work.'

'How? I'm off to LA, she's here, the band are about to set off on our biggest ever world tour, she's not long separated from her husband, and has got two kids to think about. None of it's ideal, is it?'

'What relationship is? There's always problems, I know that more than anyone, and granted not all of them on the sort of scale you've got, but problems just the same. Mate, there's always a way if you want it to work, you just have to find it.'

As they pulled up at a set of traffic lights a few minutes later, Nathan turned to Ben, a smile playing on his lips. 'Remember that time Mum tried to save a few quid by cutting our hair at home?'

Ben laughed. 'Remember it? I've still got the scar on my ear where she accidentally nicked me with the scissors because I was fidgeting so much!'

'And how about that time she managed to wangle the afternoon off work to come to our school sports day and run in the parents' race?'

Ben couldn't help but grin at the memory. 'I'd forgotten all about that!' he chuckled. 'She just took her shoes off and whizzed past the other mums and over the finish line without even breaking into a sweat!'

As the lights turned to green Nathan grinned. 'That was Mum all over, wasn't it? She was a complete and utter powerhouse.'

They continued chatting like this, trading stories of their mother, making each other laugh and smile with colourful tales from their past. But then a short while later Nathan slowed down the van and indicated to turn off the main road. As they did so Ben saw the sign for the care home up ahead. In that instant all the joy and lightness that had built up vanished. This was it. The moment he'd been dreading.

When he'd turned up at Helen's that day, what felt like a lifetime ago now, he'd never imagined that ultimately it would lead him here, to visit his father. He felt the same dread he had when he'd made this journey with Nathan before, only this time it was worse.

His heart was racing, his palms sweating, his throat dry, as if he was coming down with the worst case of stage fright in history. His every instinct was telling him to get out of the van and run, to put as much distance between himself and this place as possible, but he steeled himself to stay put. He'd overcome countless obstacles, gone through too much, to simply give up now. His time with Helen and Nathan had shown him the healing power of reunion and, whether his father was aware of it or not, it was important to Ben that the past was finally laid to rest.

As they walked towards the building Ben noticed Nathan shoot him a look as if checking he wasn't going to bail on him again. Determined to prove him wrong, Ben rang the bell at the entrance, and when a voice crackled over the intercom asking who they had come to visit it was Ben who provided the information.

The door buzzed open and, as they made their way inside and Nathan cheerfully greeted various care assistants and residents he'd clearly become familiar with, Ben started to feel even more uneasy. It had been over twenty-seven years since he'd last seen his father in the flesh, and that last meeting had been so awful, so wounding that even now he could still feel the tremors of it. And while he knew his father, at least physically, was not the man he remembered, and Ben himself was no longer a slight eighteen-year-old boy, still the prospect of seeing him again filled him with dread.

As they reached a door with his father's name sellotaped to it, Ben took a deep breath and Nathan, sensing his disquiet, turned to him. 'He's just a sick old man,' he said as if reading Ben's mind. 'He's not who he used to be.'

The tiny room, barely big enough to accommodate the two of them, was dominated by a huge hospital-style bed in which lay the gaunt figure of his father. His once jet-black hair was now snow white, his spindly arms lying limply at his sides. His eyes were open and fixed to a TV on the wall opposite, but there was no flicker of understanding or recognition in them. Ben stared hard at his father, taking him in but unable to reconcile the feeble figure in the bed with the man he had hated for so long.

Nathan gestured to a chair for Ben to sit down. 'He doesn't speak, but the nurses always say people like Dad can still hear, so it's worth talking to him. Just take his hand and say what you've got to say.'

Ben sat down, but his father didn't move, seemingly unaware of his presence. Following Nathan's suggestion, he reached out and took a frail hand in his own. It felt cool and dry to the touch, as if there was barely any life in it.

He tried to think about the man his father was, the man he used to be before he started drinking, before his world fell apart. How differently might things have turned out if he hadn't lost the love of his life, and the life he'd imagined for them both? What kind of man might he have been then? What kind of relationship might they have had?

Finally, with his eyes fixed on his father's face, Ben leaned closer to him and said the first words he'd spoken to the man in nearly three decades: 'Hi, Dad, it's me, Ben . . .'

27

Helen

Helen was in the kitchen when her phone buzzed with a text from Ben. 'It's done. Will tell you all about it when I get back. See you in a bit xxx.' Tempted as she was to call him, Helen decided against it. Judging from his message he was clearly processing seeing his dad and the last thing he needed would be an interrogation from her, even if it was a well-intentioned one. Instead, she tapped out a quick reply, 'Okay, see you soon xxx,' and had just pressed send when the doorbell rang, three short, sharp rings in succession. She sighed in irritation and, as she marched towards the front door, told herself that no matter how burly the parcel courier turned out to be, she was going to take him to task for being so impatient. She flung the door open.

'Do you have to be so—' She stopped mid-sentence. It wasn't a parcel courier after all. It was Adam.

'I think we need to talk.' His voice was cold and authoritative, not a million miles away, she suspected, from the tone he used on the children at his school. Without waiting for an invitation, he swept past her into the house, summoning his children downstairs in a gruff bark as he did so.

'What's going on, Mum?' asked Esme, looking over the banister from upstairs as her brother joined her.

'I want you both down here right now!' snapped Adam as Helen closed the front door and glared at him. 'I want to know right this second exactly what's been going on with you all.'

The children quickly came down the stairs and meekly followed their dad, who, much to Helen's annoyance, had walked into the kitchen with all the assurance of someone who still lived there. Standing in the middle of the room, he cast searching glances around the place as if expecting to find Ben cowering behind a plant pot or crouching underneath the coffee table.

'So where is loverboy? Hiding upstairs?'

Helen folded her arms tightly across her chest. 'You mean Ben? He's out. Not that it's any of your business.'

Adam snorted dismissively before turning back to his children. 'Are you both okay? I've been worried sick about you.'

His melodramatic concern for their children made Helen furious. 'Of course they're okay. You'd know if they weren't.'

Adam glared at her. 'I wasn't talking to you. I was talking to them. Kids, are you both okay?'

'We're fine, Dad,' said Esme. 'I told you that when I messaged you yesterday.'

'I know that's what you said but I needed to see for myself, especially after everything you've been subjected to.' He took the time to scowl at Helen before returning his gaze to Esme and Frankie. 'Now, tell me in your own words exactly what's been going on.'

Helen stepped forwards. She'd had more than enough of her husband and his sanctimoniousness to last a lifetime. 'They've told you they're fine, and you can see for yourself that they're telling the truth. So why are you acting like they're in some sort of imminent danger?'

Adam held up a hand as if to silence her. 'What your mother seems to be conveniently forgetting is that yesterday the gutter press were swarming around you threatening all manner of things because of her . . . her . . . so-called friend.'

'His name's Ben,' interjected Frankie unexpectedly. 'And he's dead nice, Dad. And what happened wasn't his fault.'

'So, something did happen then? What was it?'

Frankie shot Helen a look of desperation. 'Well . . . what happened was I—'

Helen cut him off. 'Frankie, you don't need to explain anything. Kids, please go upstairs and close the door behind you while your dad and I talk.'

Without needing to be told twice, Esme and Frankie scurried out of the room, and then as Helen heard the door click shut she spun around and unleashed everything she had at Adam.

'How dare you!' she screamed. 'How dare you come into my home throwing your weight around like some sort of tinpot dictator!'

'I think you'll find that legally speaking this home is still half mine.'

'Really? Well, legally speaking we're still married but that hasn't meant anything to you for a very long time.' She snatched up her phone from the kitchen counter. 'Let's see what the police's take on your "legal" standing will be when I call and ask them to sling you out!'

Adam quickly held up his hands in defeat, although Helen's guess was that this had less to do with his fear of confronting authority and more with his terror of word of any such encounter somehow making it back to his school. 'Okay, maybe I've been a bit rash . . . but surely you can see my point? The last thing I heard from you was a hysterical phone call accusing me of leaking unsavoury stories to the press! Tell me, Helen, exactly what am I supposed to think?'

'Well, for starters, that I'd never in a million years put the kids in harm's way! You know me better than that.'

'Know you? Right now, I feel like I have no idea who you are. According to Rav, who I spoke to last night after you called, you've been harbouring this mentally unstable so-called celebrity in my house, with my kids, for weeks! If that's not putting them in harm's way, tell me what is?'

Helen tried her best not to rise to Adam's baiting but it was difficult, really difficult. 'Ben's not mentally unstable, he's an old friend
who needed somewhere to stay, and unlike you I have a strong sense
of loyalty, so of course I let him stay with us. The kids were fine with
that arrangement, in fact they were more than fine, they've enjoyed
getting to know him, and at no point have they been in any danger.'

'And you were going to tell me about this little arrangement
when exactly? I was totally transparent with you about introducing
the kids to Holly and about wanting to take them on holiday with
us, so why wasn't I afforded the same level of respect?'

'Would that be the same level of respect that saw you sneaking
around behind my back with another woman for six months?'
snapped Helen. 'The same level of respect you showed in taking
that woman on *our* family holiday with *our* children?' Helen was
so angry she was relieved there was nothing close to hand she
could use as a weapon. 'I can't quite believe how self-righteous
you're being right now! You're being a pig, Adam, an utter pig,
and I can't quite work out whether that's something you've always
been or whether it's something you've become. But to be honest
I don't really care what the answer is. I just want you to go.'

Just then there was a click of the door opening, and Helen
turned to see Ben. A long silence ensued as he looked from Helen
to Adam and back again as if trying to read the situation.

'Everything okay?' Ben asked warily.

'Yes,' said Helen. 'Adam's just leaving.'

For a moment a stony-faced Adam stood defiantly, chest raised,
legs slightly apart, glaring at Ben, saying nothing. Ben met Adam's
gaze, but without the posturing of her husband.

'I think you've been asked to leave,' said Ben after a moment
or two without breaking eye contact with Adam.

Helen briefly wondered if she was going to have to prevent an altercation but, after standing his ground for all of five seconds, Adam turned to her and spat, 'This isn't over,' before deliberately brushing past Ben in a decidedly childish manner and leaving the house.

'What was all that about?' asked Ben as the front door slammed shut.

Helen sighed, and with her exhaled breath tried to let go of all the tension of the past few minutes. 'It was just Adam throwing his weight about and trying to make a point. I'm so sorry you had to see that.' She put her arms around Ben and held him tightly before looking up at his face. 'I'm so glad you're back, I've missed you, how did it go?'

He bent down and kissed her. 'As well as it could have, I suppose. He's just an old man now, a frail old man. It's hard to believe how closely the shadow of him has followed me around my whole life, and now there's barely anything left of him.'

'It must have been hard seeing him after all this time.'

'I think the dread of it was worse than the reality. The important thing is, I feel like I've made my peace with him. The anger and bitterness I felt towards him over the years . . . I don't know . . . it seems so pointless now. For the first time in a long while I feel at peace.' He looked deep into Helen's eyes. 'I can't believe tonight is my last night here.'

'Me either. It seems almost unreal.' She bit her lip. She'd told herself she wasn't going to spend their last day together crying and she'd meant it. She took a breath to compose herself. 'What time did you say the car was coming to take you down to Heathrow?'

'Four a.m. tomorrow.'

Helen looked at her watch. They had a little over fourteen hours left before Ben was due to leave. 'In that case,' she continued, 'we'd better get started making this a day to remember.'

Across the hours that followed, Helen, Ben, Esme and Frankie ate, talked and laughed until their sides hurt. They played countless games of cards, ordered pizza, flicked through all of Helen's old photos again, and even managed to watch a film too. Throughout it all Helen tried her best to remain present, refusing herself the permission to waste precious time speculating about the future: who she and Ben were to each other now, and what they might be to each other going forwards. There were times, however, when she couldn't help herself. As she sat watching Ben playing video games with Frankie while Esme did a running commentary, Helen wondered why it was that life couldn't always be like this, the four of them hanging out and enjoying each other's company.

She knew the answer of course, it was the same one she had given Gabby what felt like a lifetime ago when she'd first told her about Ben: their worlds were just too different, their time together some version of a holiday romance. Only now the holiday was coming to an end. Ben would soon be returning to his world, leaving Helen behind in hers, and they would be separated from each other by thousands of miles. Not that she hadn't allowed herself to imagine what it might be like if they could somehow make it work, him returning to visit in breaks in the tour schedule, her taking the kids to see him whenever her own work would allow, but even in her fantasies it had all seemed so fraught with complication. Adam kicking up a fuss whenever she took the kids out of the country, her constant fear of Ben being seduced by some starlet or other while moving in his old social circles, it all seemed too inevitable for words. And so, she had forced herself to conclude that any hope of them being together was impossible. All they had, all they would ever have, was what they had right now, and how could she even think about being unhappy about that, when even an hour with Ben was enough to make her heart soar?

28

Helen

It was after midnight when Ben said his final goodbyes to the kids. In the short time he had lived with them they had grown really attached to him, and she knew they would miss him terribly. Hugging an emotional Esme, he grinned and said, 'Don't forget what I said: when the tour comes to the UK, you and mates can have all the VIP guest passes you want. Of course, that is if we haven't gone out of fashion by then!'

'Never,' said a tearful Esme. 'I'll be there right at the front with all my mates. Singing along to every song.'

Ben gave Frankie a huge bear hug and as Frankie cried too, Ben vowed to practise his *FIFA* skills while on the road. 'Just you wait,' he said, 'I'm going to get so good that you won't stand a chance against me.'

With so little time and so much to say, after the kids went to bed Helen and Ben sat up talking on the sofa in the kitchen. They talked about anything and everything, all the while careful to avoid the one thing neither of them wanted to discuss: the future. Helen knew in her bones that she and Ben didn't have a hope of making their relationship work. And worse still, she knew that he knew it too. Their worlds were too different and the stress and strain of a long-distance relationship would be too much. She would end up resenting him for always being away, he would end up resenting her for not understanding the pressures of a life like his, and inevitably they would part. Far better instead to do the grown-up thing, the mature thing, to accept their time together as the happy accident it was and nothing more.

Still, even while her head accepted that there was no future for them, her heart, stubborn as always, was having far more difficulty coming to terms with it, and she suspected the same was true of Ben. With every passing moment he seemed to hold on to her just that little bit more tightly, and when he looked at her his eyes were so full of sadness that she had to look away.

In the end, it was the head that won and Helen kept all of her doubts and fears to herself, and the same must have been true for Ben, because he said nothing about them trying to make a go of things either. Instead, accepting their fate, they clung on to each other, as if trying to keep each other afloat until, at a few minutes to four that morning, Ben's phone vibrated on the coffee table in front of them.

'Is that your car?' Helen asked.

Ben checked the message and nodded. 'Yeah, he's outside. It's time.'

Walking him to the front door, Helen tried her best not to cry, not wanting his last image of her to be a snivelling wreck. But then after putting his bags in the car, he returned to the house, and, unable to hold her emotions in check any longer, she buried her face in his chest and sobbed. Finally, they kissed, a long, slow kiss that said more than words ever could, and before Helen knew it she was standing alone on the doorstep, watching his car slip away into the early-morning light.

Closing the door, Helen checked her watch. Exhausted as she was, she knew that if she went to bed she would never sleep, and so the next best thing, she decided, would be to make herself some tea and sit alone with her thoughts for a while.

Returning to the sofa, she placed her mug on the coffee table, then turned off the lights and sat looking out through the French doors into the garden now bathed in the glow of dawn. The world, it seemed, hadn't stopped turning, even though in her heart she felt as if it should have now that Ben was no longer here. A new day was getting underway, her first without him, and she wondered when, or indeed if, she would ever stop feeling his absence.

She watched as sparrows zipped in and out of the trees at the edge of the lawn, singing loudly as if they didn't have a care in the world. When a family of blackbirds landed and began pecking hopefully at the dew-drenched ground, occasionally managing to find a worm in return for their labours, she wondered how many more times in her life she would have to go through the pain of someone leaving her.

In her exhausted state, it seemed to her that her life had all too often been visited by such sorrow. She thought about her father, who walked out one day when she was five and never came back. She'd barely been aware of his leaving. One day he'd been there, the next he'd gone, leaving fragments of himself embedded in her memory. She recalled the smell of cigarettes on his breath when he kissed her hello, the loudness of his laughter as he watched TV with her mum, and his big black work boots lined up neatly by the front door, which occasionally she would put her feet in and stomp around the hallway, pretending she was the giant in *Jack and the Beanstalk*. But the pain of his departure? She had no memory of it, or even that of her mother, a young woman left to raise two small children on her own. Perhaps she'd kept her grief to herself, preferring to cry her tears behind closed doors, but on Helen herself her dad's leaving had left no impression, at least not an easily discernible one. And yet, in his abandoning of Helen, her sister and her mum, her father had set a precedent, he had been the first person to leave her life, but he hadn't been the last.

Her mind shifted to the day eighteen-year-old Ben had arrived at her house, his face etched with pain and anguish. She'd been in her room listening to music, daydreaming about what life at university might be like, when the doorbell rang, followed moments later by a knock at her bedroom door. From the moment she saw his face she'd known something was wrong, but had no idea just how terrible things were, or how bad they were about to get. He told her about his argument with his father, the smashed guitar, and his conviction that he needed to leave right away.

'I want you to come with me,' he'd said, looking deep into her eyes. 'I need you to come with me, I want us to start a life together in London away from all of this.'

His words had been so heartfelt, his love for her so pure and sincere, that for a brief moment she'd entertained the possibility of going with him, and her heart fully engaged for the first time in a pitched battle with her head. The arguments for staying were all too apparent. She had a plan for her life: exams, then university, then a good job paying decent money, a way out of the struggle she'd watched her mum go through growing up. Until that moment she'd been convinced that Ben had been part of her plans too, a long-distance relationship while they were both at university, then afterwards moving in together, living the life she'd always imagined for them. But now that plan lay in shreds at her feet. Ben was leaving; she knew she couldn't change his mind but she also knew she had to stay and pursue her own dreams. And so it was that she was left behind a second time.

She survived, of course, though it had been one of the hardest things her younger self had ever had to endure. She knew Ben had found it tough too, the letters he'd written her afterwards so full of longing and regret told her that. In the optimism of youth, they had vowed to be there for one another forever, to always remain friends. And it was a promise to which they had managed to stay true, until, a few years into Bluelight's global success, late one night, Ben had called and told her he was moving to LA.

'Wow,' Helen had said, sitting at her desk covered in lesson plans, in her shared house in Leeds. 'When do you go?'

'Tomorrow,' he'd replied. 'I know I should've said something sooner but everything's just been so manic lately.'

He'd explained that the move was because of the band, his manager having told him that it made sense to move to LA if they were going to capitalise on their successes in America. 'My management have rented a place for me and the band in Bel-Air,' he'd continued. 'You should see it, H, it's got eight bedrooms, two swimming pools, a tennis court and even its own bowling alley! It's totally mad.'

'It sounds amazing,' she'd replied, even though she had her reservations about him going, about him being so far away. 'You'll have a great time. You've worked so hard, you deserve it.'

It had crossed her mind at the time that once again she was being left, that once again she had no choice but to accept that someone she loved was leaving. But this time round it felt different, their lives were moving along such completely different trajectories as to make friendship almost impossible. Wasn't it better, she'd thought as she had prepared to say her goodbye to Ben back then, to let what they had fizzle out rather than to try to keep things going against the odds? Wasn't it wiser to accept that they no longer had anything in common than to continually try to keep the embers of what they used to have alive? She'd decided this was the case and, judging by his own lack of contact over the years, Helen had assumed that Ben agreed. Yes, he had left her, but in a way, she had left him too.

Then of course, Adam had left, a day that was forever etched on her memory, and now with Ben gone too Helen's mind raced ahead to the future. Esme would be leaving for university in a few weeks and Frankie, with only four years left at school, wouldn't be far behind her. Then there was her mum, now in her late sixties, which, while still young relatively speaking, raised the spectre of a whole different kind of leaving altogether.

Perhaps, Helen thought, picking up her tea and cradling it in her hands, the pain of someone leaving was the trade-off for having loved them. All things had to come to an end eventually. But that didn't make the ache in her heart any less keen, or the tears that fell down her face any less real. She was sick of people leaving, she was tired of being left behind. All she wanted, all she needed, was for the people she loved to stay beside her and never leave. Really, was that too much to ask?

29

Ben

The moment Ben stepped off the plane at LA-X and was herded along with the rest of the passengers in First Class towards the arrivals lounge, he knew something was up. Twelve hours earlier at Heathrow he had been whisked away by airport staff to the VIP lounge, then through a one-on-one security check before being offered the choice of being the first to board the plane or the last. Desperate to avoid scrutiny, he'd opted to be the first and was shown to the seat Rocco had selected at the rear of the First-Class cabin, chosen, he suspected, in order to reduce the number of people who would need to walk past him. Cocooned in his booth, Ben had informed the stewards that he wouldn't be requiring drinks or meal service and then, sliding his door closed, he'd slouched down low in his seat and tried his best to remain anonymous.

For the entire flight all he could do was think about Helen and how much he already missed her. Even though he'd spent much of the past few weeks as a virtual prisoner, at the same time it was the closest he'd come to having a normal life in decades. As each hour passed, as the plane took him further and further away from her, all he did was wonder what she was doing and whether she was thinking about him. Several times he even thought about using the wi-fi to send her a voice note but, every time he went to do it, he couldn't find the words to say what he wanted to express. So he'd put his phone away, closed his eyes and hoped with all his might that sleep might take him and he'd be saved, at least for a while, from thoughts of leaving the woman he loved behind.

Now he was in LA, however, and all efforts to keep him hidden had it appeared been abandoned, thoughts of Helen were temporarily overridden by those of survival as his presence in the queue at security began to cause chaos. It started innocently enough with a man pointing Ben out to his girlfriend, but then the girlfriend spoke to the couple next to him, and the news began to ripple outwards like a stone dropping into the water. Soon, people were approaching him asking if he was 'Ben from Bluelight', and the more he denied it, the more certain they became, until for his own safety an airport official intervened and sped him through security, before leaving him to fend for himself on the other side.

Having cleared customs, he stepped through the doors into the arrivals hall and was immediately blinded by a sudden supernova of camera flashes. It was only as his retinas recovered from the assault that he realised he'd walked into the midst of a sea of paparazzi and overzealous fans. The noise was disorientating, the collective clicks of dozens of camera shutters going off, the sound of people calling his name, fans screaming at the tops of their voices, and journalists yelling all manner of questions: 'Ben, Ben, where have you been all this time?' 'Ben! Is it true you've had a nervous breakdown?', 'Ben, what's the future for you and Bluelight?'

Ben didn't open his mouth. Even if he'd wanted to answer their questions, there would have been no chance they'd have heard his response over the noise that filled the air. As he concentrated on inching his way forward in what he hoped was the direction of the exit, people grabbed and pressed in on him on every side and he found himself thinking about Helen again. Had they decided to make a go of things, had they opted to stay together, she would inevitably have been caught up in something like this at some point. Photographers taking pictures of her every move, tabloid reporters digging through her bins, people believing she was public property by dint of her proximity to him. He wouldn't have wished it on his worst enemy, let alone the woman he loved more than life itself.

As he continued to shuffle forward, he became aware of a commotion ahead. Instead of being fixated on him, people were turning to look over their shoulders as if something was approaching from behind them. Finally, the crowd parted to reveal two huge bodyguards forcefully ordering everyone around to step back and make some room.

As they reached him, they each took up a position flanking him with one arm held out as they escorted him through the scrum of people. Ben thought he recognised one of the bodyguards as a man who had briefly been part of Allegra's security team, but behind the sunglasses and inscrutable expression it was impossible to be sure. Even with their help, the short distance to the exit took much longer to navigate than it should have done, and there were moments when in spite of their obvious experience Ben wondered if more assistance wasn't needed. Eventually, however, they managed to exit the building and against his skin he felt the contrast between the cool of the building's air-conditioning and the hot dry air of the LA afternoon. He was abruptly bundled into a waiting black SUV and the moment the door slammed shut the vehicle pulled away at top speed. It was only as Ben slumped back into his seat, panting and shaking, that he noticed for the first time that he wasn't the only passenger in the car.

'Hello, Ben. It's good to see you.' The familiar voice was as calm as ever.

Ben turned to look at his manager, who was wearing his trademark loud Hawaiian shirt and dark sunglasses. 'Was that your doing, tipping off the press and the fans about my arrival and leaving me to fend for myself?'

Rocco held up a quietening hand. 'A scheduling mix-up, I assure you, otherwise I would've met you off the plane myself. As for tipping off the press and the fans you know me, Ben, I don't get involved in all that.'

Technically this was true, Rocco rarely got involved in anything directly, but still Ben couldn't shake the feeling that he was behind all this. 'Okay, so how did they know what flight I was on?'

Rocco shrugged. 'You were on a plane for eleven hours, maybe someone made a call or two, I don't know, do I? But face it, photos of the return of the long-lost lead singer of the world's biggest band can't exactly do any harm, can they? As it is, your time away has given you the top two slots in the charts here and the top five in the UK, and that's with precisely zero dollars spent on promotion. Ben, you pulling a stunt like this is some sort of PR genius.'

Exhausted, Ben couldn't even bring himself to argue. 'Just tell me what you've decided the story's going to be, the way we explain to the press where I've been without dragging Helen and her family into it all.'

Rocco flashed Ben a disconcerting grin. 'You're going to love this, mate: there is no strategy. I sent out a press release two minutes ago explaining that you won't be telling a single soul where you've been these past few weeks. It'll be like when Agatha Christie went missing for eleven days back in 1926. People went mad for it, coming up with all sorts of theories left, right and centre, and the best part of a hundred years later no one's any the wiser. So, if you and your mates can keep your mouths shut, we'll be on to a winner . . .' He paused and added with a throaty chuckle, 'Who knows? Maybe they'll make a film about it one day: *Missing: the Ben Baptiste Story.*'

For the rest of the journey they sat in silence, Rocco tapping away on his phone while Ben stared out of the window watching the scenery changing as they left the built-up areas around LA-X before picking up the coastal road at Santa Monica, awarding Ben his first glimpses of the sea. Finally, they reached Malibu, and the mansion Ben had left behind what felt like a lifetime ago.

When the SUV came to a stop, Ben got out of the car without saying a word, desperate to put as much distance between him and Rocco as possible. To his dismay, however, he heard the car door open and his manager get out too, telling the driver to wait for his return. Ignoring Rocco, Ben continued towards the house, and the front door opened to reveal the smiling face of Lucía, his housekeeper.

'So good to see you back, Mr Baptiste,' she said warmly, 'welcome home.'

Lucía insisted on taking Ben's bag from him, and he knew better than to refuse. She had always taken pride in her job and wouldn't let Ben prevent her from doing it even if he was the one who paid her wages. Almost on autopilot Ben walked to the kitchen, poured himself a glass of water and then stood drinking it in front of the floor-to-ceiling windows looking out across the Pacific. He thought about Lucía's greeting and wondered if this was indeed home. It was the place he had lived for the last few years, somewhere he had spent a lot of time in between recording, tours and press junkets, but home? He wasn't sure if he'd apply that term to it, at least not any more.

'Good to be back?'

Ben turned to see that Rocco was by his side, but instead of replying to his manager's question he returned his gaze to the sea before him. As he stood watching the sun's reflection dancing across the water he wondered once again what Helen might be doing right now. The UK was eight hours ahead, so there it would be around ten thirty at night. He imagined her curled up on the sofa in the living room reading a book, or perhaps sitting in the kitchen diner listening to music, a glass of wine in her hand. Whatever view she had would inevitably pale in comparison to the one before him, and yet given a choice he knew exactly which one he would choose.

Rocco put a hand on Ben's shoulder. 'Okay, so you're not over the moon to be back here, I get it. You blame me for screwing up your one shot at happiness, or whatever you want to call it. But give yourself time, Ben, and I promise you'll see it my way soon. I'm just looking out for you. I always have done and I always will. I know it doesn't feel like it now but one day you'll get it. You see, that girl, that life isn't you, you're past all that now. We're gods, Ben. People like you and me aren't meant to be with the mortals.'

Ben didn't speak. There was no point trying to reason with Rocco, a man who had little time for anyone's opinion but his own.

Finally, Rocco removed his hand from Ben's shoulder, took a cigar from his top pocket and rolled it between his fingers idly. 'Well, I'm going to leave you to it for now. Give you a chance to have a rest and settle back in. Rehearsals are first thing in the morning at the Bunker, there's a car booked for ten a.m. and I've given them strict instructions to call me if you're even a minute late. But you won't be, will you?'

It was a thinly veiled threat, Ben knew it, but still he said nothing. While it was true that he'd made a deal with the devil, there was nothing in the small print that meant he had to like it.

Rocco sighed heavily as if Ben was trying his patience, but when he spoke his voice was back to his usual controlled manner.

'Right, I'll get out of your hair then, mate. Hope it all goes well tomorrow. Do me proud.'

The moment Ben was sure Rocco was off the premises he pulled out his phone from his jacket pocket and called Helen. She picked up on the third ring.

'Hello?'

He couldn't pinpoint exactly what quality it was about her voice that had such a calming effect on him, but in the space of a single word he felt all the tension of the past hour melt away.

'It's me, it's not too late, is it? I didn't wake you, did I?'

'No, and even if you had it wouldn't have mattered. It's so good to hear your voice.'

Ben grinned, picturing her face, her smile. 'And yours too.'

'How are you coping with everything? I saw you being mobbed at the airport on the news. It was so horrible. I thought you said Rocco would make sure that wouldn't happen?'

Ben took a sip of his water. 'I think he's been up to his usual tricks. He says it was nothing to do with him, but it's got his grubby fingerprints all over it.'

'That's awful. He's awful. You should get rid of him.'

Ben sighed and, for the first time since his stay at the Compono, wondered about the parallels between his relationships with his father and his manager. From the day twenty-year-old Ben had met him, Rocco had seamlessly stepped into the role vacated by his father. Was this why Rocco had always held so much sway in his life? Having already walked away from one father, was this the reason he was so reluctant to turn away from another?

'If only it was that simple,' he said to Helen. 'If only everything were that straightforward.' A thought occurred to him. Maybe life was always messy, maybe there were no neat solutions, maybe sometimes you had to jump first and work the details out later.

'I miss you,' he said. 'I really miss you.'

There was a catch in her voice when she spoke. 'I miss you too.'

'Then why aren't we together?' asked Ben. 'Why aren't we trying harder to make this work?'

'Because . . . because . . . everything's complicated,' replied Helen, her voice full of emotion. 'Because all the odds are stacked against us, because this is what makes sense.'

'But aren't you tired of being sensible?' questioned Ben, with an edge of conviction. 'Because I tell you what, I am. I want you, Helen, I want you more than I've ever wanted anything in my life. And I don't care about complications or odds. I know in my heart if we take the chance, we can make this work.'

30

Helen

'Helen . . . it's so good to see you, come in.'

Given the number of texts, calls and messages Helen had ignored from Gabby since their fraught phone conversation in Cornwall, it was no wonder that her friend was surprised to find her standing on her doorstep.

'Can I come in,' said Helen. 'I need to talk.'

Invited by Gabby, Helen stepped into the hallway and followed her friend to the kitchen. She'd been here a thousand times before, but never feeling as uncomfortable as she did now. She wished everything could go back to normal between them, like it used to be before it all got so complicated, but right now more than anything she needed her best friend.

Gabby filled the kettle. 'Can I get you a tea or coffee?'

'Coffee would be great thanks.' The whole exchange was stiff and awkward, nothing like their usual easy-going banter. Helen wanted to reach out to her friend but wasn't sure how. Gabby must have been feeling the same way too, because turning to look at her, her expression uncertain, she said, 'Can I just say again how sorry I am? You told me not to say a word to anyone, not even Rav, and I totally let you down. I completely understand that what I did has changed our friendship but if you let me, I'm determined to show you that you can trust me.'

'Oh Gabs, you're my best mate, of course I forgive you.' Helen opened her arms and they embraced tightly.

'I'm so sorry,' said Gabby through tears. 'I swear on my life I'll never let you down like that again.' Releasing her friend, she took a tissue out of her pocket, dried her eyes and smiled. 'I can't tell you how good it is to see you. I've missed you so much these past few days. How have things been? I saw on the news that Ben was back in America. You must be devastated.'

Helen nodded, trying her best to keep control of her emotions. 'He left early yesterday morning.'

Gabby nodded thoughtfully. 'And how did you two leave things?'

'Well, that's sort of the reason I'm here,' said Helen. 'When he left, I thought, that's it, it's over. But then he called late last night from LA and asked if I'd consider giving us a go.'

'And you're not sure, are you?' asked Gabby, reading her friend's face.

Helen shook her head and started to cry. 'I just don't know what to do for the best.'

'Well, that's what you've got me for,' said Gabby, and she reached for a clean tissue from a box on the side and handed it to Helen. 'Let me sort out these drinks and we'll talk it over.'

Gabby made two cups of coffee and then set them down on the kitchen table along with a plate piled high with expensive-looking biscuits.

'Okay,' she said, sitting down opposite Helen. 'Tell me everything.'

Helen cast her mind back to the call with Ben. His suggestion that they should carry on seeing each other had completely taken her by surprise. After all, she knew that he was as aware of the numerous obstacles standing between them, the impossibility of it all, as she was. But then he'd spoken about wanting to take a chance, said he didn't care about the fact that the odds were stacked against them, and, when he asked her how she felt, all she wanted to do was tell him how much she wanted to be with him too. But no matter how hard she tried, the words wouldn't leave her lips, until eventually the silence between them became unbearable. 'You don't think it'll work, do you?' he'd said. 'To be honest I don't blame you.'

Helen eventually recovered herself enough to speak. 'It's not that,' she protested, 'I just need time, that's all; if we're going to do this, if I'm going to do this then I need some time to think it through. Oh, Ben, if it was just me, if there was nobody else to consider, I'd jump on the next plane to be with you and never look back. But it's not just me, it's Esme and Frankie too, so I need some time.'

Ben told her that he understood and added that she should take all the time she needed to make up her mind, and that's the way the call had ended, with him promising to be patient and Helen all too aware that she had the decision of a lifetime to make. She had thought of nothing else since.

'I barely slept last night for going over it all,' she said to Gabby, having told her about the call. 'Every time I think I've made a decision, something else occurs to me and I'm right back to square one. That's why I'm here, I need your help, otherwise I feel like I'm going to completely lose my mind.'

Gabby gave Helen's hand a squeeze. 'You poor thing, of course you feel confused. It's such a huge decision. Forget about all the practicalities for a minute, what's your heart telling you to do?'

Helen's answer was instant. 'I want to be with Ben. I know I sound like a lovelorn teenager saying it, but I really love him, Gabs, he's what I want.'

'And now we've heard from your heart, what's your head saying?'

Helen groaned. 'So many things, it doesn't seem to want to shut up. The fact is I'm still technically married to Adam, for starters, then there's the whole timing issue. I mean is it all too soon? Am I just rebounding into Ben or is there something more?

And don't even get me started on the kids! I mean they really like Ben but what will they think of us being together officially? And what would that even look like anyway with me here in Manchester and him in LA?'

'So, you didn't talk about any of the details?'

'How could we, when I couldn't even give him an answer to the basic question of us being together? I think there was just too much up in the air to even begin thinking our way through it all.'

Gabby looked at Helen expectantly. 'But if the kids were all right about it . . .?'

Helen considered Gabby's question. 'Then I think I'd probably go for it.'

'Only probably?'

Helen felt her heart sink. Gabby knew her too well. 'It's the stuff I said to you before, you know, about Ben slumming it with me.'

'And what did I tell you when you said that?'

Helen grinned. 'You told me he was the lucky one.'

'Because he is,' said Gabby. 'And if you love him like you say you do then you'll trust his judgement. He wants you, Helen, he doesn't want anyone else, just you.'

Helen sighed and looked at her friend. 'You make it sound so easy.'

'Maybe it is that easy,' replied Gabby. 'My advice to you is simple: talk to Esme and Frankie, tell them what you're thinking, what it is you want from life. They're good kids, Helen, and clever with it, like their mum, so they'll understand how happy Ben makes you. They won't want you to give that up. Just be straight with them and they'll be straight with you, and hopefully together you'll work it all out.'

That evening when the kids had both returned home after spending the day with friends, Helen screwed up her courage, called them both down to the kitchen and talked to them about Ben.

'So, you mean Ben would be like my stepdad?' said Esme, starry eyed. 'I'd be the stepdaughter of an actual celebrity?'

Helen smiled, trust her daughter to focus on the wrong part of the story. 'Well . . . slow down a bit, Es, no one's said anything about us getting married. All we're talking about at the moment is the idea of me and Ben carrying on seeing each other, which of course is going to bring with it attention, not all of it positive.'

'You mean like that journalist lady?' asked Esme. 'She was a right cow, wasn't she?'

Helen found herself grinding her teeth at the thought of her. 'Yes, she was and . . . well . . . there are thousands more like her out there. They could make life very difficult for all of us if they wanted to.'

Esme's face was defiant. 'Well, I've made all my social media accounts private now, so just let them try.'

Helen looked at Frankie, recalling the lengths he'd gone to in order to keep alive the idea of her and Adam getting back together. Although they'd talked it over since, unlike his sister Frankie didn't wear his heart on his sleeve and it was sometimes impossible to know what was going through his mind.

'And what do you think about it all, Franks?' asked Helen.

For a moment Helen wasn't at all sure she'd get a response but then he lifted his gaze to her and said, 'I want you to be happy, Mum, and Ben makes you happy. So, I think you should go for it.'

'Are you sure though?' asked Helen. 'I know you've had reservations.'

Frankie squirmed, presumably at the memory of what he did back in Cornwall. 'That was then, I'm okay with it now. Es and I . . . well, we've talked about it a lot and I know now that Dad isn't coming back. I don't think it's fair that you should have to be lonely when you haven't done anything wrong.'

Helen couldn't help herself. Frankie's words were so full of kindness and sincerity that without thinking, she swept him up into a hug and for once he didn't wriggle or resist. 'I do love you, Franks, more than you'll ever know.' Reaching out, she pulled her daughter into the hug as well. 'And you too,' she said to Esme. 'I love you both so much, you're my most precious treasures and your happiness means the world to me, don't ever forget that.'

Once the kids had suffered enough fuss and kisses to last them a lifetime, they retreated back to their rooms, leaving Helen alone. She checked the large kitchen clock on the wall and calculated that it was midday in LA. In theory there was no reason for her not to make the call, but she felt as though something was stopping her although she couldn't quite put her finger on what it might be.

Making herself a cup of tea, she went to sit in the living room, and as she did so she caught sight of the family photo albums on the bookshelf beside her. Setting down her drink, Helen reached across to take one off the shelf only to discover at the last moment the one she had her hand on was in fact her wedding album. She pushed it back ready to select another but then thought better of it, wondering if perhaps this was something her unconscious mind had prompted her to do.

All along she'd assumed that her hesitation and uncertainty about making a go of things with Ben was because of the kids and the difficulty of being with a celebrity. While this was true, as she opened the album at random to reveal a smiling photo of a younger version of herself and Adam cutting their wedding cake, she realised that it wasn't the whole story.

As she flicked back to the first page, working her way through the chronology of their wedding day, Helen vividly recalled her vows to Adam. While she understood that to some people wedding vows were mere words, for her, at least, they had been so much more. To her they had been binding promises, sincere pledges, public declarations of her love and commitment to the man she'd thought she'd spend the rest of her life with. They'd never been just throwaway words, they'd meant something to her, something real, something precious.

Looking down at an image of her younger self covered in confetti outside the registry office, so full of excitement and hope for the future, it occurred to Helen that perhaps the thing that was holding her back from committing to Ben was the fact that if she said yes to them being together, she would finally be admitting to herself that her marriage was over. This wouldn't be a case of people splitting up over an affair, only to get back together later, as she had seen happen to some of her friends. Or a matter of mistakes made, lessons learned or bumps along the long road of marriage. If she said yes to being with Ben, then that would be the end, her marriage to Adam over for good, no going back, no second chances, all bridges burned.

While she had on some level accepted the fact that Adam had gone, it struck her that perhaps she hadn't quite come to terms with the idea that he was gone for good. Not that she wanted him back, it wasn't that, but it occurred to her that perhaps the thing she was struggling to let go of was the picture of how she'd once thought her life would be. The picture of her and Adam growing old together, celebrating their diamond wedding anniversary by going on a cruise of a lifetime, sharing the joy of becoming grandparents. None of it would happen, none of it would come to fruition. The finality of it felt cold, hard and unyielding. It was a death of sorts, the end of the way she thought things might be, and, as such, she felt at the very least it deserved to be mourned.

Returning to the album, she forced herself to look through every single page right to the end, before grabbing another from the shelf beside her, and doing the same again and again. There were pictures of Adam and herself when they first became teachers, and others when they travelled abroad as a young couple head over heels in love. There were snaps of their first home together, and ones capturing the gradual swelling of her belly as she grew Esme inside her. There were family holidays with baby slings and pushchairs, birthday parties featuring superheroes and princesses, Christmas mornings in matching bad-taste pyjamas, and New Year's Eves spent with Gabby, Rav and their kids, toasting with glasses of Champagne the passing of yet another twelve months. So much time, so many memories. Did she really have what it took to accept that this was the end, that these days were over forever?

31

Ben

For the fifth time in a row Ben missed his cue, causing the song Bluelight were rehearsing to collapse after its first few bars.

He shook his head as if trying to wake himself up from a deep sleep, ran a sweaty hand across his face and then apologised to the rest of the band. 'Sorry, guys, my fault completely.'

'You don't say.' Andy's tone was dripping with barely disguised annoyance.

Leona set her bass guitar down on its stand. 'Maybe we should all take a break for lunch and come back in an hour.'

'Agreed,' said Chip, getting up from behind the drums, and stretching his arms above his head. 'We'll get there, we always do in the end.'

'We do when we're all pulling together.' Andy slipped off his guitar and set it down next to Leona's. 'But I'm not convinced that's what's happening right now.'

Ben's first thought as he watched the rest of the band leave the room was that Andy's comment, barbed though it was, was probably right. Even after a significant time apart it never usually took long for them to get back into the groove of working together, to gel again, but things felt different this time and he knew without a shadow of a doubt that it was all because of Helen.

When Ben had asked her what she thought about giving their relationship a go, he'd been able to tell from the slight hesitation before she replied that she had reservations. He couldn't blame her of course, after all they weren't eighteen any more, she had her kids to think about, not to mention the chaos he brought with him, all on top of the recent collapse of a twenty-year marriage. Ben, however, had no reservations at all. In fact, he hadn't felt more certain about anything in his life.

With the exception of Allegra, his past relationships had all been little more than brief flings, nothing substantial, nothing to build a life around. And he couldn't help wondering if perhaps subconsciously he'd always been comparing the women he got involved with to Helen and always found them wanting. This thing with Helen wasn't just nostalgia, the safety of the known, but real, deep and enduring love.

In the years that had followed his move to LA he hadn't allowed himself to think about her much, reasoning that someone like her would've been snapped up straight away. Anytime he did think about her it was always in the context of her being healthy and happy, having everything she wanted, essentially living the life they would have had if things had been different. So, to have learned that she hadn't been happy, and to have been reunited with her at a time in her life when there was a chance of them being together, felt like a gift, an opportunity too good not to pursue even though the odds were clearly stacked against them.

It had been Ben's hope that having had the night to sleep on it, Helen's answer might have miraculously come to her along with a brand-new day. He'd even stayed up until four in the morning in the recording space in his home, ostensibly working on new songs, but in truth doing little more than keeping track of the time in the UK, willing his phone to ring. He must have eventually fallen asleep on a sofa because the next thing he knew, Lucía was gently shaking his arm and delivering the news that the car to take him to rehearsals had arrived. Not wanting to rile Rocco unnecessarily, Ben had refused Lucía's offer of breakfast; instead he'd dunked his face under the cold tap in the nearest cloakroom, and headed out of the house still wearing the clothes he'd slept in.

The band's reaction on seeing him for the first time in the best part of four months had been mixed to say the least. Andy, Bluelight's guitarist, barely said more than two words to him, in order, Ben suspected, to prevent yet another one of their stand-up arguments, the kind they'd been having off and on ever since they got together over twenty years ago. Bassist Leona on the other hand, ever the diplomat, had welcomed Ben back warmly, giving him a hug on arrival, and had even gone as far as telling him how much she'd missed him. And drummer Chip had simply flashed him a thumbs up, before going into a ten-minute monologue about fly-fishing, his latest in a long line of obsessive hobbies.

No one directly referred to his stay at the Compono, the events leading up to it, or indeed his twenty-one-day vanishing act. Instead, once they'd all grabbed something from the breakfast table that had been provided for them, they'd set to work on rehearsing. At first Ben put his mistakes down to jet lag and the fact that he hadn't had much sleep. And then, when they continued, he blamed the fact that he hadn't properly picked up a guitar or played any Bluelight songs for the best part of a quarter of a year. It was only when he caught himself checking the clock on the wall when he should've been concentrating on his playing that it finally dawned on him that his errors were to do with Helen and the agony of waiting for her answer.

Removing his guitar, Ben put it down on a stand, and was about to join the others for lunch when his phone buzzed. Scrambling to take it out of the back pocket of his jeans, he checked the screen and saw Helen's name. This was it: the wait was over. She'd made her decision. As his thumb hovered over the green accept call symbol his pulse quickened, and briefly he wondered if he should even take the call. It was bad news, he was sure of it. She had weighed up all the pros and cons and found him wanting. Still, he thought, as he swiped the button across, better to know now than to drag this moment out any longer.

'Ben, hey, hope I'm not interrupting.'

'No, of course not. It's great to hear your voice. How are you?'

'I'm good thanks, everything's fine here, how about you? You're rehearsing today, aren't you? How's that going?'

He thought about telling her but couldn't see what good might come of her knowing the havoc she'd been wreaking in his mind. 'It's been great. It's funny how easy it is to slip back into work after a long time away.'

'And the band? How have they been? I know you were worried about how they'd react to you being back.'

'Actually, for the most part they've been great. Really supportive.' Ben paused, conflicted by his feeling of wanting to be put out of his misery while at the same time desperately hanging on to the hope not knowing offered. 'And how's your day been? What did you get up to?'

He detected a slight hesitation before she answered his question but couldn't tell what it meant. 'Oh, nothing much.' Her tone was now light and breezy. 'Just sorted a few things out at home and then popped over to see Gabby.'

'And how did that go?' he asked, recalling Helen's anger at her friend's betrayal of trust.

'It was a bit awkward at first, but we talked things over and it's all sorted now.'

'That's good, I'm glad. And the kids? Are they okay?'

'Esme's just picked up some bar work through a friend of a friend, so she's over the moon about the prospect of earning some money before she goes away. And Frankie's mostly been in his room playing video games and, it would seem, hogging every last plate we have there.'

Ben grinned. 'At least you know what to get him for Christmas, his own set of crockery. He'd love that.'

He laughed, and then there was a long silence that neither of them filled. It seemed they had officially run out of small talk and now all that was left was her answer.

'Yes.'

Ben was confused. What exactly was she talking about?

'Are you saying yes to the crockery idea or . . .'

Helen laughed. 'I'm saying yes to you of course, I'm saying yes to us. I've done a lot of thinking and I've talked it over with the kids, and I want you to know I'm all in on this, Ben. I want us to make a go of things.'

The next half hour went by in a blur as Ben, barely able to believe just how happy he was, talked through with Helen all the details of their decision. Ben would continue with the tour as planned, with Helen and the kids flying out to join him whenever her work and school holidays allowed. It would be tough being apart for so long, but with the first leg of the tour concluding mid-December they would have a month's break to look forward to before the South America leg kicked off in the new year. That could be a month when Helen and the kids could come to LA or Ben could go back to England, or, better still, they could all go somewhere none of them had ever been and have a proper adventure.

And in the interim they would do everything humanly possible to keep their relationship from the press. Although, Ben didn't hold out much hope of their news staying secret for very long, and in anticipation of this he told Helen he would appoint not only a PR consultant to be on call, but also a security team. The one thing Ben struggled to get Helen to agree to, however, was accepting his offer to give her the money to buy Adam out.

'Like I said before, I just think money confuses things,' she protested. 'I mean, what if for whatever reason things don't work out between us? What then? You'd co-own my house and I'd be in the same position I'm in now.'

'But the money wouldn't be mine, it'd be yours, a gift, I'd have no claim on it.'

Helen was horrified. 'We're talking about over three hundred thousand pounds, Ben, you can't give me that kind of money.'

'Who says?' he retorted. 'Listen, I learned a long time ago that money doesn't always solve problems; some things you can't change no matter how much cash you throw at them. But occasionally, like here, there are issues that money can resolve, so let me help. I've got more money than I could spend in this or any other lifetime, why not let me spend just a tiny fraction of it helping you?' He laughed and then added, 'Consider it part payment, for taking such good care of me this past month.'

'But apart from anything else, this is money you've worked hard for, made sacrifices for, it just doesn't feel right.'

'But what use is it, if I can't put it to work to help out a friend in need? If the tables were turned, I know you'd do the same for me, so don't pretend otherwise. Back when I had nothing you were there for me, so now I have something, let me use it to be there for you.'

There was a long silence, which Ben assumed was Helen wrestling with the decision, then finally she said, 'Okay. But only on the understanding that this is a loan. It might take me forever, but I'm going to pay you back, every penny.'

Thinking that this was an argument for another time, Ben agreed and told her he would arrange for the money to be sent over by the end of the day.

'I can't believe it,' said Helen, after they'd finished talking over potential dates to see each other again. 'We really are doing this, aren't we?'

'There might have been a twenty-year break,' said Ben. 'But yeah, I think this is us finally getting our happy ending.'

'I know it might be a bit too soon to say this but I don't care,' said Helen, her voice uncertain. 'I love you, Ben Baptiste.'

The smile on Ben's face at these words was a mile wide. 'I love you too, Helen Greene, and don't you ever forget it.'

The first thing Ben did after the call was contact Georgia, his PA, and ask her to vet security and PR teams in the UK for him, then as soon as that was done he called his long-time lawyer and business manager Adele Shapiro.

'Hey Ben,' she said. 'I heard you were back. I sincerely hope everything is well with you.'

'I'm good thanks,' said Ben. 'And I hope everything's good with you too.'

'You know me, Ben,' Adele replied, 'I'm always good. Now, please tell me you're calling because you've finally found some space in that packed schedule of yours to complete all the paperwork I sent you months ago.'

Ben laughed. The paperwork in question was still in an envelope on his desk at home. 'I'm sorry, Adele, I'm afraid that's not why I'm calling, but I promise to take a look through it tonight and get it couriered over to your office first thing in the morning.'

'Do I have your word?'

'You have my word.'

'Good,' she replied, 'now tell me how I can help you.'

Ben told her what he needed, and in return Adele assured him she could get everything he'd asked for done in the time frame required. As he ended the call, he felt exhilarated; this was really happening, he and Helen really were going to be together. He slid his phone into his back pocket as the rest of the band returned to the room and he checked his watch, surely an hour hadn't gone by without him noticing, but it had. If only the time left until he saw Helen again would fly by just as quickly. Ignoring his rumbling stomach and keen to put the morning's fiasco behind him, Ben set aside any notion of getting food and instead picked up his guitar and began tuning up.

As everyone got into their positions, on a whim Ben suggested they should warm up with one of their old songs, 'Bluelight', the track that had not only given them their name, but had been the first of the many songs he had composed in the wake of his split from Helen all those years ago. It was one of Bluelight's biggest hits, a firm fan favourite, which over the years had not only been included on countless film and TV soundtracks, but had also, because of its lovelorn lyrics, become something of a staple at weddings as a first dance for newly-wed couples. Rather than being a sad song about the pain of loss, 'Bluelight' was instead more of a meditation on the nature of love and how it should be celebrated, and, as the band began playing, Ben sang the opening lyrics, words that recalled through the artist's eye what it felt like to love and be loved. This time around there were no mistakes, both his playing and singing were perfect, and as he closed his eyes, imagining that he was with Helen, holding her in his arms, he imbued the very lyrics she had inspired with a passion and intensity with which he had never sung them before.

32

Helen

'Is this some sort of pathetic way of playing for time?' Adam's tone, though dismissive, had an element of doubt about it. 'You know we've got viewings booked all day tomorrow, do you really think I'm going to believe your lies and cancel them? You haven't got the money to buy me out, you've said so yourself. And even if you've managed to get a full-time position there's no way you'd be able to sort a mortgage out this quick.'

Helen cast her eyes towards the ceiling and briefly held the phone away from her ear to give herself a break from her estranged husband's whining. When she'd sent him a text first thing that morning telling him of her intention to buy out his share of the house, she knew he'd have questions but hadn't counted on him being quite so bitter about it. And he was being bitter. She could tell that deep down he knew she wasn't bluffing. Everything he was saying, all of his complaints, this was him hating the fact that there might actually be a possibility that it was true, that the hold he'd had over her these past few weeks was about to disappear. It was pathetic really; this was the sound of his puffed-up ego deflating, the growing realisation that he was no longer the only person with agency in their relationship.

She returned the phone to her ear. 'No need to worry about cancelling the viewings because I've already called the estate agent and taken the house off the market. I've also just this minute appointed a divorce solicitor, so if you have any complaints about what I've done I suggest you appoint one for yourself, and get them to chat to my lovely lady. The money's ready, so whenever you decide to be a grown-up about this, let me know, and we'll get all the paperwork sorted.'

Adam laughed bitterly. 'This is all his doing, isn't it? You've taken money from him, haven't you? You know, they have a name for women like you.'

Helen wanted nothing more than to end the call but she wasn't going to let him rile her, not today. 'Yes, they do, Adam, women like me are called winners.' And with that she put the phone down and, even though she knew it wasn't dignified, allowed herself to do a little dance of joy.

When she'd called Ben the night before and told him she wanted to give their relationship a go she'd had no idea that it might lead to a moment like this. While there were many reasons she wanted to be with Ben, his wealth and fame weren't amongst them. She loved Ben for who he was, how he saw the world, his kindness, his patience, his passion and creativity. She would've loved him had he been penniless, and she had indeed done so when they were young. If she'd been the sort of girl whose head was turned by boys with money or popularity, she could have had her pick of the boys at college. But she'd wanted Ben then because of who he was, and all these years later she wanted him for exactly the same reasons.

Still, accepting the money had been hard for her. She was proud and fiercely independent. She'd always hated being so dependent on Adam's salary, and had only agreed to go part-time in the first place because one of them needed to be around for the kids, and she'd squared it with herself because she'd believed they were a partnership, two people each doing their bit to take care of the family they cherished. Adam's betrayal had shattered that illusion beyond repair, but then Ben had made his no-strings offer, and had made her see it for what it was, one friend helping another out, and under those terms and conditions it was a gift she was finally happy to accept.

Glancing at the clock on the kitchen wall, Helen calculated what time it was in LA, a process that was swiftly becoming second nature to her. It would be two in the morning there and, as tempting as it was to think that he might be awake, Helen didn't want to take the chance of disturbing him if he wasn't. She missed him though. As wonderful as it was being able to speak to him or see him on a video call, it wasn't the same as having him next to her, being able to hold and touch him, and be held and touched in return. Still, she told herself they would make this work; at half term she'd be able to fly out to see him, and then before they knew it, it would be December and they'd have the luxury of an entire month together.

In the days that followed, despite the challenges of being in separate time zones a routine of sorts was established. Waking up each morning around seven, Helen would call Ben and they'd talk for an hour at what was the close of his day. In return he would call her at four in the afternoon just as his day was beginning in LA. In between they would exchange messages, sharing passing thoughts or observations, each letting the other know that they were thinking of them, each wanting to keep the connection between them alive.

'Well,' said Ben, his voice heavy with tiredness after a long day rehearsing, 'wish Esme all the best from me for her exam results today, won't you? She's a smart kid, I'm sure she'll get what she needs.'

'I'll tell her you're keeping your fingers crossed for her,' said Helen. 'You sound shattered, are you heading to bed?'

'I wish,' said Ben. 'I'm getting too old for this, but it's Leona's birthday and she's having a thing at a club downtown. I promised I'd show my face but I guarantee I won't be staying for long, the last thing she needs is me cramping her cool by falling asleep in a corner somewhere.'

'Maybe get them to put rehearsals back by an hour or two tomorrow so you can have a bit of a lie-in,' said Helen, 'you need to look after yourself.'

'Or maybe you could jump on a flight and do it for me?' Ben laughed. 'I know, wishful thinking, still, like we keep saying, it won't be long now.'

Ending the call, Helen briefly allowed herself to entertain the idea of booking a flight to LA to surprise Ben. What a joy it would be to see his face, what an utter delight just to hold him again. Reluctantly putting an end to that train of thought, she shifted her focus to the day ahead. Today was D-day for Esme, the day her daughter would find out if she'd got the grades she needed to go to university, and also the day that might signal the end of an era: her firstborn leaving home, flying the nest, making her own way in the world. Much as she knew and accepted that this was all part of the life she had chosen, it wasn't in the least bit a prospect she was looking forward to.

Half an hour later, having got dressed for the day, Helen prepared to wave Esme and a few of her friends off as they headed to school to collect their results.

'Are you sure you don't want me to come?' Helen asked.

'Not in a million years, Mum,' said Esme, who had been adamant from the beginning that neither of her parents would be joining her that morning. 'I promise I'll be fine.'

'And you'll call as soon as you know?'

'No, Mum, I'll wait until we're all drunk in the pub first,' said

Esme. 'Of course, I'll call you straight away!' She gave her mum a hug. 'You know you worry too much, don't you?'

Helen nodded, and tried not to cry. 'Don't blame me . . . it was in the job description.'

Once Esme was gone Helen tried her best to keep herself busy, tidying the kitchen, emptying and loading the dishwasher and fussing over Frankie, but even so she could feel the anxiety in her every bone. When, an hour later, as she changed the sheets on Frankie's bed, her phone rang, Helen practically let out a scream.

'How did you do?' she asked before her daughter could get a word out.

'I did it, Mum! I got the grades!' a delighted Esme shrieked. 'I'm going to Nottingham!'

Helen couldn't help but cry; her daughter had worked so hard for so long, and had so much to contend with at home too, that it was impossible not to shed tears of joy. They were of course mixed with tears of sadness. After all, come the end of September she would go from seeing her daughter every day to once a month if she was lucky, and then once she'd graduated, who knew? Helen herself had never moved back in with her mum after university, not really, and there was a very real chance that Esme might follow in her footsteps. So, yes, it was a bittersweet moment but she was happy for her daughter nonetheless. So happy in fact that when Esme asked if Adam could join them for the celebratory meal Helen had booked that afternoon, she'd agreed. 'This is your celebration, sweetie, and you can have anyone you want there, you deserve it.'

It was only after the call was over that Helen began to have second thoughts. Since having words with Adam about her plans to buy him out a little over a week ago, they hadn't spoken, not even when he'd dropped off Frankie after a weekend stay at his flat. According to an email from her solicitor the week before, Adam had now secured himself legal representation, meaning that the process of signing the house over to her had begun. And so, while she hoped Adam would be on his best behaviour for their daughter's sake, judging by his recent track record she couldn't necessarily guarantee it.

Much to Helen's delight, Frankie's mortification, and Sue's amusement, Esme, who had spent the entire day rejoicing with Josh and her friends, all but conga-ed her way across the floor of the upmarket eatery to their table.

'What's got two thumbs, two A's and an A star?' Esme pirouetted to a halt and grinned. 'Me!' she added, victoriously pulling her thumbs towards her chest.

'Well done, sweetheart,' said Sue, standing up to give her granddaughter a hug. 'Can't quite believe it: first a daughter, and now a granddaughter, off to uni! Maybe I should think about having a go myself!'

'You absolutely should, Gran,' said Esme as she hugged Helen, and bumped fists with her brother. 'You're like the cleverest old person I know, apart from Mum of course.' She gave Helen a cheeky wink to let her know she was joking and took her seat before glancing at the empty place setting between her and Frankie. 'Where's Dad?'

Helen looked up and, as if summoned by the question, Adam walked past the plate-glass window and into the restaurant, thankfully without Holly. She had half expected him to bring her along just to spite her and was relieved that he hadn't stooped so low. This was family time, and Holly didn't belong here.

'Sorry I'm late,' he said, clearly addressing Esme and Frankie rather than the whole table. He gave Esme a hug, 'Well done, you,

I always knew you'd do it.' Reaching into his pocket, he removed a bulging sparkly gold envelope and handed it to her. 'Just a little something to say well done.'

Esme ripped open the envelope and when she saw its contents she threw her arms around Adam's neck and kissed him. 'Wow, thanks, Dad, I don't think I've ever seen this much money in one go before. How much is here?'

'A thousand pounds,' he replied, unable to keep the smug tone from his voice.

Shocked, Helen opened her mouth ready to protest that this was way too much money to be giving an eighteen-year-old, but then at the last moment she stopped herself. This gift was a dig at her, Adam's way of exacting revenge for the other day while simultaneously demonstrating that Ben wasn't the only one with money. He could have this moment, she told herself, it was no skin off her nose. Twenty years from now, Esme would still have the gorgeous necklace Helen had given her first thing that morning, while Adam's money wouldn't constitute enough to even form a faded memory.

'Oh, how lovely,' said Helen, making sure to fill her every syllable with grace and benevolence. 'You'll have great fun spending that.'

'And it isn't for sensible things, either,' added Adam. 'You've got to promise to use it to enjoy yourself and have a good time. You deserve it.'

The inference was of course that Helen didn't think that Esme 'deserved' such a lavish gift and would only give their daughter money for boring things, like books or university supplies.

'She certainly does,' said Helen calmly. 'She's worked very hard indeed.'

'So, if I work hard on my A-levels when I'm Esme's age, do I get a thousand pounds too, Dad?'

'I bet it'll be even more than a thousand,' said Helen a touch gleefully, before her husband could reply. 'That is, of course, adjusting for inflation.'

After this exchange their attention soon turned to the menu, and, after much deliberation and sending the waiter away three times, they ordered their food along with, at Adam's insistence, two bottles of Champagne.

The meal itself was a strained affair. Whenever Helen asked Adam a question directly, no matter how innocent, his answer, if he bothered to respond at all, was always directed towards one or other of the kids, as if Helen and Sue were ghostly apparitions whom he chose not to believe in. While Sue gave Helen several meaningful looks during the course of the meal, Helen was thankful that both Esme and Frankie seemed oblivious to their father's deliberate rudeness.

Later, as the waiter cleared the table, Esme picked up her phone to check on arrangements for later on. Amongst her friends, plans for the evening's entertainment had been building. There was talk of going clubbing, possibilities of a party at a friend of a friend's house, and some people had even suggested driving out to Hartshead Tower and staying all night to watch the sunrise. In typical teenage fashion, however, Esme was undecided which of these plans she most wanted to be a part of and, even after discussing it with the table, seemed no closer to an answer. Finally, she announced she was going to call Josh, but as she glanced down at her screen her phone rang.

'Josh, I was just about to—' Esme stopped suddenly, and then her expression changed as if he had just told her something important. Taking her phone away from her ear, she tapped the screen and slowly, gradually, a look of horror overtook her.

'Es, darling, what is it? What's wrong?' asked Helen, jumping to her feet. Her mind was racing. What on earth could have caused this reaction in her daughter? Was it to do with her A-levels? Or worse still her university place?

'Esme, sweetie, tell me what's wrong,' pleaded Helen, but Esme seemed to be so traumatised that she couldn't even speak. Instead, her hands shaking, she handed her phone to her mother. Confused, Helen stared down at the screen, trying to make sense of what she saw. Esme's browser was open on the BBC news page and the headline at the top of the story she'd been reading said: 'Troubled UK Bluelight frontman feared dead in car crash horror'.

Part 4

33

Helen

As the chief steward came through the First-Class cabin gently informing passengers that the plane would soon be landing, there was a small flurry of activity. Tray tables were stowed, laptops closed and seats put into an upright position, but Helen, who had done little other than stare blankly out of the window next to her for much of the flight, did nothing, aside from turn to look at Nathan in the seat beside her. The two hadn't spoken much during the journey, each lost in their own thoughts. Nevertheless, as he reached a hand across and placed it gently on hers, she knew that they were both thinking the same thing: that they were now another step closer to one of the most difficult times they would ever have to face.

As had been the case countless times since it had happened, Helen's mind went back to that night, that awful night, the night that she lost Ben. She could never recall much about her immediate reaction on seeing the news about the accident on Esme's phone, or indeed the minutes or hours it had taken for them to get back home. Her clearest memories of that time were of them all sitting in the living room, the TV on and playing the wall-to-wall news coverage: Ben's image flashing up on screen again and again, reports live from the scene of the crash, the carnage itself hidden by fire trucks and ambulances. Time and again she'd called his number hoping, praying, that somehow he was okay, that he might pick up and tell her that against all odds he had survived.

The call confirming Helen's worst fears had come in the middle of the night as she sat on the sofa surrounded by her family. Even Adam had stayed, all trace of his earlier hostility replaced with care and concern for her and the kids. She had left messages for everyone she could think of, begging, pleading for news about Ben, and had been about to book herself on the next flight to LA when her phone rang. The screen showed the call was coming from the US but it wasn't a number she recognised. Her rational brain told her she should answer it; after all, it could be someone responding to a message she'd left or even Ben on a different number. But another part of her, the part that was terrified to its very core, the part that feared the worst, hesitated.

'You need to answer it, love.' Her mum's voice had been gentle but firm. 'Whatever's happened, you need to know.'

Although she'd never spoken to Rocco, Helen recognised his voice instantly. There was a different quality to it, however, and he sounded more subdued, less assured, than she remembered him being from the TV press conference he'd given all those weeks ago.

'Is that Helen?'

'Yes.'

'It's Rocco . . . Have you got someone with you? Someone who'll look after you?'

Helen stood up and felt her head swim. Why wasn't he just telling her Ben was safe?

'Tell me he's okay,' she demanded. 'Tell me he's all right.'

'I can't,' said Rocco, sounding almost broken. 'He's gone, Helen. He's gone . . . The paramedics . . . they tried everything they could to save him . . . but it just wasn't enough. I'm so sorry.'

Helen felt like she'd suddenly been submerged underwater, all the sounds around her muffled, her vision distorted and blurry, and breathing almost impossible. Before her legs could give way she slumped down heavily on to the sofa, still clutching her phone as her family anxiously gathered round her.

Once she recovered, Rocco told her everything that he knew. That Ben had been driving home after Leona's party and some guy coming the other way had lost control of his car, crossed the central reservation and hit Ben head on. 'The emergency services were there in minutes,' he told her. 'But it was too late for both of them.'

Rocco had promised to be in touch when he had any more to tell her, and with that the call was over. Though she had fought to find the words to break the news to her family, the grief that had gripped her in that moment refused to let her speak a word. Instead, she had allowed herself to be surrounded by her family, allowed herself to be enfolded in their embrace.

It had all been too horrible to comprehend, too unreal to try to make any sense of. Ben couldn't be dead, she'd told herself, he just couldn't. Not when they'd only just found each other again, not when they had so much to look forward to, so many plans for the future. Life couldn't be this cruel, couldn't be this unfair, could it? She'd told herself that this had to be a nightmare, some awful dream from which she would wake at any second; it couldn't be reality, it just couldn't be the truth.

It had been just after midnight when the doorbell rang, shooting a shiver of panic down Helen's spine.

'Don't worry,' Sue said, reading her daughter's mind. 'If it's a journalist I promise you I'll make them regret knocking on your door! Filthy bloodsuckers, the lot of them! Nothing but vultures feeding on other people's pain!'

As her mum left the room, Helen pulled Esme and Frankie to her and held them tightly. They'd both been in a state of shock since hearing the news, and in the depths of her own grief she was wary of losing sight of them, even for a moment. 'We'll get through this, I promise you,' she told them. 'I don't know how, but we will.'

Hearing her mum talking to someone in the hallway, Helen got to her feet, terrified that a journalist had managed to worm their way in, while at the same time hoping it might be true so that she could have someone on whom to focus all of the rage and anger that now flowed through her veins. It wasn't a journalist, however, it was Gabby, who without saying a word wrapped Helen in a huge hug as Sue disappeared into the living room, closing the door behind her.

'I've only just heard,' Gabby said eventually. 'I can't believe it, I'm so sorry.'

Unable to speak, Helen sobbed in her friend's arms, finally letting out all the anguish she'd been holding back for fear of scaring the children. The sobs that escaped from her were violent and uncontrollable, convulsing her body. Again, time seemed to lose all meaning, and Helen had no idea how long they stood like that, Gabby holding her while wave after wave of pain possessed her.

Eventually, however, it had subsided enough to allow Gabby to lead her to the kitchen, where she'd sat her down on the sofa. No sooner than Gabby had presented her with a hot mug of tea, the doorbell rang again, and moments later Sue appeared in the kitchen doorway with Ben's brother Nathan by her side.

'I hope it's okay,' he said as Sue and Gabby quietly left the room. 'I didn't know what to do, where to go, but then I found myself coming here and it just felt right.'

'I'm glad you did.' Helen stepped towards him, wrapping him in her arms. His frame was different to Ben's, more solid, less muscular, but it was reassuring nonetheless.

'I just can't believe it,' Nathan said as they sat down. 'I just keep thinking there's been some sort of mistake. Have you heard anything from anyone out there? In LA I mean?'

Helen felt sick. Nathan didn't know that Ben was gone. She couldn't understand why Rocco had called her but not Ben's own flesh and blood. Hadn't Ben got around to telling Rocco about their recent reconciliation? It was the only reason she could think of why no one had thought to contact him, and now here she was, having to break the news to Ben's brother.

'I'm so sorry, Nathan,' she said, holding him tight. 'Ben's gone.'

Nathan covered his face with his hands, letting out a howl of pain, as Helen too sobbed. It was a long time before either of them could speak.

'I can't believe he's gone,' he said eventually. 'All those years . . . all that time we never spoke . . . time I'll never get back with him. How could I have been so stupid? He was my only brother. How could I have let anything come between us? How could I have been so selfish?'

Helen hugged him again as he convulsed in tears. 'He loved you,' she reassured him. 'And I know it meant the world to him that you'd found each other again.'

Nathan rubbed his eyes and looked at Helen, his expression softening. 'He loved you, you know. Not that he needed to tell me that. It was obvious. The way his face lit up whenever he talked about you . . . and, I don't know, there was just something different about him.'

Helen smiled, momentarily recalling better times, better days. 'He was a truly amazing person.'

'And a great brother too.' Nathan sniffed, and dried his eyes with the back of his hand. 'We had some right laughs as kids. This one time before Mum got sick, he showed me where our parents hid our unwrapped Christmas presents. Every Saturday morning on the lead-up to Christmas, while Mum and Dad were busy, we'd get everything out, carefully open up the boxes and have a little play before putting it all back! We were such little devils back then.' He sighed heavily. 'It was nice though, having a secret just between the two of us.'

Helen smiled, thinking of her own special moments with Ben. She couldn't believe there weren't going to be any more. She couldn't fathom that this really was the end of Ben's story.

They'd eventually joined the others in the living room, no one able to sleep, no one wanting to be alone, then just as it was beginning to get light Nathan announced that he was heading home.

'Are you sure?' she asked, not wanting him to have to face his grief alone. 'Why don't you stay with us for a bit? We've got plenty of room.'

'Thanks,' he said, 'I'll be okay. But let me know if you hear anything else . . . I mean . . . I don't know what's happening about the funeral . . . I suppose it's too early to say but . . .'

'Of course,' Helen replied, taken aback by the thought of something so horrible, so final. 'The moment I hear anything, I'll call.'

Gabby and Adam had left not long after Nathan, and eventually Helen persuaded Sue and the kids to go up to bed to try to get some sleep, before heading upstairs herself. Sitting down on her bed, she lifted up her pillow and removed the T-shirt Ben had accidentally left behind in his hurry to pack. When she'd first discovered it, wedged at the side of the bed, two days after he'd gone, she'd briefly thought about washing it and sending it on to him, but then she'd lifted it to her nose, and it had smelled so strongly of him that she'd decided to keep it. She'd felt foolish at the time, like a lovestruck teenager, but it was a way of feeling close to him while they were so far apart. Lying down on the bed, she closed her eyes and pressed it to her face, inhaling deeply the smell of his aftershave, his deodorant, his sweat. With each breath, she imagined him lying next to her, her body pressed against his, their hearts beating in unison, and for a moment, just a fraction of a second, to her at least, he was alive.

In the days that followed, Helen had barely been able to bring herself to eat or sleep. Unable to stand helplessly by, watching her daughter fall apart, in the end Sue had persuaded her to see a doctor, who prescribed anti-depressants. Although they'd undoubtedly helped to dull the sharp edges of her pain, Helen hated how they made her feel and within a week, without telling her mother, she'd stopped taking them.

She'd been lying in bed, the afternoon sun peeking through the closed curtains, when Rocco called and told her that all arrangements for Ben's funeral had been made.

'It's going to be here in LA,' he said. 'You could fly in a couple of days before, get yourself settled, and then fly out whenever you're ready afterwards. And it won't cost you a thing, it'll all be covered.'

Her first instinct had been to tell him that she wasn't coming. After all, how could she travel halfway around the world when being away from her family even for a short while caused her to virtually crumble to pieces? And anyway, what good would attending do? Ben was gone, it wouldn't bring him back and it wasn't as though she had any memories of him in LA or any desire to meet Rocco in person. In the end, she'd told him she would think about it, but then that same evening Nathan called to say he'd received the same invitation and had decided to go. 'I know I'll regret it if I don't,' he told her. 'And if you don't go, I think you'll feel the same.' Helen wrestled with the question all of that night, trying to decide what the right thing to do might be. Would she regret not going as Nathan had suggested? Would she one day be overcome with guilt that she hadn't said her final goodbye to Ben when she'd had the chance? Though it was impossible to know for sure she couldn't bear to take the risk, and the next day she called Rocco and told him she'd be there.

Rocco had taken care of everything, and a week later a top-of-the-range Mercedes with blacked-out windows had pulled up outside the house, to drive her and Nathan down to Heathrow. That night they'd stayed in two luxury suites at the nearby Hilton and the following morning boarded a Virgin Atlantic flight to LA.

And now here she was on a plane about to land in the city Ben had called home for so long. It still didn't seem real, a fact not helped by the five-star treatment meted out to them during the flight. Helen wasn't used to luxury travel of any kind, let alone the sort that served Champagne on arrival or that offered goody bags stuffed with expensive skincare products, and, even if she had been, she was in no state to appreciate it. So, the fizz sat untouched, the goody bags politely refused and the inflight entertainment left unexplored.

On landing, the plane taxied to the gate, and after a short wait the First-Class cabin was disembarked. On the tarmac, Helen and Nathan were met by airport staff and immediately escorted away from the main throng of passengers to a waiting black BMW. As the car pulled away, Helen exchanged a look with Nathan similar to ones they'd been trading since they'd arrived at Heathrow. It was a look that attempted to express the strangeness of their journey: how they were getting a glimpse into a world usually only seen by a select few and yet, because of the circumstances of their journey, they couldn't even remotely bring themselves to enjoy it. All the luxury, all the privilege, was wasted on them. The equivalent of

A Song of Me and You

showing a bright technicolour movie to people who could only see
the world in black and white.

They were taken in the car to what they were informed was
LA-X's private VIP terminal, a place normally reserved for celebrities and millionaires, but on this occasion greeting a part-time
primary school teacher and a window fitter. Inside the terminal,
Helen and Nathan politely declined the offer of a suite in which
to freshen up and went straight through to security. Here there
were none of the customary queues that normally dogged this
part of the journey; instead all the required checks were completed
in a matter of mere minutes, and with a smile. Finally, they were
shown to the exit, fully expecting to be swept into another anonymous luxury vehicle, but as the main doors slid back they
revealed a large Hawaiian-shirted figure waiting on the other side:
Rocco, the man whose actions had indirectly led to the death of
the man she had loved.

34

Helen

Helen had thought a great deal about this moment both on the long drive down to London, and on the plane on the way over: how might she react to coming face to face with this man. Had Rocco not forced Ben to carry on with the tour, her beloved wouldn't have gone back to LA, to the life he loathed, and above all the fate that awaited him there. Helen recalled some of the many scenarios she'd imagined, everything from hurling herself at Rocco in fury through to quietly and calmly saying to his face exactly what she thought of him. But in the end, as she and Nathan came to a halt in front of his huge frame, Helen was surprised to discover that pity not anger was her overwhelming emotion. Here before her was a man people both feared and admired and whose favour many courted, but in this moment she felt like she could see him for what he really was: just another in a long line of broken lonely men who had convinced themselves that power and wealth could fill the empty void at the centre of their souls.

'Helen, good to meet you, albeit under such terrible circumstances.' Rocco held out his hand but she ignored it. Seemingly unperturbed by the snub, he returned his hand to his pocket, choosing to acknowledge Nathan with nothing more than a slight nod of the head. From what Helen had gathered, Nathan and Rocco had met several times before over the years and there was little love lost between them.

'I've had your luggage taken to my car and I'll drive you to Ben's place in Malibu myself. I thought you might prefer staying there rather than in some impersonal hotel. That said, if you don't like the idea I can get you booked into the Beverly Wilshire, if you prefer.'

'My brother's place will be fine, thanks,' said Nathan pointedly, clearly wanting to remind Rocco that he had far more claim on Ben than Rocco ever could.

Again, Rocco appeared unruffled by the slight. 'Like I said, it's up to you.'

They followed him through a set of automatic doors to a silver Bentley, an attendant standing next to it holding the door open. Helen and Nathan climbed into the back of the car, while Rocco reached into his wallet, withdrew several notes and discreetly handed them to the valet, then took his keys, got into the driver's seat and started up the engine.

As he made his way out of the airport and on to the freeway, Rocco went through the arrangements for the next few days. 'I'm sure you must be tired after your journey,' he began, 'so there's nothing on the schedule for the rest of today. I've told Ben's staff to look after you and make sure you have everything you need, so if you want something just ask. While I understand you probably think you already know what you're wearing to the funeral I've taken the liberty of arranging for a stylist to drop by the house tomorrow afternoon with some alternatives. Wear their clothes, don't wear their clothes, it makes no odds to me, but I'd hate for you not to be comfortable. There's a table booked for dinner for the three of us tomorrow night at Morihiro, but if you don't feel up to it just tell Ben's housekeeper and she'll contact one of my assistants. On the day itself a car will come to pick you up and take you to Westwood Village Memorial Park. I've tried to keep the numbers attending the service to a bare minimum, but as you might imagine, Ben knew a lot of people, so that hasn't been easy.

There will be a larger memorial service in the afternoon, which you're welcome to attend,' he briefly caught Helen's eye in the rear-view mirror before looking away, 'although I understand completely if you'd rather not. As requested, your flight back to the UK is booked for the following day. Before then, I'd be grateful, Helen, if you could set aside maybe an hour or two at some point. I just need to go over a couple of things before you leave.'

Having already made up her mind that she wasn't going to sit through dinner with Rocco, Helen recoiled at the thought of having to spend yet more time in the company of this man. She guessed he probably wanted to talk about strategies for dealing with the press should they get wind of the extent of her relationship with Ben, but she would make sure that their conversation, if it happened, would take a lot less time than a whole hour.

'Okay,' she replied, 'I'm sure I can do that.'

Everyone in the car fell into silence, allowing Helen's mind to wander, and as they hit the coastal road and the sea loomed into view she wondered how many times Ben had taken this exact route, seen the same scenery flash past, the cloudless blue sky, the turquoise waters of the Pacific welcoming him home.

A panicked thought occurred to her and she turned her head to look at Rocco and found that his gaze was already fixed on her in the rear-view mirror.

'We've already gone past the spot,' he said, as if reading her mind. 'I got them to clear away all the flowers and tributes last week so you wouldn't have to see them.'

Helen supposed that he wanted her to thank him for this small kindness, but she couldn't bring herself to and so remained silent for the rest of the journey. A short while later, Rocco turned off the highway, and was soon slowing down to a crawl as they approached a set of black gates, which Helen guessed led to Ben's house. The area surrounding the gates was covered in a carpet of flowers and tributes, and there were at least a hundred people gathered there, some in groups, some standing alone, but all staring at the gates as if they imagined Ben was behind them.

At the sight of the fans Rocco swore under his breath. 'I've already had this lot moved on once today but they just keep coming back. It's because of the funeral, they want to be close to Ben and this the only way they can do it, poor buggers. I'll get someone to deal with them later.'

As the car waited at the entrance for the gates to open, the fans' attention turned to their vehicle. Even though she was hidden from sight behind privacy glass Helen couldn't help but feel exposed, as if the eyes of everyone there were upon her, and she automatically turned her head away and shielded her face with her hand. At last, the gates slid back, revealing a line of security guards who held back the crowd long enough for Rocco to drive through.

As the car made its way up a long and winding drive Helen was reminded of the approach to the Cornwall house, only this was about a hundred times grander, and the house itself about three times the size and very different in design. Where the Cornwall house had been all angular shapes, Ben's home was a series of sweeping curves and glass, designed, she imagined, to echo the stunning seascape it overlooked.

The moment the car came to a halt Ben's front door opened, and a man came down the steps and began unloading the luggage.

'So, I'll see you tomorrow,' said Rocco. 'Any problems, just give me a call, but Lucía and the rest of the staff should be able to look after you from here on.'

It was only when Rocco had pulled away that Nathan spoke his first words since leaving the airport. 'I can't tell you how much I hate that man,' he said. 'Who does he think he is?'

'I know,' said Helen, putting a comforting hand on Nathan's shoulder. 'But at least he didn't hang around. Come on, let's get inside.'

At the door they were greeted by a middle-aged woman with dark brown hair and a warm smile. She introduced herself as Lucía, Ben's housekeeper, and after expressing her condolences she invited them both inside.

'Would you like to see the house?' she asked, after leading them both to the kitchen, pouring out two glasses of ice tea from a pitcher for them. 'Mr Baptiste was always very proud of it.'

Helen sensed that perhaps the pride taken in the house was Lucía's, and that keeping Ben's home pristine for him, even though he was no longer alive, was her way of showing them how much she cared for him.

'That would be wonderful,' said Helen, even though she would rather have gone to her room. 'Please lead the way.'

The house was huge, just one vast room after another, and while it was undeniably impressive Helen was surprised by how impersonal it felt. Everything was tidy, nothing out of place. All the furniture and decoration though clearly high-end seemed strangely generic, more fitting of a luxury hotel than somebody's home.

With the tour over, Helen was shown to her room and, thanking Lucía for her time, she closed the door and sat down on the bed. She thought about her family back in the UK and tried to imagine what they might be doing with their evenings. Esme would be at work, most likely looking forward to the end of her shift. Frankie would be in his bedroom watching Japanese anime films on his laptop or playing computer games, surrounded by plates loaded with toast crumbs and glasses bearing the residue of fruit juice. Meanwhile, there would be every chance that Sue, having said that she was staying up to watch the soaps she'd recorded, would be snoring gently on the sofa downstairs. Even though it was only just over twenty-four hours since she'd last seen them, she missed them all desperately and couldn't help but wonder if they were safe. Losing Ben so unexpectedly had made her feel that nothing and no one was safe, that catastrophe could strike anywhere at any time.

She picked up her phone to call them but then changed her mind at the last moment. Was she really in the right frame of mind to talk to them in a way that wouldn't worry them? She wasn't at all sure she was. Instead, she sent a message telling them she'd arrived safely, reminding them how much she loved them and promising that she would call first thing in the morning.

Closing her eyes, she lay back on the bed, and felt a wave of exhaustion wash over her. Her body, still on UK time, was telling her to sleep, but she knew that if she gave in she would spend the entirety of her time here disorientated and confused, perhaps even more so than she already felt.

A thought occurred to her, and she went downstairs to ask Lucía if there was another way out of the grounds other than the main entrance. The housekeeper looked at Helen quizzically, and tried to talk her out of it, telling her that she would get a driver to take her anywhere she wanted to go. But when Helen insisted, Lucía finally relented, and pointed her in the direction of a service entrance at the side of the property.

Donning a sun hat and sunglasses, Helen made her way off the grounds and on to a small road leading to the front of Ben's estate. All she'd really wanted was to take a closer look at the flowers and cards the fans had left for him. She recalled her own reaction to the unexpected deaths of stars like Amy Winehouse, Prince, Jeff Buckley and Kurt Cobain. While she hadn't joined in the public outpouring of grief as some fans had done, in her own way she had felt personally affected by their passing. At the time she'd reasoned that it made sense – after all, through their art these performers had made deep connections with her and millions of others. Of course fans would feel a sense of ownership, a sense of kinship and loss when the artist whose work they adored passed away. But even so it felt odd and disconcerting to be joined in her grief by legions of strangers across the world who didn't even know of her existence, who had no idea what Ben meant to her.

Reaching the gate, Helen was surprised to find there the same number of people, if not more, milling around the entrance, and she wondered if perhaps Rocco had changed his mind about moving the crowds of fans on. She felt bad for them, these people wanting to express their grief for Ben but having no one officially acknowledge their efforts. Knowing how much Ben had loved his fans it felt wrong, and this, she decided, was a small thing she could do on his behalf without causing any trouble.

She bent down to read one of the cards, and as she did so a young woman, eyes red from crying, knelt down beside her and carefully placed a bouquet of flowers amongst the others.

'I just can't believe he's gone.'

Helen looked up and was surprised to see that the woman was addressing her.

'Me either,' she said. 'He was wonderful, wasn't he?'

Drying her eyes, the woman smiled sadly at Helen. 'There was no one else like him. He was one of a kind, a supernova. I live all the way over in Washington but I had to come and pay my respects, to be here. I just had to. His music meant so much to me, it got me through so many dark times, I felt like it was the least I could do.' She paused and looked at Helen intently. 'Is that a British accent I hear?'

Helen nodded warily, fearing that she might have said something that had revealed too much.

'Oh, that's amazing,' said the young woman. 'I'd love to visit the UK one day, especially Manchester, where Ben was from. Have you ever been there?'

Helen nodded. 'A few times.'

'And is it as great as people say? I always thought it would have to be to produce someone special like Ben.'

Helen smiled awkwardly, and was about to make her excuses when the woman continued. 'I know this is going to sound crazy, but . . . I don't know . . . it feels so good to meet someone who loved Ben as much as I did . . . can I . . . would you mind if I gave you a hug? I could really do with one right now.'

At first, as this woman, this stranger, held her and began quietly weeping, Helen felt stiff and uncomfortable, but slowly her self-consciousness began to melt away, along with all the barriers she'd put up against her grief in the wake of Ben's death. Soon she was crying too, hot tears streaming down her face, and there they stood, two strangers, bound together in sorrow at the loss of a man who in very different ways had changed their lives. And it crossed Helen's mind that even if the funeral turned out to be the celebrity circus she feared, here at the very least with this stranger Ben would be mourned properly.

35

Helen

It was just after nine the next day and Helen was showering following an invigorating early-morning walk along the beach. The day before, after her time at the front gate with Ben's fans, she'd returned to the house and immediately asked Lucía to cancel dinner plans with Rocco, and then spent the afternoon with Nathan down by the sea. They'd eaten together that evening and then got an early night, hoping to get rid of their jet lag. Despite her exhaustion, however, Helen had found it difficult to sleep, and woken almost every hour on the hour, until a little before five she'd given up all hope of sleep and had gone outside for a walk just as the sun was beginning to rise.

With the exception of an early-morning jogger, she'd had the entire beach to herself and had been glad of the solitude. Gazing out to sea and taking in the vast horizon laid out before her, the world seemed so huge and she herself so small in comparison that it had given her some much-needed perspective. There was a world outside of her head, the sea seemed to remind her, everything was not as lost as it might seem. Tempting though it was to give in to her grief, to let it subsume her, she had to stay strong, for Esme, for Frankie, and for herself too. She would get through this, she thought as she watched the dawn break over the multimillion-dollar beachfront houses lining the cliff edge, bathing the sand at her feet in its golden glow. Life wouldn't always feel this dark, she would find the strength to keep going, and once the funeral was over she would make it her mission to find both light and hope again.

Returning to the house, she had shed her clothes and showered, and, after slipping on a T-shirt and a pair of jeans, Helen did her hair and make-up before tapping out a quick message home.

'Hi gang, love you very much. Hope you've all had a great day. Love you all to the moon and back. Xxx'

She pressed send and then made her way down to the kitchen to find Nathan being waited on by Lucía. He was sitting at the kitchen island, his face bewildered at the vast array of breakfast delights, everything from platters of fruit and pastries through to eggs and bacon.

'I only came looking for a cup of coffee,' he said in a low voice once Lucía was out of earshot, 'and she's made all this!' Nathan pulled out a chair for Helen. 'You've got to help me make a dent in it, the last thing on earth I want to do is insult her.'

Though Helen didn't have much of an appetite, she sat down next to Nathan, grabbed a bowl and began spooning in chunks of mango and pineapple just as Lucía reappeared in the kitchen.

'So sorry to disturb you when you're eating, madam, but there's someone here to see you. Would you like me to send them through?'

'Is it Rocco?' she asked. She wasn't at all sure she had the stomach for him this early in the morning.

Lucía shook her head. 'No, it's one of Mr Baptiste's colleagues, Ms Ferreira.'

Helen was confused. She didn't know Ben had any colleagues.

'I think she's talking about Leona, from the band,' explained Nathan. 'Bluelight's bass player.'

The woman waiting in the lounge looked every inch the rock star that Helen now knew her to be. She was dressed all in black: a battered-looking leather biker jacket over a vintage Blondie T-shirt and tight black jeans and boots. Her dark brown dreadlocked hair was swept up into an elaborate knot on top of her head.

Without a word she rushed over to Helen, wrapping her arms around her in a tight, heartfelt embrace. It should have felt awkward, being hugged so fiercely by this woman she'd never met, but instead it felt completely natural. This was someone who had clearly loved Ben, someone who was grieving for his loss, and somehow it didn't matter that this was their first meeting, somehow it just felt right.

'I'm so sorry,' Leona sobbed. 'If things had been different . . . if I hadn't had that stupid party . . . Ben might still be here.'

'It was an accident,' said Helen gently. 'It's not your fault.' She resisted the temptation once again to lay blame at Rocco's door. Instead, she said, 'It was just one of those things: a random, senseless tragedy that could have happened to anyone . . . it was just bad luck it was Ben.'

'I'm Leona by the way,' she said, letting go of Helen and taking a step back. 'Ben spoke so much about you that I almost felt like I knew you, so when I heard you were here I just had to come and pay my respects. I know you'll be at the . . . you'll be there tomorrow . . . but I wanted to give you my condolences in private, without an audience. Ben was such a beautiful soul, it's such a shock he's been taken when he still had so much life to live.'

The three stood in silence for a moment, and then Helen, realising that Nathan had yet to speak, made the introductions.

'Hey Nathan,' said Leona, and before he could object she folded him into an embrace too. 'I'm so sorry for your loss. Ben told me you guys made up while he was in England. I'm so glad you managed to work things out between you while there was time.'

'I just wish we'd done it sooner,' he replied, and then there was an awkward pause and Helen sensed that Nathan was desperate to make his excuses. Perhaps he just needed some time alone, or perhaps he was finding it difficult talking about his brother to a complete stranger, but whatever the reason it was clear he wanted to leave.

'Anyway,' he said, nodding towards Leona. 'It was lovely to meet you and I'm sure I'll see you again at some point tomorrow but I'm going to grab my breakfast and take it up to my room, if that's okay.'

'Sure,' said Leona. 'See you tomorrow.'

Helen and Leona made their way through to the kitchen, before heading to the table out on the terrace.

'I always forget what an incredible view this place has,' said Leona, removing a pair of sunglasses from her jacket pocket and slipping them on. 'Ben really did hit the jackpot when he found this spot.'

'It's stunning, isn't it?' agreed Helen. 'It's a far cry from where we grew up in Manchester.'

Leona smiled. 'I know what you mean. I sometimes forget just how lucky we've been, and then family come over and visit and they're completely wowed by something I'm ashamed to say I take for granted. There's nothing quite like seeing what you have through fresh eyes to make you appreciate it.'

As they sat side by side Leona gave Helen a potted version of her history, how she'd grown up in Devon, her love of music encouraged by her parents who had been musicians in the Seventies, playing in a variety of bands that had come close to success but which had never quite made it. 'Because they knew how hard it could be,' she said, 'they did everything they could to talk me out of making music my life, but they were never going to stop me. Thankfully, after a few false starts, I joined Bluelight, and the rest is history.'

'And you don't have any regrets?' asked Helen. She'd meant the question innocently enough but the moment she said it she wished she hadn't. Just because Ben had come to feel trapped by the success of the band didn't necessarily mean the others would feel the same. 'I'm sorry,' she added quickly. 'Don't answer that. It was a stupid question.'

'It's not at all, I totally understand where you're coming from. I know how Ben felt. He loved music, he loved writing songs, playing them to fans, watching them fall under his spell. It was the business side of things that got him down, and I'm afraid to say that he bore the brunt of it. But the music, that was his passion.' She paused and gave Helen a look that she found hard to read. 'Has anyone taken you down to the studio yet?' Helen shook her head and, standing up, Leona reached out a hand.

'Come on,' she said. 'I'll take you.'

Thrilled at the thought of going to somewhere that meant something to Ben, Helen messaged Nathan, but he didn't want to join them. Grabbing her jacket, Helen followed Leona out to the front of the house to a bright red sports car.

'I know it's a cliché,' said Leona of the 1964 Porsche 901 as she turned on the ignition, 'but I needed a new car and wanted a vintage model. When I saw this it was just love at first sight.'

The journey to their destination flew by as they continued to find out more about each other. Leona told her all about her twenty-year relationship with her husband, who she'd met not long after the band moved to LA permanently. At the time he was a struggling music video director working on low-budget productions and now, all these years later, he was a highly regarded director, a number of whose films Helen had seen. In turn Helen found herself opening up about her and Ben and their time in England. But rather than feeling sad as she related their story, more often than not she found herself smiling. The memories she and Ben had created were so precious that it was tempting to keep them hidden away under lock and key for protection, but the more she spoke the more she realised that like a treasured piece of jewellery they needed to be enjoyed, not stuck in a box gathering dust.

'It sounds like you guys really made the most of every moment you had,' said Leona sometime later as they pulled into a parking lot just off Melrose Avenue.

'We did,' said Helen. 'I just wish we'd had more of them.'

They walked past an array of tattoo parlours, cafés, vintage-clothing stores and record shops until finally they came to a halt in front of a heavy, industrial-steel door sandwiched between a shop called Psychic Cloud and a sporting goods store called McGovern's.

'Here it is,' said Leona, pulling a set of keys from her jacket pocket. 'This is where the magic happens.' She looked at Helen and grinned. 'I know it doesn't look like much, but believe me this place is special.'

They made their way along a dimly lit corridor, through several doors, then down a flight of steps to a set of double doors, one of which Leona opened, saying with a flourish, 'Welcome to the Bunker.'

As Leona turned on the lights Helen waited for her eyes to adjust and had to blink several times before she could see well enough to look around the room. In one corner there was a drum kit and next to it a bass guitar on a stand. Opposite the drums were what looked like a set of keyboards with a sheet over the top, and in the middle of the space stood two electric guitars and one acoustic, and next to them a microphone.

'This was one of Ben's happy places,' said Leona. 'Our rehearsal studio. We could've gone to bigger or better spaces, or even built our own from scratch, but this was the first place we came to work in after we moved out here and Ben always loved it. He said it reminded him of how things were at the beginning, when we started out, when it felt like it was just the four of us against the world.'

Helen smiled; she could so easily picture Ben saying something like that and really meaning it. The beautifully decorated houses in jaw-dropping settings and expensive cars were the trappings of fame, but not where his heart truly lay. That place was here, free from the distractions of celebrity, where he could focus all of his attention on the one thing he loved doing more than anything else.

'Anyway,' said Leona, 'let me show you why I really brought you here,' and she pointed over Helen's shoulder.

Helen turned around and the sight before her took her breath away. Hanging in a frame on the wall above a battered leather sofa was a drawing she recognised instantly, even though she hadn't seen it in decades. While the paper had yellowed over time there was no mistaking it. It was the drawing she had given to Ben for his eighteenth birthday. Back then she'd had no money to buy him anything special, but in her spare time when she was meant to be working on pieces for her A-level art portfolio, instead she'd concentrated all her efforts on a detailed pencil sketch based on a photograph of the two of them taken at a party on the night they'd finally confessed their love for one another.

'I don't understand,' said Helen. 'What's this doing here?'

'It's been in every rehearsal studio we've ever used,' Leona explained. 'It hung on the wall when we wrote the first album back in London and came with us when we moved to LA. Ben said it was his favourite work of art, he called it his inspiration, his lucky charm. I suppose I just wanted you to know that you've always been a force for good in his life. Tomorrow is going to be tough, but just hold on to how much you meant to him. Hold on to the fact that even back then he always thought the world of you.'

36

Helen

It was late afternoon when Leona finally dropped Helen back at Ben's. Getting out of the car, she gave Helen a hug. 'Thanks so much for spending some time with me,' she said. 'It's really meant a lot.'

'It's meant a lot to me too,' said Helen, thinking about her framed drawing on the wall of the recording studio. 'Thanks so much for coming to see me.'

Helen watched as Leona's Porsche pulled away, and then finally she turned towards the house just as the front door opened to reveal an unnerved Nathan, dressed in a black suit and tie, looking for all the world like he was just about to walk along the red carpet.

'Finally,' he said, 'I've been trying to call you: the stylist is here.'

Helen reached into her bag and checked her phone. Sure enough, she'd got three missed calls and a voicemail message from Nathan.

'I'm so sorry,' she said, flicking the button on the side of the phone. 'I must have turned it to silent by accident.' She looked Nathan up and down again. 'I thought we'd agreed we weren't going to do the whole stylist thing?'

'I wasn't,' said Nathan, 'but then they arrived, and got everything out, and without you here I just didn't know how to say no.'

Helen followed Nathan into the house to the one of Ben's many reception rooms that had been turned into an impromptu dressing room. Along one wall were several wheeled clothes rails from which hung dozens of men's suits and shirts, and on the opposite side were about twice as many rails, this time displaying a whole array of dresses, skirts and trouser suits, all in black.

'Hi,' said a young woman dressed head to toe in black and wearing thick-framed black glasses. 'You must be Helen. I'm so sorry for your loss. I never met Ben but I loved his music and his passion. Anyway, I'm Bea, I'm your stylist,' she paused and gestured to half a dozen similarly black-clad people scattered around the room, busily arranging shoeboxes and setting out handbags, scarves and items of jewellery, 'this is my team, and we're here to help you curate your look for tomorrow.'

Helen felt her hackles rise at the memory of Rocco having the audacity to book a stylist for her and Nathan, as if they were going to be an embarrassment in their off-the-peg clothing.

'Thanks,' said Helen, 'but no thanks. I'm sorry you've had a wasted journey but I won't be requiring your services.'

The woman looked momentarily taken aback, but recovered herself quickly. 'Didn't Rocco tell you I was coming?'

'He did,' said Helen. 'But what he didn't do was check whether this was something that Nathan or I actually wanted.'

'Oh, I see,' said the stylist, adjusting her glasses. 'You've had this forced on you?'

Helen nodded. 'I know you're only doing your job, but it's not something I'm interested in thank you.'

The stylist nodded thoughtfully. 'Guys, can we have the room please?' she commanded, and immediately her assistants vacated the room, leaving her alone with Helen and Nathan.

'Okay,' said the stylist, 'reading between the lines, I'm guessing you're feeling insulted by Rocco sending me over here, like, "Who's this bitch telling me what to wear?" Am I right?'

Helen smiled at the woman's frankness in spite of herself. 'Something like that.'

'I get it,' said the stylist. 'And that's not how I want you to feel at all. Here's the thing: my guess is you guys want to get through tomorrow with the minimum of fuss, am I right?'

Helen nodded. The idea of people looking at her made her feel uncomfortable.

'Well,' continued the stylist, 'I guarantee if you wear your own clothes, lovely though I'm sure they are, you will stick out like a . . . what's that English phrase . . . I've got it . . . a sore thumb. The clothes people wear here are almost like a uniform, marking you out as one of them; if you want to blend into the background tomorrow, to attract as little attention to yourselves as possible, my advice is simple: wear their uniform.'

Helen considered the stylist's words and could see that she had a point. Ever since they'd arrived in LA she and Nathan had stuck out. It seemed as if everyone was younger, more attractive and better dressed than they were. It was obvious that they didn't fit. That this wasn't their world. And she could only imagine that tomorrow would be a hundred times worse.

Helen looked at Nathan, who shrugged back at her. It looked like he could see the sense in this too.

'Fine,' relented Helen. 'Do what you've got to do.'

The stylist called her assistants back into the room and at her command they began pulling together several outfits, which they presented to Helen for her approval. After rejecting a trouser suit, and a skirt and blouse, Helen finally opted for a simple short-sleeved black shift dress by a designer she had never heard of but which she suspected cost a small fortune, teamed with a pair of Jimmy Choo sandals. She tried on the outfit behind a folding screen they'd set up in the corner and then took a look at herself in the full-length mirror before her. Though on the face of it, it had appeared to be a fairly simple and elegant look, it was completely transformative, being so different to the clothes Helen usually wore. The stylist had been right after all. Dressed in her LA uniform, Helen barely recognised her own reflection and that was exactly what she wanted.

That night Helen went to bed early, the exhaustion of her sleepless night before finally taking its toll, and when she awoke the next morning she felt if not quite refreshed, then at least rested enough to face the day ahead.

Unable to eat much more than a few berries at breakfast, she quickly showered before the arrival of the hair and make-up artists the stylist had arranged. By the time they'd finished their work and she'd put on the outfit that had been selected for her, the old Helen was completely hidden from view. Now, all the outside world would see was just another anonymous rich person, come to pay their respects to Ben, and that was all she wanted.

Their destination that morning was Westwood Village Memorial Park, a place of which Helen had been unaware until she had looked it up online only to be astonished at the number of legendary names that were interred there: everyone from Marilyn Monroe to Kirk Douglas, and Billy Wilder to Frank Zappa. Even in death it seemed the rich and famous wanted to be together in their own exclusive club. Helen wasn't sure that this was where Ben would've chosen to end up, it didn't seem like him at all. Instead, it had all the hallmarks of Rocco once again imposing his will, managing Ben's public image even now. Still, as she and Nathan had discussed, there was no point fighting it. All that mattered, all they wanted, was to be able to say goodbye to Ben; the trappings around it were immaterial.

On their arrival at the memorial park their driver took them past the gates, where they were met by a glamorous young woman with a clipboard, flanked on both sides by two sombre-looking security guards. She checked their names off against her list as if this was an exclusive party, which Helen supposed to some degree it was. In spite of their sunglasses she had recognised the couple who had arrived just before them as a famous rapper and his model wife, and amongst the small group behind her she had spotted the lead vocalists of two rock bands, a Hollywood actress, and a world-famous tennis star.

In all the funerals Helen had been to in her life she had never seen a seating plan, and yet as she and Nathan stepped into the lobby of the chapel building there was one mounted on an easel. To her surprise she saw that spaces had been reserved for her and Nathan on the front row next to Ben's bandmates and their partners, rather than tucked away at the back as she'd assumed they would be. Helen worried that such special treatment would bring with it unwanted attention but she knew she couldn't make a fuss about wanting to be moved. Slipping on her sunglasses and keeping her head bowed, she followed Nathan to their seats, and after a short while a hush descended as from the back of the room a gospel choir began a rendition of 'Home', one of Bluelight's biggest hits. As everyone in the chapel rose to their feet, the choir led the procession escorting Ben's coffin to the front of the room, before arranging themselves to the side of the altar as the proceedings began.

Helen could barely follow the service, so focused was she on the coffin at the front of the room. It was inconceivable to think that her love, her Ben, was really in there, and it took all the strength she had to fight the urge to run forward and check. She knew it wasn't rational, but she couldn't help herself, she just didn't want to believe that he was really gone, that she would never see him again.

What she recalled of the service afterwards was vague. At one point Rocco stood up, looking strangely sombre with his customary Hawaiian shirt exchanged for a smart designer ensemble, and said a few words. Then Andy from Bluelight, speaking on behalf of the band, addressed the congregation. There were eulogies too from close friends of Ben, one a multi-platinum award-winning singer-songwriter who had formed a close friendship with him as a support act on one of Bluelight's early tours, and another an internationally renowned DJ and producer who had become friends with Ben after working on Bluelight's fifth album, *Makes Us Stronger*.

Then just like that, it was all over. Everyone stood and the choir began singing Bluelight's hit 'Love Will See Us Through' and, as the coffin disappeared behind a pair of dark blue velvet curtains, Helen had to lean on Nathan's arm for support.

Determined to hold it together at least until she was back in the car, Helen joined the line filing out of the chapel. She was almost at the door, almost free to shed her tears in private, when she felt a hand on her shoulder. She turned around to see a face she recognised immediately although they had never met.

'Allegra.'

Helen said her name as though they were on familiar terms, when the truth was she'd only ever seen this woman in the blockbuster films she starred in or in the pages of magazines. She looked just as flawless in person as she did on the big screen, if not more so. Her skin seemed luminescent, and her blue-green eyes sparkled with health and vitality. But there was something else, a warmth she exuded, which made it easy to see why she was such a popular star.

'Helen,' she said with a smile, immediately causing Helen to wonder how someone like Allegra was aware of her existence. Had

Ben told her about them? 'I'm so, so sorry for your loss.' Allegra hugged her tightly, and then, grabbing her by the hand, led her outside, taking her away from the line of SUVs waiting at the entrance.

'I'm sorry to hijack you like this,' she began, 'especially today. I know you must be hurting so much. The thing is I heard that you might not be at the memorial this afternoon, and so I wanted to reach out to you while I had the chance.'

'It's lovely to meet you,' said Helen. 'Ben told me so much about you and how grateful he was for your friendship and that of your husband.'

Allegra bowed her head for a moment and when she looked back up at Helen her eyes were filled with tears. 'He was such an amazing guy, a true gentleman and such a wonderful friend. Chris and I both loved him so much.' She reached out and rested a hand on Helen's arm. 'I need to talk to you. I spoke to Ben about a week after he arrived back in the States, and he told me all about you guys and what you'd done for him and how close you two became and . . . I don't know . . . I just wanted you to know . . . I need for you to know that I have never, and I mean never known Ben as happy as he was talking about his plans for the future with you. It was like he was drunk on joy, he was practically giddy with it all. You were all he wanted, all he could talk about, and I just wanted to make sure you knew that.'

Helen was so touched by the generosity of spirit of this woman, who herself must have been in great pain at the loss of the man she had once been married to, that she didn't know what to say. Instead, she stepped forward, and through the strength of her embrace tried her best to convey her gratitude.

'Is there anything I can do for you?' said Allegra as they parted. 'Anything at all?'

Helen shook her head. 'No, really, I'm fine. Anyway, I'm heading back home tomorrow.'

'Well, let me give you my number.' Allegra held out her hand and Helen automatically handed over her phone, watching as she tapped in her details. 'Just so you know, only six other people in the world have this number, but as far as I'm concerned you're family. If you ever need anything, months from now or even years, you call me, okay? You looked after Ben when he most needed it and for that I will be forever grateful.'

In return she made Helen put her number into her phone but before Helen could thank her for her kindness, a tall man in a dark suit, who looked like some sort of bodyguard, came and whispered something in Allegra's ear. She flashed Helen an apologetic smile. 'Looks like I've got to go. Promise you'll keep in touch, and I'm not just saying that. In fact, if I don't hear from you in a couple of weeks, expect a call from me. But beware, I'm not sure if Ben told you this, but I'm a talker, so make sure you clear a couple of hours.'

With that, she was whisked away, leaving Helen wondering if she had imagined the whole encounter. Just to make sure, she checked her phone and sure enough there was Allegra Kennedy's number looking back at her. As she tucked it away in her borrowed black Chanel clutch bag she sensed someone standing behind her and turned to see Rocco. Next to him was an immaculately dressed middle-aged woman with elegantly styled silver hair. Helen wondered briefly if this was Rocco's wife or partner, and in turn what kind of woman could bear to live with a man like that.

'Helen, I gather you're about to leave. Before you do, I'd like to introduce you to someone: this is Adele Shapiro.' He gestured to the woman next to him, who stepped forward and held out her hand. 'Mrs Morley, I'm so sorry for your loss.'

Helen shook the woman's hand. 'Thank you, but I'm not really Mrs Morley any more, you can just call me Helen.'

The woman inclined her head slightly. 'Well, Helen, I was Ben's business manager and lawyer for the past eighteen years and with my hand on my heart I can attest that he really was one of the best. He was such a kind man, and funny too, and, with the exception of his inability to complete paperwork on time, he was an absolute joy to work with.'

'Thank you so much for taking the time to say that.' Helen smiled but wondered why Rocco had felt it important that she should be introduced to this woman. 'It's been a pleasure to meet you.'

Helen turned to go, but Rocco stopped her. 'Look, I know this isn't the time or the place but with everything happening this afternoon and you leaving first thing I'm not sure when we're going to get another chance, so I'll cut to the chase. I didn't introduce you to Adele just for the sake of it, I introduced you because over the next few weeks you're going to be hearing a lot from her.'

Puzzled, Helen looked from Rocco to Adele and back again. 'I don't understand, why?'

'Because with the exception of a few small bequests,' said Adele, 'in his will, Ben left his entire estate, absolutely everything he owned, to you.'

37

Helen

It was early evening the following day and Helen was about to take her bags downstairs when there was a knock at her bedroom door. She opened it to reveal Lucía, and standing behind her was a tall, muscular man dressed in a black suit.

'Sorry to disturb you, Mrs Morley, just to let you know your car to the airport has arrived.' She gestured to the man behind her. 'If you're ready, Phillipe will take your bags downstairs.'

Although Helen was more than capable of carrying her own bags to the car, she sensed that such an action wouldn't have met with Lucía's approval and so, smiling her thanks, she stood back and allowed the man to do his job. Taking one last look around the room to check she hadn't missed anything, Helen followed Lucía downstairs to the main entrance where a tired-looking Nathan was waiting.

'Well, I suppose this is goodbye, then,' said Helen, turning to Lucía with a smile. 'Thank you so much for taking such good care of us both, you've been amazing.'

'I was just doing my job, Mrs Morley,' replied Lucía, modestly. 'But it was a pleasure to look after you and Mr Nathan. I hope you both have a safe journey home.'

If it had been up to Lucía, Helen was sure she would've left it like that but Helen couldn't help herself. Refusing to bow to convention, she wrapped Lucía in a hug and as she did so she whispered in her ear, 'And thank you for taking such good care of Ben all these years too.'

'It was my pleasure,' Lucía said quietly. 'Mr Baptiste was a wonderful man and I will miss him forever.'

As the car pulled away, and Lucía stood at the front entrance watching them leave, Helen wondered what would become of her and the rest of Ben's staff now. It was only when the car paused at the end of the driveway, waiting for the electric gates to slide back, that it dawned on her that after yesterday's news about Ben's will, the truth of the matter was that their fate now largely rested in her hands.

When Adele Shapiro had told Helen that Ben had left the bulk of his estate to her it had stunned her into silence. It just made no sense. Why would he have put her in his will when until recently they hadn't seen each other in decades? The answer to this question was quickly supplied by Adele, who seemed as intuitive as she was efficient. Apparently ever since Ben's divorce from Allegra, Adele had been badgering him to draw up a new will, but for some reason he just didn't seem to want to do anything about it. This had gone on for years, Adele chasing Ben to make the changes and Ben doing everything he could to avoid it. Then, finally, about a year ago, she'd had a meeting with him and as usual brought up the subject. This time Ben had confided the reason he'd been putting it off for so long, telling her that, as he didn't talk to his brother or his dad, there was no one besides his ex-wife he could think to leave his fortune to.

After that Adele had agreed to leave it as it was but then, following his return to the States, Ben had called her out of the blue and asked her to arrange a transfer of funds to Helen, which she'd done. Then, to her surprise he'd brought up his will. 'I want to make some changes,' he'd told her. A few days later she'd gone over to see him and after a long discussion had redrafted his will naming Helen as his main beneficiary.

'So long story short,' Rocco had added in conclusion, 'barring a few mill that he's left to his brother and some other smaller bequests to a few members of his staff, the rest is yours.'

Helen hadn't known what to do or say, and, apparently realising this, Adele had said, 'It's a lot to take in, especially today of all days. Let's agree to talk when you're ready and in the meantime, don't worry about anything, it's all under control.'

Taking Adele's business card, Helen had assured her she would be in touch and then returned to the SUV in which she'd arrived. A short while later she was joined by Nathan, and she guessed judging by the look of shock on his face that he'd been spoken to by Adele too.

'Some suit with Rocco just collared me,' he said. 'Apparently Ben's left me ten million dollars in his will.'

Helen had already made up her mind that she wasn't going to say anything to Nathan about her conversation with Adele, at least not yet. Money was awkward enough to bring up at any time but today was definitely not the day to do it. She couldn't bear to cause Nathan any more pain than he was in already. She would talk to him about it, just not now, not yet.

'It meant a lot to Ben having you back in his life,' she said, reaching across and putting a hand on Nathan's arm. 'I suppose this was his way of showing it.'

He shook his head sadly. 'It meant a lot to me to have him back in my life too. I still can't believe I sold him out like I did. What kind of brother does something like that? And now he's left me all this money, crazy money.' Nathan paused, rubbing the bridge of his nose, then looked at Helen, his eyes brimming with tears. 'I'd give it all back, every single penny, just to be able to see him again, to be able to give him one last . . .' Overcome with emotion, his voice trailed off. Taking his hand, Helen nodded to the driver and they had made their way back to Ben's Malibu home in thoughtful silence.

Now, over twenty-four hours later, here she was in yet another car with blacked-out windows, this time making her way home, her heart heavy with grief, her mind racing with thoughts and worries about Ben's bequest, and what to do about it. While it was a wonderful gift, so typical of Ben, at the same time there was no doubting the fact that because of it, overnight her whole life had become incredibly complicated. It was all too over-whelming, and the pressure of it, her desire to do the right thing by Ben, made her feel like she was carrying the weight of the world on her shoulders. It was all just too much. And so she made a decision not to make any decisions at all, at least not for the time being. Instead, she would push all thoughts of Ben's fortune to the very back of her mind and focus on taking things one step at a time, which today meant getting back home safely to her family.

It was a little after ten o'clock in the morning when they landed, and, following a swift exit from the plane, once again Helen and Nathan were swept through the VIP lanes at Heathrow and out into a car waiting to take them back to Manchester. Having been awake for the entire flight, Helen was so exhausted that as soon as they hit the motorway she was fast asleep and didn't wake up until Nathan gently nudged her to tell her they had reached his house.

'Are we home already?' she asked, rubbing her eyes. She looked out of the car window to see that it was raining and couldn't help but smile. She certainly wasn't in Kansas, or rather LA, any more.

'Not quite,' said Nathan. 'We're at my place but you're the next stop. I only woke you because I wanted to say goodbye.'

'I'm glad you did,' she said sleepily.

'Thanks for everything,' said Nathan, putting an arm around her shoulders and giving her a quick hug. 'I'm not sure I would've been able to get through all this without you.'

'And I wouldn't have been able to keep it together without you,' said Helen. 'You will keep in touch, won't you? You won't just let us drift apart?'

'Of course not,' said Nathan. 'You'll have plenty of chance to get tired of me.' He kissed her cheek. 'You look after yourself, and I'll speak to you soon.'

As Helen watched him walk up to the entrance to his building she wondered once again how she was ever going to tell him about Ben's decision to leave her everything and how he would react when he found out. But before she could conjure up answers to her questions, she reminded herself of her earlier resolution to deal with all this later. Instead, settling back in her seat, she focused her attention on the passing scenery and all the markers telling her that she was almost home.

A short while later the car pulled up outside Helen's house and, even before the driver had switched off the engine, the front door opened and Frankie, Esme and her mum were racing down the path to meet her. Even though she had only been away a few days, so much had happened it felt in many ways like a lifetime, and as they smothered her with hugs and kisses her heart leaped with joy.

'How was the journey, love?' asked her mum as she was gently corralled into the house. 'Frankie looked up your flight online, it was delayed, wasn't it?'

'Just a bit,' said Helen, following her mum into the kitchen and sitting down at the table. 'But it wasn't a big deal. How's everything been here?'

Sue smiled and looked at her grandchildren. 'We've had a good time, haven't we, kids?'

Frankie grinned. 'Yesterday, Nan didn't cook at all, and we just ordered in food all day. We had a McDonald's for lunch and Nando's for dinner!'

'Frankie!' Sue jokingly scolded. 'You're making me look bad. I thought we'd agreed it would be our little secret!'

Helen could tell from their pantomime performances that this was her mum and the kids putting on a brave face for her sake, and she appreciated it. She gave each one of them another hug and a kiss, and then sat chatting with them over tea and biscuits.

After a while Helen suddenly felt her tiredness catching up with her and yawned. Sue insisted that she go upstairs and take a nap. 'And before you protest,' she added, 'I promise I won't let you sleep all day, I'll come up and wake you in a couple of hours. But for now you need to rest.'

Helen didn't have the strength to argue, and so she meekly allowed herself to be shooed upstairs. Shedding her clothes in the bathroom, she took a quick shower, imagining that she was washing away all the tension, grief and sorrow of the last few days as she did so. Slipping into her dressing gown, she retreated to her bedroom, shutting the curtains against the afternoon sunshine before climbing into bed and falling fast asleep.

She dreamed vivid dreams, amalgamations of her time in LA. She dreamed of being on planes, walking on beaches, and even talking once again to Ben's fans outside the house in Malibu. In the dream she was just about to light a candle for him when she heard someone calling her name, and it was only when she opened her eyes and saw her mum standing next to the bed that she realised reality had spilled into her dreamworld.

'What time is it?' she asked, rubbing her eyes. 'I feel like I've only been asleep for five minutes.'

'It's been two hours,' said Sue, 'and I would've let you sleep longer except . . . well . . . I'm afraid something's come up.'

Helen sat up in bed. 'Come up? What do you mean?'

'It's Adam,' said Sue, tersely. 'He's downstairs and he's quite clearly the worse for wear, and even though I've tried to tell him to go home he's saying he won't leave until he's spoken to you.'

38

Helen

The moment Helen stepped into the kitchen she knew straight away that her mum's assessment of Adam's sobriety had been correct. He was sitting on the sofa by the French doors, an arm around each of the kids, telling them in a needlessly loud voice how much he loved them both. Helen couldn't remember the last time she'd seen Adam this intoxicated, perhaps not since they were students. He was always far too concerned about looking a fool to really let himself go very often, and the kids had certainly never seen him in this state. Something was clearly very wrong for him to be in this mess, even more so to turn up like it here in the middle of the afternoon, but whatever it was Helen didn't care. She was furious with him, and it took all her strength not to give him a piece of her mind right there and then.

The kids turned to look at Helen and seeing her, Adam leaped to his feet, swearing loudly as he smacked his shin against the coffee table, eliciting looks of shock and awe from the kids, as expletives were also something that Adam didn't do in front of them.

'Helen!' he said, as he bent down and rubbed his leg, wobbling alarmingly as he did so. 'I thought you'd never come down.' He gestured towards Esme and Frankie. 'Look at our beautiful kids, Helen, look how gorgeous they are. We did something right there, didn't we? We got those two spot on at least.'

Noting for the first time Adam's dishevelled appearance, his untucked shirt, the open flies of his jeans and the untied laces on one of his trainers, she chose to ignore his comments for the moment, more concerned with getting Frankie and Esme out of the room. She took a deep breath and tried her best to sound calm.

'Kids, would you mind nipping to the shops with Gran and getting something nice in for tea? My purse is on the table in the hallway.'

Not needing to be told twice, Esme and Frankie left the room as an almost tearful Adam called after them, 'Love you both! Never forget that! Dad loves you!'

As Sue closed the door behind her, Helen turned to face Adam ready to let rip. Here she was, jet-lagged and exhausted, and now she had to deal with this: her man-baby of a husband, standing drunk in her kitchen.

'How dare you come round here in this state!' she snapped as she angrily crossed her arms. 'You're a grown man, Adam! What do you think you're playing at?'

Adam regarded her, tears welling in his eyes. 'I'm sorry,' he said, 'I'm really sorry. I went to the pub, and started drinking, and then the next thing I knew I was in the back of a cab making my way over here.'

'So, which is it?' asked Helen, even though she already had her suspicions. 'Has she kicked you out or have work passed you over for promotion? I imagine it's one of the two, so you might as well just spit it out.'

Adam fell silent for a moment, his head hung in shame, his gaze fixed to the floor at his feet, and then finally he mumbled, 'She . . . she . . . kicked me out.'

And there it was. The news that on some level Helen had always thought she might hear, that having wrecked her marriage and torn apart her family Holly had grown tired of Adam, of playing house with a man twenty years her senior.

'So, she finally came to her senses, did she? What was it? The pants on the floor, the unwillingness to help with any of the housework or the routine lovemaking? For all I know, it could've been all three.'

'You're right,' said Adam. 'I absolutely deserve that, after the way I've treated you, the way I've behaved.' He pulled out a chair from the dining table, sat down heavily and then buried his face in his hands. 'We just weren't right together,' he said in a manner that made Helen think that he was already rewriting even this brief history, just as she was sure he had done with all the years they'd had together. 'She was too young for me,' he continued, 'when it came down to it we had barely anything in common. Anyway, after one row too many she told me to go, thinking I wouldn't, so I called her bluff. I packed a bag and left, telling her I'd be back for the rest of my things later. She begged me to stay, but I'd had enough. I told her it was over, that we were done for good and that's when I went to the pub.'

Helen doubted that the picture Adam had painted for her benefit was anything like reality. While she was sure he and Holly had undoubtedly had a row of some sort, her guess was that when Holly had told Adam to go, she hadn't been bluffing at all, she'd meant every word. And she was pretty sure it was Adam, not Holly, who had done the begging, hence his stint at the pub to drink himself senseless while he worked out his next move, which was, of course, to come back here like some sort of deranged homing pigeon and throw himself at Helen's feet.

'And so now you're here because . . .'

Adam looked up at her, yet more self-pitying tears welling up in his eyes. 'Because I'm homeless . . . because I need somewhere to stay . . . I know I shouldn't ask, I know I've got no right . . . and it wouldn't be for long, just until I find somewhere. A week, maybe two, but if you could just find it in your heart . . . it would mean the world to me.'

Helen's first thought was to throw him out on his ear, but then she thought about Ben, her lovely sweet Ben, and how in a strange way they would never have got together had it not been for Adam's actions. And while she wouldn't have asked for any of the pain of the past twelve months, without it she wouldn't have had her time with Ben. And so, she decided she would let her husband stay, for a couple of days anyway, but she knew the only reason her heart was big enough for such a selfless act was because Ben had shown her what real love was.

An hour later Helen and Adam were in the kitchen, each nursing a cup of coffee (but for entirely different reasons), when the rest of the family returned.

'I've got something I need tell you all,' said Adam, as Sue shot Helen a questioning look. 'I need to apologise for my behaviour earlier. It was wrong of me, and I'm sorry. I hope you'll forgive me.'

A wide-eyed Esme and Frankie looked to their mum before nodding in unison, and then Helen, desperate to get the announcement over with, told them that Adam would be staying with them for a short while and sleeping on the sofa downstairs.

The kids clearly had questions but knew better than to ask them at this particular moment, and her mum threw her a look that spoke volumes, but she too kept quiet. Helen felt sure that both parties would bombard her with questions later, but for the time being at least there was peace.

After dinner, the kids and Adam went to watch TV, leaving Helen and Sue alone in the kitchen.

'So, he's back then?' said Sue. 'Didn't take long to talk you round, did he?'

Helen sighed. 'He didn't talk me round, I took pity on him.'

'And how long before he works his way from the sofa back up into your room?'

Helen glared at her mother. That remark was out of order and her mum knew it.

'Okay, okay,' said Sue, holding up her hands in surrender. 'But if I'm thinking it, you can bet your bottom dollar that it'll have crossed the kids' minds too. Adam staying here is only going to confuse them and they've been through enough already.'

'And don't you think I know that?' snapped Helen. 'They're part of the reason I'm letting him stay. How would it look to them if their angry mum kicked out their own dad, even after everything he's put us through? I'd be the bad guy, at least in their eyes, and I don't want that. He's not moving in, he's not going to slide his way back into my bed, all I'm doing is giving him somewhere to stay for a few days while he sorts himself out, okay? That's the last thing I'm going to say on the matter.' Helen picked up the kettle, briskly filled it and put it on its stand. 'Now, I'm having a cup of tea, do you want one?'

That evening was strained to say the least. Although she'd been due to go home now Helen was back, Sue announced that she'd decided to stay for one more night. So it was that all five of them sat in the living room watching TV, Adam sandwiched between Esme and Frankie on one sofa, with Helen and Sue on the other, her mother casting lethal glances in Adam's direction instead of watching the action unfolding on screen. In the end Helen couldn't take any more and, just before nine, left the room, returning a short while later carrying a duvet and two pillows. 'I'm going to get off to bed,' she said, setting down the bedding on the arm of the sofa. 'I think the jet lag is catching up with me. I'll see you all in the morning.'

Not long after as she lay in bed unable to sleep, she heard Sue come upstairs, shortly followed by Esme and Frankie. She listened carefully, as one by one each of them brushed their teeth in the bathroom, before finally she heard Adam's heavy footsteps coming up the stairs and going into the bathroom, the door locking behind him. When it clicked open again Helen expected to hear him head straight back downstairs, but there was a pause, as if he were hesitating. While she was sure it was just her imagination, she couldn't help picturing him looking at each of the closed bedroom doors in turn, remembering how life used to be when they were all together under the same roof, a happy family. Finally, he descended the stairs and turned off the hallway light, plunging the upstairs into darkness, and with that Helen gave into her exhaustion and fell into a deep and dreamless sleep.

When she woke the next morning, the day before flooded back to her like a strange dream, beginning with her long journey from LA and culminating in her estranged husband sleeping on the sofa. Two very different worlds, their common denominator being Helen herself. Slipping out of bed, she pulled on her dressing gown and made her way quietly downstairs, to make a morning coffee and try to get her head around what the day ahead might look like. To her surprise, however, the door to the living room was wide open, and it was light in there, as if the curtains had been drawn. Allowing curiosity to get the better of her, she tapped quietly on the door just in case Adam was in some form of undress, and when she heard no reply she popped her head around the door to find the room empty, the two pillows and duvet neatly stacked on the arm of the sofa. On top of the bedding was a folded sheet of A4 that Adam had clearly taken from the printer next to the computer in the far corner of the room.

Opening it up, Helen saw that it was a handwritten note. She sat down on the sofa and began to read:

Dear Helen,

Thank you so much for letting me stay last night even though we both know that I didn't deserve such kindness. Apologies again for showing up in that state. I promise it will never happen again. I did a lot of thinking last night, about you, me, and especially the kids, and I can't quite believe what a mess I've managed to make of everything. You are all the very best of me, and I'm so sorry to have let you down. I'm sorry too that in all my self-absorption I neglected to even ask you how things went in LA and how you yourself are doing. For this, once again, I apologise, and I really do hope that as difficult as I'm sure it was you found some comfort in being there, and I hope you know that I wish you nothing but happiness in the future.

During my night of thinking, it occurred to me that I need to start putting the kids first, and that my presence here in the house wouldn't be doing that. For this reason, I've decided to go and stay with my parents until I find a place of my own. I can't quite believe Esme will soon be heading off to uni. It seems like yesterday we were bringing her back from the hospital, unable to take our eyes off her, or believe that she was really ours. And now here we are, this particular

327

chapter of our lives about to come to a close, it seems all too unreal.

You've been a wonderful mother to Es and Frankie, the best any child could hope for, and while only all too aware of my own shortcomings, I've made a promise to myself to at least try to be a better parent, and if I can even manage to be half as good as you, then I will consider that I've done a good job.

Give the kids a kiss from me, and tell them I'll see them soon,
All my love
Adam x

39

Helen

Standing at the bottom of the stairs, Helen took a deep breath and called up to the kids once more. 'Frankie! Esme! Can we get a move on please, your dad's going to be here any minute!'

With ears straining she heard nothing but silence. No calls of, 'I'll be down in a minute, Mum,' no cries of, 'I'm just coming,' in fact no acknowledgement that either of them had heard her at all. From experience Helen knew that when they chose to, both of her children, even when wearing headphones, had powers of hearing that were almost superhuman. They could, for instance, hear an Amazon delivery driver approaching their house from the end of the road and detect the opening of a box of Cadbury's Celebrations, even on one memorable occasion when Helen had accessed her own private chocolate stash in the cellar. So, the idea that they simply hadn't heard her just didn't hold any water. They'd heard her all right, but as usual, these children, her own flesh and blood, who had sprung from her loins, were deliberately choosing to tune her out, as if she were some kind of domestic static, like the hum of the fridge or the whoosh of the boiler when somebody turned on the hot tap.

She told herself that she would give them one last chance, one final opportunity to heed her call and show her that they were indeed capable of being summoned without the need for shouting or threats.

'Come on, kids,' she pleaded, endeavouring to keep her tone light and airy, 'we really need to get going!'

Pausing, Helen listened once again. She could hear the distant barking of a dog, the passing of a motorbike, and even her own blood rushing through her ears, but the one thing she couldn't hear was any sign her children were responding to her summons. Finally, she gave herself permission to lose it and as if possessed by the spirit of a banshee, she screamed at the top of her voice up the stairs, 'If you two aren't down here in the next five seconds I am going to lose it, do you hear me? Absolutely lose it!!!'

Esme's door opened first, followed quickly by Frankie's, and then they both appeared at the top of the stairs, wide-eyed with outrage.

'What's all the drama about, Mum? You were screaming like you were being attacked!'

Helen didn't reply straight away, she couldn't, or she'd be in danger of having a complete meltdown and that was the last thing she wanted on today of all days, the day Esme was off to university. Drawing in a deep breath, she held it for the count of ten before letting it out slowly just like they did in yoga class. Then finally, she forced a smile on to her face and said, as calmly as possible, 'Would you mind coming downstairs now? It's almost time to go.'

The past fortnight, as well as a return to work for her, and school for Frankie, had been filled with shopping trips for university supplies, family dinners and lots of late-night chats. Despite Esme's obvious excitement about this new phase of her life, Helen could tell that she was worried about leaving her and Frankie, especially given everything that had happened over the summer. They weren't the same family they used to be, they were changed, different in so many ways, and Helen guessed that Esme feared they were more fragile too. In order to assuage her daughter's fears Helen had gone to great lengths to reassure her that they would be okay, that she herself was doing fine, even though the truth was often anything but. At times, Esme's leaving, on top of the loss of Ben, almost threatened to tear her apart. It was as if every good thing in her life was being slowly taken away, making her want to hold on to Frankie all the more, and refuse to let Esme go. But she knew she had to release her hold on both of them, allow Esme to leave home and let Frankie have his freedoms too, because to do otherwise would be to stifle the very thing she knew deserved to flourish.

Despite barely sleeping more than an hour or two, churning over the hundred and one things on her mind – from the fact that she still hadn't made a decision about what to do with Ben's money, right through to the knowledge that Esme would be leaving in the morning – Helen had awoken early and felt exhausted as she had done since her return from LA. It was almost as though she was still suffering from jet lag, waking at odd hours, and feeling drained of energy all the time and almost never hungry when she should be. Mustering what little energy she had, Helen had forced herself out of bed to make Esme's favourite breakfast, American pancakes and fresh fruit, which the three of them had enjoyed together before the kids had disappeared back upstairs. Although she'd factored in plenty of time for a leisurely breakfast and getting ready for the day, as was ever the case, time had somehow slipped away, which was what had brought her to the bottom of the stairs to chivvy her children along.

As Esme and Frankie brought the first lot of Esme's things down before heading back upstairs to collect the rest the doorbell rang, and Helen answered it to reveal Adam, wearing a chambray shirt and chinos, one of a very small selection of 'non-embarrassing' outfits Esme had permitted him to choose from.

'Morning,' he said. 'You look nice.'

Helen looked down at her own outfit consisting of jeans, a navy blazer over a white T-shirt and white trainers, which had also been carefully curated by their daughter.

'Thanks,' replied Helen. 'You look nice too.'

Things had been better between Helen and Adam since his letter. In the end he only had to stay at his parents' for a couple of days, after managing to find a place to rent only five minutes away from the house, making it a lot easier for Esme and Frankie to pop in and see him without it being a huge deal. Whenever they talked, Helen no longer felt like she was battling an adversary or competing for their children's affection; instead it felt like they were building something new, parenting, but from different locations, and while it wasn't perfect neither was it awful. For the first time in a long while she felt like she and Adam wanted the same thing, to see their kids happy, to make sure that all their needs were taken care of.

'Hey Dad!' said Esme, looking gorgeous in the outfit of emerald-green crop top, black wide-legged trousers and pristine white Nike Air Force 1 trainers she had selected to make her university debut. Coming down the stairs, she put a bag of towels down on the floor next to the rest of her things.

'Hey sweetie,' replied Adam, giving her a hug. 'You look lovely. You all ready for the big day?'

'Nearly,' said Esme, 'I just need to get Frankie to change out of those hideous tracksuit bottoms and swap them for literally anything else.'

'What's wrong with my trackies?' replied Frankie indignantly as he came down the stairs holding an IKEA bag bursting with bedding. 'They're cool.'

'They're gross, is what they are,' snapped Esme. 'Just stop being a freak and put on jeans like a normal person.'

Frankie opened his mouth to protest but Helen intervened. 'It's her day, Frankie, when it's your turn to go to uni, you can make her wear whatever crazy outfit you want.'

Frankie laughed and rubbed his hands together in glee. 'So that'll be one of Dad's old shirts and a pair of Man City shorts! She'll look like a right weirdo in that get-up.'

Eventually, once Frankie had changed into a pair of jeans, they began loading the car with all of Esme's bags. And following one last check of the hallway to make sure nothing had been forgotten, Helen stood for a moment, looking at the empty space where her daughter's things had been and then finally, blinking away a stray tear, she closed the front door and joined the others in the car.

Despite Helen's initial sadness she found her spirits lifting as the journey to Nottingham progressed. The mood in the car was surprisingly ebullient, with Esme and Frankie teasing each other mercilessly and Adam tossing in the occasional 'dad' joke for good measure, all while Helen sat in the passenger seat gamely handing out sweets and snacks as she had done on countless family journeys across the years. It almost felt like the beginning of family holidays of old, perhaps even the holiday they should've had, the one they would've had this year if things had been different.

Just over two hours and a loo stop for Frankie later, Adam pulled the car up outside Esme's student accommodation. After picking up the keys they made their way to the block where she'd be living. Unloading the car, they carried everything up to her new room, discreetly staying out of the way whenever they saw her chatting to fellow students. As Helen made a return trip to the car, she thought back to her own arrival at university all those years ago. At the time she'd felt so mature, so grown up, but now with a mother's eyes she realised how young and clueless about the world she'd really been. She had a sudden urge to rush to

Esme's room, grab her daughter and take her back to the security of home, but she knew better than to act on it. This was the start of an exciting new chapter in her daughter's life and even though there might be some pain and difficulty ahead, there would also be much joy and laughter too.

They stayed for another hour but when the other parents started to go home Helen thought it best that they leave too. 'I love you, sweetie,' she said, taking her daughter in her arms, after everyone else had said their goodbyes. 'Work hard, have fun, and never forget how much we love you.'

Although close to tears, Helen managed not to give in to her emotions and the journey back to Manchester flew by in no time at all.

'Are you still okay for me to have Frankie next weekend?' asked Adam, having dropped them back home.

Helen was about to agree when it occurred to her that without Frankie in the house she would be utterly alone, just as she had been when Adam had taken the kids away with Holly at the start of the summer. While she knew it would be selfish to refuse, right now, still feeling the pain of having left her daughter behind, she wasn't sure she could bear to let Frankie go too.

'Can I get back to you on that?' she replied. 'I'm sure it'll be fine but I just need to think a few things through.'

Adam, thankfully, didn't make a fuss, she guessed because he must have known exactly what she was thinking. All he said was, 'Sure, just let me know,' and with that he was gone.

Heading inside the house, which felt different somehow without Esme's presence, Helen set about making tea, which she and Frankie ate in front of the TV. Afterwards, Frankie excused himself to his room, leaving Helen alone. It was strange to think that from now on it would just be the two of them and, in no time at all, even Frankie would be gone too. Life with its twists and turns, its tragedies and heartbreak, was at times almost too much to bear but she had to stay strong. For Esme, for Frankie, and, strange though it sounded, for the memory of Ben. He had shown her, when she'd needed it most, that she could be happy again, and having been given this gift she refused to let it go without a fight.

Eager to keep her more maudlin thoughts at bay, she set about tidying the kitchen, busying herself by not only loading the dishwasher but also rearranging the cutlery and tackling the drawer of doom, where everything from spent batteries to water bills got dumped in a bid to keep the surfaces clear.

It was early evening by the time she finished and, deciding to make herself a cup of tea and plonk herself in front of the telly, she filled the kettle. Opening the fridge, she discovered that there was no milk, just an empty bottle in the door. Rather than cursing her son, Helen, glad of an excuse to keep busy, called upstairs to let him know she was nipping to the supermarket and wouldn't be long.

Reaching her local Tesco, Helen briefly considered getting a trolley but, reasoning that she only needed one thing, grabbed a basket from a stack by the door instead. As so often happened, in addition to the milk she ended up tossing at least a dozen extra items into her basket along the way. By the time she was done, having visited all the aisles, her basket was so full she wished she'd got a trolley after all.

Paying for her shopping, Helen left the store and returned home, packing away all the items for the kitchen before taking the rest upstairs. Checking in on Frankie, who was sitting in his bedroom playing video games wearing his headphones, Helen blew him a kiss to which he responded with a thumbs up. Closing the door, she took the bag with the last of the shopping to the bathroom and began unloading the contents.

She replenished the loo roll, put away two bottles of hair conditioner that had been on offer and left a brand-new can of Lynx Africa in the cupboard for Frankie, to replace the one he'd doused himself with that morning, Helen surmised in a bid to make an impression on Esme's new university friends.

By the time she was finished there was only one item left in the bag that didn't have a home because it was something she hadn't had cause to buy in many years. As she unwrapped it, she could only wonder why she'd even bought it. After all, she was forty-five, undoubtedly perimenopausal, and there were plenty of other explanations for the symptoms she'd been experiencing.

Still, it would at least put her mind at ease and so, taking a deep breath, she opened the box, took the test and then, setting it down on the side of the bath, began the anxious three-minute wait for the result.

Epilogue

'I think that's everything, isn't it, Mum?' Helen surveyed the kitchen table now laden with party food and tried to think whether she'd forgotten anything.

Sue came and stood next to her and did a little scan of her own. 'Yes, I think so, barring the paper plates of course. I can't believe we managed to forget those. Hopefully our Esme will have managed to pick some up by now.'

Right on cue Helen heard the front door open and close, and in walked Esme, followed by Josh. She looked so grown up these days, and Helen could hardly believe that she'd almost finished her second year at university.

'Sorry it took us so long,' said Esme, 'but just wait 'til you see how cute the plates are! They're adorable!' She reached into the bag and gleefully held them up. 'Look, Mum, baby pandas! Melody is going to love these.'

While Helen suspected that her one-year-old would be too busy cramming iced biscuits into her mouth to notice the plates they were on, as she took them from Esme and inspected them she couldn't help but agree that her eldest daughter was right. 'They're gorgeous, sweetie, thank you.'

'Is there anything we can do to help?' asked Josh just as the doorbell rang.

'You could get that for me if you don't mind?' said Helen. 'I think the birthday girl's first guests are arriving.'

As Helen took off her apron and hung it on the back of the kitchen door she found herself marvelling once again at how quickly time flew by. It seemed like only yesterday when, shocked and disbelieving, she'd stared at the positive line on the pregnancy test, and now her daughter, Ben's daughter, Melody Lillian Baptiste, was celebrating her first birthday.

It took two more positive pregnancy tests and a visit to her GP before Helen finally accepted the fact that despite her age, and her assumption that her erratic cycle meant she was past all that, she was indeed pregnant. While part of her was terrified at the idea of becoming a mother again at this point in her life, most of her was overjoyed at the thought that her and Ben's love for one another wasn't lost, that it would get to live on in the form of a new life born into the world.

Gabby was the first person she told, followed by her mother, and thankfully neither had fainted with shock. Instead, they were both filled with joy for her, immediately volunteering their services for babysitting duties. Next, she knew she had to tell Esme and Frankie, something she wasn't at all looking forward to. She'd feared their reaction, worried that they might see her pregnancy as a rejection of them somehow, a shifting of her love and priorities away from them. Again, she needn't have worried. Esme had cried with joy and almost straight away had begun looking up cute baby outfits on her phone and although Frankie had initially looked a little squeamish at the news, this was soon replaced by his excitement at the prospect of being a big brother.

While Adam had clearly been thrown when he'd found out, he had at least made an attempt to seem happy for Helen, giving her a hug, and telling her that he'd help out whenever he could. And while she'd been grateful that he'd tried to be positive, she couldn't help feeling that at the same time he was disappointed, that somehow this was a drawing of a line under their relationship, that with the arrival of the baby all possibility of a reunion would disappear. Not that a reunion had ever been even remotely on the cards, at least not from Helen's point of view. Ben still had her heart, and she wasn't sure that would ever change. She wanted Adam to be happy though, and she was sure that a man like him wouldn't remain single for very long.

Nathan had been delighted to hear that he was to become an uncle and, even before Helen's first scan, had arrived on her doorstep carrying a huge teddy bear for his niece or nephew. Since their time in America they had grown close, almost like a real brother and sister. Although she'd dreaded telling him about Ben's bequest, when she finally had, part way through her pregnancy, without missing a beat Nathan had grinned and his delight for her had been evident.

As for Ben's fortune, Helen had agonised over what to do with it for months, without coming to a conclusion. But then true to her word Allegra had called to catch up. Breaking the news that she was pregnant, Helen had worried about Allegra's reaction, but the actress had news of her own: she and her husband were adopting twins. The two women had talked for hours about everything from motherhood to worries about the future, and it was during this conversation that Helen had confessed she didn't know what to do with Ben's money. 'It's too much,' she'd explained, 'I don't need that kind of money, and I don't want the kind of problems that this sort of wealth brings.'

Despite being in possession of a small fortune herself, Allegra completely understood Helen's concerns. 'Ben and I used to talk about it all the time when we were together,' she'd revealed. 'Always wondering whether the money we had was worth all the problems that came with it, and always concluding that we were both too far in to get out.'

Hearing that had pushed Helen to finally make the decision she'd been toying with for a long while, and the very next day she'd called

Adele Shapiro in LA and told her what she wanted to do. 'I want to keep all the rights to Ben's music,' she'd told her, 'but I want you to set up a charitable foundation in Ben's name with the rest to establish music and creative programmes in deprived areas all around the world.'

Adele hadn't tried to talk her out of it; after all, the rights to Ben's music would mean that neither Helen nor her children would ever have to worry about money again. She wouldn't have to work unless she wanted to, and the kids would all have enough to buy homes when they were old enough. Thanks to Ben they'd all be comfortable, very comfortable, but hopefully not to the extent they might be ruined by it.

While Helen never heard from Rocco directly again, on the day Melody came into the world an enormous bouquet of flowers was delivered to the hospital, a bouquet of blue flowers, and although there wasn't a card Helen just knew they were from him, perhaps his way of honouring Ben's memory. The last she'd heard about him via Allegra was that he'd retired from the music business and had moved to Tuscany, where he'd bought a vineyard. While she'd like to believe that in the wake of Ben's death Rocco had turned over a new leaf, determined to value what was truly important in life, at the same time she couldn't help wondering if it wasn't simply the case that he just liked a good glass of wine.

Once all the guests had arrived they ate, and afterwards Helen brought the cake out into the garden, where everyone had gathered to enjoy the unseasonably warm spring sunshine. As Frankie held Melody up to blow out her candle, everyone began singing 'Happy Birthday' and Helen felt a stab of pain thinking about Ben and all the moments like this he would miss. But then, as Melody laughed in delight in her brother's arms, someone put on some music and the air was filled with the sound of Ben singing 'Heart's Melody', a song Ben had written and recorded in LA the week before he died, the song after which their daughter was named. Calling to Josh to turn up the music, Helen stretched out her arms, gathered her three children together then, closing her eyes, imagined Ben was with them as they danced and swayed in time to the music.

Acknowledgements

First and foremost, I'd like to thank you, the reader, for choosing this book. It's been twenty-five years since the publication of my first novel, *My Legendary Girlfriend*, and I know that many of you have been with me from the very beginning – thanks so much for sticking around, it really is much appreciated! At the same time, I'm aware that lots of people have joined in along the way, which is wonderful – the more the merrier! And to those of you for whom this is your first Mike Gayle novel, I'd like to say a very warm 'welcome aboard!' Boy, have you got a lot of fun ahead of you catching up on my backlist! If you want to know where to begin, feel free to drop me a line, I always love hearing from readers. After all, without you there would be no point.

Writing a book is, for much of the time, a solitary undertaking but refining it and getting it out into the world is very much a team effort. So, I'd like to offer huge thanks as always to Nick and Ariella, the King and Queen of publishing, without whom this book would not have been possible. Thanks both for your dedication, hard work, advice and feedback over the years. Thanks also to everyone at Hodder both past and present. When I arrived in your offices twenty-six years ago, I never for a moment dreamt the day might come when we'd be celebrating a relationship that's only marginally shorter than my marriage! Special Hodder shout-outs to: Jo Dickinson, Jamie Hodder-Williams, Alice Morley, Olivia Robertshaw, Alainna Hadjigeorgiou, Sue Fletcher and Philippa Pride. Huge thanks are also due to everyone at United Agents, especially Amber Garvey and Jennifer Thomas. More thanks are due to Grand Central Publishing, especially Beth and Kirsiah.

As always, I'd also like to thank The Board, the best writing friends a scribe could ask for! Thanks too to Beth O'Leary, Ruth Hogan, Jackie Behan, Holly Miller, Jill Mansell, Libby Page, Rosie Walsh, Katie Fforde, Amanda Ross and all at Cactus, The Monday Night Lockdown Gang and The Sunday Night Pub Club. I salute you all!

Finally, thanks to my wife, for . . . everything.

About the Author

Mike Gayle was born and raised in Birmingham and moved to London to pursue a career in journalism, working as a feature editor and agony uncle. He has written for a variety of publications including the *Sunday Times*, the *Guardian* and *Cosmopolitan*.

Mike became a full-time novelist in 1997 following the publication of his *Sunday Times* top ten bestseller *My Legendary Girlfriend*, which was praised by the *Independent* as 'full of belly laughs and painfully acute observations'. Since then, he has written eighteen novels including *The Man I Think I Know*, Richard and Judy Bookclub bestseller *Half a World Away*, and *All The Lonely People*, which the *Guardian* hailed as 'a heart-breaking and ultimately uplifting look at isolation'. His books have been translated into more than thirty languages.

He lives in Birmingham with his wife and daughters. You can find him online at mikegayle.co.uk and on X @mikegayle.